Rick Brindle was born in Dorset,
family. He was educated in Gern
working mainly in pubs before joir
years. Afterwards, he trained as a .
currently working on his next novel.

Also by Rick Brindle:

Cold Steel on the Rocks

We Are Cold Steel

Rick Brindle

For Linda

We are magic in the night
We are shadow, we are light
We are forever, you and I

Prologue

2003

'Cold Steel? Never heard of you.'

Staring blankly at five scruffy longhairs, the bouncer betrayed no emotion on his Spock face. Behind him, black glass doors stood firmly closed, effectively separating Cold Steel from Earth, a West London nightclub. All around were designer clothes mixed with gem-crusted jewellery, professional manicures and cosmetically altered perfection. Beautiful people flowed in and out of the club, staring with detached curiosity at the five louts who were surely in the wrong place.

'Come on, Max.' One of the band passed around a Franks hipflask. 'We're not wanted.' The five of them swigged from the silver flask and glared at the bouncer. *Cheap flash bastards,* he thought, *there's probably supermarket booze in that five hundred quid flask.*

'We're wanted everywhere,' roared another. Long black hair tangled down his back, a large hook nose dominated his face and he probably slept with that grin in place. '*We* are Cold Steel, and we're going to be the biggest band on the fucking planet.' He strode up to the bouncer. 'Our first album's out tomorrow. It's called They Don't Like It Up 'em.'

'I'll be sure to look out for it,' the bouncer deadpanned, streetlight glinting off his crossed-rifles lapel badge.

'You like heavy metal?' Wide-eyed, questioning look.

'No.'

'So stop chatting us up and let us in.' Another longhair spoke up, dirty blonde this time, wearing a tattered t-shirt and worn combat trousers.

'We've got a strict dress code, sir.'

'Who cares about that?' He glared threateningly. 'You think we'll cause trouble?'

'I'm sure you're above that sort of thing,' the bouncer smoothed. 'And if it was up to me, I'd let you in right now. But rules are rules, and I don't own the place.'

'So?' asked the dark hair. 'What are these rules?'

'Dress code, fellas. You want in, you have to comply. Your choice.'

*

'You sure you're a metal band? You look pretty stupid to me? One card?'

The small cards room, insulated by a bulletproof door from Earth's bar and dance floor, offered just enough light for the players to see each other. Everything else was anonymised by smoke-cloud shadows.

'Look in a mirror, mate,' said Maxwell. 'Two cards.' He scowled across the green baize table at the enormous man opposite. Clad in a tent-like orange kaftan and smoking a hookah pipe that was constantly filled by a silent gofer, he seemed to make every statement into a question.

'Do you see me wearing a tie?' he asked. 'A hundred to stay in?'

'It was that or give the bouncer a blowjob.' Maxwell pulled at the striped school tie that hung over his t-shirt. 'I'll see your hundred, and raise you the same.'

'Ah, new members? Three kings?'

Maxwell shrugged. 'It's our first night here. Three aces.' He grinned and reached for the untidy pile of bank notes at the centre of the table. The rest of the band were back at the bar and Maxwell had no one at his back. In the shadows behind the orange-clad man stood an athletically curved woman in a bodycon dress, one hand resting lightly on the man's shoulder. Aside from the temporary pipe-filler, they and Maxwell were the only people in the room.

'A lucky win for you?' inflected the large man.

'Bollocks,' replied Maxwell. 'You've got too many tells.'

'My deal.' He ignored Maxwell's comments. 'Five hundred to stay on the table. What did you say your name was?'

'Maxwell Diabolo, singer with Cold Steel.' He threw a slab of banknotes on the table. 'I'm in.'

'Archimedes Wasp,' said Kaftan man. 'I own Twenty Studios? One card.'

'You make films? Three cards.'

'It's a recording studio? Fifty to call.'

6

'Ever heard of Shed Studios? I'll raise you a hundred.'

'Are they still going? They'll be closed by the end of the year? Flush, kings high.'

'Then it's a good job we made our album when we did,' grinned Maxwell. 'Straight flush, twos leading.'

*

Three hours later, Maxwell had lost count of the whiskeys he'd drunk. The small room had become humid, and his vision blurred. An insistent voice in the back of his head – which he usually ignored – was quietly telling him to stop drinking and, more loudly, to stop gambling. Had he really blown his entire advance from Ozone Records? Earth's rules were harsh. No chips, no credit, and all gambling was done with cash or mutually agreed wagers, whatever the hell that meant. Over the night, Maxwell's pile of haphazardly arranged banknotes had grown, dwindled, reappeared and then disappeared. All he had in front of him were cards and a tenner.

'Call it a day?' asked Archimedes.

'Deal me in for ten?'

'I wouldn't go to the crapper for that?'

Maxwell's jaw jutted out. 'I'm not leaving this table unless I've got all the money or none of it.' He leaned towards Archimedes. 'And you're a minute away from cleaning me out.'

'What was it about a fool and his money?' Archimedes' bushy monobrow climbed up to his tanglefoot matting of dark brown hair. He shrugged and dealt the cards. 'Ten pounds the hand?'

Maxwell won.

Then won again.

And again.

An hour after being ten pounds away from annihilation, Maxwell was level. He'd won back his advance, ordered orange juice, and remembered Archimedes' tells. He started joking, Archimedes stopped.

'Twenty Studios, you say?' asked Maxwell. 'Two cards.'

'Yes?' replied Archimedes. 'Three cards.'

'Does that mean you own twenty different studios?'

'One, and it's called Twenty?'

'Why's that?'

'It's my twentieth business venture?'

'Impressive. Call for five hundred.'

'I'll see you?'

'Full house.'

'Bastard?'

'No, mate. I knew my parents.'

'I mean, you won?'

'You want to stop?'

'Do you?'

'My deal.' Maxwell shuffled a fresh deck of cards. 'So let's make this interesting. Five hundred a hand. Can you afford it? And what's with all these questions?'

'It's called an upward inflection, and it's a mannerism, not a question?'

'It's bloody confusing.'

'Not to those of us with breeding. Two cards?'

Time passed in a blur of hands, raises and upwardly inflected statements that might have been questions.

'I hope your studio's making good money,' said Maxwell. 'A thousand to see you.'

'It will. I never fail? I'll raise you a thousand?'

'And another thousand.'

'Are you sure?'

'I've made the bet.' Maxwell flashed a white-toothed grin. 'Besides, it *was* your money I'm betting with.'

'You win this one, I fold?'

Maxwell's confidence built. It was like being on stage: fighting, working, struggling to own the crowd. He'd staggered into the cards room, had been pushed close to surrender, but now Archimedes' stash had dwindled, dried up to nothing.

'Last hand, Arch.'

'And how deaf are you? I told you already, it's Archimedes?'

'Is it?' Maxwell fanned out a wad of notes. 'We can't play with cheques or credit, so it looks like I've cleaned you out.'

Archimedes' manicured fingers fluttered over the hem of his embroidered kaftan; his eyes flickered around the murky room. 'I've never lost like this. Can we agree a wager?'

'What have you got?'

Calculating glance. 'I'll stake a free recording session at my studio?'

'No chance, we've just done our album.' Maxwell shoved his entire winnings into the centre of the table. 'There,' he said. 'All in, winner screws loser. Match the stake and we've got a game.'

A set of keys. 'Personalised Bentley?' offered Archimedes.

'An old man's car.'

Digital keycard. 'My flat in Knightsbridge?'

'Dodgy neighbourhood.'

Monogrammed letters. 'Private box at Ascot.'

'Where?'

Archimedes raised his hands in the air. 'So what do I have to tempt you with?'

Maxwell glanced at the woman, still silhouetted. She'd stood behind Archimedes through the whole game, her hand resting on his shoulder. Maxwell smiled. 'Her.'

Her straight hair whipped around and she fired a shocked look at Archimedes. Manicured fingernails dug into kaftan-clad skin.

'What do you think this is?' growled Archimedes. 'Zodiac Mindwarp?'

'Who?'

'Before your time, sonny, but I don't decide what happens to someone else?'

'Only if you lose,' smirked Maxwell.

'Winner takes all?'

'Everything on the table right now, plus your friend in the shadows. All on the turn of a card.'

'Explain?'

'Simple.' Maxwell opened a fresh deck and placed them facedown on the table. 'You cut, then me. Highest card gets the girl, the money, the car, the flat.' He grinned again. 'You can keep the bloody box in Ascot, and the loser goes home with his friends, if he's got any.'

'I don't know?'

'You do,' said Maxwell. 'You're a man with twenty businesses. You can afford this.' He swept a hand over the money. 'Maybe her as well.' He nodded at the woman.

Silence stretched around the room. 'What's it to be?' asked Maxwell.

Archimedes faced him but said nothing.

'Well, I can't hang around here all night.' Maxwell shovelled up his winnings and winked at the woman's silhouette. 'Have a drink with me? Arch can't afford it anymore.'

'Stop,' hissed Archimedes.

'What? Stop talking?'

'Leave the money there. We play.'

'You sure?'

'Of course.'

'It's just that you've stopped asking me questions.'

'Games are over. One card and it's finished.'

'What the hell,' shrugged Maxwell. 'It's your money, mostly.'

'You'll pay for this.'

'Only if I lose.'

Maxwell put the money back on the table, and then slid the uncut deck over towards Archimedes.

'You go first,' he said.

Chapter 1

Last Summer

St Clements was one of the few Caribbean islands with a rocky coastline and no beaches. Which meant no tourists. And no tourists meant very little publicity, which suited the inhabitants just fine. It meant they could get on with things their way: no interference, no hassles.

Not that St Clements was ugly. A rugged volcanic mountain sprouted from the island's centre and punctured the tropical blue sky. A beard of lush forest, interspersed with carefully managed sugar plantations, ringed its lower base. The capital, Porte Juste, was a peeling, whitewashed adobe miniature time capsule, with cobbled roads taking what visitors there were back to a colonial age, with a rust-rash of bicycles the only visible concession to modernity.

Until a week earlier.

Now the narrow roads were clogged with satellite TV vans, and news crews in white shorts and loud shirts prowled the cobblestones, interviewing locals. Everyone had an opinion about the naval blockade by the neighbouring island, Ancadia. But why had St Clements really harboured Cold Steel? Had it been too big a risk for the small island? Surely it had been crazy luck the way the band had drawn the world's attention with a life-defining concert, which in turn had mobilised flash protests around the world, sufficient to persuade the Ancadians' most powerful ally to force a de-escalation.

And with the threat of war over and the band's safety assured, stories soaked back to the encamped reporters. Cold Steel had come to the Caribbean to find a long-dead pirate's treasure. Some said they'd found it, some said they'd lost it. One group of locals said they'd been captured by the Ancadians, while another said spying, even on a secret mission for St Clements.

But just hours after delivering a miracle, and like the fade-out at the end of a song, Cold Steel's hero-status had quickly paled. With nothing to do before flying back to the studio to record their next album, the band flip-switched to character normal, seeing life as a medieval astronomer would, with all worlds and beings revolving around them.

Starting with the taxis.

Porte Juste had three motorised taxis, all resurrected from a lifetime of driving London's polluted streets. Discovered by chance in the hold of an end-of-life cruise ship that had been brought to St Clements for scrapping, they'd had the rust scraped off them, been painted bright green, and then pressed back into service for as long as they would last, running on sugar-based bio-fuel.

All three had been commandeered by Cold Steel.

'Look, man,' protested one of the drivers. 'You don't need this cab. We're here for those that can't walk.'

'You think any of *this* can walk?' Andy Stains pressed his face close to the driver's after throwing his antique telecaster onto the cab's floor. Faded combat trousers and stained t-shirt reinforced his belligerence. The cab driver shook his head and glared back at Andy, then winced as several more aged instruments were casually slung into the back of the cab.

'We're full,' slurred Maxwell. 'Let's go.'

'I'm not going in the same cab as Vince,' growled Andy.

'And you think I'd want to travel with you?' Vince Fire swayed along the narrow track outside the Coast Hotel. His normally impeccable slicked hair sprawled like a haphazard black mop, and his triangular chin beard was speckled with scraps from his last meal.

'No need,' said Maxwell. 'One cab for the gear, two for us. That way you girls get to the grove without bitching. Now pick a ride and let's go.'

*

'Nothing like national salvation for making us busy, eh, Angelo?'

Angelo looked around the Coconut Grove's packed bar and smiled. 'You said it, Nails.' He grinned at the other barman, who'd earned his nickname after nailing souvenir beer mats all around the Grove's flotsam-built interior. They served drinks in a beer-haze of activity, accompanied by roots reggae from the DJ who flowed around the bar's small raised stage.

12

Headlights suddenly cut along the harbour road and shone into the open-plan bar. Porte Juste's three taxis pulled up, the car doors were thrown open and the longhaired white boys from the night before swerved onto the sidewalk and staggered up to the bar.

'Welcome, boys,' smiled Angelo. 'Find yourselves a table. I'll get you some drinks.'

'Drinks, shminks!' slurred Maxwell. 'We're here to play.'

'No need,' smoothed Angelo. 'We got a DJ tonight. Let someone else do the work.' Quickly sensing trouble, he looked over at Nails.

'Maybe Johnny was right, man,' said Joe Dimitri, the band's bass player. His psychedelic shirt wrapped around him in the gentle breeze.

'Oh, fucking hell,' snapped Andy. 'Johnny this, Johnny that. He's our manager, not our fucking keeper, right, Max?'

'Right,' shouted Maxwell. He squared up to Angelo. 'Switch off that DJ, get him out of the way and help us set up.'

*

Gagged and bound, Johnny Faslane cracked his head against the closet wall. Iced fury fire-flickered through him, competing with the stuffy air which smelled of old mothballs. Sweating inside his trademark leather pants, he drew his ankle-bound legs up to his chest and kicked his cowboy-booted feet against the door.

Bunch of stupid bastards! They'd gone too far this time. Managing a band was worse than having children, and Cold Steel were stuck in a permanent adolescence that Johnny, their surrogate parent, was beginning to get very pissed off about.

He kicked the closet door again, again, and again. The louvre-panel rattled and bent, but stayed shut. Christ, but he was making enough noise to drag a corpse back to life. Why couldn't anyone hear?

Because you're alone in a hotel room, idiot!

And when Cold Steel had drunkenly announced an unplanned concert at the Coconut Grove, why would anyone stay inside a roach-ruled harbourside hotel in Porte Juste? Why, Johnny idly wondered, had Cold Steel booked into the place to begin with?

Because it's the only hotel on the island.

Outside the closet, Johnny's phone rang, an electro-ping of Cold Steel's traditional concert opener, Sinners Sanctuary. *Time to get that one changed.* He kicked the door once more. *Please let it be Rachel. She'll know something's wrong. She'll come and get me out of this.*

Sinners Sanctuary gouged through the phone's tiny speaker, then stopped, and Johnny was once again the guest of silence, broken only by his less occasional kicks. Intermittent lamplight flickered into the closet, but otherwise darkness shrouded him and he wondered if he'd get out before disaster engulfed the band, barely a day after their biggest success.

He lost all sense of time as he sat on the dusty, wooden floor, increasingly cramped and uncomfortable. His struggles had left him with aching legs. His wrists burned from the ropes and he'd lost count of the times his head had banged against the wall.

A knock on the room door pranged him into action and he kicked with renewed vigour. The door creaked open, high-heels tapped on the wooden floor. Johnny kicked madly, the footsteps came closer and he smelled the familiar lemongrass perfume. The closet opened and he looked up at Rachel Shaw.

'Christ, Johnny,' she gasped. A Lucy Lawless lookalike with an English accent, her long black hair flowed down either side of her heart-shaped face. 'What the hell's going on?' He muffled a reply before she freed the gag, and she looked at him with a mischievous grin. 'Actually, I kind of like you all helpless. Maybe we should do something like this ourselves.'

Johnny looked at her and despite himself, he smiled. 'Let's talk about it later.'

'Promise?'

'What?'

'Or maybe I'll leave you in here.'

'Bloody hell, Rachel. Untie me. This is serious.'

'Really serious?'

He glared at her and she slowly united his ankles. 'What happened?' she asked.

'Those stupid twats who call themselves Cold Steel, that's what.'

'Do I have to ask you sentence by sentence or are you just going to tell me?' She freed his wrists.

'They wanted to do another gig tonight.'

'And that's it?'

'An unprepared, unrehearsed gig. In a bar, for Christ's sake.'

'Is that so bad?' asked Rachel. 'Last night they played the concert of their lives. They stopped St Clements from being invaded. They started protests in cities all around the world, and they did it with a week's notice. *You* did it with a week's notice.'

'That was then.' Johnny stood up, stepped out of the closet and grabbed his phone. 'Tonight they're half pissed, their instruments are antiques that were only ever good for one show. There's no sound check, no tune up, and no road crew. After everything they achieved last night, they'll flush it all down the crapper.'

'Maybe they'll do a good show.'

Johnny sat down on the creaking metal-frame bed. 'They *think* they will, and that's the problem. They'll sound shit, they'll look shit, and then they'll get pissed off.' He looked at Rachel. 'Vince and Andy will probably have a fight onstage. Christ, Rachel, the press will slaughter them.'

'Why are you looking at *me* when you say that?' Her voice flew around the small room like a radioactive frisbee.

'Is there another other reporter in here?'

'Keep talking like that, mister, and there won't be any reporters in here at all. In this hotel, in your bed, and sure as hell nowhere near your life.'

Johnny's shoulders sagged. 'Why is it always a choice with you, Rachel?'

'It's what life's all about,' she smiled. 'The game's everything, Johnny. Haven't I taught you that? Haven't you learned that yet?'

'Bloody hell, Rachel. Cold Steel are about the commit career suicide and you're talking about a bloody game.'

'Do your job, Johnny.' She turned his legs to mush with a mountain-crumbling smile and grabbed her camera. 'Leave me to do mine.'

*

Maxwell ripped his t-shirt clear of his chest, screamed into the microphone and punched the air above his head. There was no

15

furnace-hot spotlight burning his skin, no audience roar, and no deafening wall of music from the band. Not even his own voice reverberating through the monitor speakers.

Nothing.

They competed for attention with the Coconut Grove's quirky lights flashing around the brightly coloured bar. The small speakers hijacked from the smouldering DJ just about made the band heard, and the hostility of the club's punters was starting to soak through the rum-field that cushioned Maxwell from reality. The stage was a slightly raised area at one end of the flotsam-built bar, with recycled barrel tables and bench seats crammed at the other end.

Maxwell sensed that metal wasn't the island's first love when it came to music. Maybe Johnny had been right. The bravado of an hour earlier had evaporated, but it was too late to stop. The music was playing, sort of, and what was left of the audience were watching, sort of.

Whatever they did, throw the concert or carry on playing, they were screwed. *What a choice to make.* It was all wrong and Maxwell knew it. The moves that normally came so naturally were gone. He couldn't think, couldn't feel, had no idea how to grab the feeling of playing live, of reaching out and holding the crowd. Then he heard Andy's antique telecaster sounding out a hum so loud that nothing else could be heard. He turned around.

And wished he hadn't.

In the past, Andy had talked about it, joked about it, but Maxwell never thought he'd actually do it. The part of his mind that still functioned wondered how Andy had actually *managed* it. But he had, and even in the half-out, underpowered lighting, there was no mistaking Andy's randomly tanned and naked form, clad only in guitar and filthy training shoes.

Vince scraped a furious riff along the worn strings of humbucker-filled jaguar custom, then stalked across the tiny stage. All that remained of the music was a wispy bass guitar and drum backline. 'What the fuck are you doing?' Vince fumed rum breath over Andy, who swayed slightly.

'What's the matter?' slurred Andy. 'Don't like the view?'

'Now that you ask, no.'

'Then stop eyeing me up and get on with the gig.'

Maxwell shoved his way between them. 'Fucking hell, lads. We're onstage and you're playing streaker and the pony.'

'Got something to say, Max?' Andy glared drunken belligerence at Maxwell.

'Put some bloody clothes on,' shouted Maxwell. 'Get your minds back to the music, both of you.'

'Don't look at me,' snapped Vince. '*I* was doing my job.'

'And you sounded fucking useless,' growled Andy. 'Auditioning for the next boy band, were you? It's all you're good for.'

Maxwell stepped between the two guitarists. He ducked past Vince's fist, which sailed past him like an England penalty shot and flurried the air beyond Andy's greasy blond hair. Vince and Andy locked arms in a bitch-fest wrestle, and sandwiched between them, Maxwell's arms windmilled helplessly.

Joe stepped nervously towards them. 'Hey, guys…' His weed-drenched voice was barely audible.

'A bit of fucking help,' screamed Maxwell.

'What do you want me to do, man?'

'Stopping this gangbang is a good start,' strained Maxwell.

Cold Steel's heavily muscled drummer, Mike Vesuvius, stomped past Joe and prised Vince away from Maxwell and Andy. 'Fucking grow up,' he snarled. 'This gig has turned to piss because of you two.'

'Bloody killjoy.' Vince shoved Mike, who stood like a concrete statue.

'Killjoy yourself.' Mike pushed Vince, who staggered into the gaggle of unhappy punters. They recoiled and threw him towards Andy. Andy threw a hasty punch at Vince, who grunted and fell to the floor.

'Jesus, Andy,' flared Mike. 'What the hell have you done?'

'What do you think I've done?' Andy squared up to Mike, all rum-fuelled naked aggression.

'You're an arsehole, you know that? A naked arsehole.'

'Better that then being a ponce with a perm.'

'Christ, lads,' pleaded Maxwell. 'Can we get back to the gig?'

'Who are you calling a ponce?' growled Mike. 'You're the one flashing in front of a bunch of men.'

'Get on with it.' Anonymous chants floated over the band from the remaining spectators.

'You got a problem?' shouted Andy.

'Yes,' one of them called back. 'It's called you.'

Andy's eyes glazed over. He shouted an incoherent challenge and rushed blindly forward.

'Oh no, man,' wailed Joe. 'What do we do now?'

'Joe,' said Maxwell. 'Stay with Vince. Mike, let's drag Andy out of there.'

'He might deserve the kicking he's about to get,' said Mike.

'We're Cold Steel,' growled Maxwell. 'No one slaps one of us but us. We drag that useless tosser out of there, get back to the hotel, then give him a kicking ourselves.'

'Maybe we should have listened to Johnny,' said Joe.

'Too late for that now. Come on, Mike.'

Shouting more loudly than they'd sounded through the bar's speakers, Maxwell and Mike charged into the mass of moving fists and feet that now obscured Andy's naked form.

'Max! Max!'

'Hold on, Andy.'

'Kick them in the balls.'

'No, man, not in the face.'

Chapter 2

Johnny flew down the staircase to the hotel lobby, the rusty banister wobbling like an oversized tuning fork. Rachel receded behind him, unable in her high heels to keep up with his cowboy-booted sprinting. For the first time that week, Johnny didn't care. He still couldn't take their relationship seriously. Rachel was a smouldering warrior princess, so far out of his league it was laughable, embarrassing even. He was practical enough to enjoy it while it lasted, but right now, even if Rachel Shaw *did* try to drag him away from rescuing the band, he knew where his priorities lay. He stamp-landed on the cracked stone floor, startled the receptionist awake and roared outside before she could ask for his key.

If only he wasn't too late to save the band from themselves. Again.

He stumbled along the potholed coast road that quickly narrowed to a dusty track. Porte Juste's small harbour faded into the darkness on his left, the single-storey adobe houses taking him back in time to another century, another world. If he didn't have the band to worry about, he'd have taken the time to appreciate the place. Not that it made planning the previous night's concert easy. St Clements' natural isolation had been reinforced a million times by the Ancadian blockade. He'd had to do more improvising than he thought possible, and it had succeeded in no small part thanks to the whole island's population coming out, supporting the band and making the concert happen.

But that didn't mean they'd put up with a bunch of drunk prima donnas. Johnny neared the Coconut Grove, which was nestled next to a decaying warehouse and rusting corrugated boatyard. He saw a handful of people walking out of the bar and evaporating into the adobe street warren. A few looks swayed in his direction.

'Don't bother, man. They're not even the same band as last night.'

Johnny's heart raced. He couldn't hear music, and he sprinted inside. When he'd been in the Coconut Grove before, the closely packed tables and chairs were always filled with an easygoing crowd who welcomed regulars and newcomers alike. Now he faced a war zone scattered with broken glass and furniture, with the band sat cross-legged on the floor and surrounded by the bar's staff, who growled over them if they even tried to stand up. Johnny recognised one of the barmen.

'What's going on, Angelo?'

'We didn't do anything,' whined Maxwell.

'Looks like it.' Johnny's cowboy boots crunched on broken glass. He did a double take at the sight of Andy. 'Are you naked?'

'Want a closer look?' replied Andy.

'Shit, no.' Johnny scanned Andy's spare-tyre abdomen, the bags under Maxwell's eyes, Joe's developing chin, Vince's jeans starting to stretch, Mike's muscles showing a little less definition. 'You fuckers are going to the gym before the next tour.'

'Yeah, man,' mumbled Joe. 'Change the subject, why don't you?'

'Okay then,' growled Johnny. 'Who's got the spine to tell me what happened?'

'I guess it got out of hand,' mumbled Joe.

'Really?' snapped Johnny. 'Tell me something I *don't* know.'

'Come on, mate,' pleaded Maxwell. 'You want us to embarrass ourselves in public?'

'What?' snorted Johnny. 'Like you haven't already done that? Like tying up your manager and leaving him in a closet is dignified? Like that's supposed to make me sympathetic to you?'

'You shouldn't give us shit advice, then, should you?' said Andy.

'Shit advice?' choked Johnny. 'Don't do a gig at the Grove was shit advice, was it? Look around you, lads. Doesn't look like you ended on a high.'

'You got that right,' said Angelo. 'They barge on in here, throw the DJ out, then start playing worse than me at a drunken karaoke.' He shook his head and looked at the glass-littered floor. 'The place emptied in minutes.'

'I'm sorry, Angelo.' Johnny's eyes burned towards the band. 'Say sorry, you bastards.'

Muttered apologies grudged upwards from the floor.

'That's all you'll get from them,' said Johnny. 'Angelo, we'll cover all the expenses, I promise.'

'It's not about that.' Angelo nudged his chin towards the band. 'Those boys down there, they were like heroes last night. None of us here on St Clements thought we had a chance. Then they played their show and everything changed.'

'That's right,' said Maxwell.

'Shut up,' snapped Johnny. 'You couldn't leave it there, could you? Had to play *another* bloody gig.'

Silence from the band.

'Christ,' glared Johnny. 'Arrogant, spoilt bastards. No permission, no rehearsal, no sound check, no one to tune in, no sound control, and bloody pissed. Jesus Christ, don't you bastards remember the last tour you did?'

'Okay.' Mike held up his hands in surrender. 'We screwed up.'

'Can we get up now?' asked Maxwell.

'What do you say, Angelo?' said Johnny. 'I'm sorry about tonight. All damage will be paid for by Cold Steel, with interest. Are we good?'

'We're good,' said Angelo.

'No, you're not.' Johnny looked around at a brick-built policeman. His mirror-shine boots ground the underfoot glass into dust.

'Shit,' said Johnny. 'Are we under arrest?'

'That's not up to me,' said the policeman, ominous efficiency in a starched white shirt and razor-creased trousers. 'Mister Chevalier decides that.'

*

Six months earlier, Johnny had been managing metal bands on the verge of disappearing, with obscurity their peak. He was still grappling with the changes that came with Cold Steel, who were firmly resident at the other end of heavy metal success. And he definitely wasn't used to having conversations with Prime Ministers.

Not that Henri Chevalier looked like one. Clad in faded jeans, Hawaiian shirt and scuffed training shoes, he looked like no politician Johnny had ever seen, and the thinning sun-bleached hair pulled back into a ponytail gave the two men an immediate affinity.

But while he might have still dressed like the barman he'd once been, he'd quickly learned the hard lessons behind the photo-opportunity assurances of international friendship and brotherhood. It had been easy enough for him to nationalise the sugar industry, but it was a whole different story to placate the global corporations, then diversify the island's small economy and transform it into survival. Under Henri's leadership, the people of St Clements managed to support themselves, just.

The last time Johnny had been at Henri's official residence – twenty-four hours before – he and the band had basked in Henri's tribute. Now they sat on his wide-fit sofa, and faced depleted uranium hostility. A silenced television screen played live news, a rolling feed from the Coconut Grove. A disastrous concert, a naked Andy, the rest of the band brawling.

'Compulsive viewing.' Henri's English was laced with strong Gallic inflections. 'Somehow, though, I prefer your first concert.'

'Henri...' began Johnny.

'No!' Henri interrupted. 'I do not want to hear it.'

'Good job you weren't saying that last night,' sniped Andy, now partially covered with a towel around his waist.

'And for that we have cause to thank you,' said Henri.

'Don't you think we deserve a little slack for it now?' asked Maxwell.

'As if any of us had an alternative,' replied Henri. 'Including you. What would have happened if the Ancadians had come ashore? What if we had given you over to them, as they demanded?'

'Well—'

'And why did they come here at all?'

'Hey,' said Johnny. 'You said they'd have done that anyway.'

'And so they would,' said Henri. 'But so soon? Maybe we could have anticipated them. It might have been easier had you not insisted on your treasure hunt. I warned you to avoid them, I told you what they were capable of.'

'We *know* what they were capable of,' snarled Maxwell. 'We saw it. They blew our bloody boat out of the water.'

'Whose boat?'

'What?'

'Whose boat? Yours, was it?'

'Look—'

'No, it was not. Something else the people of St Clements helped you with. And did you find this mystical missing treasure?'

'But—'

'Yes, yes. I know. It sunk with your boat. But you mean our boat, don't you? You came here with your ridiculous story about pirate treasure, which by the way we have heard a million times before. Your dealings with the Ancadians placed us in an impossible situation, which of course may or may not have happened anyway. We helped you with a boat, provisions, and last of all advice, which you clearly did not take. You did whatever you wanted, and everyone on St Clements nearly paid the price.'

'But we *did* bring the bacon in last night,' said Vince. 'And it worked.'

'Look at that screen!' roared Henri. Footage of the band at the Coconut Grove played on the large wall-mounted plasma. 'Do you see a naked performer? Do you see a fight? Do you remember terrorising the staff? Did you think you had the right to abuse the patrons, damage the fittings? Did you?'

'That's a bit harsh,' murmured Maxwell.

'And so it is with the truth. Especially with people like you. People who never have to face up to it.'

'Johnny's tried,' smirked Vince.

'I know,' scowled Henri. 'And I've heard what happened to him when he tried to talk some sense into you.'

Johnny blushed. 'You're right, Henri. About everything.'

'Thanks for the loyalty,' grumbled Andy.

'You've earned it,' snapped Johnny. 'And if you ask me you should be bloody grateful you've not been locked up.'

'Blame us, why don't you?' blazed Vince. 'What about your bird? I bet you're not bollocking her for tweeting about us wherever she'll get paid for it.'

Rachel opened her mouth to speak, but Johnny was quicker. 'That's her job,' he clipped. 'And if you hadn't been acting like twats, she'd probably be *out* of a job. Think about that, dickhead.'

23

'So what happens now?' asked Maxwell.

'That's up to Henri,' said Johnny. 'It's his bloody island, and you're the ones who've shat all over it.' He turned to Henri. 'They deserve whatever you chuck at them.'

'I do not want to appear ungrateful,' said Henri. 'And we *do* appreciate your efforts last night. But that debt is now paid. I think it would be better if you left the island on tomorrow's flight.'

'But we've got two weeks before we're back in the studio, man,' said Joe. 'What do we do until then?'

Chapter 3

Johnny's phone rang and he picked up.

'Johnny Faslane.'

'I know who you are, asshole.' A New York gang accent shuddered into Johnny's ear.

'Randall.' Johnny quaked as he recognised Ozone Records' abrasive executive. 'What's going on?'

'*You* tell *me,* motherfucker, and quickly.'

'Here?' Johnny looked at the band, contrite and powerless. 'Nothing's going on here.'

'That's not what I'm hearing.'

'What, what have you been hearing?'

'Tell me, buddy, and you'd better tell it straight. I hear things, and I know things, so don't, *don't* pull my chain, mister.'

'Well, Randall…' Johnny perspired inside his leather pants. 'The band did a gig tonight. Unplanned, impromptu, for a select crowd.'

'Wrong, dickhead.'

'Things—'

'Got a little out of hand?'

'You could say that.'

'I *am* saying it, pal. And you assholes stopped following the script so long ago, you won't get your dicks sucked for another century, you get me?'

'I—'

'Shut up.'

'Randall—'

'*Listen,* you prick. Now, last night you surprised a lot of people, including me. Tonight, you surprised no one.'

'I'm sorry, Randall.'

'Sorry don't cut it, not at this level. Do you realise the chances you created last night?'

'Sure, we—'

'Shut up. You know how many goddam doors got closed in your face tonight?'

'It wasn't that bad.'

'Get with the times, college boy. We're in the world of viral uploads, news feeds, Instagram, Twitter, Facebook. Social media is *everywhere!* You bastards wipe your asses how you shouldn't and the whole goddam world knows about it. And they know about it the next second. So guess what happens when you play a goddam lousy concert, then trash the joint?'

'Word got out?'

'No shit, Sherlock. The whole freaking universe was watching your useless asses. And holy moley, you did not disappoint.'

'Really?'

'Hey, schmo, you're not too dumb for me to be wasting my sarcasm.'

'But it's still publicity. That's never a bad thing, is it?'

'Believe that, wonderboy, and I'll can your ass right now. Your first concert in St Clements was ours, Ozone's. That publicity was leading to your next album, your next tour, and you assholes were supposed to play the goddam game all the way. You had to turn people *on* to Cold Steel, not *off.*'

'Okay, we screwed up and I'm sorry.' Panic thumped through Johnny's body. 'I swear I'll keep the band quiet till they're in the studio.'

'And I'm just about to help you do that,' chuckled Randall. 'Those jokers won't be having any more spare time with their thumbs up their asses. From now on, they work or they don't work at all.'

'Sure thing. We're due in the studio in two weeks.'

'The fuck you are. I said they work or you don't work at all, and this change of plan is down to them. You'll get Cold Steel to Twenty Studios inside twenty-four hours.'

*

'Don't look at me like it's *my* fault,' said Rachel. 'It was always going to get out.'

'Hey.' Johnny leant against the hotel room's plywood door and cradled a beer. 'I stuck up for you at Henri's, didn't I?'

'Sure you did, but oh, didn't you just hate that?'

'Come on, Rachel.' Johnny's eyebrows climbed towards his vacating fringe. 'You're following the band while they make the album, then going on tour with them. Doesn't that change anything in your mind?'

'Like what?'

'Like, like, for Christ's sake, Rachel, do I have to spell it out?'

'I think you might have to.' Her folded arms and deep-freeze blue eyes made Johnny pause before replying.

'I thought you might concentrate on the music,' he mumbled.

'Wasn't it music at the Coconut Grove?'

'You know what I mean.' He sweated inside his clothes and searched for the right words. 'Just be a bit more...'

'Selective?'

'Yes, that's it,' Johnny smiled and swigged his beer. 'That's exactly it.'

'And what kind of stories would you *select?*'

'Hey, as long as it doesn't make the band look bad.'

'So you just want the good news stories?'

Johnny opened his mouth, then closed it again. 'No.' Pause. 'Yes.' Longer pause. 'Maybe.'

Rachel shook her head. 'That makes sense. And they say women are indecisive.'

'Christ, Rachel. I've got a hard enough job keeping the band in line. Don't tell me I've got to babysit you as well.'

'What, you mean because I'm an immature, insecure musician who's stuck in teenage party mode?'

'No, you're more mature and a lot less predictable.'

'So why do you have to babysit me?'

Optimistic smile. 'It's the only perk I get after you bust my balls every day.'

She giggled. 'And you're the only one who can make me laugh when I should be furious enough to knock some sense into that strangely attractive head of yours.'

'Are you saying I'm bald?'

'No,' she laughed. 'You're a solar-powered love machine. Happy now?'

'You have no idea,' he grinned. 'So what about the band?'

'What about them? It's the game, you know that.'

'Christ, Rachel. You and this bloody game.'

'It's all there is.'

'And what about us?'

She walked towards him, snaked her arms around his head, and gently ran her fingernails along the back of his neck. His eyes rolled independently of each other like a chameleon, and his legs turned to warm fondant.

'I still haven't worked out what we are,' she purred.

'*You* haven't?' said Johnny. 'What about me?'

'What about you?'

'That's what I mean. What are we, Rachel?' He held her as though she'd run away. 'You could do better, you know.'

She took a half step back. 'And what does *that* mean?'

'It means I'm bald, skinny, *not* a rock star. I'm not as good-looking as Maxwell, not as rich as Vince, not as talented as *any* of them.'

She stepped closer. 'This beholder sees more,' she whispered. 'You're a brilliant manager, you've got more guts then the whole band put together, you never give up on the music, and you see more in me than just my body.'

'You sure about that last point?' he joked.

'Putting up with *this* girl's mood swings?' she smiled. 'One thing we're not, Johnny, is nothing.'

'So meet me halfway with the band?'

'Meet me halfway with my job?'

He tried to reply but she silenced him with a slow kiss. His grip on his beer loosened, his excitement built and she danced away from him. 'Keep them busy,' she said. 'And that'll decide how *I* keep busy.'

'Okay then.' A sudden idea slammed into Johnny's mind. 'So tell your readers, viewers, whatever, tell them about the men behind the story.'

'What do you mean?'

'Look, I can't stop you writing what you want, and that's what you're here for anyway. But how about going a bit deeper? Tell the whole world about their fuck ups if you must. Although—' he grinned — 'Cold Steel in trouble would hardly be an exclusive. I don't know why you'd bother.'

'Alright,' said Rachel. 'You've got my attention.'

'Don't just say what you see,' said Johnny. 'Let the band speak for themselves. Get to know them.'

She grimaced. 'Do I have to?'

'You might be surprised.'

'I might like them, is that it?'

'Could be.'

'You have heard of the Steel Talking Interview?' she asked.

'The one where Vince and Andy had a fight on a TV special?'

She nodded. 'That one.'

Johnny smiled. 'Followed by Maxwell mooning for the camera, Joe blazing up on prime-time viewing and the whole band getting arrested. We've *all* seen that, Rachel.'

'So what else is there to know?'

'I thought you liked a challenge, liked playing the game.'

She laughed and pressed her body against his. 'I think maybe I taught you a little too well.'

'I'm still learning.' He smiled and drank in her lemon grass scent. 'Wait until I really know what I'm doing.'

'So I get to report what I see and hear from the band, as long as I agree to show the world their real selves, their souls.' She pulled a face. 'Searching out *their* vulnerabilities and imperfections will keep me busy for the rest of my life.'

'Too busy for us?'

'Oh, I'll always make time for us, even at the studio.'

'Even?'

'You think Cold Steel will behave themselves just because they're recording?'

*

Archimedes Wasp wriggled inside the orange kaftan which shrouded his ample form. His eyes bulged at the exotic, dark-haired girl he'd hired for the afternoon. She peeled off her dress and stood before him in sheer black underwear. He groaned and she gyrated around the dancing pole inside the playroom at the exclusive A4 Club, set in the basement of a pristine townhouse in the middle of a whitewashed, immaculate block of Georgian houses. The West London street was closed to any car without a pass, and the club closed to anyone without a car, a pass, and a four-figure disposable cash wad on their person. Archimedes Wasp drove a spotlessly clean pink Rolls Royce, had been a member of the A4 club for ten years, and *always* carried ten K on him in brand new, consecutively numbered fifty-pound notes. He liked to run his life his way, and sometimes that needed privacy. Owning Twenty Studios allowed him the means to buy that privacy whenever he needed it.

'Never mind the dancing?' he whispered. 'I can see hard-body nymphos like you any time I want?' His upward inflections had survived the years.

'What do you want, Big Daddy?' the girl purred, looking at him with half-closed eyes and a feline grin.

She knew what he wanted. They all knew. And Archimedes knew they knew. They knew but they didn't tell, and that was what he liked. Girls who attended the A4 Club knew what to do, how to act, and most importantly, to keep quiet about anything they saw inside its highly polished, serene rooms. Archimedes ran a jewelled hand through his ginger beard and his eyes twinkled. 'Come through here?' he whispered, getting off the bed and opening a side door into another room.

Inside, grey plastic sheeting covered the floor. The room was devoid of all furniture, and dozens of freshly made cakes sat on the plastic. Archimedes watched the girl's face, wanting to see her reaction. That one second of recognition and acceptance was what he paid top quids for. Her eyes flew wide open. Red fingernails hovered over her open mouth and she gasped. She looked at Archimedes, her body tense and trembling. 'Oh, Big Daddy,' she gasped. 'Is all this for me?'

'You want I should give it to someone else?'

'No, no. Oh, you know what I like. You know what I want. Can I? Can I, please?'

Archimedes nodded and leaned back against the wall. He watched the girl sink to her knees and sit next to a double-decked gateau. She ran a finger along the top and collected a golf-balled sized blob of cream, then looked at Archimedes once more. 'It's good enough to eat,' she purred.

'Is that what you want to do?' he asked.

'What do you want me to do?' She knew. He knew. They both knew, and Archimedes felt his excitement building.

30

'You know what I want.' His voice was suddenly husky.

'Oh, I do, I do.' She stood up, then threw herself face down onto the cakes. With a squeal, she rolled over and rubbed cream and sponge all over her body, her underwear and skin soon merging as one beneath the hand-spread desserts.

Archimedes' arousal built as he watched the girl cavort and roll around on the plastic sheeting, although soon the walls were also splattered with random spurts. The messier the girl got, the more turned on he became, letting the pleasure build, until, with a drawn out groan, he was spent. He hadn't moved, hadn't even touched the girl, just watched her smear destroyed cake matter all over herself. She watched him with calculated judgement, speaking at exactly the right moment.

'Oh, Big Daddy,' she breathed. 'I'm *such* a lucky girl. You really know how to please me.'

*

Randall Spitz sat in a high-backed chair at an old-style leather-topped wooden desk. Slicked-back black hair showed a clean-shaven, bleach-white face, flinty black eyes, and a hostile glare that barked anger at the whole world, even in his clinically empty Los Angeles office.

Randall hadn't intended to work in the music business; it had just happened. Twenty-five years earlier, he'd stopped a mugging on his home street. Not because he was a goddam hero, but because the punk doing the mugging was from a rival family. The goddam Rossos, on *his* turf. He'd had to intervene. If Randall had seen the suited cupcake first, he'd have done the job himself. But rules were rules, and rule number one was lay down the law, *your* law on *your* turf. So he'd dragged the no-good Rosso punk off the street, knocked some goddam sense into his ugly head and sent him on his way.

The lame he'd saved changed Randall's life.

Quite what Harry Glassby, an exec from Ozone Records, was doing in Queens, much less Randall's neighbourhood, Randall didn't ask, wasn't told. What it *did* get him was a job as Harry's minder, then enforcer, then strong man for Ozone New York, then Ozone East Coast, and eventually Ozone Worldwide. He was the only member of his entire family to get legitimate work, but his

31

street instincts and natural ruthlessness made him a natural, and he recognised early on the similarities between the music business and his family's centuries-old way of doing things.

And it had helped Ozone as well. In the time Randall had been with the company, Ozone had earned a reputation for no-nonsense business and solid support for its artists – but only if they followed the company line – and absolutely zero tolerance from anyone who tried to screw them over. Cross that line, and Randall Spitz knew about it. He rarely needed to get involved with anyone a second time.

Twenty Studios were about to learn that lesson.

Randall picked up his phone, scrolled through the message list and punched in a number. On pick-up, his gravel voice grated down the line.

'Did you make the mark?' he asked, taking in every syllable of the reply, knowing he'd remember verbatim.

'So what did he do?'

'And then?'

'Then what?'

'Okay, that's great. You did real good. I'll reach out with our part of the deal, as agreed. We like your work. We'll use you again.'

*

Archimedes checked his emails and cursed. His office was a diametric opposite to Randall's, liberally splashed with purple wall hangings, wood carvings of elephants on sculptured stands and a thoroughly modern glass desk, as out of place in his office as Randall's own desk was in Los Angeles. He twitched and felt his thickly bearded face flush red, almost matching his bright silk kaftan. Cold Steel, for Christ's sake? Those bastards. *That* bastard! He was still singing for them and by shit, they'd actually made it! Their latest manager seemed to have pulled their arses out of more fires than Dante's basement, and their concert on St Clements had really put them on the map, in spite of all the tacky stories that still followed them around like herpes.

Archimedes knew that Cold Steel were pure money with their next album. The press loved and hated them at the same time; their fans made saints out of them. But for once, for Archimedes, money was beside the point. He'd die before he let Maxwell Diabolo sing anywhere *near* his studio. So what if Cold Steel were with Ozone? Archimedes *owned* Twenty Studios. He didn't have to say yes to anyone, even Ozone bloody Records. He fired back a curse-laden reply to Ozone and lit the hookah pipe that sat next to his desk. The apple-flavoured smoke fused through his lungs and he relaxed. Seconds later, his phone rang.

'Archimedes Wasp?'

'Are you asking me or telling me, you fat fuck?'

'Who is this?'

'Randall Spitz, Ozone Records.'

'Oh, so *you're* the one who wants Cold Steel at Twenty?'

'You're goddam right.'

'I take it you read my reply?'

'It wasn't the kind of answer I was looking for.'

'Well, perhaps I can comfort you with these words? Deal with it?' Archimedes felt secure, in complete control. No one *told* him who came to his studio.

'I don't think so.' Randall's reply shot down the line. 'And you're missing the point. If I want the goddam flowerpot men recording at your goddam studio, then it happens, you get me?'

'Whose studio?'

'Don't try and bend me over, girlfriend. I don't give a shit who owns the goddam place. Cold Steel's next album will be made at your place, period.'

'You don't understand—'

'No, asshole, *you* don't understand. Cold Steel are the hottest band on the planet, and it's in everyone's interest, theirs, mine *and* yours, that they do their next album at Twenty. You don't have to like it; you just have to do it. You'll make a shitload of money, so everyone's happy.'

'No.'

Microsecond pause.

'You know what, Archie, or whatever the hell your name is, you have a pure talent for pissing people off.'

'Coming from you that's quite a compliment?'

'I'm not here to be popular, friend. I'm here to get things done.'

'Perhaps,' said Archimedes. 'But the fact remains. *I* own Twenty, and I decide who records here. That does not include Cold Steel, and following this conversation, I may well have to take a long hard look at any other artists who have a contract with Ozone?'

'You trying to scare me, pal?'

'If I were you, I'd be considering my next reply very carefully.'

'You said it, douche bag. So chew on this – Cold Steel for Twenty, yes or no?'

'No.'

'It's your choice, but don't blame anyone but yourself when you read the headlines tomorrow.'

'And why should I worry about that?' A wisp of nervousness crept into Archimedes' words.

Randall chuckled. 'Hey, you're the one who cares so goddam much about who uses your real estate. I wonder how many people will give a shit about you and your studio when they read about what you like to do out of hours.'

'I'm not sure what you mean?' Archimedes took a long drag of hookah as a dread vision rinsed through him like a charcoal enema.

'Then you're either a liar or stupid. But that's the difference between me and you. I get told what to do as well, but when I do, I make sure it gets done.'

'Cold Steel aren't coming to Twenty,' shrilled Archimedes. 'And that's final.'

'Don't poker-face me, buddy, or maybe you *want* the whole world to know about your sploshing parties.'

'I don't—'

'You know, asshole. You know. Hey, it don't mean shit to me.' Randall enjoyed the thought of Archimedes palpitating at his words. 'I'm sure plenty of my staff do the same, but that's the diff between your outfit and Ozone. All we give a crap about is sales and profits, whereas you give a good goddam about opinion, am I right?'

'What do you want, Randall?'

'First, forget your threats against Ozone and our artists.'

'And second?'

'Second,' said Randall, 'Cold Steel *will* be making their next album at Twenty Studios. They'll be there tomorrow, so deal with it, unless you want your cake shots to go viral.'

*

Archimedes' fury misted through him like the hookah smoke. Jesus, were Cold Steel the *only* band that needed a studio? Shit no. But he couldn't refuse. Randall was right; Archimedes *did* care what people thought. Even the possibility of the sploshing getting out was enough to make him want to speed dial a drug dealer.

So what are you going to do?

Cold Steel. How the hell had they made it anyway? Archimedes snorted. Jesus, the only thing they were good at was tripping over their own dicks.

Then let them.

Of course. Cold Steel would do the job for him. All he needed them to do was fuck up in the right way and they'd kick themselves out of the studio. From everything he'd seen and heard, that wouldn't be difficult to arrange. He reached for the phone.

*

Dixie walked his normal uneven shuffle towards the mid-city storage unit. Half the overhead streetlights were blown, making the potholes underfoot invisible and hazardous, but he barely noticed. Christ, but he couldn't wait to get back on the road. Heading up the road crew for Cold Steel had been his life ever since the band exploded out of hard-strike poverty with their first album. And even though he hated the down time between tours, he *loved* Cold Steel. They were like his best mates and big brothers all rolled into one. Two weeks till recording the new album had been brought forward to twenty-four hours, and Dixie was a happy man. Because two weeks sooner meant the album would be finished more quickly, and then the touring could start.

First job was to make sure the band's instruments were good to go to the studio. Good? Of course they were good. Hadn't Dixie put them in storage himself at the end of the last tour? Didn't he have the keys? He fumbled in his filthy jeans pocket, his unwashed hand flickering over fag ends and copper coins until his fingers closed around the key's tattered label.

35

He approached the secured roller door. 'Piece of piss,' he muttered to himself. 'Pop the door, call the van, drums and guitars delivered. Jesus shit, even the band could manage that.' He chuckled. As much as he idolised Cold Steel, he knew their limitations. When it came to metal, they were the absolute dog-fucking best, but for most other things, they needed help. *His* help.

He clicked the padlock and the door clanked open. He stepped inside the unit and fumbled for the light switch. The eco bulb sent a gradual blanket of light seeping through the unit. He stared at what should have been a storage space full of travel-worn instrument cases, but was now empty.

'What the fuck?'

He felt a shove from behind, grunted and fell, then heard the door being pulled shut. As it rattled down to the floor, he rolled over and scrambled to his feet, only to be pushed back down again. The lights went out, he felt a knee in his chest and a torch beam shone in his face, blinding him.

'You come for the instruments?' a voice growled at him.

'What's it to you?' grumbled Dixie.

'If you want to stay connected to your balls you'll answer.'

Dixie felt cold sharp pressure between his legs. He didn't need to see the large blade to know what it was. Sudden fear soaked through his tangled hair. 'What do you want?' he stammered.

'You're here for the instruments, right?' the voice repeated. 'Cold Steel's instruments?'

'Sure, sure,' gabbled Dixie.

'So you don't tell *anyone* they've been lost, understand?'

'But—'

'Let them find out for themselves.'

'They'll—'

'Listen, fucker. They've gone and you don't know anything about it. You tell any other story and we'll come back to carry on this conversation.'

'I don't—'

'Believe it, mate.'

Chapter 4

Cold Steel sat sardined in St Clements' decaying portakabin departure lounge, while Johnny argued with the charter operator.

'No,' said Johnny. 'Cold Steel, me and Miss Shaw. No one else.'

'You're not making the rules today, man.' The charter boss sat at his desk and smiled in a relaxed, controlled way, seemingly impervious to the unfanned furnace heat, while sweat ran down Johnny's thinly covered head and into his straggly ponytail.

'What do you mean?' spluttered Johnny. 'We're paying for this flight, dammit. *We* say who goes on board.'

'Relax.' The charter boss stared at Johnny. 'One streak through the Coconut Grove and everything changes. I mean, thanks for your help the other night and all that, but let's face it, you *did* lead the Ancadians here, and you *did* trash my cousin's place.' He smiled. 'So now we're done.'

'But—'

'Look, man, it's only one person more. You'll love her.'

'Her?'

'Hey, you've already got a female reporter on board, what's one more?'

'A *reporter?*'

'A *decent* reporter.' Johnny swung around at the husky voice behind him and saw a slim-fit, shorthaired blonde in jeggings and loose white top. Slanting green eyes and a sharp nose gave her an inquisitive look that he reckoned would match her job. Her small mouth smiled easily and softened her otherwise flinty expression. 'Angie Dale, Music Post,' she whispered, ironing her body against his. The band chuckled from their squeezebox seating. 'It was good of your boys to invite me along.'

'Yeah,' he muttered. 'They're always doing stupid things.'

'A band can never have enough publicity, Johnny.' Her eyes opened wide and she stared up at him. 'If you thought about it, you'd see how much you needed me.'

'Save it, sweetheart,' sighed Johnny. 'There's nothing you could do for me or the band.'

'Are you sure about that?' she breathed, smiling even more as Johnny looked down and got an eyeful of her wonderbra cleavage. 'You need to think beyond what's inside those leather pants of yours, unless of course there really *is* another reason why you're wasting your time with Rachel Shaw? She won't give the band the same coverage I could. She won't give *you* the same attention I would.'

'And that's why he's got enough sense to stay put.' Rachel materialised at Johnny's side and he quickly averted his eyes. Rachel stood two inches taller than him, a firm-limbed package that left him reeling in disbelief at what the last week had given him. And now *another* woman, and him just the manager, a faceless entity that no one really knew or saw. 'Go talk to the band, Angie.' Rachel's voice was like a Trotsky ice pick and Johnny squirmed nervously. Angie raised her eyebrows at Johnny, spun round in a demure circle and sidled back to the band. 'Itchy feet already?' asked Rachel, a killing look in her eye.

'Christ, no.'

'Didn't stop you getting an eyeful of her undersized boobs.'

'What? No way.'

'Don't give me that. I saw you. Any closer and you'd have two black eyes.' She suddenly smiled. 'Maybe you need to know what you'd be missing if you ever, *ever* chose her over me.'

'As if.'

Rachel folded her arms. 'Are you going to kick her off the plane?'

'You mean you want me to get close enough to kick her?'

'Are you letting her get on?'

'It's not my call.'

'Really?' She skewered him with a sceptical look.

'Look,' said Johnny. 'Since last night, the band are no longer the best thing that's happened to St Clements. Which means we – *I* – can't get people thrown off a flight.'

'And whose idea was it to let her on in the first place?'

'That *reporter* is telling me the band invited her.'

'Why would they do that?'

Johnny stopped himself from blurting out the suicidally obvious. He stood open-mouthed while he waited for his brain to emerge from its foetal position. He smiled. 'I'll talk to the band.'

'Make sure it's *them* you'll be talking to.'

'Just because you didn't like her boobs.'

'You're living dangerously today.'

'Hey,' he smiled. 'I'm playing the game, Rachel.'

She smiled back. 'You're catching on fast. Watch where you look.'

'Follow me if you want.'

'I trust you.'

He laughed. 'Sure you do.'

*

'Careful, lads,' said Andy. 'He's coming over.'

'Right,' said Johnny. 'Like I was miles away to begin with.'

'Don't expect a group hug for cutting our holiday short,' sneered Andy.

'Oh, *I* did that, did I?' Johnny shook his head. 'This early trip back is on you, not me.'

'Twenty Studios, you say,' grinned Maxwell.

'That's right,' said Johnny.

'Is Archimedes Wasp still running the place?'

'Christ, Maxwell. I don't bloody know. Two days ago, we were told to be there. Yesterday we got told to be there a whole lot sooner. You want to know what I know about Twenty? That's it.'

'We might not end up there,' warned Maxwell.

'Why not?'

'Archimedes Wasp doesn't like me very much.'

'Fucking hell, Maxwell, *I* don't like you very much, but do you see *me* quitting my job.' He shot a warning look at Vince. 'And don't even go there, you bastard.'

'It's more than just personalities, man,' said Joe.

'Like what?' said Johnny.

'You mean you don't know?' asked Angie.

'And I suppose you do?' said Johnny.

'Didn't Rachel tell you?'

'Maybe she's too busy doing her job.'

'So I'll tell you,' said Maxwell. 'It—'

'Was over a woman,' said Vince.

'And money, man,' added Joe.

'And when was this?' asked Johnny.

'Straight after the first album.'

'Fucking years ago, you mean?' Curiosity flashed into Johnny's mind. He looked at Maxwell. 'What did you do?'

'Ever heard of Earth?'

'What kind of stupid question is that?' scoffed Johnny. 'I've managed metal bands all my life, Maxwell. Of course I've heard of Earth. Fucking hell, have I ever heard of Earth?'

'Not the band, mate. The club.'

'Clubs? Clubs? Do I look like I give a shit about clubs?' said Johnny. 'Cut to the gut.'

Maxwell smiled like an old storyteller. 'Back then,' he said, 'Earth was one of the most exclusive clubs in London. Getting in was a big thing.'

'Yeah,' said Andy. 'And right after we made the album, we were on fire.'

'Well,' said Joe, 'we thought we were.'

'Big new publicity,' said Johnny. 'Actually got some air play, money in your pocket, big tour arranged.' Nods all round. 'So you went slumming it with the in crowd, huh?'

'Something like that,' said Vince. 'Once the bastards let us inside.'

Johnny smiled, 'Did they make you wear ties?' Mumbled replies and no eye contact. Johnny laughed. 'Earth isn't that special.'

'Think what you want,' growled Maxwell. 'I played poker all night with the guy who owns Twenty. I cleaned him out and I staked the whole pot against his woman, all on one turn of the deck. Highest card won everything.'

'And you beat him?' asked Johnny.

Maxwell smiled. 'I've never told. And I never will.'

'Whatever.' Johnny picked up his phone. 'This is the business, Maxwell. He's forgotten about it.' Without waiting for an answer, he flicked through his contacts, punched the screen and waited for a pick-up. 'Dixie?'

'Hi, Johnny.'

'You okay, Dixie?'

'Sure, why wouldn't I be?'

'You sound a bit flaky.'

'It's nothing.'

'Hung over, huh?'

'Something like that.'

'So get off your arse, mate. We're back to work.'

'Sure, sure, I got your text.'

'The gear survived storage okay? It's on its way to the studio? It better be, Dixie, those bastards are charging a fucking fortune to record there.' A long pause and Johnny felt the first wisps of tension wrap around him. 'Talk to me, Dixie.'

'It's okay, Johnny. It's okay.'

'That's all I need to know. We're boarding the plane right now.'

Dixie had already hung up.

Chapter 5

Crammed into a Dash 8 similar to the one that had flown them into St Clements, Cold Steel and Johnny flew back to Jamaica with two extra people. Rachel sat next to Johnny, rubbed her thigh against his, and subjected him to almost vindictive levels of teasing. Across the narrow aisle and several rows back, Angie dug all ten black-painted fingernails into her interview with the band.

'So you really can't swim?' she asked.

Mike Vesuvius grinned like a spotty teenager and nodded, his corkscrew brown hair flowing around his head like a seventies shampoo advert.

'Doesn't seem important when you're a drummer,' he said.

'Bloody well does when your boat gets sunk by the frigging Ancadian Navy.' Andy leered at Angie from underneath his dirty blond hair. 'And who was it that saved the useless stupid bastard? Me. Not his pointless mate over there.'

'Hey, man.' Joe stared at Andy with vacant, stoned eyes. Dirty flared jeans and a purple shirt lent his skinny body a flowing cloudiness. 'I'd have helped if I could.'

'Leave it, Joe.' Mike glared at Andy. 'He's just trying to get a rise out of you.'

'Trying?' said Andy. 'No need. You two are busy enough getting each other to rise.' He sniggered and Mike flushed, cracked his knuckles but sat in the cramped seat and took a deep, controlled breath. 'Christ,' said Andy. 'The two of them were worse than useless. There we were...' He sidled up to Angie. 'Taken bloody prisoner by the Ancadians, threatened with God knows what, then fired at and our boat sunk. Holy shit, we'd have been drowned or roasted alive if a boat from St Clements hadn't picked us up.'

'Lucky.' Angie raised her eyebrows.

'Lucky?' spluttered Andy. 'Lucky? Fucking hell, if they hadn't found us we'd have been dead. *I'd* have been—'

'Better off dead,' Vince ran a hand through his slicked black hair, smoothed an obsessively sharp triangular chinbeard. He scowled olive-skinned Latino malevolence at Andy. 'And we'd have been better off without you.'

Angie's eyes sparked at the acrid malevolence. 'I heard about you two,' she said. 'Mike and Joe are best mates, but Cold Steel's two guitarists have never seen eye to eye.'

'It's not broken,' said Andy.

'So don't fix it,' grumbled Vince.

'Have you *ever* liked each other?'

'No,' in unison.

'Doesn't that make it hard to work together? How come you joined the same band at all?'

'Blind audition,' said Maxwell. 'We'd watch the guitarists play on their own, no back up, no support, get their essence. Shit, that's how we all came together. No point being in this band if you haven't got star quality. Vince and Andy hadn't even seen each other until they got the job.'

'Strange way to choose a team,' said Angie.

'It worked,' said Maxwell. His large, hook nose dominated his face, and his uneven-toothed smile and long black hair did nothing to hide his raw masculinity. It was easy for Angie to draw parallels between Maxwell's physical appearance and his obsession with all things pirate. His dark eyes gleamed. 'You think we'd have got this far if it didn't?'

'I suppose,' she replied. 'But some people say that left to yourselves, Joe and Mike would have hooked up with a pair of guitarists that actually liked each other, Vince and Andy would have gone off on different solo projects, and you, Maxwell, you'd have formed another band from scratch.'

'That's what they say, is it?' Maxwell's direct stare drilled into Angie's eyes and she fought to hold his stare.

'That's right.' She replied.

'Then how come we got the whole world marching after playing one concert at St Clements?'

Angie's lip's curled downward. 'No one could have written *that* script,' she agreed.

'And *you're* doubting us?' scorned Maxwell. 'Four albums, platinum sales, sold-out tours. Jesus, what do you *want* us to do?' His disreputable smile told her exactly what *he* wanted to do.

'I'm not doubting you.' A professional, slightly dismissive smile. She glanced sideways at Andy, and an idea planted itself in her mind. 'I'm just wondering how it all went so wrong the night after.'

'We screwed up,' said Maxwell, arms as wide as he could get in the cramped cabin. 'St Clements kicked us out and we deserved it, so what better time to get into a studio and do the next album?'

'And where will that be?'

'Twenty Studios, maybe.'

'Maybe?' Curiosity piqued once more.

Maxwell smiled, sat back and closed his eyes. 'We don't worry about that. That's what Johnny's for.'

Angie looked back at Johnny. 'People say it's thanks to Johnny Faslane that you're still playing.' She turned to the band. 'They say no one but he could have organised the St Clements concert in such a short time. Some say he's the best.'

'He's a good man,' said Mike.

'He's lucky,' grumbled Andy.

'Knows what he's doing,' murmured Joe.

'Replaceable,' said Vince.

'And what about your last tour?' asked Angie. 'It would have finished you if Johnny hadn't turned it around.'

'*We* turned it around,' crowed Andy.

'Nothing to do with Ozone Records giving you one last chance after another? Or Johnny Faslane laying down the law?' Angie faced Maxwell. 'Looks like it's a fifty-fifty split on the manager and you've got the casting vote, Maxwell. What do *you* say?'

Maxwell looked over to Johnny, whose attention was monopolised by Rachel. He turned to Angie and smiled once more. 'He knows what he's doing right now.'

*

Dark rainclouds hovered over Jamaica's Norman Manley airport and climbed into infinity. Silenced by the VIP lounge's air-sealed interior, the miles-high nimbostratus matched Johnny's mood. He glared at Maxwell who looked back at him with choirboy innocence.

'I don't see the difference.' Maxwell sipped a Red Stripe as singer and manager sat on high-leg bar stools in the Club Kingston Bar. 'It's good enough for you.'

'What is?'

'Your bird.'

'My *what?*'

'Oh, sorry, I meant *Rachel.*'

'And you'd be fucking wise to stick with her name.' Johnny glared balefire at Maxwell. 'So what about her?'

'*She's* got a ticket back with us,' said Maxwell.

'So?'

'So how come you're the only one taking a squeeze on the flight home?'

Johnny saw Rachel looking curiously at him and Maxwell. She went back to photographing the band. 'She's not my fucking squeeze,' he hissed.

'Well, she's not shagging anyone else. What would *you* call it?'

'She's a reporter, an embedded reporter.'

'Embedded,' chortled Maxwell. 'In bedded more like. Don't be shy about it, mate, I've seen worse, she's definitely a good pull for you.'

'And what the fuck does *that* mean?' Johnny's skin burned and he felt his face flush.

Maxwell shrugged. 'What's in it for her? Have you ever thought of that?'

'And I suppose she wouldn't be seen dead with me if it wasn't for my job. Is that what you're saying?'

'I'm just—'

'Listen,' fumed Johnny. 'Rachel is reporting on the band. What goes on between me and her is nothing to do with anyone else, *get it?*'

'Yeah, and she'd have blown the Ancadian story wide open if you hadn't caught her.'

'That's her job, tosser, and she's on our side now.'

'Sure looked like it last night.'

'Reality check, Maxwell. You and the rest of the band were out of order last night. You deserved it. If you don't like it, talk to Ozone. Rachel's reporting on the whole story as it happens. Album, rehearsals, and the tour. Even *I* don't get to change that.'

'Not that you'd want to, right?'

'Get this,' fumed Johnny. 'I can't stop her telling the whole world every time you act like children – only *you* can do that, by growing up. But what I have done is challenge her to show you lot as more than just depraved party animals.'

'What?'

'She's got the job of showing the world your caring, fluffy, human side.'

'I don't think we've got one.'

'Start growing one,' snapped Johnny.

'And this will make us look good?' asked Maxwell.

'Just be yourselves.' Johnny sighed in exasperation. 'When Rachel asks, tell her.'

'That's all?'

'That's all.'

'We can say all that to Angie.'

'No,' growled Johnny.

'You can't stop her getting on the same flight as us.' Maxwell's lower lip pouted.

'Maybe,' said Johnny. 'But if you've got any sense, you'll avoid her like a dose of Ebola.'

'Yeah, right. Because that applies to you as well, doesn't it?'

'What?'

'We all saw Rachel coming on to you on the flight from St Clements. We know what *you'll* be getting up to in first class.'

'Right,' said Johnny. 'Surrounded by you lot it'll be like a royal bloody wedding.'

*

The last Johnny saw of Angie, she was standing at the crowded departure gate, talking rapidly on her mobile. *She's trouble,* he thought, before ushering the band through the VIP lounge and into the dreamliner's spacious first-class cabin. Ozone had paid for the whole section, and Johnny, feeling like the weediest bouncer in the world, had entry rights for the entire flight. It was himself, the band and Rachel allowed in, and no one else.

'Better than kipping under the stars on that bloody treasure hunt,' whooped Andy, bouncing up and down on his extended pod seat like an excited schoolboy. 'We should crib like this all the time.'

The plane's doors whispered shut, the cabin crew motioned Johnny to his seat and he buckled up next to Rachel. Her cobalt eyes bored into him from beneath her raven-black fringe. 'Are you going to watch over them for the whole flight?' A small grin tugged at her lips.

'I don't know.' He smiled back at her. 'Are you going to be taking pictures and talking to them for the next nine hours?'

'What do you mean?' Her eyes flashed wide open. 'It *is* what I'm here for.'

'And I thought you were here to distract me and lead me astray.'

She chuckled. 'That's my hobby, not my job.'

*

Johnny dozed off halfway through the new-release sci-fi movie on his in-flight screen. He awoke with a start in a darkened cabin and pulled his earphones free. Next to him, Rachel was scrolling through a set of images on her camera, while behind him he heard muted male mutterings and unmistakable female giggling. 'Jesus,' he groaned. 'They'd find a groupie on top of an iceberg.'

'She's not a groupie,' said Rachel absently. Her eyes remained fixed on her camera screen.

'What?'

'It's Angie Dale.'

'You mean the reporter?'

'I'm glad you didn't remember her *that* well.'

'They let her in here?' he gasped. 'I *told* them not to, the simple bastards.'

'Did you expect them to do as they were told?'

'After everything we've been through, I thought they might.'

'It'll never happen, Johnny. You'd better get used to it.'

'Happen or not,' he growled, 'I'm kicking her out.' He stood up and stepped around Rachel. She grabbed his bony wrist in a steel grip and pulled him towards her. Her perfume wafted over him and blurred his thoughts. He looked down at her, sleeveless blouse and leggings uncreased and wardrobe-fresh. It seemed to Johnny that she was the only person in the world who could travel and still look good.

'She won't get them to say anything they haven't already told everyone else,' she whispered. 'It's *you* she needs to talk to for the inside track.' She inched her face next to his. 'And do you *really* think I'm going to let you?'

'What?'

'I need the rest room, walk me there.'

'What? It's just there.' He flung an arm towards the front of the plane. 'You won't get lost.'

She tightened her grip on his wrist. 'Come with me,' she whispered.

Two minutes later, Johnny stood outside the first-class but still tiny restroom, waiting for Rachel and wondering why the hell she needed an escort. *Maybe she doesn't like the dark,* he thought, staring around the subdued cabin. An air stewardess undulated past him. Her fitted blouse and skirt showed off her figure and snared his eyesight. He didn't hear the restroom door opening, didn't see the sudden wedge of light. He yelped in surprise as he was grabbed and dragged backwards.

The door snapped shut and Johnny crashed against the toilet wall. Rachel pressed into him. Her hands roamed over his body and sent live electricity shooting along his nerve endings. With barely enough room for one person, he snaked his skinny arms around her, painfully turned on after the earlier flight. They linked together, closer than a pair of Siamese twins in shrink-wrap, and his hands felt glued to her body.

'Still thinking of Angie Dale?' Her whispered words soaked into his ears like molten honey.

'You think I'd prefer her over you?' He gripped her buttocks and pulled her closer. She gasped and smiled invincible seduction.

'Maybe you should prove it,' she purred.

'What, here?'

'Have you done it this high up before?' Her fingernails slipped beneath his sparse ponytail and stroked his neck, sending shock waves exploding through him.

'Well—'

'Really?' She chuckled a throaty laugh. 'That experienced?' A light kiss danced across his trembling lips. 'Or that eager to find out?'

He growled and pressed against her. She squealed and pushed back at him, her back against the small mirror above the washbasin. He kissed her and moaned with pleasure at her taste and feel. She wriggled against him and sat perched on the basin. Johnny held her slim waist and slid her camera behind her. She took a firm hold of his head and they kissed. He felt the lightning rush of blood inside him roaring in his ears, louder than a post-gig bout of tinnitus. Her perfume floated around them like an intoxicating lemongrass cloud, the feel of her firm curves, the taste of her lips, the sound of her own heavy breathing and quiet gasps. His hands traversed her body and translocated him to nowhere and everywhere. He could have been on the plane, the moon, at the bottom of the sea. Where he was meant nothing, *who* he was with meant everything. His leather pants quickly mingled with her leggings on the tiny floor.

'Oh, God,' she gasped. 'I should tease you more often.'

'Yeah,' groaned Johnny. 'And I should look at other reporters more often.' Her nails dug into his neck and he yelped in sudden pain, then moaned in pleasure while she ground into him and they did a pelvic motion dance. His hands alternately twitched and held her close. Her camera swung back and forth behind her in time with their rhythmic movements.

'My camera,' she said distractedly. 'It'll get broken.'

'Bollocks,' grunted Johnny. 'We're not stopping now. I'll buy you another one.'

'Do you know how much they cost?'

'I don't *care* how much they bloody cost.'

A quiet ring-tone advertised the camera being inadvertently switched on by their piston-like movement. Johnny's hands fumbled behind Rachel's back in an attempt to switch it off, not wanting a candid picture of the two of them enjoying a top-budget tropospheric coupling. All he managed to do was turn on the water, soaking them both as well as the camera.

'Oh, Johnny,' moaned Rachel. 'Forget about the bloody camera, think about *me!*'

He grabbed a twin handful of firm flesh and groaned, the camera forgotten. He didn't notice the crack as it hammered against the toilet wall, breaking the casing.

'Faster, faster,' she gasped. 'Oh, God, do it, do it, you scrawny, bony, slaphead wonder-man!'

Johnny tried to shut off the tap, but he turned the switch the wrong way and even more water sprayed over the broken camera.

'Keep going, Johnny. Yes, yes, oh, yes.'

A sharp crack and a smell of burning wafted through the air.

'Rachel,' panted Johnny. 'Your camera.'

'*Screw* the bloody camera.' She silenced him with a kiss and he surrendered to the moment. The cramped, uncomfortable reality of the washroom featured nowhere in his mind. He wasn't on a plane with Cold Steel, he was an invincible love-God, soaring through the heavens with a smouldering beauty at his side, sharing an endless ecstasy that eclipsed all other pleasures. Rachel's long black hair brushed against his face, her perfume wisped around his head, and he heard nothing but her breathing and words of encouragement as her lips hovered next to his ear. He was oblivious to the acrid smell of a burning electrical circuit in contact with running water, and completely missed the sharp, insistent beeping of a smoke alarm.

The toilet door crashed open and an ice cloud of carbon dioxide hosed over them. Johnny started coughing and he and Rachel struggled apart. He grappled with his leather pants, and Rachel slammed into him and locked her arms around his neck. He looked towards the solid wall of light that poured into the small cubicle from outside, then saw the pinpoint red light a microsecond before a camera flash illuminated them both.

Chapter 6

'For fuck's sake, it wasn't a bomb.' Johnny sat in a sparse police cell, somewhere in the bowels of Heathrow Airport. Cuffed to the back of the steel chair, he fidgeted impotently, while across a chipped table the sky marshal who'd held him on the plane had a muttered conversation with a weary-looking detective. The detective faced Johnny.

'The evidence says otherwise, Mister Faslane. Is that your real name?'

'No,' said Johnny. 'It's not my real name. You've seen my passport, why ask me the bloody obvious?'

'Don't fuck with me,' snapped the detective. 'You're the one who set off the fire alarm. You know what kind of world we're living in, Mister *Faslane,* and I've lost count of the number of people I've met who claim they didn't do anything wrong.'

'But I—'

'Didn't?' asked the detective.

'Look.' Desperation pitched Johnny's voice higher. 'It wasn't a bomb. It was a camera. It got broke, it got wet, it caught fire. Surely that's happened before.'

'What, in the toilet? With two people in there? The toilet closest to the flight cabin? All of a sudden, for no reason, a camera that you've both got in there breaks, gets wet and catches fire. You mean a chain of events like that happens all the time? Often enough for us to overlook it? Is that what you're saying?'

Johnny flushed and looked helplessly at the two men opposite. 'Jesus, lads, give me break. Do I *really* have to tell you what I was doing?'

'No,' replied the detective. 'You can say nothing and go down for ten years. I wouldn't dream of removing your right to remain silent.'

'It might be safer at that,' sighed Johnny. 'What did Miss Shaw say?'

'What?' snorted the detective. 'You think I'm about to let you know what your accomplice said? So you can both come up with the same alibi? You think I'm stupid?'

'No, I—'

'You started a fire at thirty thousand feet, Johnny. How do you think *that* looks?'

'We didn't mean to.'

'Oh, you didn't mean to? What *did* you mean to do?'

Johnny looked in mute appeal at the two men, then shrugged. 'Rachel's my girlfriend,' he murmured.

'What?' asked the detective.

'She's my girlfriend,' said Johnny. 'She pulled me into the restroom because, because, well, because we wanted some privacy.'

'Privacy? What for? So you could prime your bomb? So you could blow the plane up?'

'No! No!' wailed Johnny. 'Jesus Christ. We were having sex, the water was switched on, the camera got wet and caught fire, alright?'

'Sexual activity on board an airliner?' snapped the detective. 'Are you aware that contravenes paragraph three, subsection four of the Civil Aviation Act?'

'Oh, really?' said Johnny. 'Fucking hell, what's the penalty for getting laid on a plane? Are you going to castrate me?'

'Don't get cocky, mate.'

'No, I did that up in the air.'

The sky marshal guffawed. The detective kept a deadpan face for a few seconds, then started to chuckle.

'That's what she said as well,' laughed the detective. 'And if you're half the man she says you are, you can stay the hell away from my wife.'

'She said that?' asked Johnny.

'We couldn't shut her up.' The sky marshal stepped behind Johnny and unlocked the cuffs. 'And the forensics on the camera came back clean, so I guess you're telling the truth. Do it again, though, and you'll be more than just interviewed. Now, I suggest you get hold of as much redwing as you can cram down your neck before tonight, and for the next twelve months, you and Miss Shaw do *not* even enter the same airport together. Understand?'

Johnny stood up and rubbed his numbed wrists. The detective opened the door and waved him through.

Johnny gripped Rachel's hand, they walked through customs and were ushered into the VIP arrivals lounge where the band waited. 'Christ,' he muttered. 'They'll never shut up about this.'

'Don't worry,' said Rachel. 'They'll have enough on their minds with the new album.'

'And what about that photo of us doing it? It'll be viral by now. Oh, Jesus, it should be the band doing stuff like this, not me.'

'Any regrets?' Frosty enquiry.

'No, no. Shit, no.' Sheer terror response. 'I'd rather it wasn't splashed over the net, that's all.'

'You leave that to me,' growled Rachel. 'I can handle Angie bloody Dale.'

'I almost feel sorry for her.'

'You make damn sure you don't feel *anything* about that grasping little bitch,' hissed Rachel.

'Ashamed, Rachel?' Angie Dale glared open hostility as she stood backed against a prefab wall in Heathrow's arrivals hall. Suited commuters rushed past them, pulling cases on wheels and ignoring the conversation.

'Jealous, Angie?' Rachel pushed into Angie's personal space and stared back at her.

'Of what?'

'A healthy sex life.'

'Maybe I should cruise the ladies' toilets more often.'

'Well, the flight deck is out of bounds these days, so a girl didn't really have much choice, did she?'

'And no pride, either. Couldn't you have waited a few hours?'

'Don't lecture me, Angie.'

'You're right, why should I waste my time saying something you'll never listen to?'

'And what will you listen to?'

'You tell me, Rachel.' She looked left and right. 'I didn't ask for this encounter.'

'Delete those pictures, Angie. They're not news. Christ, the manager in a snoop shot while the band get ignored. You'd be laughed out of the business for putting your name to that. Call yourself a pap.'

'I'm not a pap,' blazed Angie.

'So don't come on like one. I swear if I see your pictures, or read your stories, or even *think* you've uploaded any of it, I'll find your agent, editor, contacts, whoever or whatever pays your bills and I'll tell them the truth about you.'

'The truth,' laughed Angie. 'And what's that? Christ, what does anyone care about the truth as long as I give them what they want?'

'No one wants pictures of Johnny. I'm warning you, Angie.'

'You're not scaring me, Rachel.'

'Maybe not, but I heard it was an insider who tipped off the Roberts enquiry.'

'That wasn't—'

'You want me to prove it? You want everyone to know about the journalism hacks that were made public by one of our own? Well, I use the term loosely. You're nothing to do with me.'

Angie broke eye contact. 'I didn't do it.'

'Sure, and I'm a blonde.'

'Believe what you want, Rachel, but there's more to my current assignment than getting a picture of you and Johnny. Be careful.'

'Oh.' Rachel's eyebrows climbed to her fringe. '*You're* warning *me?*'

'My brief was to get bad publicity, anything that would stick, including Johnny.'

'And who's paying you?'

'I don't know.'

'I don't believe you.' She moved nose to nose with Angie. 'Bad publicity, you say?'

'That was the brief.'

'Anything else?'

'That's all.'

'The assignment's over, Angie.'

'I can't—'

'Think about Roberts, Angie. You can.'

'You'd do it, wouldn't you?'

'Believe it.'

Angie lifted and then dropped her shoulders. 'So I'm unemployed again, but I hope you've got a thick skin, Rachel. I can't stop the pictures I've already passed over.'

*

Archimedes Wasp sat in his purple-lined office and simmered pot-roast fury. The bubbling hookah pipe seemed to echo his emotions like an old friend. The new game was containment, and that meant letting Cold Steel, *the bastards,* into his studio.

His emergency plan hadn't gone well. All he'd got were a few blurred pictures of their manager getting it on at thirty thousand. *As if that's going to stop anything, it'll just encourage them, for Christ's sake.* He picked up his desk phone and seconds later his secretary picked up.

'Fawn,' he said. 'I want to see Kurgan?'

'But he's—'

'Now?'

Five minutes later, Archimedes looked across his desk at his best producer. Kurgan wore faux-fur lined imitation animal skins that only just gave his broomstick build an illusion of masculinity. Dark blue hair sprouted from his head like exploding fireworks. And although he was the boss, Archimedes felt Kurgan's hostility at being summoned. His attitude rankled, and Archimedes fought to curb his anger. 'Cold Steel are coming here to record an album?' he bluntly announced.

'Are you asking me or telling me?'

'Do I sound like I'm bloody well asking you?' yelled Archimedes.

Kurgan shrugged. 'Metal, huh?' His nasal voice meshed through blocked nostrils and Archimedes felt a desperate urge to ram a handful of menthol up his nose. 'I *could* do it, I suppose. You *are* my boss, after all.'

'You *suppose,* you cheeky bastard?'

'And *I* suppose there's something else going,' said Kurgan. 'You've never brought me in here before to dish out your orders.'

'The whys don't concern you?' commanded Archimedes. 'As you said, I'm the boss and you'd better remember that. Now, it wasn't Cold Steel who asked to come here, it was Ozone, their recording company. And they didn't ask, they told?'

Kurgan stifled a yawn. 'Whatever,' he said. 'And you want me to do their album?'

'I don't want it released?'

'Good idea,' snorted Kurgan. 'Are you really so pissed off with Ozone Records that you'll sign your own studio's death warrant?'

'Meaning?'

'Meaning that if you shaft a band that Ozone specifically wanted to send here, they'll send all their other acts elsewhere. We'd never survive that kind of boycott.'

'You're not as stupid as you look?'

'And you're not as dumb as you sound. So what's the story behind this?'

'What?'

'Not what, why?'

'Why?'

'Yes. Why not let Cold Steel make the album here? They're hot prop after their Caribbean trip. Everybody wants a piece of them.'

'I'm not going to turn them away, but I don't expect to release the album?' Archimedes paused and stared at Kurgan. 'Do you know *anything* about Cold Steel?'

'Brit metal, four albums. Had a nuclear wobble on their last tour. New manager is universally accepted as having saved them from themselves. They stopped a war in the Caribbean with a concert organised within a week. Did I miss anything out?' His eyes shot wide open. 'Hang on a second, their singer's Maxwell Diabolo!' A crooked grin pasted itself to Kurgan's stubbled face. 'Something about a card game a few years ago.'

'Shut up.'

'Stash of money and a woman on the turn of a card, wasn't it?'

'Shut up!'

'Yes, she told the red tops a whole *load* of stories about you.'

'Shut UP!'

'And didn't you get kicked out of that club after that? You lost it and trashed the cards room.'

'SHUT UP!'

Archimedes stood up, fists planted on his desk, eyes wide and bloodshot and staring murder at Kurgan, who sat inside his fake furs and giggled.

'Ozone sent them here,' muttered Archimedes. 'And I can't stop that. I can't kick them out, either, but I'll die before I let those bastards get rich out of *my* bloody studio.'

He sat down and glared at Kurgan, as though everything was his fault. Kurgan smiled. 'So, just like Police Academy, we don't throw them out, they must be encouraged to leave on their own, right?' Archimedes nodded. 'But you do realise, Archimedes, they *are* going to make another album. If not here, somewhere.'

'I don't care what they do, as long as it's not here.'

'And we're going to achieve that, how?'

'They won't be able to record anything without instruments?'

'Come again?'

'Their instruments. They won't have them.'

'I don't—'

'All you need to know is that they think their instruments will be at the studio when they arrive.' Archimedes shook his head. 'They've already disappeared, and I've seen to that?'

'But they'll get replacements,' said Kurgan. 'They're a big band, they've got money, endorsements, sponsors.'

'Sure they will, but it all takes time? And that's the one thing Cold Steel haven't got.' Archimedes laughed. 'Their tour dates are already booked and the album has to be recorded before the tour starts, before they can rehearse. Even a short delay will either make their album less polished, or their tour less prepared. Delay them, Kurgan. It's a war of attrition, and you can play your part by keeping them off balance, and helping them in a very unhelpful way?'

*

From the outside, Twenty Studios looked like just another anonymous corporate building. The small, brushed-silver nameplate next to the gloss-painted wood-panel door suggested a modest, conforming business, completely in keeping with all the other doorways on the Regency townhouses that stretched the length of London's Squire Street.

No chewing gum stuck to Squire Street's scrupulously cleaned pavements, no bird shit spattered the ground beneath the television aerials. A gleaming collection of Bentleys, Astons and Maseratis parked along the street, and none of them showed a speck of accumulated dirt on waxed paintwork. Gucci and Prada footwear walked on the pristine paving stones, and the few of those who might have known what heavy metal was would never have expected to see it on Squire Street.

'Doesn't look much to me.' Maxwell stepped out of the oversized taxi, and the rest of Cold Steel followed, forming a longhaired molasses-pool outside the studio. Maxwell's black hair blew around his lean, stubbled face in the summer breeze.

'Judging by appearances?' Johnny stepped out of the taxi after the band, his ponytail and mostly visible head reflecting the sunshine. His matt yellow cowboy boots tapped on the pavement. He shoved a hand into the pocket of his beige leather pants and looked at Maxwell with mock seriousness.

'That's always a *big* mistake.' Rachel grinned at Johnny. He returned her smile.

'Maybe you can keep the attention coming *our* way instead of tabloid shots of you and Johnny,' grinned Maxwell. Johnny blushed brighter than a traffic light and Rachel fired a bullet stare at Maxwell. He deflected her hostility with an armour-plated smile and nodded towards the studio door. 'I'm still surprised they let us in here.'

'Forget about the past,' said Johnny. 'You're getting a real chance here, so use it.' His phone rang.

'Johnny, it's Lucy Penhalligan. Are you there?'

Johnny pictured the slim, dark-haired executive from Ozone Records, who headed the company's UK artists and relations department. 'We've just arrived.'

'Keep a tight rein on your boys. We had to lean hard to get them in.'

'Oh?' said Johnny. 'Any details?'

'That's need to know, just be aware.'

'Don't tell the hired help too much, eh?'

'Don't be a bitch, Johnny, it doesn't suit you. You know what Twenty Studios means for an artist, what kind of albums get made there?'

'Absolute classics. Every time.'

'Which brings us to Cold Steel. The St Clements publicity makes this an ideal step. This album could make the band a household name. They're big metal, we want them big, full stop.'

'There's easier ways.' Johnny checked. 'I heard about some sort of history between Maxwell and the guy who owns the place.'

'Personality issues are *your* job to sort out.' Lucy paused. 'What kind of history?'

'A card game years ago.'

'Is that all?'

Johnny shrugged. 'The band seem to think it might still be live.'

'A little friction is a price worth paying,' said Lucy. 'Anyway, it's a done deal, so keep your boys sweet and they won't need to talk to me.' She hung up and Johnny looked back at the band.

'Problem?' asked Maxwell.

Chapter 7

Six feet inside the studio, Johnny's irritation simmered to potboil overflowing. 'What do you mean, we're not expected. Check again. Cold Steel.'

The receptionist, with a grey power suit and silver fingernails that flashed like scalpels, stared cold-war hostility at Johnny before looking at her computer screen. She drummed her nails on the polished ebony desktop, tutted to herself, then looked at a solitary printout on her desk. She looked up at Johnny through blue-grey storm eyes beneath arrow-straight platinum hair.

'Cold Steel, you say?'

'Do you want me to spell it?'

'And you're musicians?'

'You work in a recording studio,' said Johnny, 'and you're asking me that?'

'I only know bands of consequence.'

'Meaning?'

Arctic smile. 'How many Grammys have Cold Steel won?'

'Oh, Christ,' gasped Johnny. 'I didn't know you had to be such a musical snob to work here.' He looked at the black and white square marble floor. 'I guess it comes with the territory.' He turned back to her. 'Check with your boss. *Somebody* hasn't told you we're due.'

'They don't want us here,' chuckled Maxwell. 'And I know why.'

'We're here. We're staying and they'd better get used to it.' Johnny glared at the receptionist. 'Where's the control room?'

'Through the lobby, first on the left.'

'Right,' said Johnny. 'We're setting up now, find the producer.'

'But—'

'Do it.'

*

'How can they be gone?' spluttered Johnny. 'I phoned Dixie; he said it was all arranged.'

Kurgan slouched on a Freedom Task chair and propped feet in dirty sneakers on the control room's computer-festooned mixing desk. Fake fur rode up his unattractive and spindly legs. 'What can I say?' he whined. 'They're not here.'

'I told you,' said Maxwell. 'I told you they didn't want us here.'

'Do you want us here?' asked Johnny.

Kurgan shrugged. 'You're here.' His voice rumbled indifference. 'I thought you'd be coming with instruments, though.'

Johnny felt the awkwardness slide around the control room like hot butter in a saucepan. He picked up his phone and called Dixie. 'Where the hell are the instruments?'

'I'm sorry, Johnny.'

'What the hell does sorry mean, Dixie? We spoke on the phone the other day and you never said a bloody thing.'

'They told me not to say.'

'*Who* told you not to say? Fuck me, I thought you were one of us.'

'Hey, Johnny, I'd like to see how big *your* balls are when they're being threatened with a pair of garden shears. You weren't there, man.' Dixie paused. 'Shit, Johnny, you're not going to fire me, are you?'

'Dixie, what's your job?'

'Roadie, man. All the way.'

'Can you get me a trainer?'

'What?'

'A trainer,' said Johnny. 'You know, someone who trains people, gets them fit.'

'I don't—'

'Look, Dixie, the band are getting slack. We need them lean again, so a gym is definitely in. Along with a real bastard of a trainer who won't take their shit, but who *will* get them into shape.'

'Well, I know one bloke who might be alright.'

Johnny turned and looked at the band. 'Get him on side, Dixie, and we're mates again.'

'I don't know, Johnny. Are you sure you want him?'

'I don't know, Dixie. Are you sure you want your job?'

'You—'

'I want him. Get him.'

'He's a bit—'

'Just get him, Dixie.'

'And then what?'

'I'll message you Ozone's budget code. Book a gym, get this guy. When the band aren't recording, they're training. I want them fit enough to run a bloody marathon. And Dixie, if the instruments go missing again, find *some* way to tell me, alright?' Johnny hung up and turned back to the band. 'We've had some bother at the storage unit.'

'I wonder how that happened.' Maxwell stared at Kurgan.

'How do I know?' asked Kurgan.

'So what do we do now?' asked Maxwell.

Johnny flicked through his phone contacts. 'It's a temporary thing, we'll get replacements. Even if you lads don't know what the hell you play, I do. Leave it with me.'

'And is our gear going to magically arrive right now?' asked Vince.

'What kind of dumb question is that?' snapped Johnny.

'Okay,' said Vince. 'What kind of dumb question is this – what do you want us to do in a studio with no bloody instruments?'

'Well,' smirked Kurgan, 'we've got a few left behind by the last band who were here.'

'Fine,' smiled Johnny. 'It'll be two days max before the replacement stuff is here. So until then, we'll use what you've got.'

'There's only one guitar, though.'

Johnny looked at Vince and Andy. 'What's it to be, lads? Take turns till your own guitars arrive?'

'I'm not touching the same guitar as him,' spat Vince.

'Me neither,' said Andy.

'What then?' snapped Johnny. 'In fact, don't bother. Tell it to Rachel. I'm not fucking interested.'

'Tell it to Rachel?'

'All part of the new three-point plan. When you're not making music, you're telling Rachel why you're all such a bunch of tossers. And when you're not doing that, you're in the gym.'

'The gym?' yelled Andy. 'I'm not sharing a gym with Vince.'

'Oh, fucking hell,' gasped Johnny. 'Look, one of you is playing guitar, and I don't care who, so just sort it out.'

'How?'

'Christ, just flip a coin, can't you?'

'I've got a better idea,' smiled Maxwell. 'Blue flame.'

'What?' asked Johnny.

Vince looked at Johnny. 'Got a lighter?'

*

'What the hell is this blue flame shit?' asked Johnny. Vince and Andy sat on plastic chairs in a live room, eating cold beans.

'Lighter,' said Maxwell.

Johnny fumbled in his pocket and threw him a fake Zippo. 'What do you need that for?'

'What do you think?' belched Andy. He put his empty beans bowl on the floor and undid his belt.

'Oh, shit,' groaned Johnny. 'Not naked again, Andy.'

'Can't get the flames with clothes on.' Andy's grubby combat trousers dropped, he pulled down a pair of once-white underpants and bent over. 'First one cooking up, standard rules apply.'

Maxwell flicked open the lighter and spun the flint-wheel. A guttering flame hovered near Andy's pale, brillo-hairy buttocks. Seconds later a growling burst of flatulence was ignited, sending a foot-long blue flame streaking across the live room, followed by a musty, burnt-egg after-smell.

'Top that,' crowed Andy, his face obscured by his trousers. 'First one and we've got a twelve-incher.'

'Jesus Christ,' muttered Johnny. '*That's* the blue flame?'

Maxwell laughed and looked absently at his phone. 'Timer's set. We've got an hour of lighting farts and measuring the flame. Longest one wins.'

'Fucking hell,' sighed Johnny. 'Do you mind if I don't watch.'

'You got something better to do?' Vince unzipped his Escada jeans and bent over next to Andy.

'*Anything's* better than watching this,' said Johnny. 'Shout me when it's over, I'll be next door in the real world.' He walked into the control room and saw Kurgan's questioning look. 'Don't ask.' He sat down and pulled out his phone.

'Can I ask?' said Rachel.

'No,' snapped Johnny.

Muffled cheers wafted through from the live room.

'Can I look?' Rachel peered through the live room window. 'I thought you wanted me to find out about the inner them.'

More cheers, more highly pitched this time.

'If you look in there, you'll never be curious about anything ever again.'

Johnny touched his phone screen. 'Dixie, how's our trainer going? Have we got the gym?'

Rachel looked at the live room window and her mouth dropped open.

'He needs the job,' said Dixie. 'He's in.'

A faint insistent tapping at the window.

'Good,' said Johnny. 'I want the band there straight after recording.'

The tapping got louder,

'They won't like that,' replied Dixie. Johnny turned his back on the live room and tried to concentrate on his phone call.

'Johnny,' said Rachel.

'In a second,' said Johnny. 'Dixie, I want them playing all day, getting in shape for the tour, and too damn knackered to do much else.'

'That's never happened before,' said Dixie.

'Johnny,' said Rachel, louder this time.

'It's happening now, Dixie.' Johnny waved Rachel to silence.

'Johnny!' screamed Rachel.

A grating claxon blast semtexed through Johnny's ears. He looked up and saw a flashing red light above the control room door. Kurgan mimed 'fire' and jerked his head towards the live room. Johnny spun round and looked through the reinforced glass window.

'Oh, shit.' Flames climbed up the felt-lined wall covering while the band ran around in circles. He turned to Rachel as he grabbed the door handle. 'Did you see this?'

'*You* told me not to be so curious.'

'Christ.' Johnny grabbed a fire extinguisher and yanked open the door. 'Why are you still in here?' He strode past the band and squeezed the extinguisher handle. 'Get the fuck out.'

'Not without Vince.'

'What?' A stream of foam coated the wall and a cloud of acrid black smoke poured towards them.

'Vince is down,' shouted Maxwell.

'Then pull him out,' yelled Johnny. 'We're leaving, now!'

The band retreated before the smoke cloud, while Johnny squirted a dwindling stream of foam into the thick darkness rolling towards them. Last man out, he slammed the door shut and turned around. Soot-blackened faces and a writhing Vince greeted him in the control room. The fire alarm still shrilled its deafening tattoo.

'Out,' shouted Johnny. 'Out! Out, right out, now!' He herded the band, Rachel and Kurgan across the pristine lobby and outside into the drizzling rain.

Vince had been dragged out by his Ralph Lauren shirt. His equally expensive jeans lay around his ankles and his underpants were nowhere to be seen. His face was screwed up and his dull moans spoke of unexplained pain. Johnny knelt down beside him, rainwater soaking through his leather pants. 'What's wrong, Vince?'

'Bloody flame,' he grunted. 'Fucking well blew inside me instead of out.'

'Jesus.' Johnny reached for his phone. 'I'm calling an ambulance.'

'What about the contest?' asked Andy.

'Fuck the contest,' roared Johnny. 'Vince could have all sorts of internal injuries and you're talking about a bloody contest.' He stab-dialled three nines and waited for the pick-up. 'Ambulance, Twenty Studios. Shit, we've got a male with internal burn injuries. How? How do you bloody think? He was lighting his own farts, haven't you ever seen that before? And send a fire engine as well. No, not for his arse, for the fucking building.' He looked down at Vince. 'So if the flame went inside you, how did the fire start?'

'Can you see my bloody underpants?' Vince asked through clenched teeth.

'What?'

'Course you fucking can't. They caught light and the lads ripped them off. I reckon they hit the wall. Christ, Johnny, why are you so bloody curious?'

'Why are you lot so bloody stupid?'

'Good job it wasn't a cock slamming contest,' said Maxwell.

'And I *really* don't want to know about that,' replied Johnny.

Wailing sirens and the ambulance and fire engine screeched to a halt outside the studio. Vince was strapped to a stretcher and disappeared into the ambulance, while a squad of firemen rushed inside the studio with a trail of hosepipe snaking behind them. Black clouds smoke-signalled out of the studio door and Johnny ran to the front of the ambulance. He bashed on the window. 'What hospital?' he shouted.

'University Central,' came the reply. 'A ten-minute drive.'

The ambulance wailed through the streets and disappeared. Johnny looked back at the studio. Archimedes stepped heavily out of the building, his kaftan now soaked though – Johnny guessed by the firemen – and he glared at the four remaining band members.

'See that, Johnny.' said Maxwell. 'See how he looks at us? He thinks this is our fault.'

Chapter 8

Plastic piping stretched outside the studio doorway and micturated the fire brigade's leavings onto the road. A taxi brought the band back from the hospital, with Vince sitting gingerly in the front, perched on an air-filled cushion and holding a paper bag full of prescription painkillers. After paying the driver, Johnny climbed out and stood in front of the studio door.

'You letting us in?' asked Maxwell. 'You *said* we were losing time.'

'Yes,' said Johnny. 'And you're straight back to work. Don't wind *anyone* up, and if anyone talks to you, the first and last words you'll be saying to them is sorry. Understand?'

'What?' said Maxwell. 'Sorry, Kurgan, can we do that vocal again? Sorry.' Arm and shoulder raise. 'We'll sound like fucking idiots.'

'You *are* fucking idiots,' snapped Johnny. 'Get inside, get to your live rooms, and play your songs. End of.'

'What do I do?' asked Vince.

'Go to the control room, sit down, shut up. If Rachel wants to do an interview, answer her questions. When your guitar arrives, play it. Sounds pretty simple to me.' His cold gaze search-beamed over the band. 'Inside.'

Johnny's cowboy boots splashed through puddles that sheeted over the stone tile flooring. The receptionist looked up and shot them a cold-eye broadside. Inside the control room, a small electric pump slowly sucked the water from the floor, random whorls of soot patterned the ceiling, and Kurgan was slouched at the mixing desk.

'How's your buddy's arse?' he asked.

'Sorry, Kurgan,' the band unisoned before subsiding into quiet.

'It's nothing to me,' said Kurgan. 'I don't own the place.'

'So what about these spare instruments?' asked Johnny.

'All set up. Who gets the guitar?'

'Me,' said Andy.

'Live room opposite.' Kurgan looked at the band with blatant surprise. 'Do you lads really record all together?'

'Doesn't everyone?' asked Maxwell.

'Shit,' said Kurgan. 'Some bands aren't even in the same country when they make their albums.'

'Not us,' said Maxwell. 'This'll be the first time we record anything with even one of us on the sidelines.'

'And you'll be shit because of it,' moped Vince.

'Enough,' snapped Johnny. 'Get used to the gear and show us why you're the best.' He folded his arms and the band filed into the live rooms, each one cocooned with sound-absorbing material that looked like egg boxes stapled to the walls.

'For fuck's sake.' Andy's voice cut through the speakers. 'You expect me to play *this?*'

'Didn't you tell him?' asked Kurgan.

'Come in here, Johnny.' Andy's voice filtered into the control room. 'I'm fucked if I'm coming out.' Johnny opened the live room door and looked inside. 'Don't let anyone else in here,' said Andy.

'Too late,' laughed Maxwell.

Cold fury and indignation was stamped across Andy's face as he held a pink, penis-shaped guitar. The neck and machine head were made to look like an erect shaft and glans, while the body had been shaped into a bulbous scrotum.

'Fucking hell,' howled Vince. 'I'm so glad I lost that contest.'

'Piss off,' muttered Andy.

'Jesus,' chuckled Mike. 'It's even got pubic hair.'

'Joke's over, lads.' Johnny smiled despite himself, and herded the band out of the room.

'Hey, Johnny.' Andy nodded towards Rachel. 'No pictures, right?'

'Ask a bit more nicely,' said Rachel.

'Please?'

She smiled. 'Be a boring subject and I'll point my camera elsewhere.'

'Like I can really do that with a cock for a guitar.'

'No different to normal,' sniped Vince.

Johnny closed the live room door and looked through the plate-glass window. Andy pressed his fingers into the strings on the unfamiliar fret board. 'I don't care what he looks like,' said

Johnny. 'And I don't care how bloody annoying he is. He's a guitarist first, last and always.'

'Let's see what he sounds like,' said Kurgan.

Johnny nodded nervously. He'd been in studios with bands before, although his pinnacle until managing Cold Steel had been a self-financed demo. But some things stayed the same, and he knew there was more than just modern technology behind making a great album. He watched Kurgan's reluctant, almost hostile attention to the music and sensed what everyone was thinking. The all-important chemistry, the spark of understanding between crew and band, impossible to quantify but easy to spot, simply wasn't there. No one seemed to have a choice about Cold Steel recording at Twenty, and nobody who was there seemed to like it.

Andy's riffs sliced through the control room speakers like a sonic buzz-saw. Perfectly timed from separate rooms, Mike's drumming and Joe's supporting bass line deepened the sound and defibrillated Johnny's sagging spirits, then Maxwell's piercing voice firebombed across his synapses. Johnny listened to the lyrics and heard the story of the band's recent adventures in the Caribbean, smiling at the memories they evoked. Andy cringed as his hands flew over his phallic guitar, but his razor-scream solo carved a stone-line furrow through Johnny's skull.

*

Vince sat at the mixing desk and stared into Andy's live room. Note-perfect riffs piked through the speakers. Rachel could almost taste Vince's frustration. A grimace of ill-concealed pain creased his face as he shifted position. 'Wishing you were in there?' she asked.

'What do you think? Andy's killing this song.'

Rachel raised her eyebrows. 'Sounds okay to me.'

'Exactly, *only* okay. Oh bollocks, he's missed another one. He could have put another two picks on top of that half-riff. We'll have to do the whole thing again.'

'He's playing the way he plays.'

'He's playing wrong.'

'You think he should be more like you?'

'Of course he should.' He looked at Rachel. 'If he wasn't so bloody stubborn he'd have a few lessons.'

'Lessons?'

'Like me.' His back straightened as he spoke. 'Properly trained, classically trained.'

'That's unusual in metal.'

'Which is why Andy's a metal guitarist and I'm a *rock* guitarist.'

'There's a difference?' smiled Rachel.

'Of course there is.'

She silently invited an explanation.

'Well...' Vince looked anywhere but back at her. 'Oh fucking hell, Rachel. What's the difference between rock and metal? That's like asking what's the difference between Jehovah and God.'

She stifled a chuckle. 'So what about your training?'

'The best, like everything else I do.'

'Where was that?'

'Royal College of Music.'

'In London?'

'Are there any others?'

Her eyes went wide. 'Impressive.'

'You'd better believe it,' growled Vince. 'I'd been playing for years before then as well.'

'Did you always want to be a musician?'

He shook his head. 'It was a hobby at first. My family wanted me to join their business. And not just your local-run corner shop, either.' Pride laced through his words. 'A proper stock-exchange, multi-national, gilt-edged business. That's how I got to the Royal College, that's where I got my first SG, and that's why I didn't starve to death before we got the break.'

'A different world to Andy's.'

Vince sighed and looked up at the ceiling. 'Look, Rachel, I had the same audition as him; I had to play just as well as him to get into this band. So don't think I had it any easier just because I didn't grow up in a bloody council house, whatever the hell one of those is.'

'Have you said all this to Andy?'

'Hey, I was dead set to be mates with him, but he was always out to prove that talent's something you've either got or you haven't, you can't be taught.' He shrugged. 'There was no chance we'd ever agree.'

'And if it was up to you,' said Rachel, 'you'd be friends?'

'Sure I would,' snapped Vince. 'He's the one with the bloody attitude. He's the one who wants to be the victim.' He shifted on his chair and winced in sudden pain. 'Christ,' he gasped. 'He's sure as shit not the victim right now.'

*

The new song tack-hammered to a stop and Maxwell looked through the glass with his trademark smile. 'Sound good?' His voice filled the control room.

Johnny pulled over a spare microphone. 'It's good,' he nodded. 'What's it called?'

'Little Men and Big Boys.'

'It's a good take,' said Kurgan.

'Not without me it's not.' Vince sat up and glared at Kurgan.

'Sounded good to me.'

'What? Christ, Kurgan, that solo was kid's stuff. Andy might have done a half decent riff, but come on. Guys—' Vince spoke into the microphone — 'Kurgan thinks we've got a take on that one. Comments?' He turned to Kurgan and smiled. 'Incoming.'

'I *need* a strat.' Andy looked down at his guitar. 'Whatever this thing is, it's no Fender.'

'Do you need Vince's help?' asked Kurgan.

Johnny's senses screamed suspicion, and he looked around at Kurgan.

'He might be able to add something, I suppose,' said Andy. 'Want to play this and be a cock star, Vince?'

Vince shook his head. 'You're in front till my SG gets here.'

'So we hold off on that take,' said Johnny.

'Nothing wrong with the vocal,' said Maxwell.

'Drums was alright,' said Mike.

'I don't want alright,' snapped Johnny. 'And nor do you. This album goes out perfect, nothing less.'

'Fine.' Kurgan clicked the mouse and his screen flashed. 'It's gone.'

'What?' gasped Johnny.

'Gone. You said you didn't want it.'

'You mean you've fucking *deleted* it?'

'Oh.' Blank look. 'You wanted to *keep* it?'

'Christ, yes. At least until we've heard it.' A tendril of suspicion smoked around Johnny's mind.

'Time for a beer break and team meeting,' said Maxwell. 'Johnny, we need to talk.'

'Tell me about it,' muttered Johnny.

Chapter 9

'This whole setup is bullshit,' Maxwell slammed his beer glass on the table and Johnny looked around the small pub's interior. Low-timbered ceiling and uneven plastered walls made the John Lacey seem as though the very building was pressing in on him. He and the band sat in murky emptiness; pictures of guillotines hung from the walls at skewed angles, somehow different to the traditional French ones Johnny had seen. It all made him feel slightly uneasy, and he swerved his mind back to the band.

'The first song was pretty good,' he said. 'Even with one guitar.'

'It's our *only* song,' said Mike.

'What?' choked Johnny. 'What the fuck? What kind of band turns up at the studio with *one* song?'

'What kind of band gets *told* to turn up at the studio?' asked Vince.

'*Every* band,' said Johnny. 'And it might have been brought forward by a fortnight, but everything else was carved in concrete.' He stared up at the low ceiling. 'Jesus, after everything you – *we* – went through since the last tour, you should have enough inspiration for a dozen new albums.'

Andy slouched in his chair, hands buried in the pockets of faded combat trousers. 'It's just not right. Twenty and us, it should never have been.'

'It might help if we had our instruments,' said Vince.

'Full replacements within twenty-four hours,' said Johnny.

'Come on, Johnny,' said Maxwell. 'It's not just that. They don't want us there.'

'That's right,' said Mike. 'And did Kurgan *really* delete the first take?'

'I've had a word,' said Johnny.

'You shouldn't need to,' said Mike. 'Something's going on.'

'*What's* going on?' asked Johnny. Silence from the band. 'What, you want another studio?'

'Good idea,' said Maxwell.

'*Bad* idea,' said Johnny. 'Look, we've got no choice. Everyone at Ozone wants you there. Everyone, including Randall and Lucy. You think I can change *their* minds? Christ, all the studios are booked solid for the next six months anyway, and don't forget the tour straight afterwards.' He jaw-clenched and looked at the band. 'You lot need to stop pissing around and get this album made, because the sooner it's done, the sooner you can start rehearsing.'

'We need the right place,' said Andy. 'And that's not Twenty. Even if they weren't trying to screw us over—'

'We don't *know* that,' replied Johnny.

'We know enough,' said Maxwell. 'That studio's not right for us. It's so, so...'

'Empty,' said Vince.

Mike slammed his glass down on the table. 'That's exactly it.'

'So,' said Johnny. 'How do we fix this?'

*

'I need a piss.'

Johnny looked up at Andy. 'You need to ask?'

'Just saying.'

'So piss and get back,' snapped Johnny. 'The clock's ticking.'

Andy scowled and stomped into the men's room. The door closed behind him and he pulled out his phone. He knew who the text was from before he read it and his chest tightened. He wanted it to be her and he didn't, but she was already inside his head. He speed dialled the number.

'Hello.' He recognised her voice.

'Stop calling me.'

'You don't mean that, Andy.'

'I bloody well do. You're trouble.'

'Nothing else?'

He remembered the way she'd looked on the plane, the way she'd looked at *him*. Him, not Vince, which was *really* part of the rush. Sure, he could get groupies, even *he* could get groupies. But away from the concert circuit it just didn't have the same buzz. *Maybe I'm getting old.*

But that didn't mean he wanted complicated, and Angie Dale brought complications *and* trouble. 'What do you want?' he growled.

'Hey, I'm just missing my rock star. Where are you?'

'Making an album. You know that.'

'You're not at the studio.'

'How—'

'I'm a reporter, Andy. A proper one. What's going on?'

'I can't say.'

'Can't say? Won't say?'

'I don't know.'

'You don't know if you want to tell me?'

'No,' he shouted. Christ, this woman wound him up. 'I mean I don't know what we're doing.'

'Oooh, how exciting. So what can you tell me?'

'We've hit a wall in the studio.'

'You haven't got much time to waste with that.'

'No shit.'

'So?'

'So we're in a pub and we need some inspiration.'

'And?'

'And Johnny's sorting it.'

*

The game was everything.

Rachel sat in the studio's press room. Condemned furniture from the rest of the studio had been dumped there, along with a motley collection of cast-off landline phones and white boards. She sat in a collapsing armchair and reviewed the interview with Vince. Rivalry, differences, dislike even. All expected, but maybe not quite so intense. Why *was* this band still together, she thought. How did they manage these differences and still succeed? Even Angie Dale, *not in my league on any level,* had suggested that no other band would have survived. Why shouldn't Rachel put forward that view? Johnny wanted the band's depth, inner conflict, naked vulnerability. What was more vulnerable than a band on the edge of splitting?

That's not what Johnny wants.

Really?

I don't know.

You do.

The game was everything, but that didn't make it easy.

'We need to talk.'

Archimedes looked up from his desk and saw Kurgan's blue hair through a haze of hookah smoke. 'I thought they were back from hospital?' he said.

'They are.' Kurgan dropped into the vacant chair opposite Archimedes.

'And the bloody fire engines have gone,' growled Archimedes. 'So why aren't they making their damned music?'

'*I* thought you didn't want them to.'

'I don't. Have you talked them into leaving?'

'They're survivors,' said Kurgan. 'And that manager of theirs has arranged for replacement instruments inside twenty-four hours.'

'What? How did he manage that?'

'He's good at his job. If you want my advice, sink their manager. They won't last six months without him.'

'I tried, but it's not personal with him, he didn't—'

'Didn't what?'

'Never mind? So where have the great Cold Steel gone now?'

'The pub.'

'What? I thought you said their manager was good. Why isn't he busting their balls to get the album recorded?' Archimedes' eyes narrowed. 'Not that it'll ever get released, right?'

'I deleted the one song they recorded.'

'Was it any good?'

'You really want to know?'

'No' snapped Archimedes. 'And when they get back, do your best to discourage them. Any way you can?'

Kurgan's phone rang.

'Kurgan, it's Johnny. Look, mate, the band need to do a bit of self-exploration, find some inspiration. Are we good to call it a day and come in tomorrow?'

Kurgan looked at Archimedes and smiled. 'That's fine, Johnny. Take as long as you need.'

Chapter 10

'I don't know about this, Johnny.' Maxwell stood in the wicker basket and gripped the edge. He looked out at the ground that suddenly released its hold on the balloon. A lightweight helmet was crammed onto his head, and his hair fingered out from underneath in all directions.

'Hey.' Johnny smiled and hid his nervousness. 'You wanted danger, you wanted excitement, and you *didn't* want to go back to the studio.'

'This wasn't what I had in mind.'

'So next time be careful what you wish for. Now soak up the experience and search your emotions for the next song.'

Joe lit a joint and his eyes glassed over. His brightly coloured shirt wind-wrapped around his skinny body in the steadily rising altitude. 'We don't need to be way up here to think of them.'

'Staying at Twenty didn't help,' Johnny gripped a securing line, and forced himself to look at the band's strained faces instead of the dwindling earth beneath him. 'Christ, you lot are all talk and no trousers. I give you what you want on a plate, and you moan like a bunch of hairdressers. You'd better record a bloody classic tomorrow, that's all I can say.' Clear flames roared upwards into the balloon's arena-sized belly, and the super-warmed air carried them higher. Keeping his own fear of heights canned tight, he swept his arm outwards. 'Take a look, lads. All this uninterrupted view, is that stirring any song-writing stuff in you?'

'Shit.' Maxwell looked over the basket. 'You never said anything about going over the sea.'

'You never asked,' replied Johnny. 'Always bloody moaning. And by the way, you're in the gym tonight.' He looked at the operator, who shrugged beneath a quilt of warm clothing. 'We are supposed to be going over the sea, right?'

'Is okay.' The pilot spoke with an indistinct East European accent. 'The winds will take us back.'

'You're sure?'

'I do this flight four times this week, always return safe.'

'I wasn't worried.' Johnny forced a smile.

'Then let go of that rope,' said Maxwell.

Andy watched the coast of Eastern England slip silently away beneath them. 'Hey,' he said. 'We've dropped something.'

'Is ballast,' said the pilot. 'Bag of sand.'

'Won't that make us climb higher?' asked Johnny.

'Fuel running low, balloon start to cool, it makes us sink more slowly.'

'Christ,' said Andy. 'We're sinking?'

'Oh, bloody hell,' said Johnny. 'Think of it as landing. Did you think we were going to stay up here all day? We've got to come down sometime. This is obviously how it happens.' He looked at the pilot. 'Right?'

The pilot looked over the side, then back at Johnny. 'Is right, we come down slowly, wind pushes us back over land. Land is warm, warm air rises, keeps us level, we descend slowly.'

'There,' said Johnny. 'Nothing to worry about.'

The basket suddenly lurched. Johnny yelped and gripped even tighter on the stays. He looked at the pilot, who edged to the basket's centre and fiddled with the fuel burner. 'Are we supposed to move around like this?'

'For sure,' replied the pilot. 'Strong winds coming.' He looked at Joe. 'No smoking, I check the fuel tanks.'

The pilot shuffled from one tank to the next. Johnny looked out at the grey expanse of the North Sea. He began to feel stirrings of disquiet. Drifting over the sea, dropping sandbags to stay aloft, the wind that was getting stronger, and the pilot, who, now that he thought about it, didn't seem like the fastest runner on the track.

A wedge of geese flew below the balloon. Joe flicked out his joint and Johnny watched the reefer's glowing tip spiral downwards, then gasped as it hit the lead bird's eye. The goose cawed in pain and shot upwards, followed blindly by the rest of the flock.

'Oh, shit.' Johnny looked back at the pilot, who gazed over the basket's side as the geese sped towards them.

'Is alright,' he said. 'They see us, will fly around.'

As though they heard, the lead goose carved a line through the sky, straight towards the slowly moving balloon. Johnny's faith in the pilot melted like beach ice cream. He wailed in fear and ducked behind the basket. The birds rushed towards them and straight at the balloon's huge, multi-coloured canopy. Flapping wings buffeted the air, small grey feathers snowed down, and loud goose calls and the sound of solid, beaked objects hitting the canopy's fabric echoed around them.

Panicked beaks pecked and tore, looking for escape. Johnny heard the ripping sound of the canopy being breached. Black and white bird shit mingled with downy grey feathers, and Johnny's insides lurched at the unmistakable sensation of their descent picking up speed. Still crouched beneath the basket's rim, he looked up at the pilot. 'Was that supposed to happen?' he asked.

'I said no smoking.' The pilot picked up the empty fuel canisters and threw them over the side.

'I did what you told me, man,' wailed Joe. 'You said no smoking, I put it out.'

'You throw your hashish straight at the birds,' accused the pilot.

'I didn't know, man.'

'And now the birds go crazy. Balloon ripped, no altitude to get to land, and we're sinking.'

'Oh, shit.' Terror tram-lined through Johnny. He gripped a cylinder and helped the pilot. 'So what do we do now?'

'Throw all overboard, make lighter, we sink more slowly.'

'But we *are* sinking?'

'Look up, look down. What do you think?'

'Christ,' said Maxwell. 'Cold Steel and the sea don't go well together. Where's the life jackets?'

'No life jackets,' said the pilot. 'Never need before, none here. We ditch, we swim.'

Johnny looked over the side of the basket at the sea that was now rapidly coming towards them. A whistling, flapping noise sent his gaze upwards. The ripped balloon was collapsing. Once warm air escaped through the geese-pecked rents in its skin. 'Listen, lads,' he said. 'As soon as we ditch, jump overboard and start swimming.'

'You fucking what?' asked Mike. 'Look, Johnny, there's no life jackets and my swimming isn't the best in the world. If the basket floats, it's the nearest thing we'll have to a boat.'

'The balloon will come down right on top of the basket, and there's a chance it'll push us under and drown us.' Johnny heard the shrill tone to his words.

'Shit.' Mike looked at the pilot. 'Is he right, mate?'

The pilot stood on the edge of the basket and looked back at Mike. 'Is right,' he said. 'Goodbye.' He jumped over the side.

'No time to argue,' Johnny watched the pilot splash untidily into the foaming waves, pull off his coat and clumsily swim away. 'Over the side, now. Feet first, legs together, and start swimming as soon as you land.'

'I wish we'd stayed at the studio, man,' wailed Joe.

'Think up some lyrics while you're swimming and you'll be able to. And don't forget Mike's your mate.'

'What, man?'

'He can't swim, remember? So bloody well look out for him, alright?' Johnny shoved him over the basket's edge, made sure the rest of the band had done the same, then went over himself.

He felt the air whoosh through the remains of his hair. Silent waterspouts erupted where band members splash-landed and quickly surfaced, each struggling away from the descending balloon with clothes-slowed strokes. He looked down at the sea beneath his cowboy boots. He tensed his legs and took a deep breath, then felt as though the soles of his feet had been whacked with a cricket bat. He smashed into the sea and plunged beneath.

Fucking hell, that's cold! He struck frantically for the surface, staring through murky salt water. His head broke through and he spat spray, shook his head and looked around for the balloon. The basket settled into the water behind him, and he launched into a schoolboy crawl, fear of being trapped beneath the canopy driving him on.

He swallowed mouthfuls of cold, salty seawater and gagged and spluttered. He stroked for a full minute before looking back. Behind him, the balloon settled on the sea like a multi-coloured oil slick, covering the basket and looking like some weird, misshaped priapism. Safe from the immediate danger of drowning, he began to wonder how long before they'd be picked up. Swimming back to the coast was definitely out.

A black and grey shape hoved into his portside view. He blinked seawater out of his eyes and focussed on an approaching police launch. *Bloody lucky,* he thought, waving his arms and shouting. Then he looked around and saw another four similar boats, circling and picking up the band, and his elation at imminent rescue quickly turned into nervous suspicion.

Strong hands hauled Johnny over the side and he squelched onto a small open area at the back of the boat. 'Thanks, lads,' he coughed.

'Save it.' A folded blanket was chucked at him and he was left to cover himself up. Booted feet clambered back inside and the door slid shut, leaving him to dry naturally in the cold sea air.

Chapter 11

'It was an impulse booking, I've never heard of them before.'
Wrapped in a now damp blanket over his still wet clothes, Johnny
nursed a lukewarm cardboard cup of tea and shivered. Detective
Sergeant Debden's iceberg face looked back at him over a mouldy
table in the harbour police station's tiny interview room.

'That's not what Oleg's saying.' Debden ran a dry-skinned
finger under his tight shirt collar and loosened a coffee-stained tie.

'You mean Oleg, the balloon pilot?'

'You know him then?'

'No, I don't. What's he saying?'

'You tell me.'

'I don't *know.*'

'Look, Johnny.' Debden's voice softened. 'We know the
balloon company Oleg works for is a front for smuggling. They
drop packages of diamonds into the sea, which are picked up by—'
air quote — '"fishing boats". And when they do balloon trips to
the continent, they pick up drugs and bring them over here.'

'News to me,' said Johnny.

'Sure.' Deadpan disbelief.

'And you know it,' said Johnny. 'Look, you've done your
checks, you know who we are. Why would Cold Steel want to get
involved in any of that?'

'Really, Mister Faslane? Didn't your predecessor do that very
thing?'

'But he was a junkie,' snapped Johnny. 'And the band had
nothing to do with it.'

'So you're innocent of all charges?'

'Of course we are. We haven't done a damn thing wrong. You
know we haven't.'

Debden smiled.

'Christ,' gasped Johnny. 'You got the bastards, didn't you?
Jesus, you should be thanking us for making their balloon fall into
the sea right next to you.'

'That was a bit of luck for us,' admitted Debden.

'You're fucking welcome.'

'And you had no idea about their smuggling?'

'Why would we shit on their smuggling route if we were in on it?' countered Johnny.

Debden sighed. 'All right, Johnny. We believe you.'

'*Now* you believe me?'

'You might thank me.'

'Thank you?'

'Some people might think you brought that balloon down deliberately.'

'What, by Joe Dimitri, the stoned goose whisperer?'

Debden chuckled. 'It sounds unbelievable, but Oleg's employers may see things differently. We've been on this operation for months now.'

'So?'

Debden sipped his coffee. 'So, we didn't find this out all by ourselves. We've got informers, and they know that.'

'So, again?'

'Who's to say that you're not part of the informant ring?'

Johnny's eyes snapped open.

'Being brought in and questioned helps you. Makes you look innocent, from their point of view.'

'We're a bit out of that bloody league,' sneered Johnny. 'Look, I don't want to blow our trumpets, but we *are* Cold Steel, and we can organise our own protection. Besides, in a couple of months we're on tour, which starts in Spain, not here.'

'Have you ever heard of someone called Julio Ramirez?' asked Debden.

'No,' said Johnny. 'Should I have?'

'He's the main man.' Debden's face flushed. '*He's* the bastard we want.' He looked at Johnny. 'You're not immune from him, either. He's diversified, made his money legal. From what I hear he's bankrolling singers as a way to make his cash look honest.'

'Don't look at me,' said Johnny. '*Or* the band.'

'We've no reason to doubt you, Johnny.'

'Is that a warning?'

'Advice. Ramirez is global, so when you think you're safe on tour, if he wants to get in touch, he just might.'

*

83

London's Excelsior Hotel boasted imperial grandeur and comfort on a commuter's budget, achieved through the use of interns and apprentices, and a chain of similar hotels in aspirational cities worldwide. Rachel sat at the small bar cramped next to the thick-glazed revolving doors and watched one damp band member after another squelch into the lobby.

'Bar's open,' roared Maxwell. 'And it's your bloody round, Johnny.'

The band trooped inside behind Maxwell and followed him to the bar, lank hair shaking seawater remnants around the lobby. Johnny emerged last through the doors; he smiled at Rachel and lock-kneed towards her, sea salt caking his leather pants.

'How was the trip?' she asked.

'Fucking wet,' said Andy.

'Which was my fault, apparently,' added Johnny.

'Well, it wasn't bloody mine.' Andy glared at Joe, who was hunched at the bar, and ordered a Campari Lush.

'It was just bad luck, man.'

Andy planted his elbows on the bar. 'Bad luck that you were there at all, and worse luck that you're still in this fucking band.'

'Don't say that, man.'

'That's right,' said Mike. 'You're out of order, Andy.'

'Oh, and did you rescue your special mate when his bloody joint landed us in the North Sea?'

'Did you?'

'Did I fuck, but I wish I'd drowned the bastard.' Andy turned and glared at the student barman, whose eyes twitched nervously from one band member to the next. 'What's going on with underage here? Pint of top shelf, right fucking now.'

'Sorry?' stammered the barman.

'Top shelf,' repeated Andy. 'One measure of every spirit you've got, in a pint glass.'

'He'll have a pint of lager,' said Johnny.

'Top shelf,' said Andy.

'Lager.'

Andy turned, marched into Johnny's personal space and growled nose to nose. 'Don't push it, Johnny, it's been a shit day.'

'You don't say.' Johnny level-stared Andy. 'I was there too.'

'And you're telling me I don't need a drink?'

'Have a lager.'

'I'm having a *real* drink,' snarled Andy. 'Not a pint of cold piss.'

'You'll wish you hadn't.'

'Why? Are you going to tell me off?'

'No.'

'What then?'

'You're all going to the gym.'

'Fuck off.' The rest of the band looked at Johnny.

'Gym,' repeated Johnny. 'And you need it. Christ, have you seen yourselves?'

'What do you mean?' asked Andy. Johnny sneered and poked Andy's recently appeared abdominal bulge.

'That's hard-earned living,' said Andy.

'That's past it,' said Johnny. 'You already look it, and pretty soon it'll be showing onstage.'

Mike stared at Andy, raised his eyebrows and nodded. 'Johnny's got a point.'

'I thought you'd stick up for him,' muttered Vince.

'You don't have to like it,' said Johnny. 'But you *are* going to do it. Now drink your drinks, get upstairs and get changed. Work out in half an hour. *Not* negotiable.'

'I'll wait down here,' said Andy.

'Not on your own, you're not,' said Johnny.

'I'll stay with him.' Rachel looked at Johnny. 'I'm here to report, aren't I? Plenty of time for Andy to talk about himself.'

'It's my favourite subject,' he grinned.

'Fair enough,' said Johnny. 'The rest of you, half an hour and back down here. Don't make me come and get you.'

*

'A large white wine.' Rachel sat at the bar and stared at Andy.

'We have Greek white or Canarian red?' stammered the barman.

'Assyrtiko,' said Rachel. 'Leave the bottle.'

'Not working out with us tonight?' asked Andy.

She poured herself a large glass. 'You think I need to?'

'Yeah, right,' He barked a laugh. 'I'm not stupid enough to answer *that* one.'

She slid a tablet across the bar. 'You're stupid enough for that.'

His eyes flickered over the screen and Rachel saw the facial twitch, a subconscious reaction that gave away the lie. He shook his head. 'Nothing to do with me.'

'Bullshit.'

'What?' Andy slung back his drink and ordered another. 'You bloody own me?'

Rachel shook her head. 'Someone else does.'

'I don't know what you're on about.'

'Read it again.' She nudged the tablet. 'You've just got back, how the hell did Metalnet find out about your trip when you hadn't even planned it?'

'Oh, and why is it *me* who blagged it?'

'Who else would it be?'

'There were—'

'Johnny's got more sense than the rest of you put together.' Rachel counted off her fingers. 'Maxwell hates the press, Vince only goes through his agent, Joe's too embarrassed about whatever happened out there, and Mike is Joe's mate.'

'So?' Andy folded his arms and glared at Rachel.

'So what made you such a hero out there?'

'Maybe Angie Dale spiced the story up a bit.'

'Who said anything about Angie Dale?' asked Rachel.

Andy's mouth dropped open and his eyes snapped to the tablet screen. 'It's on—'

'No it's not. What did she promise you, Andy?'

He fidgeted and stared at the floor.

'Whatever it was,' said Rachel. 'She didn't pay up, did she?'

'I don't—'

'Know what you mean?'

Andy's mouth slacked open but he said nothing.

Rachel shook her head. 'Did she call you her very own rock star?'

'How did—'

'Because I know her,' said Rachel.

'Really? Were *you* her rock star as well?'

'You wish.'

'I bet Johnny would as well.'

'Don't even go there, Andy.'

'But you can?'

'Hey,' snapped Rachel. 'I didn't spill the goods to a hostile reporter.'

'*I* didn't, either.'

'Save it, Andy. It's pathetic.'

'What are you going to do?' Andy ordered another drink. 'You going to tell Johnny?'

'That's down to you.'

'Shit, Rachel. If you think a shag's more to me than the band, you've got me wrong.'

'Prove it.'

'I do that every time I play.'

Rachel's lips corner-creased. 'You could have fooled me.'

'Bollocks,' sneered Andy. 'Next time, listen, really listen. Cold Steel works. It works because of me and Vince. I don't know how, but it does. And when you're in a band that's got it, even if you don't know what it is, you'd have to be a fucking idiot to walk away.'

'That's not what Angie thinks.'

'I don't care what she thinks.'

'Really?'

Andy hesitated. 'Maybe.'

'Drinks down, Andy.' Johnny stepped out of the hotel lift, wearing dry leather pants and a Cold Steel t-shirt. 'Gym time.'

*

Total Sport and Fitness' corroded sign clung to a pockmarked brick frontage, held in place by rust and crumbling fixings. The taxi pulled up on a potholed street, and Johnny looked at the uninviting gym and then stared at the band, who looked more than vaguely ridiculous in mismatched, ill-fitting sports clothes. 'Are you sure about this, Dixie?'

'You wanted a gym, a trainer and no attention,' said Dixie. 'The third one's always a bitch to organise when you're talking Cold Steel.'

'Am I banned from here as well?' asked Rachel.

'Open season for you,' grinned Johnny. 'Five sets of guns like you've never seen before.' He herded the band inside. Warped panel flooring creaked, and tired wooden climbing frames emerged into view through underpowered lighting.

'Empty.' Johnny wrinkled his nose at the musty smell of mouldy wood. 'You sure he's here, Dixie?'

Suddenly, ice-cold water dropped on the band. Shouts and screams pealed around the neglected gym, and a thick hemp rope flashed into view. A fast-moving figure slid down it, landing on the ground with a combat-booted thump.

'Christ on a fucking bike,' shouted Johnny. 'Bloody soaked again.'

'Didn't look up. That's why you got the bucket.' Clad in faded green trousers and threadbare white sports vest, a middle-aged man stood in front of them. Close-clipped hair shot through with grey crowned his lined face.

'Fuck me,' spluttered Maxwell. 'Is that Bruce Willis?'

'Do I look like some poncy actor?' he growled. Toned chest and arms bulged, and he prowled the gym floor.

'Doesn't sound like him, man,' said Joe.

'Fucking right I don't. I've heard you lot sound shite as well.'

'What did you say?' Andy squared up to him.

'*And* you look like poofs.' The stranger's hands moved in a blur; Andy's arm was dragged up and then propellored backwards. He flew through the air and landed flat on his back. A loud grunt escaped his lungs.

'Whoa there, Tex.' Johnny placed himself between them. 'Dixie, is this guy the trainer?'

Dixie shuffled forward and nodded.

'Johnny Faslane.' He held out a hand. 'Can you get these guys into shape?'

'Sawyer,' he grunted. 'Faslane, you say? That's a fucking stupid name.'

'It's not my real name.'

'Bloody glad to hear it.'

'So can you get these lads fitter than they are right now?' repeated Johnny.

'I'll sort them out for you. Why aren't you dressed for it?' Sawyer looked at Johnny's leather pants as though he'd been made to eat them.

'I'm not in the band, I manage them.'

'Officer, huh?'

'What?'

'Never mind. A word of advice: your blokes will respect you more if you do what they do.'

'Do a good job tonight,' said Johnny. 'Don't throw any more water over me, and maybe next time.'

A slight nod from Sawyer acknowledged Johnny's words. 'Alright,' he shouted. 'Let's shake a fucking leg.' He glared at the band. 'You five pussies who need a haircut, gutkiss the floor and give me press ups.'

'How many do you want?' asked Maxwell.

Sawyer sprang over to Maxwell and pushed his face so close they almost rubbed noses. 'Don't ask fucking stupid questions, Rapunzel. On the deck, now. Press ups, right now, gentlemen.' To Johnny's mild surprise, the band did as they were told. 'And to answer your girlfriend's question, you'll do as many as I bloody well tell you to. One, two, three, four. One, two, three, four. Don't slack off, don't slow down. Jesus Christ, you lame bastards, we've only just started.'

Hard living and virtually no exercise had an instant effect on most of the band. Mike's build and resilience drew Sawyer's attention. He placed a boot on Mike's back and pressed down. 'At least someone round here's making an effort,' he snarled. 'Let's make it a bit harder for you, level up the competition for your mates here.'

Sawyer ran into the dark recess of the old gym, came thudding back with a paint-chipped weight and put it on Mike's back. The rest of the band slowed and watched what he was doing.

'Did I give you fuckers time off for a fondle-break?' he shouted. 'Press ups. You can stop when you puke.'

Johnny edged around the sweating and grunting longhaired press-up gaggle in the middle of the gym. 'Christ, Dixie. Where the hell did you find this head case?'

Sawyer bawled the band into running on the spot.

'We drink in the same pub.'

Sprinting to the far end of the gym.

'Bloody hell, I *don't* want to go there. You shared a pint with him?'

Star jumps.

'Well, I probably let my mouth run away with me.'

Conveyor-belt leapfrog back the other way.

'What do you mean?'

Crunch sit ups.

'He didn't say a word while he was sober, just listened to me telling a few band stories. Don't tell me you haven't bragged a few tales when you're pissed.'

Rope climb to the damp-stained ceiling.

'I guess,' murmured Johnny. 'So what happened next?'

All five band members picked up a long wooden gym bench and jogged around the gym, hounded by a screaming Sawyer.

'Said he liked a good story and offered to tell a few himself. He's real hardcore, Johnny.'

The band shuffled slower and slower in their shrinking circuit. Sawyer kicked Andy's arse. He yelped and they picked up speed.

'He looks the part. What is he, ex-squaddie or something?'

Vince's normally olive skin had taken on a pale, clammy look.

'Or something is right.'

Maxwell started hyperventilating.

'So spill the beans, Dixie. Is he going to train the band or fucking kill them?'

Joe broke ranks, bent double and staggered outside.

'He used to be in the military,' said Dixie. 'Wouldn't say what he did. Told some scary tales about being kicked out, though.'

Joe tottered back inside, wiping green slime from his mouth with the back of his hand.

'Kicked out? What the hell for?'

'He didn't say, exactly.' Dixie tapped the side of his head with a finger and rolled his eyes towards Sawyer, who'd stopped the band and was now herding them into a straight line.

'Let's hope it wasn't for killing recruits.' Johnny saw five expressions of near collapse, each different, yet each the same in their terrified appeal for it to stop. 'I reckon that's enough for one night.' He walked towards Sawyer. 'You got a first name?'

'I suppose it's Sean,' grunted Sawyer. 'My mates used to call me Shot Away.'

'Fucking hell,' wheezed Maxwell. 'He's that all right.'

'Call me what you want,' said Sawyer. 'I'll get your lads into shape, whatever they've got to face.'

'Easy, fella,' said Johnny. 'I just want their beer guts gone and them looking five years younger by the time the tour starts.'

'Fuck looking younger,' gasped Mike. 'I feel ten years older.'

'How long have we got?' Sawyer ignored Mike.

'About two months,' said Johnny.

'Piece of piss.' Sawyer turned to the band. 'In two months, you lot'll be able to tab across country with a full bergen, dig a fire trench, put in for pre-para.'

'Right,' said Johnny. 'I didn't understand any of that, but I guess it means you'll get us all fit, right?'

'Us, you say?'

'What?'

'Including you?'

'Why not?' Johnny shrugged. 'I wouldn't want you lads thinking I wasn't suffering alongside you. Okay, thanks, er, Sean. We'll see you tomorrow. You fancy a pint at the Lacey?'

'No thanks, mate, I'll turn in for the night.'

'Got far to go?'

'I live right here.'

'In a bloody gym?'

'Better than outside.'

'I guess.' Johnny looked sideways at Dixie. 'Lads, pub. First round's on me.'

Andy was the last band member out. Rachel gripped his arm and pulled him back. 'Check your texts,' she whispered. 'And send it to Angie.'

Chapter 12

'It was Andy who saved me.' Mike sat in the John Lacey and sipped a smoothie after the band had crawled inside. He was the only one not drinking alcohol, and he chuckled at Rachel's look of surprise.

'*Andy* saved you?'

'Sure.' He glanced sideways at the rest of the band, sitting at the next table and ignoring him and Rachel. 'It was that or let me drown. He knew I couldn't swim, and he *is* a knob sometimes, but when you're being chased by the Ancadian navy, even he knows when to stick together.'

'That whole Caribbean trip must seem like ages ago.'

'Christ, yes, look at what we've crammed into just over a month.'

'And all the new friends you've made.'

Mike laughed. 'Friends and nothing else, as always.'

'Ever wish you drummed for another band?'

'Not a chance.' Mike's lips set into a hard line. 'Sometimes you wonder how long all this will last, especially the way Vince and Andy go on. But this feels right. *We* feel right. I can't explain it any better than that. Maybe you should talk to Joe.'

'He's next on my list,' smiled Rachel. 'It's a much different conversation with you than it is with a guitarist.'

Mike smiled. 'Sure it is, I've got brains.'

'And what's it like always being at the back?'

'It's where the drummer goes,' he shrugged. 'It's like asking Maxwell if he'd rather sing from backstage.'

'Never wanted the attention?'

'You seen my solo?'

'Okay,' laughed Rachel. 'I've got a confession, will you forgive me?'

'What have you done now?'

'The only Cold Steel concert I've seen was the last one you guys did.'

'And you're a music reporter?'

'Hey, much as I'd like to, you can't see *every* band out there.'

'But we're—'

'Yes, I know.' Rachel rolled her eyes. 'You're the great Cold Steel.'

'That's right,' said Mike. 'And the drummer sits at the back and keeps it tight.' He smiled. 'We can't all be like Mister Killjoy.'

'You and Joe are a great team.'

'Hey, the band is a great team.'

'Even Vince and Andy?'

'That's just talk,' said Mike. 'Come on, Rachel, you think they'd live in each other's socks for months on end if they *really* hated each other?'

'I've interviewed them, and I'd bet a million pounds they weren't friends.'

'They're not close mates, not like me and Joe.'

'Why's that?'

'They're showmen, performers. It's only right that they try and outplay each other.'

'And you and Joe?'

'Hey, we're the rhythm section. We give the rest of the band a solid platform. It works, so we don't analyse it.'

'And your solo is your only extravagance?'

'Onstage, at least.'

'Oh?'

'We're not on the dole anymore.' Mike grinned. 'Not that Vince ever was.'

'So you like shopping?'

'Yeah, I shop for wheels.'

'Wagon wheels?'

'Cars,' laughed Mike. 'Fast, expensive cars.'

'Johnny told me a story about that.'

'The Porsche? In France?'

'Crashed on a test drive, something about being chased by hillbillies.'

'No need to go over that again.' Mike suddenly blushed.

'Change the subject?' asked Rachel.

Mike nodded.

'What do you think happened to your instruments?'

'I don't know.' He spread out his arms. 'But this is Cold Steel, it could be anything.'

'You think it'll affect the album?'

'What?' Mike grinned once more. 'With Johnny in charge?'

*

Andy woke up in his hotel room with a hand on his balls. A firm female body rubbing against him dispelled his first terrified thoughts of a Russian castration squad. He reached for the light switch and felt a strong hand on his wrist, holding him still.

'Hey, rock star.' Husky whisper.

'Angie?'

'Who else?'

Andy lay on his back with Angie on top. He reached for her in the darkness. She gripped his wrists and pinned them to the mattress. 'Not so fast,' she purred. 'What was that bullshit message you sent me? All systems go with the album, no problems with recording, the best songs ever? You weren't saying that when you got dropped in the sea.'

'What can I say, Angie? It got our juices flowing.'

'Yeah?'

'Would I lie to you?' He tried to wriggle free but she held him down.

'Maybe I should ask Vince.'

'You'd need to go through his agent. At least you're dialling direct with me.'

'*You're* the one who should be having the high-powered agent, not Vince. He's not even in the same league as you.'

'Really?'

'Would *I* lie to *you?*' She chuckled. 'So *you'd* better stop lying to me, mister.'

'It's complicated,' breathed Andy. 'The rest of the band—'

'*You're* the band, Andy.'

'I'm not.'

'You could be, you *should* be.'

'You think?'

'I'm here, aren't I?' Her grip on his wrists relaxed, but she stayed in control. 'You're the star,' she whispered. '*Be* the star.

94

The others are holding you back. You know it, you just need to do something about it.'

'I don't know, Angie.'

'You know,' she husked. 'You've always known. And don't forget…' She brushed his lips with a light, teasing kiss. 'The star always gets the girl.' He strained his head upwards to try for more contact but she rolled off him and stood up. By the time he'd found the light switch and flicked it on, Angie had gone.

*

'It's the wrong bloody colour.' Vince pouted at the brand new SG custom and glared around the live room.

'Is everything else right?' asked Johnny.

'Well...'

'Well nothing,' snapped Johnny. 'It's got what you want, what you play, what you always use, and it got here in a day. How fucking wrong can the colour be? It's black, for fuck's sake, and you play a black SG.'

'*My* SG is tropical midnight. *This* SG is burnt carbon.'

'Can you really tell the difference when your head is that far up your arse.'

'I'm just saying—'

'I know what you're bloody saying, and I don't want to hear it. You want a different black one for the tour? No problem, but right now, you're playing *that* fucking black one. It's an SG custom, made exactly for you.'

Vince grimaced. 'Apart from the colour.'

Johnny clenched a fist and held it in front of Vince. 'Custom pick-ups,' one finger flicked up. 'Inlaid Latin motto on the neck,' two fingers. 'Named, numbered plectrums,' three. 'Hand-coated beeswax on strings cut to the exact length you normally use,' four. 'Letters instead on numbers on the dials,' thumb. 'Hand-sewn, monogrammed strap,' fingers curled in a wanker sign. 'All *as* you requested, so fuck the colour, Vince, just play the pissing thing.'

'I don't know if I'll do a good job with this shade of black,' whined Vince.

Johnny's eyes turned into chips of flint. 'Andy played a blinding job yesterday on a penis-shaped guitar with pubic hair. So I guess that makes him better than you.'

95

'If you put it like that.' Vince stuck out his chin and his beard bristled.

'Jesus Christ, but you bastards are hard work.' Johnny spun round and walked into the control room, his cowboy boots stomping loudly on the Norwegian wood floor. As he walked in Kurgan quickly stuffed his phone back into his furs.

'Starting now?' He flushed red beneath his blue hair.

'I bloody well hope so.' Johnny wondered what Kurgan's furtive call had been about. 'And listen, mate, maybe this time we can keep the takes, all of them.'

Kurgan shrugged. 'I'm just the technician, what do I know?'

'A lot more than you're bloody saying,' muttered Johnny.

'What?'

'Nothing.' Johnny leaned forward and spoke into the microphone. 'Ready?' Longhaired nods visioned mutely through the soundproofed windows. 'So let's make some music.'

*

Song after song peeled out of the live rooms as the lowering sun sent thick beam shadows creeping across the mixing desk. Mike's double-tap snare drum finale reverberated around the control room, and the music bouldered to a shuddering halt. Kurgan felt the energy flowing, and wondered if Archimedes really needed to think through his hate for Cold Steel. Their album was going to be brilliant. He finger-typed an email on his phone: 'are you sure you want to trash them?' The affirmative came back almost immediately, and Kurgan sighed. *What the hell, it's not my bloody studio.* He quickly cleared the phone screen just as Johnny leaned over.

'The band sound good,' said Johnny.

'They're on fire,' agreed Kurgan.

'Finally turning into a rocker?' asked Johnny.

Mike looked through his live room towards the desk. Seeing Johnny, he picked up a microphone. 'You like?' he asked.

'You'd better tell him, man,' Joe's voice ghosted into the control room.

'Tell me what?' asked Johnny.

'I've got an idea,' said Mike.

'Great. What is it?'

Johnny stood outside the studio's polished front door and gaped in disbelief at a huge brass gong propped against the brickwork.

'Big, isn't it?' grinned Mike.

'Fucking enormous,' said Johnny. 'What's it for?'

'Didn't you ever see them old movies where the bloke hits a gong right at the start? What an intro. It's amazing, man, a real sound.'

'So you want to use this at the start of a song?'

'Yeah.'

'And that's it?'

'Well, yeah. Is that okay?'

'Fine by me.'

'So how come you're looking so pissed off?'

Johnny looked at the gong, the studio door, then back at Mike. 'It won't fit inside.'

Kurgan followed the band outside and stared at the gong. 'Maybe we shouldn't write this off, Johnny.'

'What do you suggest?' Johnny's suspicion rose at Kurgan's suddenly helpful attitude. 'If we can't get the thing inside, how are we going to record a single, never-to-be-used-again note?'

'Well,' said Kurgan, 'we've got a mobile studio. It's designed for concerts, but it can be used for any outside event.'

'Great,' said Johnny. 'Just set it up here, Mike can whack the gong, then we can all go back inside.' He looked up at the darkening sky. 'Hopefully before it starts raining.'

'We can't just park the van up and bash on the gong.'

'Why not?' asked Johnny. 'That's exactly what Mike was going to do in the studio.'

'Look, Johnny,' said Kurgan. 'This is an ephemeral, ethereal sound we're creating here. We can't just record it anywhere.'

'Angie Dale.' Sitting at her desk and concentrating on the laptop, she answered without looking at the phone.

'And that's the only honest thing you'll say this week.'

'Rachel? How sweet of you to call. I'm fine, thanks.'

'Get your claws out of Andy Stains.'

Unseen by Rachel, Angie smiled. 'Hey, Rachel. I'm no different to you. I'm just following a story. The only difference is our taste in men.'

'You've got an agenda, Angie.'

'And you haven't?'

'I'm reporting the story, that's all. It seems to me you're creating one.'

'Andy's not appreciated in Cold Steel,' said Angie. 'I'm just telling him what he already knows.'

'So maybe I should tell everyone what *I* know about you and the Roberts enquiry.'

Angie chuckled. 'That threat's getting old, Rachel. And maybe it stopped me selling pictures that might have been lacking in taste, but being the first to spill the goods on Andy Stains moving on, that's a legitimate story.'

'You're saying it like it's already happened.'

'What can I say, Rachel? Maybe I'm talented like that.'

*

Porn flick ringtone.

'Yeah.'

'It's me.'

'Yeah, yeah, mate. Look we're off to a sound test, I can't talk right now.'

'Out of the studio again, Andy?'

'Something like that.' He looked around the mini bus. No one else seemed to be paying attention to his call. He looked out of the window in case his face gave anything away. 'Not a good time, mate.' Christ, she'd do more than caress his balls if he called her mate again. She'd already warned him about it.

'Get out of there, Andy, before they drag you down with them.'

Shit, he thought, *why did I even mention it to her?* 'Yeah,' he muttered. 'Thanks for the update.' He switched off his phone.

'Alright, Andy?' asked Johnny.

'Sure,' replied Andy. 'New shoulder strap for the strat. Gotta keep up with Vince and his fashion statements.'

Johnny nodded and looked away. The rest of the band completely ignored the byplay, and Andy's insides tied themselves in knots.

What the hell was he going to do about Angie Dale?

*

A chill wind stabbed through Johnny's t-shirt. He stood on an exposed hilltop in the threatening rain and listened to Mike hammer away at the gong that now hung between a set of thick log beams. Two hours of city and then motorway driving had taken them right out of London, and he surprised himself at how much he missed Rachel. *Not that she's missing anything here.* He stared at rustic emptiness all around him.

'I'll stay here and get to know Archimedes,' she said.

'Really?' asked Johnny.

'Jealous?'

'No.' He flushed.

'Sure.' She grinned. 'That's why your face has turned into a stop sign.'

'Just don't start wearing kaftans by the time I get back.'

On the hilltop, Mike stood on the cloud-swept hilltop, and an array of dead cat microphones hovered over the gong on thin tubular stands. At the mobile studio's control van, an operator stood holding a direction mic at the gong from fifty yards away.

'Christ.' Johnny looked at the windblown grass. 'How many times do you have to hit the bloody thing? It's only going to be used once.' His eyes fetched upwards. 'It's going to piss down any second.'

'We want it to be right,' said Mike.

'You'd be the first to moan if we did a bad take,' said Vince. 'Mike wants to do it, so let him.'

'Fine,' snapped Johnny. 'Just get a fucking move on.'

Mike hammered, struck and drummed on the gong, hitting the centre, the edges, using ripple beats, solid sticks, padded sticks.

'Once more,' said Kurgan. 'I want you to speak to the gods this time.'

'We should be done and back at the pub by now,' grumbled Johnny.

'Harder,' called Kurgan. He hunched over a pair of laptops planted on a hastily put together pasting table. Cables spider-webbed out from the laptops to the microphones that surrounded Mike and the gong.

99

'Softer,' said Kurgan.

'I think Kurgan's reaching him,' said Vince.

'I'll be reaching for his fucking neck if he doesn't hurry up,' said Johnny. Rain drizzled down on them with unsurprising British summerness.

'That's it for today,' said Kurgan.

'Today?' shrieked Johnny. 'Jesus H, Kurgan, what do you mean, *today?* All he has to do is hit a fucking gong.'

'You're missing the intricacies.'

'I guess I am.'

Kurgan looked up at the building rain, then pulled a hoodie over his hair and windblown fake furs. 'You'll see,' he said. 'Wait till I'm finished with the takes.'

'Which you *won't* delete, right?'

'Of course not.'

'And tomorrow?'

'Hopefully an hour's gong-bonging will see us right.'

'So we've got to come all the way out here again tomorrow?' said Johnny. 'Fuck me, Kurgan, how early a start will that be?'

'Don't worry,' smiled Kurgan. 'The studio owns a property five miles down the road.' He looked at the band. 'Your boys will love it.'

'Why's that?'

'Because it's a castle.'

Chapter 13

The convoy of people carriers bounced along a rapidly puddling country track, and the band yelped with pre-pubescent joy at the thought of sleeping in a castle. Johnny imagined huge stone walls, battlemented towers and a moat to welcome him. 'How come Twenty own a castle?' he asked.

'The land,' said Kurgan. 'It's not just the castle. Twenty have diversified their wealth. They've got tenant farmers, forestry, water treatment plants, you name it.'

'Jesus,' said Johnny. 'And all that from making albums.'

'All that from Archimedes' business sense.'

'You mean there's more to him than kaftans and question marks?'

Kurgan looked over at Maxwell. 'More than you'd think.'

The castle emerged through the squalling rain. It stood nestled close to an encroaching wood and was ringed by neglected fields that seemed to be slowly returning to nature. Ivy climbed the once-smooth walls and bearded the crumbling battlements. The gateway yawned open and toothless, and the people carriers bumped over the uneven track, crossed a moat that was now little more than a drainage ditch barely a foot deep. The vehicles crept past the gateway and through an abandoned gatehouse. The walls, old, crumbling but still solid and very thick, pressed in on Johnny and his nerves only relaxed when they emerged into a small courtyard, overgrown with weeds and strewn with fallen chunks of medieval masonry. They pulled up next to a collection of motor homes.

'They look pretty established,' said Johnny.

'Of course,' replied Kurgan. 'We send wardens out here from time to time.'

'What for?'

'To keep the trespassers out.'

'Trespassers?'

'It's not just inner cities that have squatters.'

'Oh, shit.' Johnny looked around nervously. 'Are they dangerous?'

*

A campsite-style electrical point sprouted out of the ground between the two lived-in motor homes. Mike started frying camp food in one of the small kitchenettes, while the rest of the band sat on an uncomfortable foam sofa in the tiny living room and dwindled the beer stocks.

'Guess they knew we were coming, eh, Johnny?' Maxwell pulled off a bottle top with his teeth and grinned.

Johnny opened his beer with a bottle opener and glared at Mike, who stood over the cooker. 'How much longer do we have to stay here until you get that bloody gong strike just right?'

'I know, I know.' Mike flipped the eggs. 'Look, Johnny, I *was* going to just bash the thing and be done with. But Kurgan's got a few good ideas.'

'I'm more worried about the ideas he's *not* telling us about.'

'Maybe we were a bit twitchy at the start,' shrugged Mike. 'But it's going well now, isn't it?'

'Let's hope.' Johnny took a pull of his beer.

*

'Why would I want to talk to you?' Archimedes stared with instant dislike at Rachel.

'You don't seem keen on Cold Steel being here.' Rachel deflected the statement and stared back at him across his glass desk. 'Seems a little strange to me.'

'Not to me? The gutter's too good them, so why should I welcome them in *my* studio?'

'You don't like Cold Steel.' Rachel thought she saw a blob of white hair product nestled among his unruly curls, but was it sugar-coated?

'So?' Archimedes half smiled.

'So you're making it personal.'

'Let's understand this, what's your name?'

'Rachel Shaw.'

'Ah yes. Well, Rachel, Twenty is a very successful, very profitable studio, yes?'

'Agreed.'

'So even if Cold Steel weren't here, Twenty would still be in business?'

'But—'

'*I* decide who records here, and I always have. By setting the bar high, we keep standards high?'

'And Cold Steel don't meet your standards?'

'That's all.' Another semi-smile. 'So you see, it's not personal?'

'You're saying that even if you liked them, you wouldn't want them here?'

'Correct? Good business for Cold Steel isn't necessarily good business for Twenty?'

'Okay,' said Rachel. 'So if you don't want them here, why *are* they here?'

'I can't answer that?' Archimedes fidgeted and looked uncomfortable for the first time.

'It's an interesting story.'

'There are many more stories of interest in this studio,' he snapped. 'Artists who have recorded here, careers that have changed as a result of being here? Do you know the talent we normally accommodate in this studio? Have you considered the genius of Kurgan, and how he stoops to even listen to that band you follow around? All of this information you could glean, and you ask about Cold Steel?'

'That's my job.'

'You sell yourself short?'

'I don't think so.'

'Really? Tell me, do you ever eat dessert?'

*

Glass smashing on stone walls jolted Johnny awake. In the darkness, shouts and curses landed on top of him, draping a quilt of virtual fear on top of his real sleeping bag. He fumbled for his phone and switched on the torch, saw Mike and Andy climb out of their sleeping bags and head towards the motor-home door.

'What's going on?' he asked.

'Intruders,' growled Maxwell.

'What? Christ, Maxwell, this isn't the bloody Tower of London, who the fuck's intruding around here?'

'Must be those squatters Kurgan spoke about.'

'Hey, that's what he's got security for.'

'Security?' Maxwell squeezed free of his sleeping bag and pulled on his shoes. 'What fucking security? Did *you* see any guards around here?'

'That doesn't make it *our* job,' hissed Johnny.

'Do what you want, mate, but we're heading outside to crack some heads and show them who's boss.'

'Maxwell.'

He stopped and faced Johnny. 'What?'

'Be careful.'

'And what does that mean?' asked Maxwell. 'You can stay in here till it's over, or come outside and join the party.'

The band pulled on clothes and squeezed out of the motor home. Torches flickered and shouts punctuated the darkness. Johnny tried to make sense of the random noises, most of which were unrecognisable, and when any of the band spoke, it was just to swear into the night. He grabbed his cowboy boots and climbed over the haphazard, abandoned bedding towards the door. Outside in the darkness, shouts and curses whirled around his senses, along with the unmistakable sound of fists hitting bodies.

Torchlight stabbed into the void, shadows danced around the peripheries of Johnny's vision, and he heard footsteps running in different directions, then growls of pursuit.

He stepped nervously on the metal mesh step and then onto the courtyard's uneven floor. He looked around, and as he faced right, a fist whacked into his left cheek, snapping his head back and turning his legs to collapsing timber. He sank to the ground and heard a gruff voice above him, gradually receding as he slipped into unconsciousness.

'That's not him.'

Then who the hell am I? Johnny's confused thoughts followed him down a tunnel of forced blankness, accompanied by disembodied grunts of pain and random shouts in the dark.

*

'Johnny. Johnny.'

Johnny weakly flapped his arms and slowly opened his eyes. Then he yelped in pain as an unseen hand slapped him around the face.

'Hey, fuck off. That hurts.'

'He's awake,' said Maxwell.

Johnny sat up and brushed courtyard dust off him. In the multiple torch beams, he saw the rest of the band kneeling around him. Kurgan was staring wide-eyed at the band, and Johnny shook his head clear of the remaining cerebral clouds. 'Punched,' he slurred. 'Bastard. Shit, lads, what's happening?'

'It's the squatters all right,' said Maxwell. 'Barricaded themselves in our own bloody motor-home and locked us out.'

'That's alright,' said Johnny. 'They can't get past us, we'll just call the police, get them arrested.'

'No way,' snarled Maxwell. 'Those fuckers are ours.'

'Hang on, lads.'

'Hang on, bollocks,' said Andy. 'They come in here, take what's not theirs, then bloody well kick us out when *we're* supposed to be here.'

'Wait,' said Johnny.

'No,' roared Maxwell.

'Wait!'

'No!' The band chorused like a barber's quintet and in the shifting torchlight leaned against the motor-home and pushed. Trapped inside, the squatters taunted the band until the vehicle started swaying and then the wheels on one side began to bounce off the floor.

The vehicle recoiled back and forth, the tyres hitting the ground and then, propelled by the band's pushing, lifted off further each time. Each time the motor-home leaned over and teetered on the verge of tipping before crashing back on its tyres, the band cheered. The vehicle edged closer and closer towards tipping point, the desperation from the unseen occupants clearly audible.

The motor-home balanced on an unwieldy axis for five seconds, crashed back onto its tyres and was immediately pushed back by the band. The heavy vehicle slowed, slowed, almost stopped, then slid past its critical point. The squatters felt the moment and screamed even louder, and the motor-home flopped onto its side.

Flimsy wall panels split and perspex windows pinged free of their mountings, and a rising dust cloud drifted through the weak torchlight. Frantic sounds of movement came from inside the shattered vehicle, and Johnny saw arms, legs and torsos ooze from the empty window sockets. None of the squatters seemed harmed by their experience, and they rolled into view, clambered upright and ran off into the darkness, clutching great armfuls of belongings as they fled.

'Got rid of *them!*' crowed Maxwell.

Johnny approached a bent window frame and gingerly climbed inside. The motor-home's remains creaked like a sinking ship. Everything inside had tilted through ninety degrees, and he and the band walked along a trashed wall towards what he guessed was the spot he'd picked to sleep. Cushions and mattresses had been thrown around and the flimsy table ripped from its fittings. He switched on his phone torch and threw the narrow beam around the motor-home's interior. 'Wrecked van, nowhere to sleep and bloody robbed,' he said bitterly.

'Relax,' said Maxwell. 'It's not like we're homeless.'

'Right,' shrugged Andy. 'There's still the other RV.' He slouched into the remaining vehicle.

*

Johnny disappeared inside the remaining intact motor-home and Kurgan, now alone in the courtyard, reached for his phone.

'Were they yours?' he hissed.

'Were *what* mine?' Archimedes whined into Kurgan's ear.

'Don't play dumb with me. We're at the castle and some bunch of halfwits just invaded the vehicle pitch.'

'Anyone hurt?'

'Not Cold Steel. They beat the snot out of them, overturned one of the motor-homes, and your mates ran off.'

'Really?'

'What did you think was going to happen?'

'Well, I—'

'Well, shit, Archimedes, you need to stop underestimating Cold Steel. They're smarter, *and* tougher than you think.'

'Their luck will run out soon enough.'

'Not with their manager around it won't.'

'He's not indestructible?'

'He's got more savvy than Brian May at an astrophysics convention. No matter how deep a hole they fall, or get pushed, into, he'll pull them out.'

106

'And this time?'

'He didn't need to. Cold Steel and fighting go together like Axl Rose and a late arrival.'

'Shit?'

'So tell me, Archimedes, what exactly were you hoping to achieve tonight?'

'Those lads were supposed to be tasty,' said Archimedes. 'I thought they could have landed a few punches, broken a few guitarists' fingers, terrorised a lone hippy, maybe?'

'You're really crossing a line here, Archimedes.'

'Developing a conscience?'

'No,' said Kurgan. 'A survival instinct. So fucking well tell me what you're planning next time.'

'Fine, fine. Are they still making music?'

'Of course they bloody well are. It's what they came here for.'

'Are they still getting on?'

'You've never seen anything like it, Archimedes. All in the same studio at the same time, recording in real time. Jesus, it's like a heavy metal version of the Brady Bunch.'

'Don't fall for it,' said Archimedes. 'The guitarists hate each other. Didn't you know that?'

'Seems more like rivalry to me.'

'When you get back to the studio, turn it into something more.'

*

'Christ, Rachel.' Johnny sat at the hotel bar, his fingers clenched around his beer glass. 'I thought we'd seen the last of her.'

'Has Andy been acting any different?' asked Rachel.

'In what way?'

'Not being happy with the band, not getting on with Vince, talking about quitting?'

'Are you serious?'

'Angie's getting Andy to give her the juice on what's happening with the band,' said Rachel. 'And in return, she's telling him he's the best part of the band and would be better off going solo.'

'Is that where that Metalnet story came from?' said Johnny.

'What did you think?' asked Rachel. 'But I did convince him to start sending Angie good news stories instead, in return for me keeping it quiet.' She shook her head. 'But it won't last. Angie's not stupid.'

'I thought it was maybe blowback from Twenty' Johnny rubbed his forehead. 'Jesus, we don't need this.'

'Do you think Andy'll quit the band?' asked Rachel.

Johnny shook his head. 'He's not that stupid.'

'He and Vince aren't mates,' said Rachel. 'Maybe he *has* had enough of their bickering.'

'It brings out the best in both of them. Everyone knows it. Including Vince. Including Andy.'

Rachel raised her eyebrows. 'So what are you going to do?'

'What the hell *can* we do?' asked Johnny. 'They're both consenting adults.'

'So you're just going to let Andy walk?'

'It won't come to that.' He looked at her. 'Jesus, will it?'

Chapter 14

'He *said* that?'

'I swear, Vince.' Kurgan spoke softly, despite the live room door being closed. 'Back at the motor-home. I wish he hadn't told me. I mean, I thought you and Andy liked each other.'

'Dream on, Kurgan. You think I like that useless wanker?'

'Maybe he's feeling the pressure.'

'And so he bloody should, the way he plays. Christ, he doesn't appreciate *any* of the times I carried his useless arse.'

'Maybe if he'd had the same education as you.'

Vince nodded enraged agreement. 'He wouldn't have slagged off my music school if *he'd* been there.'

'Andy just hasn't got your training, your control. Everyone knows that. I know that.'

'See? See? Even you know. Bloody hell, Kurgan, he can't even read sheet music.'

'Really? I didn't know.' *Christ, this guy is the most egotistical snob I've ever met.* 'I mean, okay. But he can still play. I mean, not as good as you, of course.'

'Bloody right not as good as me, and that's why. And it's about time it was spelled out to him.'

*

Vince and Andy mouthed silent insults from inside their live rooms and fired musical broadsides at each other. The result was an intoxicating blend of addictive, ear-compressing guitar, which would have left Johnny crying with joy if he had nothing else to worry about.

The album.

The studio.

The whole Andy/Angie Dale thing.

Climate change.

Half an hour later, his anxieties transferred to his bladder and he hurried outside. Standing at the polished ceramic urinal, he sighed with contentment, his concerns temporarily forgotten in the stream of rapidly emptying body fluids. The urgency of the moment passed, he zipped up his leather pants and turned around.

The toilet door flew open and smacked him in his face. He fell flat on the marble floor and looked up, his vision starring. A large man dressed in jeans and a faded combat jacket over a blue striped t-shirt stepped through the doorway. He slammed the oak panel door shut and grabbed Johnny, yanking him up and throwing him against the wall. 'You owe!' he roared.

'What?' muttered Johnny.

'Police take Oleg.' He sprayed vodka spit over Johnny's face. 'I follow, they take him. Your fault.'

'Oleg? What the fuck are you talking about?'

'You know.' Violence seethed through the Russian accent. 'You make pipeline closed. You owe my boss. You pay with your band.'

Johnny suddenly remembered Debden's warning about Oleg's boss. Someone called Ramirez, who was looking to make legitimate money from the music business.

'No,' stammered Johnny. 'I don't know anything about it.'

'You lie!' The Russian clenched handfuls of Johnny's t-shirt and pulled back a sledgehammer fist. Johnny closed his eyes and prayed for unconsciousness before the pain. With his eyes shut, his other senses picked up and he heard the sound of heeled footsteps on the floor.

'What's going on?' Rachel's voice cut through Johnny's resigned torpor. He edged open one eye and saw her standing before them, hands on denim-clad hips and gunshot anger in her cobalt eyes.

'Stay out of this, *suka!*' spat the Russian.

Johnny knew a chance when he saw one. With the Russian glaring street murder at Rachel, he pushed back and kicked as hard as he could. Designer Italian cowboy boots connected hard with Russian testicles. Johnny's assailant grunted, his legs stayed as solid as pinewood tree trunks, but it was enough. Johnny hurled himself to the left, stumbled a few steps, bounced off two ornate walls and ran into the corridor.

Managing a hurried 'Thanks, babe', he shot past Rachel and on into the control room, the Russian close on his heels. At the mixing desk, Kurgan sat fully absorbed in the music pumping around the room. Johnny zoomed past and into the first live room. The

110

Russian thundered after him, his shouts still audible over the music.

Inside, only Mike's brown corkscrew hair was visible over the bank of concert toms that fringed the two bass drums. Hands holding drumsticks flew up and down, and Johnny's scream of pure fear went unheard. He stumbled through the small room and scrabbled at the next door.

A reeking wall of cannabis smoke slammed into Johnny and he almost collided with Joe. He sensed Russian booze-fumes breathalysing over him. He streaked past Joe, shot into the next room and nearly smacked into Andy's fretboard. Johnny swerved around and scampered past.

Bursting into the next live room, he saw Maxwell standing at a static mic, hips moving to the music, eyes closed and hands over the headphones. A tattered pirate flag that he'd had fashioned into a t-shirt draped over his upper body and moved with him.

'Maxwell, heeeeeeeeeeeeeeeelp!'

Maxwell's eyes opened, he looked at Johnny, then pitched forward as the Russian barged him out of the way. Johnny switched his focus to the door and thundered through to the last live room. Vince glared at Johnny, then the Russian exploded through the doorway. Johnny flashed through the next connecting door and back into the control room. He lightninged past Kurgan, who watched the double-body flash-past like an open-mouthed F1 spectator. Johnny sliced back into the drum room, then yelped in surprise as his arm was grabbed and Mike pulled him aside. The Russian surged through and the solid flatness of a bass guitar slammed into his face. He collapsed in a man-sized heap on the floor.

Joe looked at Johnny. 'Next time you want a backing singer, man,' he droned, 'let us know first.'

*

Firmly outside the building and waiting for the police to arrive, Johnny's former pursuer stood on shaky legs, clamped between two security guards. Johnny sat and trembled in the control room. Even Rachel's protective arm and warm nearness did little to calm him.

'You should have told us,' said Maxwell.

Johnny dragged a cold beer to his lips, his shaking hands causing it to froth close to overflowing. 'Told you what?' he quavered. 'That maybe the arseholes who dipped us in the North Sea were working for some badass euro-thug, who *might* come after us for some payback?'

'No might about it, man,' said Joe. 'He did.'

'So he did,' glared Johnny. 'But that didn't mean he would have. Anyway, you're here to make an album. Everything else is my problem.'

'He's got a point,' muttered Andy.

'Back off, Andy,' growled Mike. 'Standing up to underworld crime kings isn't Johnny's job.'

'Yeah,' chuckled Maxwell. 'Did you get a load of his bitch-wail when he ran through the vocal room?'

Johnny flushed and the rest of the band joined in the laughter. 'I can filter it out if you want,' offered Kurgan.

'Shit, no,' roared Maxwell. 'It's pure scream. You don't get more metal than that.' He smiled at Johnny. 'Fame at last.'

'Yeah,' muttered Johnny. 'Next thing you know I'll be guest singer.'

'No one sings in this bloody band but me,' crowed Maxwell.

'Mister Faslane?' A voice came from the control room door.

Johnny turned and saw Debden standing in the doorway. 'We need a word,' he said.

*

Johnny sat opposite Debden in a small studio side room and felt as if he were back at the police station.

'Did you tell Vladimir anything?' asked Debden.

'That's his name, is it?'

Debden nodded over a plastic cup of cold coffee.

'And what, exactly, would I have told him?' asked Johnny. 'I don't *know* anything, for fuck's sake.'

'Okay, so what did *he* say?'

'Something about owing his boss, closing the pipeline, paying with the band.'

'Do you believe me now?'

'All right, lesson learned.' Johnny held up his hands. 'We can't just count on the band's fame for security.'

'That's right,' said Debden. 'You need to get yourself some protection.'

'Any chance of some help from your lads?'

'You've already had help from us. We fished you out of the sea the other day, remember? Besides…' He raised his eyebrows. 'What are you thinking? An officer outside the front door?'

'I wouldn't mind.'

'Dream on, Johnny. You'd only attract attention.'

'Cold Steel are hardly low profile.'

'So make sure your protection is.'

Chapter 15

'A word, Andy.' Johnny stepped into the live room and closed the door.

'What now?' moaned Andy, holding his guitar like a slung rifle. 'My playing was there, man. Not like bloody Vince, or his arse.' He sniggered. 'Fire by name, fire by nature.'

'I hear you're thinking of quitting the band.' Transparent guilt washed over Andy's face and Johnny smiled grimly.

'Look, Johnny—'

'Are you really that stupid?'

'You all think that, anyway.'

'Is that what she's feeding you?'

'And who says she's not bang on?' snapped Andy. 'Plenty of bands out there are actually mates. Maybe some of that would be right up my street.'

'I'm not hearing this, Andy.'

Andy folded his arms, sat down and scowled at Johnny.

'Look,' said Johnny. 'We all know about this love-hate thing you and Vince have got going.'

'You mean hate-hate.'

'Call it what you want,' said Johnny. 'But it works. You know it.' He looked at the egg box wall and ran a hand over his thinly covered scalp. 'We *all* know it works. You won't get that anywhere else.'

'Is that the best you can do?'

'Hey, no one's offering you a blowjob to stay in the band. Just remember that Angie's after a story, and if she has to, she'll make the story.' He stared at Andy. 'That's what she's doing with you.'

'That's—'

'Think about it, Andy. What's a bigger story, Cold Steel making an album, or you quitting the band? And was that ever really in your head before she landed in your pants?'

'She's not—'

'And don't expect her too, either.' Johnny raised his eyebrows. 'It wouldn't surprise me if she dumped you straight after she got the story.'

114

'How does all that love and peace stuff fit in with Cold Steel?' Rachel and Joe sat in the empty control room after the day's recording had finished.

'Music's just a part of me, you know,' he warbled. 'Same as anyone. Look at Alice Cooper, man – owns a restaurant and plays golf. Is that metal?'

'But Cold Steel,' said Rachel. 'Heavy metal, aggressive music, the posturing, the image. I mean – and don't be offended – the only thing you've got in connection with any of that is your long hair.'

Joe sipped his drink with a lazy grin. 'These days, most metal bands don't even have that.'

'Which kind of makes my point,' laughed Rachel.

'Hey, never underestimate the music, and the image is just that, nothing else. We're all different in this band, but the music is what we've got in common.'

'Do you mind being called a hippy?'

'Why should I mind, man?' Lazy smile. 'It's what I am.'

'And how did you end up in Cold Steel?'

Joe shrugged. 'I played bass, they were auditioning, I got the gig.'

'Just like that?'

He lit a joint and smiled at her through the lung-clogging smoke. 'What do you know about my past?'

Rachel smiled. 'What do you want to say?'

'It's no secret,' he shrugged. 'Kinda boring really.'

She leaned forward slightly. 'So tell me anyway.'

'It was a long time ago, and the police know about it.'

'The police?' quizzed Rachel.

'Yeah, like, I know a bit about explosives.'

'Legally?'

'I was like Max California,' said Joe. 'Bass guitarist in the film 8mm.'

'You mean you worked in a sex shop?' grinned Rachel.

'No, man. I mean I couldn't get a job with my music.'

'And?'

'And I'd studied all about blowing stuff up. It became a hobby, and I got a few under the counter jobs.'

115

'Under the counter?'

'Robbery, safe-cracking, burglary.'

'You talk about it like it's nothing,' said Rachel.

'Nothing but stupid.' He drew on his joint. 'But I was young, no job, and I needed the money.'

'I'm guessing you didn't make it as a criminal mastermind?'

Joe shook his head and smiled. 'None of us could keep a secret. The gang was caught before their first blag, I turned informer and got off. I had to join Cold Steel, it was the safest place for me to be.'

'And now?'

'What do you mean?'

'Not thought about joining another band, going solo?'

'No way, man. Even with that ball-breaking gym Johnny's got us into, this band is the best job ever.'

*

Johnny slowly poked his head around Total Sports and Fitness' creaking door. He looked up to see if Sawyer was waiting with another bucket of water. The band shoved impatiently from behind and he hissed at them. 'A bit of fucking space, lads.'

'Can you see him?' whispered Maxwell.

'The place looks empty.' Johnny crept inside, his boots clunking on the uneven wooden floor despite his attempted stealth. 'It's okay,' he breathed. 'There's no one around.'

The band filed inside and Johnny made out longhaired silhouettes against the gym's unwashed, off-white wall. 'So where the hell is he?'

A sideswipe wave of cold water slammed into them. The band screamed out in shock. Hit and miss lights came on and Sawyer appeared from seeming emptiness.

'Christ,' spluttered Johnny. 'What the fuck are you, a bloody ghost?'

'Ghosts are dead, mate,' grinned Sawyer. 'I'm a long way from that.'

'Are you going to soak us every time we come round here?' asked Maxwell.

'All you've got to do is stop me.'

'How the hell can we do that if we can't even bloody see you?'

'Your problem,' shrugged Sawyer. 'And where were you nancy boys last night?'

'Fighting,' boasted Andy.

'And you beat them?' grinned Sawyer.

'Why wouldn't we have?'

Sawyer walked up to Andy, stood nose to nose and growled. 'Because you couldn't beat a bucket of bloody water tonight.'

'I didn't say we were fighting you,' murmured Andy.

'Hey, Shot Away,' said Johnny, making Sawyer spin round. 'That's what you like to be called, right?'

'What about it?'

'Cold Steel clearly aren't as tough as you, so why give them a hard time about it? Does that make you tough?' He laughed. 'Makes you a bully in my book.'

'They could do with your balls, Johnny.' Sawyer squared Johnny, who forced himself to stand still. He might have fled from Vladimir earlier that day, but he was damned if he was doing it a second time. *Not with Rachel watching.*

'Fact is,' said Johnny. 'We need more than just help to get the band into shape.'

'Meaning?'

'There are some new players in the game. Ever heard of someone called Julio Ramirez?'

'Maybe.'

'He's some scumbag who thinks it's the band's fault his smuggling pipeline got shut down.'

'And now he wants a piece of your action?' Sawyer smiled a grey-stubbled grin. 'Sounds about right. Best you start writing some cheques.'

'No way,' snarled Maxwell. 'We might not have had the same knocks as you, but we didn't work as hard as we did for our wedge to have some lowlife take it from us.'

Sawyer nodded slowly. 'So you *have* got some stones, even if you do look a bit stupid.'

'Have you seen yourself lately?' sniped Maxwell.

'What do you want?' asked Sawyer. 'Fitness or protection?'

'Can you do both?' asked Johnny.

'Murderball,' said Sawyer.

'What?'

'Wait there.'

Sawyer disappeared into the gym's dim recess, pulled open a fire door leading to the storeroom and vanished inside.

'What the fuck is he talking about?' asked Maxwell.

'Damned if I—' A medicine ball whooshed across the gym and slammed into Johnny's gut. He grunted and bent in half.

'Good catch,' said Sawyer. 'So here's the game. I take it your girlfriend and Dixie aren't playing?'

'I—'

'Rachel's not playing,' snapped Johnny, straightening slowly. 'She's here to take pictures.'

Her lips tightened and she reached for her camera.

'Dixie, you in or out?' asked Johnny.

'Mind if I watch the door? My ankle's playing up.'

'Sure.' Still holding the medicine ball, Johnny turned to Sawyer. 'Can you do security for us or not? We can find someone else if you're too busy.'

'Didn't say I was too busy.'

'You haven't said much at all. Christ, mate, it's not multiple choice. Yes or no?'

'Murderball first. I need to see what you've got.'

'What we've got?'

'Look, even I can't look after a bunch of complete no-hopers. You need to be able to stand on your own, to a point. If you want one person to make the difference, you lads need to meet me halfway.'

'I've got his number,' said Andy. 'He wants to know if we're all talk and no trousers. Right, mate?'

Sawyer nodded. 'Play one game and I'll know. Then I'll let *you* know.'

'What *is* this game?' asked Johnny.

'Simple,' said Sawyer. 'Two teams, one ball. A bench at each end of the gym is the goal. Highest score after ten minutes is the winner, or the team with the last man standing.'

'Any rules?'

'I've just explained them. You work as a team, score your goal any way you can, *and* stay on your feet till the end. The game's as tough as you make it, and there's no prize for the losers.'

Johnny grinned, 'Vince? Andy? Want to play on the same team?'

'Fuck off,' they unisoned.

'Mike and Joe?'

'We're on the same side, man.'

'No one else would have you,' grumbled Andy.

'That's sorted then,' said Johnny. 'Vince, you're with Mike and Joe. Maxwell and Andy, you're with me.'

'But—'

'Are you going to bitch all night, or do you want to show Shot Away here what you've got.'

'We—'

'You're Cold Steel,' said Johnny. 'Start bloody well showing it.'

'This all seems a bit violent to me, man,' said Joe.

'Supposed to be,' said Sawyer. 'But it's more. When you're down, hurting, and it seems impossible, are you going to give up or keep on trying? That's what murderball finds out. That's what *you* find out. About yourself. Show me what you are, lads. Players or pussies. I'm not sure about you myself, so how about convincing me?'

Sawyer blew a whistle. Its shrill tone made Johnny twitch. He still had the ball and he looked uncertainly at Rachel.

'Move!' she shouted.

'What?' Johnny faced front, then Vince body-slammed into him. He grunted and landed back first on the hard floor. Vince snatched the ball from his numbed fingers.

'Sorry, man,' Joe stepped over a writhing Johnny.

'Screw him.' Vince ran past Maxwell and threw the ball to Mike. Andy sprinted towards him, eyeing the chance to damage his guitar rival. Mike scooped up the ball, held it under one arm and sprinted to the far end of the gym. Maxwell charged after him but the distance widened by the second. Mike threw the ball at the bench, which slammed back against the wall with a crash that echoed back and forth around the gym.

'First point to El Cid and the two buddies,' drawled Sawyer.

Rachel ran over to Johnny and shook his shoulders. 'Get up,' she hissed. 'They're all over you.'

'Don't worry.' He stood up shakily. 'I'm fine.'

'If I was worried about you, you'd know it.'

'I love it when you get protective.'

'You want me to start crying and ask Vince to go easy on you?'

'Come on, Johnny,' said Maxwell. 'We need to work fast on this.'

Muscle aches wrapped around Johnny's ribs and Sawyer retrieved the medicine ball. 'Huddle in the middle,' he called, then threw the ball up in the air. Both teams roared and jumped up to reach it.

Johnny dropped first, the pain closing like a python around his chest. Joe and Mike followed. Vince and Andy forgot the ball and went for each other, leaving Maxwell a clear path for the ball. His hands gripped round it. A clear second faster than anyone else, he streaked towards the gym's far end. Joe and Mike raced after him; Vince and Andy were locked together in a street-wrestle on the floor. Johnny shuffled after them, his pain slowly easing.

An echoing crash trumpeted an equalising goal. Maxwell roared and raised his fist in the air as though he had just stepped onstage. Sawyer's whistle blast cut through the gym's humid air. 'All square and everything to play for.'

'Step up, lads,' growled Maxwell. 'We're going to win.'

Rachel's camera worked the building and Dixie fiddled with a portable speaker. Seconds later Cold Steel's first album, They Don't Like It Up 'em, flowed around the gym.

'What the fuck is that?' roared Sawyer.

'Better get used to it if you're coming on the books,' grinned Maxwell.

'Is that what you sound like?'

'You got a problem with that?' Andy fronted up to Sawyer, this time with a solid gaze and a straight back.

'Did you lot do a song called In the Pipeline?' asked Sawyer.

'Fucking right we did,' preened Andy. 'Got to number one as well.'

'Holy shit,' grinned Sawyer. 'I've actually heard of you bastards.'

*

Sawyer's whistle shrilled around the gym and he watched the two teams work to their strengths. It wasn't about who won, but he wasn't going to tell them that. When Sawyer played murderball, fists, feet, knees and elbows always connected. There was usually more blood on the floor than a Tarantino film but it forced people to work as a team. He watched the band: they wanted protection, but he needed to know they could make a stand till he got there, and murderball would tell him if they had what it took. *One man on his own never gets far, but a team is unbeatable.*

His mind flashed back to the time he'd been part of a team.

Chapter 16

1998

'Stand clear.'

'Lifting.'

'Watching.'

'Stand clear, lifting, watching. What a load of bollocks.'

'You secure that shit, Sawyer.'

'Sorry, Corp.'

'Corporal! You prick.'

Senior Aircraftman Sean 'Shot Away' Sawyer muttered under his breath.

'What was that, Sawyer?'

'Nothing, Corporal.'

'Good. Keep on saying nothing and you'll stay out of the guard room tonight.'

Low-angle autumn sunlight stabbed into the storage bunker's interior. Sawyer screwed his eyes against the glare and looked through the light dust haze at the gently swaying gantry. Eleven feet of drab green, torpedo-shaped metal hung suspended on lightly oiled chains. Sawyer, his best friend Johno 'Fist' Farrell, and Corporal Bates wheeled the gantry and its cargo outside to the olive green Air Force truck, its tailgate down and blue-overalled crew waiting.

'Christ,' said Sawyer. 'These things are older than me. Do they even work?'

'Want to drop one and find out?' grunted Bates. 'Now shut up and keep pushing.'

'They're probably not even real,' said Farrell.

'They're real,' said Bates. 'You think they'd have a whole squadron of us guarding them if they weren't?'

'Just saying.'

'And I'm just saying you're stupid, Sawyer. These things are real and they work, alright?'

'Let's find out.' Sawyer stopped pushing the gantry and with one less man pushing, it crunched to a slow halt. He picked up a hammer from the back of the vacant truck and walked to the bomb's pointed nose.

'Sawyer,' said Bates.

'What?'

'Sawyer!'

'Fuck off.'

'Sean, mate.' Farrell placed a hand on his friend's shoulder.

'Bollocks.' Sawyer jerked violently against his friend's gesture. 'Two years of walking the wire for these things,' he growled. 'They should have been binned years ago, let us do some real soldiering.' He swung the hammer and brought it down hard. It clanged against the bomb's nose, which swung in its chains.

'Stand down, Sawyer,' roared Bates. He stepped towards Sawyer and grabbed at the hammer. Sawyer swerved out of reach, bunched his fist and jabbed towards Bates. Bates saw it coming and jumped back, striking the gantry and knocking the release lever. With a heavy clang, the bomb dropped to the ground and rolled towards the truck.

'Take cover!'

*

'Bring in the accused.'

'Prisoner, by the front, quick, march. Leftrightleftrightleftrightleftright, right wheel, mark time, halt! Attenshun! Atease! 'Tenshun! Atease! Shun! Atease! Shun! Eyes front, face front. Look straight ahead, you bastard. Don't you eyeball me, or the CO.'

Squadron Warrant Officer Pinn prowled malignant circles around Sawyer, who risked a downward glance at his commanding officer. Squadron Leader Church's remaining eye fired belt-fed hatred right back at him. Above Church's head, a battered AK was mounted on the office wall. Sawyer knew the stories. Back in '91, as a Flight Commander, Church had been part of a wing-strength assault on Kuwait International Airport against the occupying Iraqis. Leading his men personally, he followed his exploding grenade into an enemy sangar, grabbed that very Kalashnikov from a dead soldier at his feet, and returned fire that came from the survivors. His flight followed him through the breach, but not before he'd been hit and lost his eye. And so, looking like an unsmiling Moshe Dayan, Church became the only one-eyed member of the Corps on the active list.

'I hear you've been hitting nuclear weapons with a hammer, Sawyer.' Church spoke with glacial hostility.

'Yes, sir.'

'Got a death wish, have you?'

'Frustrated, sir,' said Sawyer. 'I'm a soldier, not a gate guard.'

'Guarding those weapons are the orders,' said Church. 'And around here we follow orders. We don't have to like it, but we do have to do it. Unless you feel we need your approval first?'

'No, sir.'

'Shut up. These weapons are being retired, Sawyer. You were escorting the last one out of here. And no weapons means no need to guard them, which means new duties for the squadron.' Church flickered through a sheaf of papers in front of him. 'What's your nickname, Sawyer?'

'Shot Away, sir.'

'By name and by nature, it seems. The bomb you struck didn't have a warhead fitted, but I presume you were switched on enough to know that its detonator was?'

'Yes, sir.'

'And the resulting explosion would have been enough to kill not only you, but also your mates.'

'Yes, sir.'

'Fucking dangerous way to make a point.' Church sat back in his chair. 'I've heard all about you, Sawyer, getting pissed at the station bar, then running around the base in your camouflage, giving it the big I am to the scuffers.' He shook his head. 'It doesn't impress me. I was in Baghdad when you were still in your Dad's bag, you moronic little shit. You've damaged Air Force property, you disobeyed a direct order from an NCO, and more importantly, your actions have risked the lives of my men. You'll be stuck at Honham until long after this squadron has been reassigned, Sawyer. By the time you leave here, the entire Regiment will have forgotten all about you.'

*

Johnny tapped his feet in the control room and smiled at Sawyer, who seemed to be enjoying the music. *For once he's wearing jeans,* thought Johnny, although the faded green t-shirt displaying crossed rifles over an astral crown seemed to be the only other piece of clothing Sawyer owned.

The band's recent experiences had translated into rapid-fire inspiration and the songs sloughed away from them like exfoliating skin. Cold Steel's product was tight, clinical and addictive.

Nocte Battle, Swimming for Justice and Feathered Death spoke of their newest brushes with drama.

Vince and Andy sparred with each other just like they always had.

Angie Dale seemed to be keeping her distance.

Even Kurgan seemed happy. Almost.

Which only made Johnny more suspicious.

'I like it,' gushed Kurgan.

'You should see them live,' said Johnny.

'With this look?' He ran a blunt-fingered hand through his blue spiky hair.

'No one give a toss what you look like at a gig,' said Johnny. 'All eyes are on the stage.'

'And it's down to guys like me to make sure their ears are, too.'

'What do you mean?' said Johnny. 'This music could stand up anywhere.'

'So record it in a garage and save us some trouble,' muttered Kurgan.

'What?'

'Nothing.' Smile back in place.

Johnny looked at Kurgan and wondered if he should push it. 'I need to talk to Rachel.' He held up his phone. 'I'll be in the press room.'

*

'He liked *cake*?' spluttered Johnny. 'What was that all about?'

Rachel's lips corner-creased into a half-smile. 'I don't know, and I didn't ask him.'

'So what's with him and the band?'

'He doesn't like them.'

'Because of this old-time card game with Maxwell?'

'He didn't say.'

'And is that a problem?'

'Could be.'

'Christ, Rachel, why did we have to come here?'

'Because Ozone said so,' smiled Rachel. 'You know the game, Johnny. From a business perspective, you can see why. Twenty should know that as well. But...' She looked at Johnny. 'Maybe there's more.'

'What do you mean?'

'I don't know. A hunch, that's all. This thing with Archimedes, there's something else, I know it.'

'Explore a little further,' said Johnny. 'We've already had our instruments disappear, been dropped in the North Sea, and then attacked by squatters.'

'None of that's down to Ozone.'

'You think?'

'You're a suspicious son of a bitch, Johnny.'

'Come on, Rachel. You said it yourself, you've got a hunch. And what about Kurgan? He binned the first song the band recorded.'

'That's hardly conclusive.'

'*And* Archimedes doesn't want the band here. He hates Maxwell over something that happened bloody years ago.' Johnny frowned. 'I wouldn't be surprised if all of our bad luck was down to him.'

'And all I have to do is find it out, right?'

'You did on St Clements,' said Johnny. 'You worked out the whole thing before any of us wanted you to. Shit, Rachel, we'd have been greased turkey snot if you'd spilled the story when you wanted to.'

'But I didn't, did I?' She eyeballed Johnny.

'Yeah, watched over by the St Clements Army is why you didn't, nothing else. You didn't do it for me.'

'I was doing my job.' She folded her arms. 'What did you expect?'

'And now?'

'I'd never hurt you.' Her voice softened. 'But I'm still a reporter.'

He smiled. 'The best one I know.'

'I'd better be the only one you bloody well know, mister.'

'I'm too damn scared of you to do otherwise,' he laughed.

She snaked her arms around his neck and ground her body into his. 'So you're only with me because you're scared?'

'You sound more like a wife every day.'

'Is that a proposal?'

'You want to know?'

She chuckled and stepped back. 'What exactly are you worried about?'

'I think someone at Twenty's up to something,' said Johnny. 'Maybe more than someone, maybe the whole bloody lot of them.'

She grinned. 'Maybe you've got a point.'

'Can you find out?'

'Is that a challenge?'

Chapter 17

'Don't you even *think* about saucing my wiener, you goddam cake weirdo. Don't think, don't *dream* that Cold Steel aren't going to complete their album at your studio.'

'You've made that very clear, Randall?' Archimedes blew a cloud of apple-smelling smoke around his office while he spoke to Randall on speakerphone. 'And you know what, I'm not arguing?'

'What then, douche bag? You sure as hell didn't call me up to wish me a goddam happy Labor Day. I blackmail you, I know I did, and now we're *friends?*'

'No?'

'Don't give me wise-ass shit. Are you goddam asking me or telling me?'

'I'm telling you?'

'So tell me.'

'You want Cold Steel to record here?'

'You know it, and you'd better not freaking try and stop it.'

'I don't need to stop anything, they'll do that all by themselves?'

'The fuck they will. Faslane would have told me. Shit, that's why we put him to them in the first place. He'd *never* let them lose control like that.'

'He's already used to it?'

'What does *that* mean, asshole?'

'The band's guitar players?'

'Old news, pal. They don't like each other, but neither of them are dumb enough to blow their ride. They know it, I know it, and Jesus Christ, Archie, *you* should know it.'

'That's not what I'm seeing?'

'And that don't turn you on?'

'No? Especially if you thought *I* had anything to do with it. I don't want them here, but I want you to tell the world about my… my preferences even less. What am I to do? Especially when one of them seems to be getting some outside suggestions to spread his wings.'

'What are you saying? Has one of those faggots got religion?'

'Of the female variety?'

'Dumbass bastards.' A pause. 'You did the right thing coming to me with this, Archie. I'll take care of it.'

'You're coming over here?'

'A man in my position doesn't have to sweep up the shit after the storm, he sends someone else to do it.'

Randall ended the call and Archimedes looked at Kurgan, who was sitting opposite him and had heard every word. 'Make sure they *really* hate each other?' growled Archimedes.

*

'Have Vince and Andy caused any problems on this album?' Lucy Penhalligan's Knightsbridge accent was steel beneath silk and her brown eyes stared assassin ruthlessness at Johnny. She sat opposite him in the press room, dressed in her meet-the-band uniform of jeans and faded combat jacket.

'What do you mean?' Johnny's throat tightened.

'I mean you're hiding something.'

'I—'

'Would you rather be talking to Randall?'

Johnny's pretence deflated. 'Okay,' he said. 'On the surface, it's the usual. They can't stand each other, or so they say.'

'No shocks there,' said Lucy. 'So tell me why I'm really here.'

'Andy's got an admirer.'

'Well, why didn't you say so?' Lucy threw up her arms in mock despair. 'Let's stop the album right now till he goes back to living like a monk.'

'It's—'

'Christ, Johnny, is that it?' She stared at him. 'Did we sack you after you got with Rachel? Do you think I shouldn't be in the same building as the band without an armed guard?'

'That's not what I meant.'

'Oh. You mean he's hooked up with a man?'

'No,' chuckled Johnny. 'He's with a woman who's putting ideas into his head.'

'That's more like the women we need to worry about, right, Johnny?'

'I didn't—'

'Really?' said Lucy. 'Seriously? Is that what I should be worried about?'

'She's a reporter and she's telling him he should leave the band.'

Lucy's head snapped round. 'Now *that's* not the kind of idea we like. Have we had any delays?'

'A few wobbles at the start but we're doing alright now.'

Lucy shook her head. 'Archimedes is complaining.'

'What about?' asked Johnny. 'Look, Lucy, Cold Steel are musicians, they're unpredictable, but they're doing their job.'

'We need more than that,' said Lucy. 'Cold Steel are in a top studio, and straight after this, there's a tour to rehearse for.'

'I know.'

'And we're through with any excuses, any problems, *any* shit. That includes Andy or anyone else thinking they're going solo. Their contracts say otherwise. Maybe you should remind them of that.' She glared iced hostility at Johnny. 'From now on, everything goes by the numbers or they'll be more gagged than the Rock City Angels.'

'Who?'

'Google them if you don't know, but don't doubt we'll do it. And make damn sure Vince, Andy and everyone else do what we want, what we say, *when* we say.'

'You want them in bed on time as well?'

'Don't, Johnny. Not now. Not when so much is at stake.'

'I'll keep them on message,' said Johnny.

'I think I'll hang around and see for myself.'

*

Andy's anger burned like a white-hot slave brand. Tab charts, fucking tab charts! Bollocks to Johnny, Angie was right. Vince was goading him, looking for a reaction, and the fact that it worked annoyed him even more. He stood in the live room and attacked his strings, gouging into the riffs he'd created with Vince. *Just like we always did. No sheet music, nothing written down, just the sound, you bastard!*

Tab charts left in Andy's live room. By Vince. A calculated insult. They were six lines on paper, representing six guitar strings, and a number over each line telling the player which fret to rest his finger on. A simple, effective way for many guitarists to learn, but Vince was telling Andy that he was too stupid to read sheet music.

Andy's fingers blurred along his guitar's maple neck, inlaid with miniature pirate flags. He could hear Vince through his headphones, clinical, note-perfect, and he knew his own playing matched the precision, which he overlaid with a surging rage. It was all part of the rivalry. Neither one of them would give the other the excuse of poor timing or slack riff discipline, and the solos were a straight fight. The band chose the best one. *You're lost without me, you bastard. Just wait till I'm gone.*

He pressed the sustain and his plectrum scraped from the pickup, along the top string and stopped at his left hand, his fingers pressing down on the string. Both hands fluttered along the fretboard and he blasted a trademark improvised solo that poured molten notes over Vince's power chords. His very existence telescoped down to his playing. He harnessed the emotion, letting it build his determination to outplay Vince.

Andy's solo knifed through the live room. He sweated, felt living pain. He attacked the strings, ploughing a metal tsunami that surged towards the control room. His fingers, though hardened by a lifetime of pressing strings, felt new agony as he pressed for more sustain, heard the terminal screech of strings that endured musical overdose. He twisted the tuning key and at the same time leaned back on the tremolo. One of the strings shot past its end-point and snapped.

Still anchored at the bridge and machine head, the string's split ends whipped though the air. The top half pinged away from Andy, the other flicked up to his face and dug into his nose like a fly hook. His solo melted like a slushed drink. He gasped, grabbed his face and collapsed to his knees. Vince carried on playing, pouring an acid burn onto Andy's torment. He barely heard the door being thrown open and footsteps rushing towards him.

*

Johnny stood behind the curtains in the hospital's emergency department. Looking at Andy's blood-squirted face, he felt his lunch fighting for reappearance. A shirt-sleeved doctor and latex-gloved nurse busied themselves injecting local anaesthetic in and around Andy's nose. Twisted ends of bloodstained guitar string poked out of two holes in his skin as though he'd had a bizarre body piercing.

'Of all the days for you two to act like arseholes,' fumed Johnny.

'What do you mean?' Trying to keep his nose still, Andy's voice had a strange nasal twang.

'Lucy from Ozone turned up today.'

'So?' Gauze squares soaked up spatters of blood on Andy's face.

'So she's heard about delays in recording and the studio aren't happy with us,' said Johnny. 'She specifically asked about you and Vince, and she knows about a certain someone putting ideas about a solo career into your head. Any of that sound familiar?'

'And?' Brown iodine was liberally wiped over Andy's swollen, pierced nose.

'You don't get it, Andy. Ozone *own* Cold Steel. Completely, utterly, unconditionally. And right now they want an album recorded on time. Taking time out for an unplanned nose job could mean the difference between band and no band at all.'

'Bollocks, Johnny. We're worth too much. And I'm worth plenty, in or out of Cold Steel.'

'Because Angie says so?'

'Yeah.'

'Shows how dumb she is,' said Johnny. 'Look at your contract again, the one you were stupid enough to sign *before* I came along. It's Ozone or no zone, and if they want to, you'll be more gagged than the Rock City Angels.'

'Who?'

'Google them. Something like this is exactly what we didn't want Ozone to see. Christ.' Johnny looked at Andy's nose. 'Don't tell me this is normal.'

'Have *you* ever seen anything like this before?'

'*Nothing* you lot ever do has been seen before, why should this be any different?'

Andy winced as the doctor syringed numbing drugs into his face. 'Jesus Christ, Doc.'

'So what really happened?' asked Johnny.

'Bloody string broke, flew back and stabbed me.'

'And how come it snapped? Anything to do with Vince?'

'Look, Johnny, strings snap,' he gasped as the needle stabbed into his cheek. 'Fucking hell, Doc, I thought you said I wouldn't feel anything.'

The doctor pursed his lips and flicked Andy's hands back from his still bleeding face. 'I said you wouldn't feel anything once the anaesthetic takes effect.'

'And how long will that be?'

'A few minutes, be patient.'

'Can't you just pull it out?' asked Johnny. 'It's only a guitar string.'

'Thanks for the sympathy, you bastard,' growled Andy.

'Earn it, you'll get it. Maybe you'd like Vince in here to hold your hand.'

'Yeah, right. It was his bloody fault.'

'Finally the truth,' said Johnny.

'He's been winding me up for bloody days,' said Andy. 'Don't tell me you haven't noticed. And don't tell me Angie's wrong on this.'

Johnny laughed. 'What, you mean I haven't noticed the fact that you and Vince hate each other? Fucking hell, Angie Dale's hardly the genius of the century to work that out.'

'You *might* have noticed how cosy Vince has been getting with Kurgan.'

'How could I have missed a musician talking to the producer?' said Johnny. 'Yeah, that's really suspicious.'

'More than you'd think,' said Andy. 'Vince doesn't talk to the producer.' He shook his head. 'He doesn't talk to anyone at the studio. He thinks he's above all that shit with his fancy music school learning. As far as he's concerned, he's the artist, the *only* artist who counts, and it's way beneath him to talk with the hired help at the studio. *Then* he leaves bloody tab charts lying around.'

'Tab charts?'

'Yes, fucking tab charts.' Andy winced as the doctor gently pulled on the blood-slicked string. 'You know what they are, right?'

'Sure, but what—'

'So he's telling me how thick I am. He's telling me I'm too bloody stupid to read sheet music.'

'And?'

'And it wound me up. Wouldn't you be? Jesus, Doc, that bloody hurt.'

The doctor held both ends of the sheared string, jagged, twisted. 'When the anaesthetic has taken effect,' he said, 'we'll cut the string again, and then pull it out with clean ends. There's a risk of infection, so we'll put you on antibiotics.'

'Shit,' said Andy. 'Vince is going to walk all over me with the solos.'

'No he won't,' replied Johnny.

'What do you mean?'

'All recording's stopped till you get back.'

'What?'

'And it doesn't happen again, you bastard. Look, shag Angie Dale if you must, *if* she lets you, but by Christ, don't believe a word she says about leaving the band. Any shit from just one of you lot and none of you will ever perform again, together or solo.'

'Right,' said the doctor. 'I think the anaesthetic's had enough time to work. Mister Stains, are you ready?'

Andy clenched his jaw. 'Do it.'

'Mister Faslane.' The doctor looked at Johnny. 'You might want to look away.'

'Leave it out, mate,' said Johnny. 'I've seen worse than this.'

*

'He's coming round.' Johnny heard distant voices radiating through a thaw of cold unconsciousness. He opened his eyes and groaned, felt a thudding pain at the back of his head.

'Bloody pussy.' Andy's face floated into Johnny's vision far above him, his nose double-sized and obscured by a wad of white hospital dressing. 'You sure know how to interrupt an artist at work.'

'What?' Johnny slid around on the hospital floor and sat up.

'The doc was two seconds into sorting me out when you decked at the sight of blood,' sneered Andy. 'Some people will do anything to get groped by a nurse.'

'Don't tell Rachel,' slurred Johnny. 'She wouldn't understand.'
He rubbed the back of his head.

'I'm finally starting to like her,' grinned Andy. 'Right, Doc,
Johnny's woken up, my snout's sorted, can we get back to the
studio?'

*

'But you *can't*!' gasped Johnny.

'I can.' Lucy stood in the control room and glared at the band.
Andy popped an antibiotic the size of a memory stick into his
mouth and grimaced as he forced it down with a large gulp of
bottled water. 'This is just the kind of shit we've been hearing
about, and it's getting old.'

'Andy's guitar string snaps and you're going to pull the plug on
Cold Steel?' said Johnny. 'It could have happened to anyone.'

'Cold Steel aren't just anyone,' snapped Lucy. 'Ozone Records
aren't just anyone, and no, Twenty Studios aren't just anyone.'

Johnny shot a shut the fuck up stare at Vince, who opened his
mouth, caught Johnny's look and kept quiet. The rest of the band
faced Johnny as though everything was his fault.

'And I suppose,' said Lucy, 'it's just coincidence that this
happened today, when I came down to see what's going on?'

'What's so special about you?' asked Vince.

'*This* special,' she flared. 'You're all just one comment away
from being history. *Complete* history.' She picked up her phone
and brandished it around the control room like a detective's ID.
'I'm just one swipe away from calling Randall Spitz.' Collective
groan from the band. 'You remember him? Well, know this, I
speak for Randall. I've had it with you, he's had it with you.
We've worked bloody hard to get you into Twenty, and you
bastards need to appreciate that fact. One more single delay, even
one minute, one more bad report from Twenty, one of you even
swears out of line, and it's over. For good.' She looked at her
oversized Russian watch. 'Right, there's absolutely *no* point
getting you back to work today. Here. Eight o'clock tomorrow
morning. I'll be watching.'

'You heard Lucy,' snapped Johnny. 'We're done for the day.'

'No gym tonight?' asked Maxwell.

135

'No. The last thing I want is you lot chucking medicine balls around when you're hormonal. I'll see you in the hotel foyer tomorrow morning with your minds back on the job. Maxwell?'

'What.'

'Interview time.'

*

'So far,' said Rachel, 'I've heard Cold Steel described as rock, metal, rock 'n' roll, and plain old music. So how about you, Maxwell – what music do Cold Steel play?'

She and Maxwell were in the drum room, with Mike's gleaming kit standing silently behind them like an empty watchtower. 'Sometimes,' said Maxwell, smiling at her, 'it's all of those, or any of those. Sometimes none at all. Must be why metal's so hard to define. Even we don't know what it means.'

'Okay,' laughed Rachel. 'I guess we're no nearer to solving *that* riddle.'

'Have you *ever* had that question answered?' asked Maxwell. 'Have you ever been able to define heavy metal, really, truly? Has anyone? Ask a hundred different fans, you'll get a hundred different answers. Ask a hundred different bands, you'll get the same.'

'So what about this pirate fixation?'

'If you're asking *that*,' said Maxwell, shaking his head, 'you haven't really listened to our songs.'

'So I've got to listen to all of Cold Steel's albums before I interview you?'

His killer smile bounced off her armour-plated, blue-eyed stare. 'You might call it research.'

'It's research enough to be surrounded by you five for the duration, enough to watch you record your new album, then follow you on tour. Don't you think that earns a little information?'

'Well, alright.' Maxwell nodded. 'Did you ever read Treasure Island?'

'It wasn't on my school reading list.'

'Wasn't on mine either, but I'm glad I read it.'

'Why?'

'Forget about good and evil.' Maxwell's eyes glittered. 'Forget right and wrong. That's down to each one of us to decide. It means what it means to each of us.'

'Just like metal?' asked Rachel. 'Different meanings to different people?'

'That's right,' said Maxwell. 'You read Treasure Island and you decide for yourself who's good, who's bad, who's right, who's wrong. It's make up your mind time, but that's only part of the story.'

'What's the rest?'

'It's all in there. Everything about life that defines living, that defines metal. Individuality, free spirit, adventure. Christ, if that book isn't about metal, what the hell is? If Long John Silver was alive right now, he'd be fronting his own band.'

'Singing for Cold Steel?'

'No one else does that,' growled Maxwell.

'And the rest of the band?'

'What do you mean?'

'You've never wondered what it might be like with other personalities in the band?'

'It'll never happen. *We* are Cold Steel. It works, we work.' Maxwell scowled, folded his arms and non-verbalised a change in subject.

'So,' said Rachel. 'You see a lot of common ground between pirates and modern-day heavy metal?'

'Oh, it's there,' breathed Maxwell. 'It's so there. Being an individual, choosing your own destiny, not being preached to, deciding for yourself what you like, what you don't, not fashionable, but never out of fashion. Those lads did things their own way, they were always the underdogs, undergunned, outnumbered, but they never gave in, never sold out. Sounds like metal bands, and metal fans, to me. How about you?'

Rachel smiled. 'It sounds like it's the perfect match.'

'You know it.'

'So how's Johnny doing?' she asked.

Again, Maxwell turned his full grin on to Rachel. 'What do you think?'

Her eyebrows climbed to her fringe. 'I think I'm the only one around here who appreciates him.'

'You're appreciating different things,' said Maxwell. 'He's a manager, never a singer.'

Chapter 18

'Christ, Johnny,' whispered Maxwell. 'Why don't we just try knocking on the door?'

Johnny turned around and glared at Maxwell, while the rest of the band lurked behind him in the shadows, a longhaired yeti-clump silhouette. 'Quiet,' he hissed.

'But he *knows* we're coming,' said Maxwell.

'There's no windows,' said Johnny. 'And if he can't hear us we've got the edge.'

For the first time since he'd been managing Cold Steel, Johnny was wearing trainers instead of cowboy boots, and in his mind this allowed him to float along as silently as a midnight assassin.

They crept towards the gym; Johnny sensed the band's tension behind him. The starkly lit door stood closed, silent and menacing. The light bulb above it swayed lightly in the gentle night breeze. Birds cawed in the darkness, lending an almost tropical air of mystery to the atmosphere. The gym seemed deserted: no sign of Sawyer.

Johnny reached out and slowly, quietly, opened the door. The swinging light threw a wedge of illumination onto the uneven wooden floor. He froze, listening for any sound.

Nothing.

He sneaked through the doorway. The band's collective shadow stretched into the door-framed block of light, surrounded by solid, malevolent darkness all around.

Silence crashed into them.

'No sign of him,' whispered Johnny. 'Follow me, lads.'

'What happens when we get inside?' asked Maxwell.

'Fucked if I know,' said Johnny. 'If we can switch the lights on without getting soaked I guess we've got him beat.'

Step by step, the band toothpasted into the gym. Silence embraced them and Johnny edged towards the single light switch and reached out for it. *We're there!* he exulted. *We've beat him. We got inside without getting soaked. Result!*

Cold water splash-boarded over the band. Johnny, who had been leading them single-file, took the full force of another near-ice soaking. The lights flickered on and there was Sawyer, hanging upside down, gripping a rope between his legs and holding a now empty bucket. He let go of the rope, his body blurred into a summersault and then his combat boots thudded onto the gym floor, so he landed on his feet like a thrown cat. 'Not bad,' he nodded to Johnny.

'Didn't stop us getting wet, though,' spluttered Johnny.

'Hey,' said Sawyer. 'Get too good and I'm out of a job.' He held a whistle and blew a shrill blast. The band tensed at the sound. 'In pairs,' roared Sawyer. 'We're going back to our childhood, ladies. Wheelbarrow race.'

'You fucking what?' blustered Maxwell.

Sawyer ballet-leapt over to Maxwell. 'You heard me, girlfriend. Competition, upper body strength, teamwork. It's amazing what you can learn from simple exercise.'

Maxwell looked at Johnny, who shrugged and nodded.

'Now pair up,' shouted Sawyer. 'And you two bitches—' he pointed at Vince and Andy — 'you're working together.'

'Fu—'

'Don't even *dream* about it,' snapped Sawyer. 'You pair of handmaidens need to work out what everyone else already knows.'

'And what's that?' grated Andy.

'You actually depend on each other. Shit, I don't know anything about your bloody music and I've worked that out. And until you admit it, I'm going to make you do it. You'll team up in this gym or you'll answer to me, alright?'

Vince and Andy glared at each other but said nothing.

'Positions, gentlemen,' snapped Sawyer. 'I take it you're not participating?' he asked Rachel.

She picked up her camera. 'I've got a job to do.'

'Always my luck,' muttered Sawyer.

'Fucking hell.' Johnny planted his hands on the gym floor and felt slightly sick. Maxwell grabbed Johnny's legs and lifted. He looked left and saw Mike holding Joe, and after a brief squabble, Vince held Andy's legs.

'This is going to be more exciting than Silverstone,' grinned Sawyer. 'On my mark, and the last one to puke wins.' He blew his whistle. 'Go!'

*

'Call yourself a rock star.'

'No,' snapped Andy. 'I'm a fucking musician. You're the one that keeps calling me a bloody rock star.' Holding his phone, he stared up at the peeling artexted ceiling and drank room-service whiskey. He ached all over from the gym and he was still pissed off with Johnny.

Or was he? Did he really want to quit the band? Before he'd met Angie he knew the answer was no. Now he wasn't sure, but the fact that he knew he couldn't was infuriating.

'You're not quitting the band?' asked Angie.

'I can't. Johnny was right. I've checked my contract. It's Cold Steel or nothing.'

'Haven't you heard of a lawyer?'

'Loving your sympathy, Angie.'

'Check your dictionary, lover, sympathy's between shit and syphilis.'

'Must be why I've been shagging my fist lately.'

'Don't expect a better offer from me while you're wasting your time in Cold Steel.'

'Sounds like I'm wasting *your* time,' snapped Andy. 'Staying put gives you no story and you know what? That bald bastard's always been right. Screw you, Angie.' He ended the call and grinned to himself. 'Hung up first,' he chuckled. 'That means *I* dumped *her*.'

Chapter 19

Silas 'Mad Monk' Moss sat in his cluttered office, ran a hand through his tonsured hair and pondered the latest metal news via a patchy internet feed. He needed to get a better connection. But his office landlord wanted regular rent payments first, so how could he do one without the other? And the number one rule was find out what they're saying about your band.

Because unless you were Peter Mensch, you only managed one band, and you hoped like hell they made it.

Silas Moss wasn't Peter Mensch.

Silas managed Chainsaw, who, despite supporting Cold Steel on part of their last tour, hadn't made the progress in terms of album sales he felt they deserved.

An unrecognised number came up on his phone.

'Silas Moss.'

'Silas. Angie Dale.'

'Do I know you?'

'No, but you will.'

'And why's that?'

'We can help each other out.'

'That's what all the girls say. Sorry, love, I'm spoken for.'

'Her name's Florence, isn't it?'

'That's right, and we're tight.' Silas googled Angie Dale while he spoke.

'That's not why I'm calling,' said Angie.

'Glad to hear it,' said Silas. 'And time's wasting with you telling me nothing.'

'I've got an idea that'll give Chainsaw some top publicity.'

'How many times have I heard that? Really, love, sounds like it's your publicity you're selling.'

'Is that a problem?'

'It is for me. What's in it for Chainsaw?'

'Payback from Cold Steel.'

Silas sat up. 'Talk to me.'

*

'A week?' asked Maxwell. 'Then what?'

The band lounged on mismatched chairs in the control room while Sawyer prowled around the entire studio.

'Did you think you were moving in?' asked Johnny. 'You've got songs to record, you've got a week to do it, and while they're being mixed and produced, you rehearse for the next tour.'

'Jesus,' moaned Andy.

'So what happens after a week?' asked Mike.

'Rehearsals,' said Johnny. 'Have you thought about what you want?'

'What we want?' said Maxwell.

'Effects, lights, stage setup, playlist. Any ideas at all?'

'What about support bands?'

'You want Chainsaw again?' asked Johnny. 'They're doing an interview on Blue Metal tonight.'

'Fuck off,' snarled Maxwell.

'Just as well,' Johnny smiled. 'Support's already decided. In each country you play, their biggest metal band will be opening up for you.'

'Who've we got for Spain?' asked Maxwell.

'Damas Infernales.'

'What does that mean?'

'Hell's Belles,' said Vince. 'More or less.'

'What?' said Maxwell. 'You mean like the song?'

'Belles,' sneered Vince. 'Not bells.'

'And there's a difference?'

'Belles, belles. Women, for fuck's sake.'

Maxwell sat up like a meerkat with rigor mortis. 'A girl band?'

'Haven't you heard of them?' asked Johnny.

'Should I have?'

'They're big news in Spain.' Johnny tapped his phone screen and passed it over. 'They really know what they're doing, and it'll be the same everywhere you play. You *will* have to do good shows every night on this tour.'

'Jesus.' Maxwell showed Johnny the phone screen. 'Is that them?'

'Why the amazed look?' asked Johnny.

'They're dressed like bloody secretaries.'

'I think you'll find they call it commerce metal.'

'Commerce metal?' spluttered Maxwell. 'What the fuck is that?'

Johnny snatched his phone back and his finger fluttered over the screen. 'Watch and listen. And maybe even learn.'

The band crowded around Johnny's phone. Deep, riff-laden music seeped around the control room. Quick appreciation flew across their faces, followed by a wisp of apprehension from Maxwell.

'Good?' asked Johnny.

'Not bad,' pondered Maxwell. 'But seriously, what the hell are they wearing? They look like bloody stockbrokers, for shit's sake.'

'Is that a problem?'

'I guess not,' said Maxwell. 'It's just a bit weird.'

'Don't be so quick to judge them,' said Johnny. 'They pay their bills with investments, stocks and shares. And—' he smiled — 'they manage themselves, by choice.'

'Don't get any ideas, man,' said Joe.

'I wish,' said Johnny. 'Anyway, it all starts on the north coast in Barakaldo. The Bizkaia. It's the biggest arena in Spain, and I don't need to tell how much you've got to prove to the Spanish, and then the Portuguese.'

'Yeah yeah,' said Andy. 'We cancelled last time round.'

'That's right,' said Johnny. 'You owe them, big time.'

'Old news,' said Maxwell.

'Bad news,' replied Johnny. 'Look, lads. You're good. I know it, you know it. But you've got to stay good. And that's up to you.' He shrugged. 'I can't make you play well, all I can do is give you the best chance.'

'And how do you intend to do that?' asked Maxwell.

'One week, and you'll see.'

*

Honham was a disused airbase that clung to Suffolk's last scrap of dry ground before it gave way to reeds and marshes. Crumbling concrete fence posts leant at awkward angles around the vast flat area, and the once pristine fencing now resembled broken fishing nets after a year's storm exposure.

144

The band drove along a deserted, potholed road that skirted the perimeter. Crammed into a minibus, they led a small convoy of vans that had driven with frustrating slowness from London.

'Doesn't look much like a rehearsal location,' mused Maxwell.

'It won't.' Johnny's mind drifted back to his conversation with Rachel in their hotel room that morning.

'I'm supposed to be embedded.' Her eyes flickered molten hostility.

'Sure you are,' he replied. 'And we know that.'

'Looks like it.'

'Hey, if this was an ordinary session, we'd love to have you there with us.'

'And when are Cold Steel *ever* ordinary?'

'Rachel, you know what we need.'

'You need me to be a snoop. That's *not* my job, Johnny.'

'It was when you tracked us down to the Caribbean.' Johnny took a deep breath. 'Look, Rachel, you know we need you.'

'Fair enough when the band were here,' she blazed. 'But I'm not getting any hits while I'm hacking into Kurgan's dirty underwear.'

'You might get a real exclusive.'

'I might get nothing.'

'Come on, Rachel. You know something's not right. We need to look into it.'

'We?'

'Okay, you. But you're us, you're one of us.'

'When you want me to be.' Her dark red lips tightened.

'Come on, babe,' he smiled. 'For me?'

She smiled back. 'You're such a meat-head when you're on a mission. Two days, Johnny. I'll ferret around for two days and then I'm straight up the A whatever it is to Honham. Is that what the place is called?'

'Stageright, C Hangar, Honham.'

'Christ, what a place. Only Cold Steel could go there.'

'We're not the first.'

'Just make sure you're not the last. Two days.'

'We'll be waiting for you.'

'You'll be waiting for me. And you'd better be damned grateful once I've proved to you what I've wasted my time here for.'

*

'You sure pick the places,' grumbled Vince.

'You'll see,' said Johnny.

The minibus nosed off the road and stopped at a barrier. A blue-uniformed security guard walked over and Johnny handed him a sheaf of paperwork. Sawyer shrunk into his faded camouflage jacket, hiding the green and black crossed rifle badge sewn untidily onto one sleeve.

'Cold Steel.' The guard looked disinterestedly into the minibus and Johnny felt the band's irritation rise at not being recognised. He grinned at their indignation and the guard lifted the barrier. 'C hangar,' he said. 'They're expecting you.'

Johnny looked out of the minibus window. Weeds burrowed up from cracks in the neglected road and reclaimed the paved paths that led towards boarded-up, decaying barrack blocks. Empty window frames yawned dark abandonment. The once bustling base that used to house hundreds of airmen and the aircraft they served was a distant ghost, the sorry present suggesting only to the most vivid imagination what might have been.

'What the fuck is this place?' asked Andy.

'Your last home,' sniped Vince.

'Shut it, you two,' snapped Johnny. 'Eyes front.'

'Hey, man,' said Joe. 'We might be on an airbase, but we haven't joined up.'

'In your dreams,' muttered Sawyer.

'Just look,' said Johnny.

A clean and new-looking sign, out of place on the rest of the decomposing estate, pointed towards a hangar. C Hangar. Fresh black paint on its huge, end-mounted metal doors shone against the late summer. The doors clanged open to the sound of a warning horn, anticipating the band's approach. The minibus drove inside and the band looked around the interior in hushed awe.

'Out.' Johnny rapped the order and the sliding door flew open. The hangar's vast floor was mostly empty, while stretched along each side were two stages, facing each other like a pair of duellists.

146

'Cold Steel. All right!' A slightly round man with greasy hair, grimy cargo pants and a stained t-shirt shuffled up to the band. 'I'm Hickey.' He pulled a burger out of a packet and stuffed it into his mouth, holding out his free hand.

'Hickey?' asked Maxwell.

'Sound engineer for the tour,' said Johnny.

'I've wanted this trip for years, man.' Hickey sprayed burger debris as he spoke. 'You guys are the best.'

Maxwell looked at Johnny with raised eyebrows, Vince laughed openly.

'Since when did you bastards judge by appearances?' asked Johnny.

'Since we met you,' said Andy.

'You want to look at yourselves sometime. Hickey comes highly recommended.' Johnny nodded. 'Hickey. Are we good to go?'

'In a fucking hangar?' asked Maxwell.

'Here's where we plan the tour,' said Johnny. 'And rehearse.' He looked at Maxwell. 'What did you do in the past?'

'Well,' stammered Maxwell. 'It kind of just happened. Andreas knew we always had the pirate ship at the back of the stage. He did whatever we wanted with that.' He shrugged. 'We jammed a few times at some small clubs beforehand.'

'And that's *it*?' asked Johnny.

'What the hell else do you want?' asked Vince.

'Yeah,' said Mike. 'We've known each other a long time. It doesn't take much to bring it all together.'

'Sounds to me like you're going through the motions,' said Johnny.

'We'll be playing the set list every night, man,' said Joe. 'It's gonna get routine.' He shrugged. 'We'll work it out.'

'No,' snapped Johnny. 'You'll work it out now.'

'And which stage do we rehearse on?' asked Maxwell.

'Both,' said Johnny. 'We've got four different stages to cover the different-sized venues. I want you fluent on them all within a month. Today you practise these two. Tomorrow, the other two. And it'll give the roadies all the practice they need as well.'

'We never did this before,' grumbled Maxwell.

'I don't give a shit,' said Johnny. 'You're doing it now.'

'Hey, Johnny.' A tall, thin man with wavy grey hair walked towards the band on long, stretchy legs that skimmed the concrete floor two seconds before the rest of him arrived. 'Welcome to Stageright.'

'Stageright?' asked Maxwell.

'Sure.' The tall man held out his hand. 'Ryder Tall, we turn stage fright into Stageright.'

'Good hook,' grinned Maxwell.

'It's more than that,' said Johnny. 'We've got the entire Cold Steel touring machine right here. Roadies, lighting and sound, film crew, and of course the band.'

'Good of you to remember,' muttered Andy.

'For the next month,' glared Johnny, 'this place is home. You'll get to know your set list, and everyone else will learn their jobs inside out.'

'You lads are our fifteenth band in two years,' said Ryder. 'They all saw the difference, and we can do the same with you.'

'Fifteen bands?' asked Maxwell.

'Sure.' Ryder smiled easily. 'Come into the chill room, I'll show you what they said.'

'Thirty minutes,' rapped Johnny. 'Then we start.' He spun around. 'Where the hell is Shot Away?'

Chapter 20

Sawyer scampered away from C Hangar, emotions surging inside him at seeing Honham for the first time in years, even decades. Why did he feel so overwhelmed? The place had ruined him, robbed him of his youth, his dreams. He jogged back the way the minibus had driven in. It felt as though every square inch of the base held memories. The site of the old NAAFI bar, where without fail he'd had a fight every Thursday night. The barrack block where he'd lived, and the older one by the gates, which once had a full-size plane on display outside, earning it the nickname The Buccaneer Suite.

But it was all secondary. There was one place he needed to go, needed to see more than anywhere else.

It made absolute sense that security were based where the Guard Room used to be, right next to the main gates. Ghost memories screamed into Sawyer's mind, unheard and unwanted. Orders, taunts, humiliation, it all happened at the Guard Room. He'd never told anyone that part of his past. Sure, he'd impressed Dixie with a few stories, but he hadn't told him everything. The physical confirmation of his memories, his past, was painfully personal. It was between him and what happened there, no one else. He walked into what he knew as the Guard Room, now called the security hub. Inside, one of the blue-uniformed guards sat with his feet resting on an old wooden desk, separated from Sawyer by a chest-high wooden counter.

'Can I help you, mate?' he asked.

Sawyer looked around the white-painted brickwork. Unchanged, just as he remembered. An open door at the back of the main room led to a corridor. He knew what lay beyond: the cells, *his* cell.

'I used to work here,' said Sawyer.

'Which company?'

'No, mate,' smiled Sawyer. 'When it was an airbase, I served here.'

'Really? No way.' The guard stood up and walked towards Sawyer with a smile. 'I bet you could tell a few stories, right?'

'Sure. Any chance of a look around? I spent quite a bit of time in here.'

'Well…' The guard paused. 'I shouldn't really.' His gaze shifted. 'Between you and me, right?'

'Like my life depended on it.'

The guard lifted the hinged counter and Sawyer walked through. Like a hound on a scent, he sped through to the back, along the corridor and towards the three cells, now used as store rooms. He knew where to go. Middle cell, metal door still there. He strode inside, knowing exactly what he'd done the last time he was there, what he was wearing, what he'd eaten. And he knew what he was looking for. He crouched down by the side of the door, pushed a cardboard box to one side and stared at the wall.

As though he'd written it the day before.

F8408432 SAC Sawyer, where's my hammer?

*

The hangar doors clanged shut, giving two seconds of numbing darkness before the lighting rig burned illumination on the main stage. Maxwell's familiar grin pixelated onto his face, he raised his fist and prowled back and forth, singing Sinners Sanctuary with virgin freshness. Hickey's hands flew over the touch screens of the brand-new mixing desk. The music flowed with an intoxicating combination of familiarity and new-song freshness, then steam-hammered to a juddering halt. The lighting crew turned the hangar into a summer day.

'Good enough?' Maxwell's voice thundered though the speakers.

'It's a start,' said Johnny.

'He's never frigging happy,' snapped Vince.

'We all know you can play Sinners,' said Johnny. 'How about the new stuff, and it better be good.'

'The new songs are good,' said Andy.

'Prove it. I want the new album, now. Start to finish.'

'They're still mixing it,' said Mike.

'Oh, they're still mixing it.' Johnny aped Mike's words and added an effeminate whine. 'You've just written and recorded those songs. Play them.'

Maxwell sighed, his hands dropped to his sides and he looked around at the rest of the band. 'I can't remember the lyrics.' His murmured admission hammered around the hangar. As he spoke, Andy's gaze fell to the floor.

'I'm not a hundred on some of the riffs.'

'Which is why we're here.' Johnny's expression dropped. 'Right?'

'Wrong.' Vince stared at Johnny. 'We should be a lot more ready than we are right now.'

'So what's going on?' asked Johnny.

'The bloody studio.' Mike stood behind his drums. 'We're all thinking it. I'm saying it.'

'What are you saying?' Johnny felt anxiety-sweat building. 'Come *on*. This is tour time, *your* time. What happened at Twenty doesn't matter.'

'It does.' Maxwell shook his head. 'That whole album was forced. It'll never sound good.' He leaned against the mic stand and looked at the back of the hangar. 'We've always had a studio's backing before; they've always *wanted* us there.'

'So that's it?' asked Johnny. 'The last album never happened? You're just going to do some sort of Greatest Hits tour? You won't play *any* new songs?'

'We can't—'

'Yes you can.' Johnny ran a hand over his sparse forehead and clenched his ponytail. 'Right. Stick with what you know, for now. Give me the St Clements set. You played it, you know it. Get good, stay good, and believe it. Then we'll work the new songs in.'

'I don't know,' breathed Maxwell.

Johnny looked up, unsure that he'd ever heard such hesitancy from the dark-haired singer. 'Hey,' he said. 'Hey, you won't make the legend because of what you were, you've got to *be* the legend because of what you are.' He raised his eyebrows. 'Impress me.'

Vince and Andy looked at each other and shrugged. A quick-riff gallop snarled through the speakers and Spider Woman shotgunned round the closed hangar. Johnny tapped his cream cowboy boot against the concrete floor and hope sparked.

For one song.

In the Pipeline started with a missed beat; Vince and Andy's riffs were microseconds apart. They both knew it and over-compensated. On the last tour, Maxwell had sung No Nation with a binding, visceral emotion. Now it was flat and monotone. After an hour of what Johnny could only describe as mediocre, support-band metal, the music drained to a halt.

'It's a start,' he intoned. 'Okay, take a break till the opposite stage is ready. Then you can do it again.'

'What?' gasped Mike.

'Hey, this isn't going to fix itself, lads. So make the most of today. Tomorrow I want new songs.'

'How long have we got till the turnaround?' asked Vince.

'As long as it takes,' shrugged Johnny. 'You want some fresh air?' He raised his arm and pointed at the hangar end. With a hollow clang, fifty-foot high doors railed open to the sound of the warning horn. Bright sunlight swept in and, after a permissive nod from Johnny, the band shuffled outside.

The crew swarmed over the newly vacated stage and a whooshing roar from outside made Johnny slew his head around. A sudden gust of wind blew into the hangar, and the band fled back inside. 'Scared of a little wind?' he asked.

'See for yourself,' Maxwell pointed with a trembling hand.

Johnny followed the band back outside and they skirted the hangar's edge. In front of the building, and taking up much of the flat, former airfield, stood a legion of wind turbines. 'Jesus,' he gaped. Powered by a building wind, the turbines picked up speed, creating a low moan as they turned. He felt the power of their motion, slow and majestic, providing a mute, if less than silent illustration of the power of nature.

'Bloody big,' said Maxwell.

'They're beautiful,' said Joe.

'I thought you'd like them,' sniped Andy.

'We'll all be using them soon, man.'

'Whatever,' said Johnny. 'Back to work when I say, alright, Joe? Even if you want to hug those damn turbines. Understand?'

'I wouldn't get too close, lads.' A voice crept up on them. Johnny turned around and saw Ryder, grinning loosely.

'What do you mean?' said Johnny. 'Are they radioactive?'

Ryder's lazy laugh competed with the turbines' moaning roar. 'You'd be safer if they were. Walk from one side of that field to the other in high winds and you'd be sliced to bits before you got a hundred yards.'

Joe stared at the turbines like a disciple. 'No,' he whispered. 'You just have to feel your way. Be at one with the wind, with nature.'

'Interesting thought.' Johnny turned to Mike, miming 'watch him'. 'But it's just wind turbines whichever way you look at it, right, Ryder?'

Ryder's lip curled. 'Unless you believe the fairy tales the engineers told when they set the place up.'

'What's that, man?' asked Joe.

'Nothing anyone really took seriously. Ghosts, prowlers, someone living in the bunker. Stuff like that.'

'Bunker?'

'Right in the middle of the turbine field,' said Ryder. 'Some sort of bomb dump.' He shook his head. 'It's been deserted for years. Most likely crumbled back to nature by now.'

'It's still there.' Sawyer suddenly appeared at Johnny's side, making him jump.

'What did you say?' asked Johnny.

'It's still there.'

'You've been out there, man?' asked Joe.

Sawyer nodded.

'But this place used to be an airbase,' said Johnny.

'So?'

'Well... well, I mean, no offence, but I thought you were in the army.'

'I never said I was in the army,' whispered Sawyer.

'But, but, you look, you dress—'

'I was a soldier, mate, but that doesn't make me army.'

'Oh, wow, man.' Joe's eyes blazed and he looked at Johnny with carbon-arc intensity. 'Hey, if there's a fortress right at the centre of this natural energy, man...'

'No,' said Johnny.

'You don't even know what I'm thinking, man.'

'I don't want to.' Johnny looked at his watch. 'Right, break's over. Smaller stage and let's see you bust those moves when there's less room for posing. And forget what I said earlier. Work out the new songs, and start doing it now.'

Joe looked wistfully out towards the field of turbines.

'Now,' snapped Johnny.

*

As well as C hangar, Stageright had also bought Honham's Officers' Mess, an old brick building with large, square-framed, single-pane windows surrounded by crew-cut lawns and meticulously-kept shrubbery. Inside, the grandeur had been preserved, although the subject matter of the old military prints was unexpected. 'I thought there'd be more planes,' puzzled Johnny.

'We were surprised as well,' said Ryder. 'The place was empty when we got here, but even before Honham closed, there weren't any aircraft here.'

'What then?' Johnny was intrigued. He stood in the wood-panelled bar and cradled a beer, keeping a wary eye on the band, who in turn looked back at him with the frustrated hostility of children denied their sweets.

'Honham was a flying station till about twenty years ago.' Ryder nodded to two framed pictures of low-flying Tornados and desert-painted Buccaneers. 'Then the planes got sent somewhere else and all that was left was the bunker. It was used for storing bombs or something like that.'

'And these were the guys who guarded them?' Like modern-day Stanley Wood paintings, stylised prints of heavily armed camouflaged soldiers stared down at Johnny. He looked at Sawyer, who was slouching over a table on his own and scowling at anyone who came close to him. He hadn't even wanted to step inside once he realised where they were sleeping.

'I wasn't an officer,' he muttered.

'And you think we were?' asked Johnny. 'Christ, Sean, we weren't even *in* the military. Whatever this building was in your time, right now it's a place to doss for the night. Nothing else.'

Sawyer muttered and stomped past Johnny.

'Blokes like them guarded whatever the air force had.' Ryder nodded towards one of the prints. 'Planes, equipment, even whole airbases. But they were long gone by the time we came along. All that was left were these pictures, and a lot of rumour and hearsay.'

Johnny looked around the mess. 'It was a shrewd move, buying this place. You could add two hours onto our day if we had to commute in.'

'All part of the service.'

'So who else uses this place?'

'What, the base or the mess?'

'Both.'

'The base is currently split between us and the wind farm. A few years ago, some weird type of yoga cult wanted to create an academy and school, but what locals there are around here didn't like it, they had enough clout with their MP and the plan was shelved. But *someone* had to set up, and that's where the wind farm came in.' Ryder smiled. 'And we're all right, because we haven't changed the way the place looks. People don't like that around here – change.'

'Bloody great wind turbines are a bit of a change,' said Johnny.

'But a bit less of a threat than a yoga academy.'

'I suppose. So what about this haunted bunker?'

Ryder shrugged. 'Not much to say. Some of the wind-farm lads say there was a sealed building right at the centre of the base.' He shook his head. 'They say that a few years ago they think they saw someone, something, out there some nights.'

'Could be anything,' said Johnny.

'I think it was an animal myself. The wildlife have adapted to the turbines better than us. The birds have got some way of knowing they're there, they just fly around them, and anything on four legs is small enough not to get in the way of the blades. It's only us that's at risk out there.'

'Us?'

'You can hear them moaning from a distance, like you did today, right?'

'Yes.'

'Get in among them and it's weird silence. Those turbines are big, and when the wind's got them, they move fast. They create all sorts of turbulence at ground level, and if you get caught up in it, you'll be lucky to get out without being chucked around like a leaf, thrown into the towers, even carved up by the blades.'

'Jesus,' shivered Johnny.

'Not as bad as working on an oil rig though.'

'I guess.'

'One other thing. You might want to keep an eye on your lads tonight.'

'Why?'

'Who's the one that looks like a hippy?'

'Joe?'

'He's really bought into the whole renewable thing, hasn't he?'

'Knows his stuff too,' said Johnny. 'Done all the research, he should be running PR for them.'

'Well, he's not up on the risks around here,' said Ryder. 'And I don't know what he thinks he'll find at what's left of the bunker, but he's dead set on getting there.'

*

'You mean there really *was* a fortress out there?' Joe stared at Sawyer, his Sangria and Southern Comfort forgotten.

'They're called bunkers.' Sawyer's reply was barely audible.

'A bunker?' wowed Joe. 'It's just that I've never seen one.'

'Don't encourage the simple bastard,' said Andy. 'Christ, he'd have us all communing out there.'

Vince slicked an imaginary hair back into place. 'So there were bombs and shit out there?'

'Something like that,' said Sawyer.

'Oh, man,' said Joe. 'That's unbelievable. Here we are, right on the edge of the wilderness, man. Those turbines are giving us power from nature. It's the ultimate good, and right at the centre is the remains of ultimate evil.'

'Is he always like this?' Sawyer jerked his head in Joe's direction.

'No,' said Vince. 'Sometimes he's fucking nuts.'

'I'm serious, man.' Joe stared at Sawyer. 'Shot Away here is like, like… you were there, man. You're part of what this place was. A reminder, a sign.'

'And now?' asked Sawyer.

'Now it's the future,' Joe's eyes burned fanatic intensity. 'These turbines, they've surrounded the past, kept it in, protecting us from ourselves. Green and clean, man, it beats where we've been.'

Although he faced a wall of blank stares, he kept going. 'You don't get it, man. This is big, huge, bigger than us, bigger than the band, bigger than the music. If we go out there tonight, we'll be at the centre of a cosmic power. We can tune in to that, harness it. It'll change our music, transform us. We can use this, guys. Just *think* what it can do.'

'Don't you remember what Ryder said?' asked Vince. 'Those turbines are a bloody death trap if you walk in amongst them.'

'What does he know?' said Joe. 'We need to go out there.'

'No you don't,' said Sawyer.

'Why not?'

'That place is off limits.'

'Maybe when you were there,' said Andy. 'A hundred fucking years ago.'

'Siding with your hippy mate, are you?'

'No, but—'

'You *don't* go near the place.'

'But we—'

'You never served,' snapped Sawyer. 'Hey, you're a decent bunch of lads, but you weren't in the same mob as I was, and that means two things. You don't go out there, and I don't bloody take you.'

'Look,' said Maxwell. 'This place ain't Fort Knox anymore, and you ain't GI bloody Joe anymore. If we want to go *anywhere,* we go. We're Cold Steel, no one tells us to do anything.'

Sawyer smiled. 'Apart from your slaphead boss.'

*

The bar closed and the band weaved back to their rooms. Johnny took up station in a gloomy hallway corner in sight of the front door. The lights in the mess slowly winked out, and he wondered how long he'd have to wait. After an hour, he yawned and decided it was safe to get some sleep. Then he heard creaks and hushed whispering on the shadowed staircase.

The stairs spilled out onto a reception hall the size of a bowling green, and sumptuous dark blue carpets swallowed up the sound of

157

footfall. Johnny saw longhaired silhouettes creeping towards the door.

'Where the hell are you going?' he asked.

The band yelped in surprise and stared in all directions. Johnny flicked a switch and bright lights flooded the hall. They stood like a mannequin challenge, with blackened faces and torches.

'Nowhere,' said Maxwell.

'Jesus,' laughed Johnny. 'Are you out to steal the crown jewels?'

'No.'

'You're not heading into the wind farm either.'

'What do you mean, man?' asked Joe.

'What do you mean?' Johnny copied Joe's voice. 'It's a wind farm and nothing else.'

'But it's a pure, spiritual—'

'It's a wind farm, Joe, and that's it.'

'But the bunker?'

'What about it?'

'Shot Away said we shouldn't go there, man.'

'Which is why you're headed there, I guess. Christ, he's got more loose screws than a flat-pack wardrobe, but that is one piece of advice you should be taking.'

'I think he served here when he was a squaddie,' said Maxwell.

'Did he say anything else?' Scepticism oozed from Johnny's words.

'Jesus, mate,' said Maxwell. 'You bloody hired him.'

'Yes, to get you fit, not to scare you into a bloody midnight jaunt through a fucking wind farm.'

'But we've *got* to see it, man,' said Joe.

'You've *got* to get your live act together, all of you. And that doesn't involve trekking into the middle of a slice you up into little bits and pieces wind farm.'

'It's—'

'You're not going,' snapped Johnny. 'Now get washed and go back to bed. Christ, you look like a bunch of hippy commandos, and I sound like your fucking parents. Jesus, how old are you lot?'

'Old enough to be treated like adults,' grumbled Vince.

'Then fucking well act like it. I've got better things to do than babysit you.' Johnny thought of Rachel and wished she were there.

Chapter 21

Sawyer's rapid-fire fists pounded on solid wooden doors. He prowled along the corridor where the band's rooms looked out over immaculately kept hedges and pot plants. Early morning sunlight slanted through the net curtain windows and washed against the varnished door panels. No answer. Sawyer went back to the first door and repeated his call, adding his voice to the alarm. 'Get up, you lazy bastards. The day's wasting away.'

Still no answer. Sawyer growled, grabbed a fire hose and rammed the end close to the bottom of the nearest door, not knowing and not caring who was inside.

'Last chance,' he bawled. 'Ten seconds or it starts raining.'

He turned the tap. Squeaking resistance from years of never-use succumbed to bicep pressure, and a torrent of loch-cold water hosed out. The first door flew open and a soaked Maxwell roared into the corridor, stopping short in front of Sawyer.

'What the fuck, you bastard?'

'You're awake.'

'Bloody right I'm awake. You soaked me.'

'So next time I tell you to get up, bloody well do it. Now turn your mates out and get outside.'

'Please?'

'What?' growled Sawyer.

'You might want to say please.'

'Outside in five minutes.' Flatface response. 'Or Mister Fire Hose returns.'

*

Standing alongside the band on a bare grassy space, Maxwell scowled in his damp gym clothing. They'd scrambled out of the mess in three and a half minutes, hounded by a screaming Sawyer. Clothes had been haphazardly thrown on, shoes were unlaced, hair uncombed.

'I've been hired to get you lads fit,' barked Sawyer. 'And we're *still* working on that. Now you bunch of limp dicks want me to protect you as well? Jesus Christ, talk about mission impossible.'

'You not hard enough?' sniped Andy.

Sawyer paced around the band, his voice quiet with menace. 'I can handle my end of the log, lads. But like I said, I'm not everywhere all the time. Suppose some evil bastard shows up and wants to kidnap you, rob you, take your wedge, your drugs, your pissy instruments?'

'Hey—'

'You keep telling me you're big business, that bad guys like Ramirez want a slice of you, right?'

'Right,' said Johnny.

'So don't expect them to be impressed if you just tell them you can take care of yourselves. You need to do it as well.' He spread his hands. 'That's never a bad thing, right?'

'I don't know, man,' said Joe. 'Are you teaching us, like, violence?'

'Call it self-preservation,' grinned Sawyer. 'Lesson one. You stick together. You lads are a band, you do your job on the stage and in the studio, but you're not a team, not a real team. And that needs to change if you want to survive in my world, because ever since your balloon trip, people who live in my world are living in yours. Buddy up, lads.'

'What?' asked Johnny.

'Get in pairs,' growled Sawyer. 'We don't have time to be perfect, but we'll make a start. First off, screw the rules, dirty tricks keep you on your feet. And here's where we start learning them.'

*

Lisa Blue pushed the red button and the on air light winked out. Then, having learned the hard way, she unplugged the microphone before taking off her headphones and placing them on the sound desk. Her hour-long radio show for Sun FM was over and now the mic was unplugged she could swear without being sacked.

She flicked through her hard-drive mind, already focussing on the next show. She always knew which bands were touring, recording, splitting up, getting back together, sacking their singer, poaching a guitarist, or sleeping with other band members' girlfriends. And what she knew, her listeners found out soon afterwards.

She tried to keep her show varied, shifting between interviews, comments, phone-ins and occasional competitions. Always a mixture of old and new metal, a music-taste tightrope between retaining the increasingly aging original fans, right through to the kids whose idols were now the new bloods, shaking the foundations of the old guard's fortresses. Something for everyone, but all of it good.

And it worked. It took Lisa a whole week to prepare, to get it right, and to do the fill-in jobs that paid the bills: columns in two metal magazines, answering mail, and various celebrity appearances at beach shows, concerts, album releases and store specials. Metal ruled her life as much as it did for any band or fan.

But after last week's disastrous interview with Chainsaw, she needed something big. 'Chainsaw,' she muttered to herself. 'What a bunch of pricks.' They'd supported Cold Steel on the last tour several months previously – a gig most bands with any sense would have killed *and* died for. But all that Chainsaw – correction, Zip Fly, the singer – could talk about was how crap Cold Steel were, and how it should have been them headlining.

Lisa couldn't understand Zip's stance. In the space of a week, he'd alienated not only Chainsaw's fans but also Cold Steel's. Zip Fly, with his long hair split down the middle in a black-white divide, was equally on-off in his personality. Dominating the band; what he said, Chainsaw said, and he even belittled them for backing him.

'So,' she asked no one in particular. 'What's next?' As if she didn't know. Cold Steel. After the accusations by Chainsaw the week before, it had to be. Besides, she'd done Cold Steel specials, phone-ins and competitions. It was time they paid her back with an interview. She picked up her phone and flicked through the contact screen.

*

Sitting alone in the hotel room, Rachel suddenly realised that for once doing her job wasn't a passion, it was simply something to help her forget how much she missed Johnny. Although what she'd found out was all the story she could have hoped for. She'd hacked into Twenty's cloud drive and her eyes had stretched wide as she'd sat at her laptop and sifted. She'd dug and downloaded, then backed up onto two memory sticks and covered her tracks with an expertise she kept a guarded secret even from Johnny. Her loyalty was to him, but not necessarily to the band, and while they were on the same side now, that might not last forever. And back in the Caribbean, she'd had no second thoughts about exposing the real reasons for the St Clements concert. It had only been Johnny's intervention that had stopped her.

Johnny Faslane, a walking contradiction. She could drop him to the floor with a single look, but she'd never been able to get him to put her before the band. And she didn't want him to, but she knew it was part of the challenge, part of what drew her to him. She smiled to herself; he *was* learning the game, but only what she was teaching him. How would the dynamic of their relationship change once he started learning for himself, and she knew that one day he would.

It was possible, and not *just* possible, but entirely possible, that Johnny could become the next Peter Grant or Ed Bicknell. And if that happened, a lot of it would be down to Rachel. She smiled again. *I always did like a project.*

More than the story?

Logging off from her assumed cyber identity, she was about to shut down her laptop when her phone buzzed in her handbag and belted out Sinners Sanctuary. She knew all about appearances.

'Rachel Shaw.'

'Hi, Rachel. It's Lisa Blue from Sun FM, presenter of Blue Metal.'

'Yeah, I know, the radio show.'

'Sure, so how are you?'

'Like this is *really* a social call, Lisa. I might know about you, but I've never met you. We *do* play the same game, though. So why are you really calling?'

Lisa's throaty chuckle crackled in Rachel's ear. 'Spoken like a true professional. We're going to get along fine.'

'That's not what everyone says about me.'

'Nor me. I hear you're shadowing Cold Steel while they make their new album.'

'Mostly.' Realising possible bluetooth interference, she shut down the laptop. 'I hope you're not thinking of muscling in on my territory.'

'I wouldn't dream of it. I'd love to do an interview with Cold Steel, though, on my next show.'

'And that's up to me? I'm just a reporter, Lisa. You need their manager.'

'Johnny Faslane?'

'So you know who he is. Why do you need me?'

'I hear you're in a position of… influence with him.'

'He's my boyfriend, if that's what you mean. It doesn't make me his boss.'

'Come on, Rachel. We're all girls here.'

'Look, Lisa. You want Cold Steel, talk to Johnny and ask him. I daresay he'd agree anyway, but it's *not* up to me.'

'I wouldn't want you to think I was treading on your toes.'

'Only two ways you'd be doing that.'

'Oh?'

'If you turned up here and started following the band around, or if you jumped into bed with their manager.'

Lisa chuckled again. 'I don't want your territory or your man. Embedded can be a drag sometimes.'

'Tell me about it,' said Rachel. 'Especially when I've got to head off to the middle of bloody nowhere in Suffolk later this week.'

'What for?'

'The band will tell you all about it. Talk to Johnny.'

'Can I say I've already spoken to you and you think it's a good idea?'

'You can tell him we had lunch and talked about sex with our ex's if you want.'

*

The playlist jigsawed together, new songs slowly meshing with the old, and the last ten years of the band's musical history layered into a caustic tapestry of sound. Progress was slower than Johnny would have liked and he worried about the first shows. His phone rang and he walked away from the stage.

'Johnny Faslane.'

'Johnny, hi. It's Lisa Blue.'

'Who?'

'Lisa Blue. Cloudy Blue. I present Blue Metal, the Sun FM radio show.'

'I've heard of that.'

'Shame you haven't heard of me as well. I've heard of you.'

Johnny smiled. 'So why are we speaking?'

'I hear the band's next album is out soon.'

'Couple of weeks.'

'And the tour starts straight after that?'

'First show is Barakaldo Bizkaia, Spain.'

'Rescheduled from the previous tour, right?'

'Old news, Lisa, and everyone knows we'll honour all tickets bought the first time round. What's your point?'

'They haven't done much radio lately.'

'They've had an album to record, and right now they've got a tour to rehearse for. It doesn't leave much spare time.'

'Interviews and publicity are hardly recreation. Damas Infernales certainly don't think like that: they're doing interviews every day, and they're the band everyone in Spain will be seeing before Cold Steel.'

'Meaning?'

'Meaning there's no such thing as bad publicity, except no publicity.'

'Cute line, but we've got it covered.'

'Is that enough?'

'It's a whole lot easier for me to keep an eye on the band, which you can take from me isn't easy.'

'I know,' chuckled Lisa. 'I've spoken to Rachel.'

'Don't tell me,' sighed Johnny. 'You want to do an interview with the band.'

'It would be great for everyone.'

'So why not save everyone some time and come straight out with it?'

'Oh, Johnny. You've come a long way in the last year, but you shouldn't let it show, at least not too much.'

'And I suppose taking ten minutes to come out with a simple question is how it's done at the top table, is it?'

'It's called finesse.'

'It's called bollocks. Give me a direct conversation any day.'

'So how about a direct yes or no?'

'Fine,' said Johnny. 'You want to go around the houses, I'll call you back in half an hour.'

Chapter 22

'Yeah,' drawled Vince. 'We'll be at the hangar for a whole month. Not going anywhere else. You got that right, Johnny.'

The band's at-odds-with-society dress sense and appearance sat incongruously with their in-line, seat-belted rows in the Stageright minibus. Sitting next to the driver, Johnny turned around and speared Vince with a killing glance. 'You fancy another morning of Shot Away's training?'

'No.'

'Then give it a rest. You've all done radio interviews before?'

'You've managed bands before?' sniped Vince.

'Cool it, man,' said Joe. 'I hate to say it, guys, but I could do with a break from rehearsals.'

'For this morning and no longer,' snapped Johnny.

'Christ,' said Andy. 'If your bird was doing her job properly, we wouldn't need this poxy interview. Where is she, anyway?'

'Doing her job.' Slow-burn anger filtered through Johnny's clenched teeth.

'Really? I can't see her anywhere. Maybe she's stuck inside those leather strides of yours, doing her other job.'

Andy cackled, and Johnny kept his hands out of sight and balled them into knuckle-cracking fists. He pressed his lips tight together and his eyes iced over.

'What can we talk about at the interview?' asked Mike.

'Anything you want,' replied Johnny.

'Anything, man?' said Joe.

'Sure,' said Johnny. 'It's not like we're fugitives anymore.'

'And it won't matter if we swear like troopers?' asked Vince.

'Won't bother me a bit,' smiled Johnny.

'That's too easy,' said Maxwell. 'You're not even *trying* to ask us to be polite.'

'Hey, you moan when I try to rein you in, and then you bitch when I let you loose. I'm the bad guy either way.'

'What's Cloudy going to ask us, then?' asked Andy.

'She hasn't said, but let's face it, you've got a new album coming out, you're about to start a tour, and you got a right royal slagging from Chainsaw two weeks ago. What do you *think* she's going to ask?'

'What if she wants to know about St Clements?' asked Maxwell.

'Tell her,' said Johnny. 'Everyone knows about it anyway.' He smiled again. 'But you might want to do a bit more than just swear.'

'What do you mean?' asked Maxwell.

'Cloudy's got the most listened-to metal show on the radio, but it comes with strings.'

'Here we go,' said Andy. 'What do we have to do, stand up for the bloody national anthem, make endorsements for their advertisers?'

'Just don't swear.'

'Why not?' asked Vince. 'It's a metal show, it's late at night. What's the problem?'

'No problem with me,' grinned Johnny.

'What then?' asked Maxwell.

'The show's recorded this morning, mixed in with songs, timed to run for an hour. There's no time to do extra stuff and edit, and that's not what Cloudy or Sun want. They want a one take, spontaneous run, which means you don't get to know what you're being asked, and your first answers go out on air. They won't cut time, but they'll bleep out any profanity.' Johnny laughed. 'So just stick to answering the questions.'

*

Seventeen-year-old new pop sensation Angel Face sat in one of Sun FM's otherwise empty and dust-free live rooms and sulked with toxic levels of naturally occurring petulance. Straight black hair slid down one side of her face, half obscuring prominent cheekbones, while on the other side her shaved head made her look like a cross between monk and infantryman.

Sitting opposite, Alphonse cracked his knuckles and glared hostility at the entire universe. His black business suit only emphasised that he was in the wrong place.

'Did you really think taking your tie off would get you down with the kids?' sneered Angel.

'Shut up,' he snarled, thin lips exposing yellow, uneven teeth. 'I don't care what the weirdoes around here think of *me*. I'm the big man, remember?'

'Julio's the big man, *you're* just his message boy.'

Angel scowled and stared around the live room. Alphonse was too easy. She could wind him up in seconds but there was no challenge in that, and besides, he wouldn't *dare* do anything about it. Julio Ramirez was a different case altogether. In fact, he was just a case, full stop. Maybe she shouldn't have been so keen to get him to finance her singing career, but when had she ever taken anyone's advice, even her own? Although she *should* have shown her contract to a lawyer, even if it was just Pepe, Julio's slimy brief.

But things had moved too fast to think. When her first single I Want a Boy, her own composition about teenage pregnancy, hit number one, Julio had proudly claimed her as his own, and who was she to argue? Everything she ever wanted was now in sight.

Apart from the low-life criminals who were part of Julio's life. Business associates, he called them. How dumb did he think she was? Still, all he had her for was one song; she wasn't *that* stupid. Although it hadn't stopped him from putting Alphonse onto her, following her, tailing her, even sitting outside her flat in his crappy, flashy car.

True, even with his large cut of the royalties, Julio *had* been there with the money to get the song out there. But he had no idea who to contact to get her in with the best people to make an album.

An album: that was where she wanted to be. With a band, a proper band, making real music that wasn't just there for the single, the one second of fame. Which was all she looked like getting with Julio running her career. She needed to get rid of him, quick.

Julio had only agreed to the interview because he thought she'd be talking about her single. No chance. She was there to see just who else she could network with, *and* to announce on the airwaves what her *real* plans were. Let Julio stop *that* if he could.

Angel had drawn papp attention, which then brought the attention towards Julio, which he didn't like. In an effort to control it, he'd ordered Alphonse to drag Angel to the studio twenty minutes before her interview was due to start. Which he duly did, and then dumped her in the empty live room. 'I'm thirsty,' she whined.

'What do you want *me* to do about it?'

'Get me something to drink.'

'I'm not your slave, little girl.'

'Fine. I'll tell Julio you let me die of thirst in here. And I'm *not* a little girl.'

Alphonse glared at her malevolently. 'Wait here,' he growled.

*

'Are you sure about this?' Walking into Sun FM's studio area, Zip Fly flashed an uncharacteristically nervous look at Silas. 'We really shouldn't be here after that interview we did.' They walked down narrow corridors and avoided looking at anyone who came their way.

'Have I ever let you down?' asked Silas.

Zip raised eyebrows into his long straight hair, jet black on one side, white on the other. 'Telling us to bitch about Cold Steel wasn't your best idea. The press crucified us.'

'Angie made the play, we follow the plan.'

'Angie, Angie, bloody Angie. Jesus, Silas, don't let Florence hear you.'

'This is business.' Silas kept his voice low. 'Chainsaw's big break is just around the corner, and this could be the move that gets you there.'

'By shafting Cold Steel? Again?'

'We're not shafting them,' hissed Silas. 'We're levelling the field. Shit, Zip, we're not even interfering with their interview. All we're doing is putting Cold Steel's words against Chainsaw's music. Mix that with Angie's scoop about one of their guitarists leaving the band, problems at the studio, and what do *you* think the listeners will remember?'

Zip replied with a look of silent misery.

A large man in an open shirt and black suit walked towards them, growling hate and carrying a brace of drink cans. Silas and Zip flattened themselves against the narrow corridor between the live rooms. 'Out of the way,' snarled the man.

'I thought we were,' muttered Zip.

170

Black Suit whipped around. 'You have a problem?' he snapped.
'What do you want us to do?' asked Zip. 'Dig a bloody tunnel?'
'You might wish you had.'

Zip took a hesitant step forward and rolled his eyes. 'Oh, Christ, listen to this drama queen, Silas. Acting like a hit man and he's just the servant who carries the drinks.'

'Not now, Zip,' whispered Silas.

'Bollocks.' He squared up to Black Suit. 'I'm Zip Fly, whose bitch are you?'

Black Suit threw the drinks to the floor. They exploded and sprayed sugar rush around the corridor. He roared psycho anger and pinned Zip against the wall. 'Who's the bitch now, *BITCH?*' His fingers turned into steel cables around Zip's throat.

'No,' croaked Zip. 'Not my throat, please. I'm a singer. Oh God,' he choked. 'Punch me instead.'

'Put him down, Alphonse.' A wire-strong female voice cracked over them.

Standing motionless in Alphonse's grip, Zip edged his eyes sideways and down, focussing on an emo-clad waif with long black hair straightlining down one side of her head and the other half shaved. Thoughts of his own half and half hair flashed through his fear-sludged mind. *She must have got the idea from me.* 'Hello darlin',' he whispered. 'You know this guy?'

'You're Zip Fly, right?'

'You know it. Who are you?'

'Angel Face. My single's number one.'

'Number one, huh? I'll have to pay more attention to the charts.' Zip flicked his head towards Alphonse. 'So what about your boy here?'

'Alphonse,' snapped Angel. 'Let him go.'

'I'll let him go,' said Alphonse. 'I'll tear him a new arse first.'

'You think Julio wants you to get arrested at a radio station? You think he wants that publicity? Don't be stupid.'

Alphonse dropped Zip like a wet rag. He breathed with relief as Alphonse spun round and faced Angel. She matched his stare with implacable directness.

'Don't call me stupid,' he hissed.

'Don't act stupid,' she shot back and then flicked past him. 'So, Zip. I'm looking for a band to make music with.'

'No, she's not,' growled Alphonse. Angel spun around and slapped him. A stony silence descended and danger crackled up and down the corridor.

'You don't own me,' said Angel. '*Julio* doesn't own me. He's already making enough money out of my single. *I* decide what happens next.'

Alphonse grabbed Angel's arm and walked her back towards the live room she'd come from.

'What the fuck was that about?' Zip massaged his throat.

'Christ if I know,' said Silas. 'Come on, Zip, let's get this done and get the hell out of here.'

'Yeah, and thanks for backing me up with that psycho, you bastard.'

'Anytime. What are friends for?'

Chapter 23

Cramped inside Lisa's live room, the band jostled to sit opposite her. Ceiling-mounted boom mics swung towards them like huge spider legs, and Johnny stood at the back, happy to be out of sight.

'Welcome to Blue Metal.' The show's tight signature tune grated to a halt and Lisa smiled into the microphone. 'And tonight we're host to Cold Steel. Fresh from the studio and rehearsing for their next tour. Welcome, listeners, and welcome, Cold Steel.' Lisa clicked her mouse and the first track on the playlist ratcheted through the speakers.

'Isn't that Chainsaw?' asked Maxwell.

'That's not what I uploaded,' frowned Lisa. 'Still, they're not bad as long as you focus on their music. Is it a problem? You toured with them, right?'

'Yeah,' growled Vince. 'Those loose bastards tried shafting us from every point of the compass.'

'And now they're first track on *our* interview spot,' said Maxwell.

Lisa moved her mouse and the music faded down. 'Sorry about that, guys. I'd planned on starting the show with Sinners Sanctuary.'

'There's nothing better,' grinned Maxwell.

'And the new album?' asked Lisa. 'Out any day now, and the tour starts soon after. What can the fans expect? More of the same? Anything different?'

'Both,' said Andy.

'That's right, man,' said Joe. 'Like, we always try new directions, new avenues. But it's always Cold Steel at the end of the day. No one does it like us, and we don't do it like anyone else.'

'What's the new album called?'

'Rock in a Hard Place,' said Maxwell.

'Is that a personal statement?'

'It's about all of us,' said Mike. 'Us, the band, our music, our fans. It's about being the underdogs, and we've all been there.'

'That's right,' said Vince. 'And whatever it was that put us down, it's always been the music that brought us back.'

'Same for us, same for the fans,' said Maxwell. 'Listening to us or watching us play live. They get us and we get them.'

'A pretty potent theme.' Lisa's lips curved downwards. 'Not too original though.'

'Depends how you tell the story,' said Maxwell.

'Don't you ever worry about getting stale?'

'All the time.' Maxwell smiled at Johnny. 'Keeping that thought at our backs means we'll never have it in front of us, right, lads?'

A testosterone chorus of approval roared over Lisa's mixing desk. 'And on that note,' she said, 'this *is* Cold Steel, and Sinners Sanctuary.'

A barely recognisable riff shot through the live room.

'What the hell,' roared Maxwell. 'It's Chainsaw again.'

Johnny suddenly felt six sets of eyes boring into his soul, as though it were *his* fault. 'How the fuck am *I* supposed to know what's going on?'

'So what are you going to do about it?' asked Maxwell.

'That's more like it. Johnny the super-hero will solve all of your problems, even when I know bugger all about it.' He facepalmed for a second before a thought pinged in his mind. 'Lisa, where's the station's hub computer?'

'Down the corridor, first right.' She threw her photo ID at him. 'Give them my name and that, and you won't get kicked out.'

Johnny looked at the band. 'Concentrate on the interview, forget what songs are playing, and no piss-arse swearing.' He turned around and stepped out into the corridor.

*

'Now sit there and just wait.' Alphonse thrust a single undamaged drink can at Angel and stood like a granite sentinel at the door. 'Once you're done, you're leaving, and you're not talking to anyone else.'

'I'll talk to anyone I want,' she screamed. 'I'm a singer, not a fucking prisoner.'

'You're Julio's employee, little girl. He's invested in your career, which means you owe him.'

'He's made more out of me than he ever put in. I don't owe him a thing.'

'That's not very grateful.'

'If he wants grateful he should talk to *you*. I'm not interested. Zip Fly's manager will help me more than Julio can.'

'Careful, little girl. You're talking trouble.'

'Why? What are you going to do?'

'You don't want to know.'

'Ha! You won't do anything. Not unless Julio tells you first. And then you'll just do what he says. He owns *you*, not me.'

'You talk like a child, you act like a child.'

'And you're the big man, are you? Doing everything Julio tells you?'

'You know nothing.'

'I know *you*.' She saw her laughter grating away at his limited self-control. 'You don't even wipe your arse unless Julio tells you first.'

'Don't push me, girl. Just don't do it.'

'That's all you're good for,' sneered Angel. 'Shouting at a girl. Call yourself a man? You're nothing, not like Zip Fly, *or* his manager. You babysit me because Julio tells you. *They* make their own decisions.'

'Shut up!' shouted Alphonse. 'You wouldn't have even made your single if it weren't for Julio. You want to see those real men? Well, you stay here, little girl. I'll show you just how wrong you are.'

*

'Hurry up, Silas.' Zip sweated in an empty live room's doorway and kept watch over the corridor.

'I'd like to see you hack the playlist any quicker.' Silas flung the cursor around the computer screen.

'You said you could do this.' Zip nervously scanned the corridor.

'I *am* doing it. Bloody hell, but they're a bunch of idiots here. Unencrypted, piss-easy password. I'm surprised it hasn't happened before.'

'What, swapping one metal playlist for another? Yeah, I bet the virus kings are queuing up twice round the building to take that crown. No one's even going to notice what we've done.'

'They'll notice all right,' said Silas. 'At least half the songs on this list are Cold Steel. A couple of clicks and they're all Chainsaw. *Then* you'll see the benefit of this. Angie's story will help sink Cold Steel, and all eyes will be on Chainsaw.'

'In a good way, I hope.'

'I checked Angie out. She's a known reporter, she gets the controversial stories, but her plants always benefit.'

'Yeah,' groaned Zip. 'I always wanted to be a fucking plant. Will I have big leaves and everything?'

'Christ, Zip, but you whine like a lonely bridesmaid. What happened to the streetwise, heavy metal anti-hero, the man no one could faze.'

Zip turned away from the corridor and gave Silas a wilting stare. 'Fucking hell, even *I* don't believe that shit. Just hurry up.' He turned and felt a hammerblow snap his head back and lift his feet off the floor. He collapsed in a onesie-soft heap on the floor and unconsciousness shrouded his senses.

Alphonse gripped Silas by the throat, dragged him over the desk and held him against the wall like a chicken ready for slaughter. Silas completed the illusion by kicking his spindly legs and squawking.

'What did you say to Angel?' he roared.

'What are you talking about?' croaked Silas.

'Don't bullshit me. She said you'd help her out.' Alphonse pressed his face close to Silas. 'Listen, she's got all the help she needs.'

'Right,' wheezed Silas. 'That's why I sent her to Johnny.'

'Who the hell is Johnny?' spat Alphonse.

'Johnny Faslane, Cold Steel's manager. He said he'd sort your girl out. He's still in the building. Isn't that right, Zip?'

Zip writhed at Alphonse's feet and groaned wordlessly.

'Where is this guy?' Alphonse shook Silas.

'I don't know.' Silas' arms flopped about like a rag dolly.

'Then how do you know he spoke to Angel? Where is he?'

'Jesus,' shrilled Silas. 'I don't know. Look, we're not mates, he doesn't tell me where he goes.'

'But you know he spoke to Angel?'

'I'm sure of it.'

'How do you know?'

'What? Young girl like that, she's right up his street, know what I mean?' Silas dredged up a dirty man leer.

'That perverted bastard,' hissed Alphonse. 'I'll rip his damned head off.'

'I'd do the same thing, mate.'

'Where is he? *Where*?'

'He's with Cold Steel. They're doing an interview with Lisa Blue.'

Alphonse slammed Silas against a wall. 'Stop talking in riddles, you shit. WHERE IS HE?'

Silas rolled his eyes and his head shook. 'Put me down,' he quavered. 'And I can help you.'

Alphonse opened his hand and Silas dropped to the carpet-tiled floor. He massaged his throat and coughed, then glanced at his watch. 'Well, their interview will have started. That means Johnny Faslane will have worked out something's going on, so he'll be headed towards the hub room to try and sort it out.'

'The hub room,' said Alphonse. 'Where's that?'

*

Surrounded by a mass of quietly humming computers, Johnny sat in the hub room and logged into the station's portal. Standing over him, a bespectacled teenager in an oversize Sun FM polo shirt directed him to Lisa's account.

'Click there,' he said. 'And you're in.'

'Thanks, mate,' said Johnny.

'Call me Spotty. Everyone else does.'

'Better than Baldy.' Johnny rubbed a hand over his sparse covering of hair.

'That'll happen soon enough,' muttered Spotty.

'It's the mark of a man,' said Johnny. 'Now, where are the playlists?' He flickered around Lisa's files and folders, looking for anything relevant. He found the list of songs for the latest show featuring Cold Steel. 'That's weird,' he said.

177

'Looks like a normal setup to me,' said Spotty. 'Just a list of songs.'

'Do you look any deeper than that?'

'What, at a radio station? I'd never get anything done if I did that.'

'Fair point.' Johnny looked at the screen. 'It *is* a collection of songs, but none of them are by Cold Steel.'

'So?'

'So they're being interviewed by Lisa – you'd expect at least *something* by them.'

'Are you Johnny Faslane?' An unknown voice barked from the room's doorway and Johnny looked up at a large man in a black suit.

'That's me,' he said. 'What can I do for you?'

Alphonse strode across the room, flicked Spotty out of the way and dragged Johnny out of his chair. 'Leave Angel alone, you bastard.'

Johnny squirmed in the man's grip and found himself pushed flat against the wall. He looked at Spotty who, standing behind Alphonse, hand-signed a telephone and mimed the word 'help'. Johnny nodded. *Christ,* he thought. *Training, training, remember Sawyer's training. Look him in the eye; he's just as scared as you.* 'Who the hell is Angel?' he asked, digging a fingernail into his palm to cause distraction pain and force down his simmering fear.

'Don't give me that shit,' hissed Alphonse. 'I know you've been talking to her. Taken a liking to her, have you, you fucking nonce?'

'You're out of line, mate. I've never seen her, heard of her, wouldn't recognise her if she was standing right next to you.' Inside, Johnny was melting with fear, but he forced himself to appear calm. *Impose your will on the enemy,* he remembered Sawyer's training. But – *How the fuck do I do that?*

'Liar,' hissed Alphonse. 'You haven't got the bottle to admit it.'

Johnny forced a patronising smile. 'What makes you think I'd be interested in her anyway? Who told you this crap? And how come you're so damned gullible?'

'Don't mock me, you bastard.'

'You're doing that all by yourself,' muttered Johnny. 'I think maybe you've been played?'

'Nobody plays me.'

'Look, calm dawn, mate.'

'I'm not your fucking mate.'

'I got that message.'

'And here's another one for you.' Alphonse drew back his fist.

'Step back, sir.' A quiet voice loaded with authority spoke from the doorway. Johnny looked over Alphonse's shoulder and saw two security guards, bulked out with stab vests.

'Stay out of this,' said Alphonse. 'This guy's a paedo nonce.'

'If you've got an allegation to make,' said the security guard, 'I suggest you contact the police, from *outside* this building.' They moved forward, flanking Alphonse, who looked left and right. His grip on Johnny relaxed.

'I need to get back to Angel.' He struggled for a moment before his moves were stilled by strong hands. 'Let go of me,' he shouted. 'Do you know who I am? Do you know who I work for?'

'Sorry, mate.' The guards gently but firmly removed him from Johnny, who sank back and felt cold relief gush through him.

Alphonse was marched out of the room and Johnny turned to Spotty. 'Who the fuck was that? And who's Angel?'

'Angel Face. She's number one with her first single, and he's the hired muscle. I think his name's Alphonse. He takes his orders from Julio Ramirez.'

'Yeah, I've heard about that guy.' Johnny remembered Debden's warning and tremulous fear sucked at his insides. Was this a coincidence? Or was it something else? He picked up his phone and scrolled Lucy Penhalligan's number.

*

After Alphonse had charged off to the hub room, Silas grabbed Zip and dragged him in the opposite direction.

'What's the bloody hurry, Silas?'

'Do *you* want to talk to him after he's finished with Johnny?'

They rushed for the exit; Silas reached for his phone, ricocheted off a wall and bounced into Zip.

'Fucking hell, Silas.'

'Quit your bitching and get outside.' Silas speed dialled a taxi, then called Angie.

'Angie Dale.'

Silas yanked open the door as the taxi was still moving.

'It's done.'

He shoved Zip in the back and jumped in after him.

'Details, Silas.'

Arms and legs tangled on the back seat like spaghetti.

'Drive! We owned the playlist, Angie. It's Chainsaw all the way. Stitched Johnny Faslane right up as well. Zip, fucking sit straight and stop groping me'

'How did you do that?'

Silas sat up and pushed Zip to the other side of the seat. 'Some girl there called Angel or something like that. We wound up her minder and set him after Johnny.'

'Angel Face?'

'Christ, I don't know.'

'What did she look like?'

'Weird as fuck. Long black hair one side of her face, bald on the other.'

'That's Angel Face, and she's run by Julio Ramirez.'

'Who?'

'You don't want to know.'

'Whatever, Angie. We've still got a deal, right?'

'Deal's a deal,' laughed Angie. 'Interview rights for Chainsaw, a negative story for Cold Steel, and thank you, Silas.'

'You're welcome. Thank you for what?'

'Oh, for bringing an old assignment back to life.'

Chapter 24

'Of course we'll do a good job.' Lucy Penhalligan's Knightsbridge accent rolled out of Johnny's phone. 'We'll liaise with child protection, get her a business coach and her own lawyer.'

'Just like that?'

'No, not just like that, but it *is* easier when you're premier league.'

'Well, whatever you're going to do, you'd better be quick. A few days ago a detective warned me that Ramirez was looking to get into music, prey on bands for a take of their action.'

'Why would a detective warn you about that?'

Johnny paused. 'The band wanted a distraction, so I organised a balloon trip. Turned out it was a front for Ramirez and his smuggling, or something like that. Anyway, the balloon crashed in the sea, we got picked up by the police.'

'And Ramirez thinks you might have caused it or tipped off the police?'

'That's what the detective said.'

'You should have told us about this sooner.'

'Look, Lucy, we faced down the Ancadian war machine and we didn't bitch about it. Do you think I'm going to cry in my beer over a scumbag like Ramirez?'

Lucy laughed. 'That's what we like about you, Johnny. You don't come whining to us for help every five minutes, even if you *do* screw up now and again.'

Johnny looked at his watch and groaned. 'I think another screw-up's just about to happen.'

'Get back to Cold Steel. We'll take care of Angel from here.'

*

Feral hostility fused around the Stageright minibus on the bumpy road back to Honham.

'On the case, were you?' grumbled Vince.

'Hey,' said Johnny. 'I nearly had it solved.'

'Only nearly? It's never enough for you when we're only *nearly* good enough.'

'You know what, Vince,' snapped Johnny. 'It wasn't me that allowed whoever it was to put nothing but Chainsaw songs on the playlist. It was only a guess that led me to the hub room.'

'That didn't stop it from happening,' said Maxwell.

'So it happened,' said Johnny. 'You still got the interview, didn't you?' He looked at the band. 'You *did* do that, didn't you?'

'We would have,' said Andy, 'if the playlist hadn't wound us up.'

'I'm not sure I want to hear this,' groaned Johnny.

'You might not have to, man,' said Joe.

*

At ten o'clock, the oak-panelled bar in the Officers' Mess was full. *Might as well make our humiliation public*, thought Johnny, although the band remained silent about what it had actually gone on.

The barman flicked on the radio and Chainsaw's tightline riffs grated through the large, packed room.

'What the *beep*-ing hell are *beep*-ing Chainsaw doing on our *beep*-ing special?' Maxwell's affronted tones played through the Mess speakers.

'*Beep, beep, beep*-ing *beep*-ers, for *beep*-s sake.'

Irreverent laughter rippled around the Mess.

'Was that you, Andy?' Johnny forced down a grin. 'I didn't hear enough of your voice to be sure.'

'Just answer the *beep, beep, beep*-ing *beep*-tch.'

'That was Vince,' said Mike.

The beeps subsided, and another Chainsaw song played.

'Was the *whole* interview like that?' asked Johnny.

'Look,' said Maxwell. 'It wasn't our fault. Somebody shafted us, pissed us about, and *you*—' he stabbed Johnny's chest with a bony finger — 'were supposed to sort it out.'

'Okay,' said Johnny. 'So I didn't stop the Chainsaw hijack. Did I make you swear right through the interview?'

'Well—'

'In fact, didn't I warn you not to?'

'But—'

'I'll hold my hands up to not sorting out the playlist, but having the whole damn interview bleeped out on you. Shit, I wasn't even in the room when it happened.'

'So what do we do now?' asked Mike.

'Get back to our jobs,' replied Johnny. 'Rehearsing for the tour. And you'd better be spot on with everything by next week.'

'Next week, man?' asked Joe. 'I thought we had two weeks of rehearsals left.'

'We do,' said Johnny. 'But next week it'll be more than just the crew and me watching you. You'll be playing to the Cold Steel fan club.'

'*All* of them?' asked Maxwell.

Johnny shook his head. 'Rolling admission, five hundred for each set with a meet and greet in between.'

'And the album?' asked Maxwell.

'Released for download on the same day we let the fan club in. CD version goes worldwide halfway through the tour.'

*

The bar crowd thinned out, and Andy scrolled through to Angie's number and dialled.

'Are you still in the band?'

'Yeah, I missed you too.'

'Along with the good advice.'

'Quitting Cold Steel was a good idea?'

'You could be the greatest guitarist alive, Andy. You could have been a rock star, *my* rock star. Now you're just part of a band.'

'Hey, Cold Steel are more than just a band, and I'm already a rock star.'

'Always happy with second best, Andy. Always happy *being* second best, behind Vince. Is that what you wanted?'

'Look, Angie.' Andy's voice rose and he looked around to see if he was being heard. 'Even if I did want to leave the band, my contract says Cold Steel or nothing. It's unbreakable.'

'Haven't you heard of lawyers?'

'Christ, Angie. You're fucking unreal. Busting someone's balls isn't how you get them to like you.'

'I don't want you to like me.'

'What, then?'

'We could have been great together, Andy. You and your music, me making the story.'

'Hang on a second, did you say *making* the story?'

'They don't make themselves.'

'Shit, Angie, you're taking this journalism thing a bit too far.'

'You've no idea.'

Andy didn't know what to say.

'What's it to be?' said Angie. 'Andy Stains or Cold Steel?'

'I can't leave the band.'

'Can't, or won't?'

'Both, I guess.'

'Then you're no good to me.' She ended the call.

*

The bar closed and Johnny weaved back to his first-floor room. He groped for the key and wondered where the second keyhole had suddenly sprouted from, before closing an eye and seeing just one again. He turned the key and the suddenly unlocked door flew open. He stumbled inside and his legs John Cleesed underneath him in a frantic effort to remain upright.

'I can guess how tonight went.' A throaty chuckle and hint of lemongrass came from the far side of the small room, and the table lamp winked on. Rachel was sitting in an armchair and looking at Johnny with a mixture of mirth and embarrassment.

'Hi, babe,' he slurred. 'I thought you were busy at the studio.'

'I was, and now I'm here. I need to talk to you, but I think it should wait until morning.'

'If it's that important, tell me now.' He said each word with drunken correctness.

'I don't think you're up to it just yet.'

'Are you saying I'm pissed?' he hiccupped.

She wrinkled her nose at the smell of Johnny's beer-laden breath. 'Yes.'

He drunkenly reached out for her. 'Well, how about helping me get through my impending hangover?'

'And you're *definitely* too drunk to appreciate me,' she laughed. 'I'm next door tonight. I'll see you in the morning.'

'Can't wait.'

'You say that now. You won't like it tomorrow.'

'What? Cold Steel's new album?' Johnny mispronounced the band's name.

Rachel nodded.

'Jesus, Rachel, what's not to like? I'm *already* liking it.'

'Hold that thought, kinky boots. I'll remind you what you said in the morning.'

Chapter 25

'What do you mean, they've lost it?' Johnny stared at Rachel, his hangover churning up his insides. Sawyer stood like a camouflaged statue, immovable with folded arms and simmering distemper at another morning of lost training. The band sat on the small stage in the otherwise deserted C Hangar and glared Tigranes-like hatred at Johnny and Rachel.

'That's what Twenty are going to tell you in a few days' time,' said Rachel.

'But we recorded it,' spluttered Maxwell.

Rachel turned towards him. 'Haven't you got some history with Archimedes?'

'Shit, that was years ago.'

Rachel raised her eyebrows and said nothing.

'Has the album really disappeared?' asked Johnny.

Rachel nodded.

'Christ on a sedgeway,' said Johnny. 'We are so up Shit Street now.'

Rachel smiled back at him.

'Is there anything else to this story?' he asked.

'Maybe.'

'Well, *maybe* you could tell us what you're so bloody happy about.'

'Who's the best?' she asked.

'Oh, bloody hell, Rachel. You're the best. Alright? Happy now?'

'Of course, and you don't listen, do you? Any of you.'

'What do you mean?' asked Johnny. 'We've got no album. We're screwed.'

'No, you're not,' said Rachel. 'They're going to *tell* you they've lost the album. Doesn't mean they have. Archimedes told Kurgan to think of any way to trash the album. If Kurgan couldn't get the band to walk, then it was up to him to make sure the album never happened.'

'And how did you find out all this?' asked Maxwell.

She smiled. 'You gave me a job to do, Johnny, and I did it. Luckily, some of the players at Twenty don't play as well as us. Right?'

'Right,' said Johnny.

'I found out plenty from emails that were stashed on the cloud and should have been deleted. They probably still put un-shredded paperwork in landfill bags.' She wrinkled her nose. 'But I'm damned if I'm going through that, even for you, Johnny, and your narrow, yet strangely attractive butt.'

'Okay,' said Johnny. 'So Twenty never wanted us to do the album. How does knowing about it help us?'

'Because unofficially, Kurgan's still got the master copy. Officially, the original files have already been lost.'

'Why's he done that?' asked Johnny.

'He's thinking about worst case scenario,' said Rachel. 'He was told to lose the album, so he *said* he did.'

'Then why keep it?' asked Maxwell.

'In case he has to sell it back to you.'

A growl of rage surfed around the stage and Johnny's insides tightened. 'They were going to *sell* Cold Steel's own music back to them?' he muttered.

'If you're lucky,' said Rachel. 'If Twenty stand by him, Kurgan wouldn't even think of approaching you with a deal. Cold Steel would be left with no album at all, and no time to record one. The only way he'd be coming to you with your album is if Twenty shafted him and went back on their word.'

'Which, given the music business,' said Johnny, 'is a more than even chance.'

'So what do we do, man?' asked Joe.

Johnny felt the laser gaze of five sets of eyes. He looked at Rachel. She was still smiling. 'Is there something you haven't told us?' Pregnant pause. 'Yes,' he snapped. 'You're the bloody best.'

She held up a memory stick. 'Here's the lost album.'

'You got it?' asked Johnny.

'Did you doubt me?'

'Not for a second.' Johnny plugged the stick into a bluetooth speaker and flicked up the volume. Minimised metal played from the speaker at their feet.

'It's a bit tinny,' frowned Maxwell.

'That's just a small speaker,' said Johnny.

'No,' said Andy. 'It's the first take. Skip to the next track.'

Johnny pressed the triangular forward button. The second song surged out from a drum explosion.

'He's right,' said Mike. 'That's how we started, but it's not the finished thing.'

'So we just tart them up a bit,' said Johnny. 'How hard can it be?'

'A piece of piss,' said Maxwell. 'If you can find a producer.'

Chapter 26

'I assume you've got proof of all of this?' Lucy's cut-glass accent sliced down the phone.

'Email intercepts and downloads.' Johnny stood outside the hangar and stared at the wind turbines, wishing they somehow had the answer. 'Twenty were never going to make the album.'

'Just don't say I told you so. Shit, Johnny, we sent your boys there for a reason, and now *this* happens.'

'It's one of those things, Lucy. We can't change what's happened.'

'So what *can* we do? The whole world is expecting Cold Steel's album. You've got the tour just around the corner and there's no time to start from scratch.'

'We don't need to.'

'What do you mean?'

'You'll have your album, Lucy.'

'How?'

'Trust me, it'll be on time.'

'Johnny, all you've got right now is a demo on a memory stick.'

'We can do it, Lucy.'

'You'd better.'

*

'What the hell do you want from me?' Hickey crammed a cheeseburger into his mouth and chewed with venom hostility. 'I'm a sound engineer, *not* a fucking producer.'

'Christ, Hickey.' Johnny swept his arm around the mixing desk. 'We don't need it produced from scratch. Just smooth the edges, give it a finished feel.'

'A finished feel?' choked Hickey. 'Are you nuts? This is a concert setup, not a bloody studio. It'll sound like a demo made in some bastard's garage.'

Johnny shrugged. 'It wouldn't be the first.'

'It would from Cold Steel. Holy crap, Johnny, they're about big sound and production, not some half-arsed grunge put together by a bloody student.'

'On St Clements—'

'Fucking hell, that was a one-off. It'll never happen again. And besides.'

'Besides what?'

'I'm a sound engineer. A *live* sound engineer.'

'Fuck me, Hickey, you've got the demo, you've got the best mixing desk money can buy.'

Hickey raised clenched fists and looked up at the hangar ceiling. 'Look, I work with live sound, instant sound. Recording takes days, weeks to get one song. Onstage it's music straight away, no delays, no reruns.'

'But—'

'You don't get it, Johnny. It's like asking a car mechanic to fix a fighter jet with a socket set. Shit.' He stuffed another burger into his mouth and Johnny moved to one side before he spoke again. 'You must be *really* desperate to ask me this.'

'How desperate do you want?'

'What do you mean?'

'Right now, this is all Cold Steel have got.' Johnny handed him the memory stick. 'And if you lose it, I'll fucking kill you.'

'Fuck me,' gasped Hickey. 'Is that it?'

'Can you can *do* this, Hickey?'

'I'll do my best,' he chewed. 'But it'll take a couple of days.'

'Two?'

'That's usually a couple of days.'

'You've got one.'

*

'They might say you're finished,
They might say you're done.
They'll take away your hopes and dreams,
Tell you you're alone.
But don't ever believe them,
Or let them think they've won.
You never were, never are, you've never been alone,
Stand tall, raise your fist
And shout out WE ARE ONE!'

Under the looming shadow of the album mix, We Are One
scorched out at the end of every rehearsal. Hickey flicked a switch
on the desk, the sound was doused and light flooded the hangar. He
unwrapped a burger and took a bite. 'Don't look at me like that,
Johnny.'

'Look at you like what?'

'Like I'd killed you in the night and turned you into my next
burger.'

'If Ozone don't get an earful of your remix in the next twenty
minutes you just did.'

'Stop being so bloody dramatic, Johnny. It's done.'

'What?'

'Bald, anorexic *and* deaf. What the hell does Rachel see in you?
I SAID, IT'S DONE!'

'The album?'

'No, my nails. Of course the bloody album.'

'Well, don't stand there bitching,' Maxwell jumped down from
the stage and landed with a thud next to Johnny. 'Let's hear the
damn thing.'

*

'Brilliant.' Johnny beamed at Hickey. Pared-back metal grated
through the mixing desk speakers and slashed a jagged furrow up
and down his spine.

'Liking it.' Maxwell added understatement to the verdict.
Johnny's scream of concentrated fear as he was chased through the
studio by Vladimir rasped around the hangar, followed by the intro
to Pieces of Hate. The band looked at Johnny and chuckled.

'You really like it?' Hickey chomped through an egg and bacon
burger and smiled nervously, his cheeks bulging like a stubbled,
carnivorous chipmunk.

'Well,' said Vince. 'It's basic.'

'It's raw,' said Andy.

'It's not very polished, man,' said Joe.

'Sure, it's unrefined,' said Mike. 'And that's just what we
want.'

'Only half of you seem to like it,' said Hickey.

'It's a fucking sight better than no album at all,' growled Maxwell. Murmurs of assent from the rest of the band hedged around him.

'Basic is good,' said Johnny. 'A change from your other albums.'

'He's right,' said Andy. 'Metal's gritty, dirty.'

'Dangerous,' said Vince.

'On the edge, man,' said Joe.

'Deafening you,' said Mike.

'And sleeping with your wife and daughter,' roared Maxwell.

'Let's hope Ozone see it that way.' Johnny glanced at the band, then rolled his eyes and nodded towards Hickey.

Silence.

'Thank you, you bastards,' growled Johnny.

'Now what have we done?' asked Andy.

'Nothing, for a change, but Hickey's just saved you.'

'Oh, yeah. Cheers, mate.' Muttered mild gratitude seeped out of the rest of the band.

'What if Ozone don't like it?' Hickey paused halfway through his burger.

'That won't happen.' Johnny looked around for a reason to change the subject. 'Right then, last rehearsal before the fan club get here tomorrow, then a week later all this shit gets shoved in trucks and driven out to Spain.'

Maxwell leered at Johnny. 'I can't wait to share a drink with this girl band you've been speaking about.'

'Dream on,' said Johnny. 'They don't do parties. And nor are you after the last time you hit Europe. Jesus, you laid waste to France, and your first concerts were shite. That is *not* happening again.'

'What?' Andy's lip jutted out. 'Bad gigs, or going on the rampage?'

'Both,' snapped Johnny. 'The kit goes overland, you fly there and get a feel for the first venue. We start this tour right.'

Vince muttered in the background.

'What was that, Vince?' asked Johnny.

'I said, I remember our last album going platinum in every country we toured in.'

'Yeah,' said Johnny. *'After* me and everyone at Ozone spelled out how close your arses were to being used for ashtrays. Look, I've seen your disasters onstage. Christ, *you've* seen your disasters onstage. Head-butting each other into unconsciousness.' He glared at Vince and Andy. 'Too stoned to play.' He shot a poisonous stare at Joe. 'Hair on fire.' Eyes on Maxwell. 'Is it really so bad to have to admit that nobody, not even Cold Steel, can make it without hard work?'

Chapter 27

'And that's the plan.' Johnny slung back his fifth beer and thumped the empty bottle on the solid bar of the Officers' Mess. 'Ozone have got Hickey's remix. Tomorrow they tell us if it's good enough to release, and we let the fan club in to watch rehearsals.'

'It's the best you could do.' Rachel sipped her first glass of wine and pulled her long jacket tightly around her. 'Don't you think you should ease up on the booze?'

'Are you saying I can't handle my drink?'

'I'm saying you need to watch the band.'

Johnny head-swayed to the left and glowered at the band, who sat morosely at a small table and glared back at him. 'They're not going anywhere,' he slurred. 'Tomorrow's as big a day as they're facing. Trouble's the last thing on their minds right now. All they want is a decent album, and now someone else decides if it all happens or not.'

Rachel looked over at the band. 'I've never seen them looking so miserable.'

'Shit on a stick, Rachel.' Johnny ordered a coconut rum and pineapple juice. He sipped it without managing eye contact. 'Twelve hours from now could be an absolute triumph or the complete end. And the way they're looking at me, you'd think it was *my* fault.'

'Come on, Johnny,' said Rachel. 'Owning their problems is your job. And you're not going to quit just because the band you manage are idiots, are you?'

'It's not—'

'Of course you're not. You *care* about the music, and as long as you do, you'll carry on doing what you do best. And that means Cold Steel will be okay.' Half smile and a shrug. 'Eventually.'

'Less than a day away from either a basic album or no album at all,' said Johnny. 'You're pretty bloody optimistic.'

'You've got a plan, it's going to work.' She edged towards him and effortlessly removed his glass from unresisting fingers. 'Now call it a day down here, give yourself the night off and come upstairs with me. We've got something to talk about, something more important than the band.'

'I thought you thought I had to watch them.'

'And I thought *you* thought they weren't going to play up tonight.'

'So?'

'So you need to work out how to spot a yes.'

*

'Are you *sure* it's a good idea, Joe?' Mike looked nervously at Johnny. 'We've got enough shit on our plates right now.'

'And that's exactly why we need to go, man.' Joe spoke with rare assertiveness.

'Johnny said he'd take care of it,' said Maxwell.

'And he will,' Joe swirled the remains of his drink and put the glass on the small table. 'But we're in a bad place, guys. We were fucked over by the *studio*! How many more times are we going to get doggy-styled by people who are supposed to be our buddies, man?'

'Okay,' said Vince. 'But how is fucking off into the middle of the damn airfield in the middle of the bloody night going to help? Even that mad ex-squaddie thinks we should stay away.' He swivelled his head like an exorcist dolly. 'By the way, where is he?'

'He took off as soon as we started talking about this,' said Joe. 'I think it's a touchy subject for him.'

'He's not the only one,' muttered Andy.

Joe's eyes blazed. 'Can't you feel it, man? We're on sacred ground, the edge of civilisation. Just out there—' he flung out a haphazard arm — 'are the marshes, man. Nothing. And that wind farm is nature's guardian. It's powerful forces, and we can harness it.'

'What the fuck has all this tree-hugging shit got to do with us?' asked Maxwell.

'Natural energy.' Joe's stoned eyes flamed. 'It's invincible. We harness that for ourselves, man, and we can channel that into whatever Johnny's got worked for the album. That album is us, and we can link into it. If we can do that with the force of nature, we can't lose.'

195

'What have you been putting in your ganja?' said Vince.

'Don't blow this off, man. I'm right.'

'And what are we supposed to do once we get there?' asked Mike.

'Don't tell me you're actually agreeing with this bollocks?' said Andy.

'Let's hear what he's got to say.'

'Christ,' said Vince. 'You two are so far up each other's arses.'

'I'll leave the bitching and backstabbing to you and Andy,' growled Mike. 'You do enough for the whole band put together.'

'It's served us pretty well so far.'

'Yeah, like Andy going to hospital because you wound him up.'

Vince's eyes narrowed. 'If you can't take it, get out of the kitchen.'

'That's right,' laughed Mike. 'Cooking gingerbread, leave being a musician to the grown ups.'

'Enough!' snapped Maxwell. 'What is this? We sound like a fucking boy band on their period. What are we?' Four blank stares faced him. 'We're Cold Steel!'

Chapter 28

Joe yelped as a turbine blade whooshed past him, inches from his head. The huge white length of carbon fibre disappeared into the night, its low noise vanishing almost to nothing before the next one approached out of the darkness. He looked around and saw the rest of the band sprawled facedown on the windblown grass.

'Shit,' spat Maxwell. 'This *is* fucking dangerous.'

Joe gulped down his fear and took a step back, watching the blade turn in the wind. He saw where it came closest to the ground, then plotted a safe path.

'Alright, guys,' he whispered. 'As long as we know where they come down, we'll be fine.'

'Sure,' muttered Andy. 'Until the bastard wind changes direction.'

Joe looked at the swishing, moaning turbine blades ghosting in and out of his vision. First he saw a confused mass of jumbled movement, then he concentrated, thought about patterns, *felt* for a safe way through.

'I know where to go,' he said. 'I *know.*' He turned around. The rest of the band stayed on the grass like downed statues. 'Has one of you lost a contact lens?'

'Very funny,' growled Maxwell.

'Come on, guys.' He held his hands out in front of him. 'Walk in my steps.'

Mike stood up first, and then Maxwell, who looked down at Vince and Andy. Neither showed a sign of getting up. 'Finding each other, are you?' chuckled Maxwell. 'Bloody jaffa boys.' They stood up like a pair of electrified lizards.

'Christ,' choked Vince. 'We've done some fucking stupid things in our time, but this really pushes it.'

Joe focussed on the turbines and where he was leading the band. For one of the few times in his life, people were depending on him. He took a hesitant step into the darkness, then another. He felt his confidence flame-growing inside him.

'Are you with me, guys?' He turned around and saw creeping longhaired silhouettes.

'Don't look at us, you stupid fucking hippy,' snapped Andy. 'Find a bloody way through this.'

Joe stepped through the turbines. Moaning blades swarmed in and out of view. The winds inside the farm were a cyclonic, random movement, and the low-pitch oscillating blades added to the confusion. Joe's lank hair billowed outwards like a slo-mo shampoo ad. He heard the band's nervous mutterings subside. *They trust me*, he thought. His steps became quicker, more assured. He no longer looked up, and despite the darkness, he knew where turbines would be. He didn't know how he knew, he didn't even want to know. It was enough that he did.

Joe's thoughts guided his feet, turning, swerving, but always edging closer to the centre of the field. He didn't even know what they'd find, but there *had* to be something, something the whole band could feed into and take strength from, now, when they really needed it.

Striding past the final blade, he found clear ground. He stopped and grunted as the next band member nearly clambered over him.

'About bloody time,' said Andy. 'We can still get back to the bar before closing.'

'What do you mean?' asked Joe. 'We've only just got here.'

'Here being a patch of ground in the middle of a pissing wind farm.' Andy spun around in a circle, clenched his fists and raised his shoulders as he strode towards Joe. 'Fucking hell, Joe. There is fuck all here.'

'It's nothing you can see,' said Joe. 'It's what you can feel, man.'

'You'll be feeling my boot up your arse in a minute,' growled Andy.

'Hey,' said Mike. 'He got us here in one piece, didn't he?'

'And for what?' said Vince. 'To risk eco-castration on the way back. Joe's way of helping population control.'

'Wait a second.' Maxwell pointed towards the centre of the field. 'What's that?'

'What's what?' Andy glared into the distance. 'I can't see anything.'

'There's a raised area,' said Maxwell.

'What?' said Andy. 'A clump of grass ten feet higher than the rest? This is so not keeping me from my beer.'

'Ryder said something about a disused bunker being out here.'

'So?'

'And Shot Away said he was based here.'

'Did he?' asked Vince.

'Well,' shrugged Maxwell. 'He sort of hinted.'

'He didn't bloody deny it,' said Mike.

'And he's also madder than Varg Vikernes,' said Vince.

'Who?' asked Maxwell.

'It doesn't matter,' said Vince. 'He's a mad bastard is all you need to know, just like bloody Shot Away. Do you really believe anything that nutter says?'

'There's something scary about him,' said Andy.

'Scary, mad, and a bastard fitness instructor,' said Vince. 'But that doesn't mean he was ever out here. And I think you'll agree it's a bit of a bloody coincidence if he was.'

'Where do you think he's gone?' asked Maxwell.

'Oh, who cares?' said Vince. 'He's not dumb enough to hang around out here, is he? Christ, we're the only ones stupid enough to listen to bloody Captain Green over there.'

'We're here, man,' said Joe. 'May as well make the most of it.'

'You just get on with your bloody séance,' snapped Andy. 'Leave the exploring to the normal people.'

'Yeah, man. Like getting your nose pierced with a guitar string is my idea of normal, too.'

'Funny bastard. How'd you like your hair yanked out and left as an offering on top of one of these bloody pylons?'

'Leave it,' said Maxwell. 'Joe said he'd get us here and he has. Let's see what's here before we head back.'

'Well, what the hell *is* over there?' asked Andy.

With Maxwell in the lead, the band fanned out and approached the misshaped dome of grassland in line abreast. A sudden mist slipped down and the raised ground became blurred and uncertain. On the right, Joe felt a tingle of apprehension. 'This doesn't feel right, guys.'

'Give me some reasons,' said Maxwell.

'It's just a feeling, man, but it hasn't let me down yet tonight.' Joe felt a slight, barely perceptible resistance against his flared jeans, and seconds later heard faint metallic clatters. 'Will that do you, man?' he asked.

'What, that noise?'

Joe's reply was drowned out by a startled cry from Maxwell, immediately followed by a solid thud and a grunt. Joe rushed towards the sound. 'Shit, man,' he burbled. 'Where are you, Max?'

Wind turbines moaned through the emptiness.

'Max? Max?'

'What the fuck is this place?' asked Andy.

'It's just an open area,' soothed Mike.

'Then where the fuck is Max?'

'He can't have just disappeared,' said Vince. 'Could he? *Could he?*'

'Oh, no, man,' wailed Joe. 'Oh, heavy heavy. This isn't happening, man. It can't, it just can't.'

'It fucking well is.' Vince grabbed Joe's psychedelic shirt and shook his wire-thin body. 'You dragged us out here, you stupid bastard, now Maxwell's bloody missing and we're surrounded by killer wind turbines. This is *really* going to set us up for the fan club tomorrow. Christ, I'll be playing worse than Stains.'

'A fucking improvement, then,' growled Andy.'

'Can it, girls,' snapped Mike. 'We're in trouble, and all you can do is bitch.'

'What are we supposed to do?' asked Vince. 'Join hands and skip in the bloody wilderness until Joe comes up with a plan?'

'I know what to do, man,' said Joe.

'You do?' Mike looked at Joe in surprise. 'I mean, of course. Sure. Yeah, you do. So, what's the plan, Joe?'

'Back to the ranch. Let's get Johnny.'

*

'Ho-lee shit!'

Johnny lay back on the bed, staring at Rachel with wide-eyed, schoolboy lust. Slowly, teasingly, she removed her raincoat. He vaguely remembered realising she was wearing it at the bar, but hadn't questioned it. The drink, the stress, the band, the album, all had conspired in an unholy alliance to keep his eyes and mind away from such weighty matters.

Not any more.

'Don't tell me you've never seen this before?' she smiled, and he writhed on the bed, his leather pants making his arousal extremely uncomfortable.

Her coat fell to the floor and Johnny's eyes bulged in their sockets. She stood before him in a pristine white tennis dress, the short hem ending tantalisingly close to the top of her firm thighs and the top half hugging her curved figure. He growled and surged to stand and up and grapple with her predominantly on-view flesh. She halted him with an outstretched arm and finger-point that carried more power than a cattle prod.

'Stay right there,' she commanded, her voice empress-like.

'But—'

'I'll come to you.'

'How did you know I'd like you in that outfit?'

'How did I *not* know?' she chuckled, slowly walking towards him with a maddening, hip-swaying walk. 'In the short time we've been together, the one group of women you stare at more than any other are tennis players.'

'But we've never been to a tennis match.'

'And we never will, either. This is as real as it gets for *you*.' She stood on the edge of the bed and pushed him back. He flopped onto the mattress. 'Besides, you *really* don't need to be at a match to give it away.' She climbed onto the bed and straddled him, the dress hem riding up her thighs. Johnny gasped and reached for her, but she slapped him away.

'I don't know what you mean.' He tried to grope her once more but she twisted his fingers, and only released them when he yelped in pain.

'Sorry,' she said. 'But you need to learn to do as you're told, *and* how obvious you are, leering at the sports news every time the tennis gets a mention.'

'I don't—'

'You do. Don't argue.'

'Oh, God, Rachel. You've got a hell of a way of punishing me.'

She laughed. 'That'll happen if your eyes or any other part of you strays.' She slowly leaned forward, kneeling over him with her hands planted on either side of his head. Her long straight hair brushed against his face. He stared up at her body, only just encased in the flimsy white dress. Once more, he tried to reach her, but she grabbed his wrists and pinned them to the mattress. 'If you *told* me what you liked, instead of me having to find out, things might go a little easier for you.'

'I'd love it if you wore a tennis dress,' he moaned. 'Please, Rachel, *please* wear a tennis dress for me, just once.'

'That's more like it,' she whispered. Slowly, she lowered herself on top of him. He felt her breasts flatten against his bony chest. Her long black hair settled around his face. He felt her breath on his skin, heard her rapid breathing, giving away an excitement that matched his own, then he smelled the lemon grass and his senses plunged into freefall.

Followed by the shattering crash of panicked knocking on the door.

Chapter 29

Maxwell groaned and shook his head, the movement sending a pack of pain-devils running around behind his eyes and down his spine. He tried to move and found that he couldn't, then realised he was hanging upside down with his wrists bound tightly behind him, and his arms pinned to his sides with strong nylon rope.

Panic surged through him, his hammering heart rate threatening to make him sick. He shook his head and focussed his eyesight on a corroded steel bar locking an equally neglected but formidable metal door in place.

Solid footsteps approached from behind. He tried to swivel his body and see who was approaching, but all he did was swing from side to side. How the hell had he got there? *Think, Maxwell, think!* He remembered walking through the wind turbines, seeing the grassy mound. Then what? *Then what?*

Christ, yes! That bloody mad bastard Shot Away. Twatted him senseless. And then? *And then you were strung up, you fucking idiot.* He didn't need Johnny Faslane's quick mind to know he was in trouble. But why? So they'd walked into the middle of a wind farm, so what? What did that have to do with Shot Away? Maxwell vaguely remembered him alluding to having served out here bloody years ago. *So what again?* he thought. *What does that matter now?*

'You made it though those turbines, then.' Maxwell turned his head, long dark hair dangling beneath him and pooling on the dusty, concrete floor. He saw a pair of legs clad in faded camouflage trousers, and dull boots with the soles almost worn through.

'Fucking hell, Shot Away,' groaned Maxwell. 'What is this shit? Some twisted new training thing?'

'You lads aren't as useless as you look.' Shot Away's grey-stubbled face peered down at Maxwell, cropped hair hidden underneath a tattered green bandana. Ice-chip grey eyes sent a bayonet of fear into Maxwell's thudding heart. This wasn't the same eccentric who made their life hell in the gym, who kicked them out of bed at dawn and sweated them down before rehearsals. This was a whole different world.

'What the fuck is this about?' tremored Maxwell. 'Are we in this bloody bunker you told us not to go to?'

'Never let civvies onto an air base,' muttered Sawyer. 'They're worse than bloody herpes. You'll never get rid of them.'

'Look, mate,' soothed Maxwell. 'This isn't an air base anymore, it's civilian. In fact, *you're* a bloody civilian as well.'

'Not here,' snarled Sawyer. 'Never here. Do you know what this place was? Do you know who was here?'

'You were?'

'You know it.' Sawyer smiled insanely.

'But nobody's here anymore,' said Maxwell. *Including you,* he thought.

'No one's *supposed* to be here.' Sawyer spun around in a camouflage circle before piercing Maxwell with an intense stare. 'These turbines are surrounding the place, approaching us, getting closer. The doors have been forced, people have been inside, people have been in *here.*'

Maxwell swung his head round and scanned the place from his upside-down viewpoint. 'Does it really matter? For God's sake, the place is fucking empty.'

'It always matters, even more so now.'

'What do you mean?'

'You wouldn't understand. You'd never understand.'

'So tell me,' said Maxwell. 'Why is this place off limits to everyone except squaddies, even knackered old past-it ex-squaddies?'

'This place was *ours,* ' snarled Sawyer. 'We secured it, kept it safe, we said who, we said when anyone else came inside.'

'Fair enough when there was something here to protect,' reasoned Maxwell. 'But that was years ago. This place has moved on. *You've* moved on.'

'But we were *here!* ' said Sawyer. 'WE held this ground, and we don't give it up.'

'Were you meant to stay here for ever?'

'The squadron was about to be posted out. I had to stay.'

'Why?'

'Why? Why? Why am I always being asked that?' Sawyer screwed his eyes shut. 'It's all wrong. I shouldn't have been left here. I shouldn't.'

'But you just said—'

'Don't question me.' Sawyer thrust has face into Maxwell's, brushing his nose with a stubbled chin. 'They've got eyes on us, we need to close the blast doors, take cover, cam up.'

'What the fuck are you talking about?'

Sawyer stared around the empty concrete room, paced back and forth, then glared back at Maxwell. 'Scope the grey, mate, I'm not straight out of basics. I know how to make this place invisible.' His head flickered around as though he were surrounded by a swarm of insects, while a muscle twitched in his left cheek. 'You lot coming *here* of all places to do your bloody rehearsals. Do you think I'm stupid?'

'You're something alright, but stupid isn't it.'

Maxwell spun his head around and took in the upside-down, dusty, empty concrete nothingness.

'This place was my home when everything in here was turning and burning,' said Sawyer. 'One fuck-up on the job and the bastards left me here to keep the pilot light on. Then they tossed me aside when it finally closed.'

'Come on, Shot Away,' said Maxwell. 'That's old news. You've got that gym of yours. Coming to this place, wanting to turn it into something it used to be, well, that's stepping back. I'm right, mate. You know it. So how about putting me right way up and I'll buy you a beer back at the Mess?'

'Trying to talk me down, are you?'

'As it happens.'

'Think you'll get me to give up?'

'Christ, Shot Away, this place is empty, has been for years. And don't take this the wrong way, but no one cares anymore.'

'Don't say that.'

'It's true.'

'It matters to me.'

'But no one else,' pleaded Maxwell.

'Maybe,' twitched Sawyer. 'Maybe not. But they won't get me without a fight, and they won't get in here.'

Sawyer disappeared from view, and Maxwell struggled and swung around and looked up. He saw the rope tied between his bound feet, fed through a gap in the ceiling joist and secured to a rusting steel hook drilled into the wall. He studied the joist the rope stretched through, and saw his weight being taken by a thin, if not sharp edge. *It's worth a shot*, he thought.

Chapter 30

Dawn slithered across the wind farm and Johnny glared molten fury at the band, minus Maxwell. 'Fucking bastards.' His acid words burned across the light mist that quilted the grass.

'Hey, man,' whined Joe. 'What were we supposed to do?'

'Number one, not go out into the turbine field at all. And number two, leave me the fuck alone when I'm—'

'What, man?'

'When I'm… when I'm… when I'm busy, you bastards.'

'Busy booking the tour hotels?' asked Andy.

'Booking his own extras, more like,' sniggered Vince.

'Never mind what I was doing. What the fuck where *you* lot doing out here? Ryder *told* you how dangerous it was. Didn't you listen? No, don't answer that, you twats *never* listen. Jesus shit. The fan club are coming today, the pissing album is being released today—'

'Maybe,' grumbled Vince. 'Only if Ozone like it.'

'Shut up,' snapped Johnny. 'Either way, you fuck-ups have got far too much going on to be out here in a bloody wind farm in the middle of the bloody night.'

'It wasn't the wind farm, man,' said Joe. 'Max disappeared.'

'Sure he did,' said Johnny. 'Of course he did. Jesus Christ, it's like having five kids. Shit on a stick, if there's some new way for you lot to need your arses wiped, you'll find it, won't you?'

'We weren't looking for trouble,' said Mike.

'You never are.' Johnny looked up at the turbines looming into sight. 'But isn't it amazing how it always finds *you?* Right, let's find a way through these fucking things.'

'Hang on, man,' said Joe. 'I'll help there.'

'What, like you helped lose Maxwell?' sniped Johnny. 'Just shut up and follow me.'

'Are you sure you don't need any help?' asked Joe. 'It took all my powers to get us through there last night.'

'What fucking powers?' snapped Johnny. 'Look, I've got eyes, I can see the blades, and it doesn't take the brains of a bloody archbishop to work out where they'll come down.'

207

'Joe got us through in the dark,' said Mike.

'Christ,' blazed Johnny. 'He's the bloody wind-farm whisperer, is he? Well, it's bloody daylight now, so we don't need Joe with his fucking weed goggles to lead us all to disaster.' He held his hands above his head. 'Just stop coming out with this bullshit for an hour, follow me and show me where you last saw that stupid bastard singer.'

With anger fusing through him, Johnny alternated between glancing up at the blades as they turned in the steady wind and making sure the band were still following him. His mind took him back to the moment he left Rachel behind, and he hated all things Cold Steel with a heat that would have melted the Koh-I-Noor diamond. 'One hour.' He'd looked up at her white-clad form, and she whispered above the foaming roaring desire inside his ears, 'Get back by then, and you'll still get your treat.' He'd been tempted not to go at all. Time and again she'd told him she was teaching him the game, the publicity sport of half-truths and omission. It was a game she played as well. With him. She'd wait the hour, but only if he left in the first place and carried on proving himself, proved himself the only man to either control or rescue Cold Steel. Johnny may have hated doing it, may have despaired at times, but he also knew it defined him. With a string of vile curses he'd opened the door and stared at the remaining four band members who stood before him in unseeing panic.

*

'Last seen around here, you say?' Johnny looked at the grassy expanse of nothingness in the centre of the wind farm.

'This is where we were, man,' Joe insisted. 'It was here.'

'Do you think we made it up?' asked Mike.

'Fuck me,' said Johnny. 'You pricks might have planned the whole thing just to keep me occupied while Maxwell gets bailed out of a police cell, discharged from hospital, runs away from some tart's husband, bloody anything.'

'Why would we do that?' asked Vince.

'Fucking hell, why would you *not* do that?'

'And what about this, man?' Joe edged forward and picked up a thin strand of line. Small strips of tinfoil were tied to them, almost invisible among the cropped grass. 'This shouldn't be here.'

'Hey,' said Andy. 'Didn't we hear some sound like that last night?'

'Just about the time we lost Max.' Joe looked at Johnny. 'Believe me now, man?'

'So where is he?' asked Johnny. 'You drag me out here on some half-arsed story about a missing Maxwell, then show me a length of string with some tinfoil tied to it. Of *all* the times to be playing your bastard games. Do you *know* what I turned my back on to follow you wankers out here to this godforsaken piece of shit-fucking nowhere?' He looked at his watch. 'Jesus, forty-five minutes to get here, I'll never be back in time.'

'We don't give a fuck about your deadline,' said Vince. 'Maxwell's *disappeared!*'

'Has he?' hissed Johnny. 'Has he really?' He spun a fast three-sixty. 'Look, this place is emptier than your bloody brains. Maxwell is clearly not here and there is fuck all else to see. Back to the hangar. Now. And by Christ if Maxwell's there, I'll bollock you bastards to the moon and back.'

'And if he's not, man?' asked Joe.

'Then you'll *really* be in trouble.'

*

Twenty minutes later, Johnny glared around the empty hangar, wanting to see Maxwell gloating about what a great wind-up they'd done, or how he'd been there all night, and where the hell had they been? He also *didn't* want to see him there, but only if that meant the rest of the band had been telling the truth, if it meant he'd actually had a reason to abandon Rachel at her absolute seductive, teasing best. 'He's not here,' he muttered.

'Of course not, man,' said Joe. 'He was taken.'

'Taken?' Johnny stared water-board interrogation at the band. 'By who, for fuck's sake?'

'Don't know, man.' Joe's denial was barely audible.

'Well, what *do* you know?' Brick-wall stares bounced back at Johnny. 'Oh, Jesus.' He looked at the hangar. Both stages stood ready to host the band, wires and cables hung from lights, and propped-up instruments waited to create the music. An expectant silence hummed around the empty building. 'We're filming in front of the fan club today.' He palmed his forehead. 'Fuck me.'

'What are you going to do?' asked Vince.

'We've got a missing person.' Johnny pulled out his phone. 'That's a job for the police.'

'You think they'll find him in time?'

'In time for what?'

'Rehearsals.' Surprise rinsed through Johnny as he saw a tense face, saw genuine concern in Vince's features.

'A bit of reality hitting, is it?' he asked.

'Look, mate,' said Andy. 'Why would we *want* to face the cameras and our own fan club without a singer?'

'Deal with it,' snapped Johnny. 'Because right now that stupid bastard's vanished, which makes Cold Steel a foursome.'

'No way, man,' said Joe. 'We can't go out there without a front man. We *need* Max.'

'He's not here.' Johnny's firm voice was a black-white contrast to the anxiety chomping through his organs. 'You say you need a singer, so what do you suggest?'

'We need a stand-in.' Mike folded his arms. 'Someone who knows the band, knows the songs, knows the music,'

Johnny started to speak and then felt his throat shrink. Four pairs of eyes stared back at him with cold decision. His mouth opened and closed like a beached goldfish.

'I guess we've got no choice,' said Andy. 'Looks like Johnny's the new singer.'

*

'Last seen in the wind farm, and now he's gone.' The middle-aged policeman scribbled in his notebook, then scanned Johnny and the band with seasoned apathy.

'That's right, man,' said Joe. 'Someone took him.'

'Here?' The policeman's eyebrows rose fractionally. 'At Honham?'

'Is that significant?' asked Johnny.

'An abduction? Too right.' The policeman snapped his notebook shut and looked in the direction of the wind farm. 'There used to be a bunker out there in amongst those turbines. Closed down and sealed years ago. You know anything about that?'

'Is there a connection?' hedged Johnny.

'I'm here to help, lads.' The policeman's eyes sparked open and centred on Johnny. 'What *do* you know?'

Johnny fidgeted and looked at the floor. 'One of our, er, crew said he used to work there.'

'Are you sure?' Raised eyebrows.

'It's what he said, but he's not the most level of guys. He's our fitness instructor. Said his nickname was Shot Away.'

'Oh, shit.'

'Why "oh shit"?' asked Johnny.

'Do you know what was stored in that bunker?'

'No,' frowned Johnny.

'Nukes.'

'What?'

'That bunker housed nuclear bombs.'

'Holy crap,' breathed Johnny. 'But let's be clear about this. "Were", not "are", right?'

'You're missing the point.'

'I am?'

The policeman nodded. 'I used to be a mechanic in the air force. This shit hole in the middle of nowhere was my last posting before I left and joined the police.'

'You fixed nuclear bombs?' asked Johnny.

'Well, I was supposed to keep them working. They were bloody old by the time I got there. Two years into my posting, I helped deactivate and retire them.'

'So what's the point?' asked Johnny. 'Did you need police to guard them?'

'No,' laughed the policeman. 'To guard the guards, maybe.'

'What?'

'Imagine you had a shed-load of nukes to guard, who would you get to do it?'

'The toughest bunch of bastards I could find,' said Johnny.

'They were tough all right,' said the policeman. 'Hardest cases that ever wore the uniform. With those lads on the job there was no way those tins of sunshine were going *anywhere* the air force didn't want them to go.'

'So?'

211

'So, they were also bloody crazy, and the last one to leave was the absolute worst. I don't know the details, but he got into trouble on the bunker's last day as an active unit.'

'What did he do?'

The policeman shrugged. 'It must have been bad. They kept the poor bastard there till the place was empty. I heard he ended his military days sweeping the tarmac and checking the padlocks hadn't been tampered with. By the time the base closed and he was turfed out into Civvy Street, he'd lost what few marbles he had to begin with.'

'Shot Away,' said Johnny.

'Sound like your man?' asked the policeman.

'Got to be,' replied Johnny. 'What more do you know about him?'

'Just rumours. At one time all he wanted to do was leave here and do something exciting, but when he flipped and they kept him there, he became fixated with the place. Some say he lived like a hermit nearby. The lads who work the wind farm say they've seen what they think is someone prowling around at night.'

Johnny shook his head. 'One of our roadies came across him in London, living in a run-down gym. We hired him to get the band fit.'

'But he wasn't happy about coming out here,' said Mike.

'Yeah,' said Vince. 'And now we know why.'

Johnny turned towards to policeman. 'Has he ever shown up on your radar?'

He shook his head. 'After the stories came in, I fed his name into the computers. He didn't show up anywhere: tax, residence, crime, nothing. As far as the world is concerned, once he left the air force, he disappeared. Just another unhinged Rockape.'

'Rockape?'

'It's what he and the rest of his unit called themselves.'

'Never heard of them,' said Johnny.

'Not many people have, but if you knew what they were about, you'd know he's capable of anything. And if there are strange tales about this place, then a feral Rock may be the reason. We'll swing over to the bunker site and have a look around.'

'Are you going inside it, man?' asked Joe.

The policeman shook his head. 'Can't. It's still owned by the MOD and locked down.'

'But what if Maxwell's inside?' asked Johnny.

'If we find signs of entry, we'll notify the appropriate authorities, and *then* a search will happen.'

'Do you really think he's out there?' asked Johnny.

'That would be too obvious. If it is him, he won't want to draw attention. And breaking into a secure bunker isn't how you stay off the grid.'

'I thought you said he was nuts.'

'He's not mad enough to forget his training.'

Chapter 31

Maxwell pendulumed across the concrete emptiness like an oversized bat roosting in a ship's hold. Creasing his abdominal muscles and contorting into mid-air sit-ups, he generated movement, then swung his body to build momentum. Pulled taut through the joist, the rope creaked and strained against his weight.

He arced further and further to each side of the suspension point, coming close enough to the concrete walls to read faded graffiti on the once smooth greyness. Above him, he heard the rope fray and snap, strand by strand. Sweat dripped up his forehead and into his hair, and he wondered how much time he had before Sawyer came back.

A dull twang rang out from the taut rope and Maxwell felt a one-inch drop. He tensed for a sudden fall to the unyielding floor and wondered what he'd look like with a broken nose. But the rope, slowly giving way, kept a tenacious hold on its six feet of hanging meat. He flicked sweat out of his eyes and carried on swinging.

A second, louder strum reverberated above Maxwell and he shot to the floor. His shoulder hit with a solid thud and he groaned in pain. He lay on the cold floor like an oversized caterpillar and looked for anything that would help him untie himself and get away. At the far end of the cavernous room stood an old workbench. Like a human witchetty grub, he bent his body and then straightened his legs, slowly edging towards the table. Half rolling, half crawling, he reached the solid wooden bench. He rolled over and looked up, quickly realising that he'd have to stand up to see what was on the tabletop.

Think, Maxwell. Johnny's not going to tell you what to do this time. His tortured synapses screamed out at being tasked with something other than screwing around. He rolled onto his side and brought his knees to his chest. A few sways back and forth and he was on his knees. The ropes bit into his flesh and he felt his hands go numb. He had to hurry but he knew he had to be careful. His balance was shot with his limbs being tied to his body, and slowly he bent his toes to the floor and rocked back. His feet were now planted firmly on the floor and he was in a tightly bound crouching position. He forced his breathing to stay even, using the tricks he normally only practised onstage. Then he tried to stand. Every time he tensed, the rope bit into his muscles and arrested his movement.

Maxwell ignored the numbness in his hands and the pain in his arms and legs. He leant forward, his head over his knees. Jesus, this was impossible. *It'd bloody well better not be!* his thoughts screamed back at him. Slowly, shakily, and nearly falling, he gradually stood up. Elation surged through him. He felt as though he'd climbed one of the wind turbines single-handed.

He looked down and to his left, and hope exploded inside him. Littered on the tabletop was an array of tools, and among them a Stanley knife. He crouched slightly and then jumped, bunny-hopping sideways like a hairy pogo stick. Closer and closer to the table, then he was leaning against it.

Maxwell pulled and wrenched at the ropes binding his wrists. There was limited movement, but he could just about get a finger onto the knife's blade. He winced as the blade sliced into his finger, gritted his teeth and tried to get a tighter grip, his scrabbling fingers now slippery with his own slowly oozing blood. Millimetre by millimetre the knife edged towards him. Now he could grip it with more than one finger; now he could touch the handle. He spun it around and brought it close towards him, attacking the ropes in a frenzy fuelled by fear.

One, two, then three ropes snapped apart under the blade, but Maxwell didn't feel any less bound. He calmed his breathing once more and focussed on the ropes around his wrists. Working by touch, he felt for the individual strands and ran the blade through them. He gasped with pain as the circulation returned. It was like stepping inside on a snowy day. Moving quickly now, cut by cut; his power of movement returned. Less than a minute after freeing his wrists, the remains of the ropes that had bound him lay in a sundered heap at his feet. There was no time to lose. Gone was the amused, patronising view he had of Shot Away. The man was fucking nuts and could come back at any time.

Maxwell looked wildly around and saw blank concrete walls. He ran back to where he'd been hung upside down, and pulled open the rusting steel doorway. The walls narrowed down to what

215

was little more than a tunnel; soon he had to crouch down under the low roof, and he felt the walls closing in on him. Claustrophobic panic made him feel sick, but he kept on going.

After a minute of scampering along, he came out into a dimly lit room. It looked like a store room filled with long empty bags and boxes, while in the corner lay a small, orderly collection of sealed packages. *Fuck me, how long has that food been there?*

Never mind that, you're in a dead end!

He spun around and saw a dark hole near the room's floor. The concrete wall had been smashed open and a dark tunnel led somewhere. He hadn't seen any other way out of the cavernous hold; he crouched down to crawl inside, and then heard sounds of movement coming towards him. He squawked with fear and dived beneath the empty food boxes.

In a flurry of arms and legs, Maxwell burrowed into the paper-thin cloud of discarded wrappers and packaging. He lay on the cold floor covered by a duvet of crumpled foil-wrap, his heart madly hammering. The sounds from inside the improvised tunnel became louder, but covered by his makeshift concealment, Maxwell couldn't see a thing. The shuffling crept closer, and he heard heavy breathing as a man laboured along the tunnel, always getting closer.

Then the rustle as someone crawled through the waste littering the store room floor. Maxwell stopped breathing as Shot Away cleared the tunnel, stood up and walked down the corridor, the sound of his footsteps receding.

Maxwell leapt up and dived into the tunnel, clawing his way forward. He had as long as Shot Away found him gone before he would be after him. Utter darkness blanketed Maxwell's senses. His hands clawed into soft earth, and the void that pressed in on him smelled of damp soil and roughly hewn planking, which he guessed kept the tunnel from caving in. He felt like he was starring in a remake of The Great Escape. His laboured breathing rasped loudly in his ears and he crawled mechanically, automatically, going as fast as he could and straining to hear for any signs of pursuit.

The tunnel right-angled left and right, and Maxwell quickly lost his sense of direction. Once, he slammed into a roughly planked step. Sweating with exertion, he climbed over it and carried on crawling along the upwardly edged tunnel. There seemed no end to the corners and perpetual darkness. He couldn't hear any sound of pursuit, but he didn't slow down. He felt as though the walls and roof of the primitive tunnel were pressing in on him; at any moment he'd be buried beneath tonnes of Suffolk dirt.

He looked down at the ground and gasped, suddenly able to see his hands, pale blurs against the dark soil. He looked up and saw vague shapes. Light, it was light. He crawled faster, spurred on by the pale illumination, daylight, and escape. He wondered where he'd come out. The light got brighter; the tunnel became damp and then wet. His hands and knees squelched through cold mud. He looked behind him and saw nothing, heard nothing. *Just a few more yards and we're there.* He sprint-crawled towards the tunnel's opening, sobbing with exertion, his clothes filthy with splashed mud. He erupted into daylight, flopping onto his back and sucking in lungfuls of sweet, free-range air.

He rolled over and stood up, spun around and saw the wind turbines all around him. At his back was the raised hillock he and the band had been walking to the night before. He ran towards the turbines. How was he going to get through the blades without Joe? He didn't have time to work it out with a nutter on his tail and nowhere to hide. He'd just have to take his chances.

*

Bowel-loosening fear pulsed through Johnny, and all thoughts about whether Twenty would release the album were mashed from his mind. He slowly strapped on a spare Les Paul and looked at the rest of the band. 'I *really* don't think this is a good idea,' he said.

'Nor do we,' snapped Vince. 'But Maxwell's not here, so live with it. And for fuck's sake at least *look* like a singer.'

'Look like one?' stammered Johnny. 'What the hell do you mean, look like one? Shouldn't I be sounding like one?'

'You're the front man, you're the one telling everyone how fucking great this band is, so look like you believe it.'

'That's right,' said Andy. 'It's like you deserve the attention. Don't go creeping out there like you've asked to go onstage, go out there like you fucking well own it. It's your *right* to be there.'

'They've never seen you before,' said Mike. 'So make sure you connect with them straight away.'

'And how do I do that?'

'Hey, only you can decide. It's what's inside you, what you are. A word, a gesture, whatever feels right. Don't worry, the music'll start straight away, and then it'll be on us, not you.'

'I turn up instead of Maxwell and they *won't* be looking at me?'

'Don't worry, man,' said Joe. 'We'll do a bit more poncing around than usual, soak up the attention.'

'Look, lads.' Johnny gripped the guitar as though it would save his life. 'I know the songs, fair enough, but I've never sung in my life, and I sure as shit can't play a guitar past power chords.'

'Who says you'll be playing?' asked Vince. 'Here's a trick we learned from you on the last tour. You look like you're plugged in, but you're really switched off. Trust me, Johnny, a first-time front man *without* a guitar to hide behind, you really would look as naked as you're going to feel.'

'Shit, don't remind me.' Huddled behind stage props, without a backstage area to speak of, Johnny saw the fan club filling the hangar. They might have looked like an ordinary cross section of metal fans from across the generations, but they were the elite of any audience. If people going to a concert were an army, the fan club were the shock troops. Fanatical about the band they followed, they soaked up the rewards, like having their own dressing room, backstage meets or, for Cold Steel, seeing their band rehearse for the tour. If there was a change in the line up, they'd expect to be told first. *And I'm just about to spring it on them,* Johnny thought.

He looked around the hangar. There was none of the background noise before a normal concert: the metal playlist, the muted chatter of conversations that got louder as the hall filled up. None of the usual smells of close-packed humanity, cold burgers and spilled beer. Instead, the constant calls among the road crew working the props and both stages, and a perpetual humming in Johnny's ears that he took for abject fear at having to go onstage as Cold Steel's singer.

'You can do it.' Rachel smiled and squeezed his arm. 'It'll be good for Maxwell to know there's some competition.'

'Yeah, right.' He looked around, desperate hope searing through him that Maxwell might suddenly stride into the hangar.

'You're on, lads.' Dixie gave a shaggy-haired nod. The hangar lights were doused with a multi-decibel click, the audience cheered and spotlights sabred onto the stage.

They walked onstage and Johnny felt the band close-clouding around him. The audience, smaller than the band had known for many years, still sounded painfully loud to Johnny's heightened senses. The spotlights burned bright, and the static energy from the onstage monitor speakers felt like a punch in the guts. Johnny saw Mike sitting at the drums, almost unseen behind the bass and toms. He looked around like a condemned prisoner seeking a final reprieve. He saw bewildered faces from the mosh pit, picking up on Maxwell's absence. He saw Vince and Andy staring intently at him, fingers primed on their strings.

Johnny's fear crescendoed. He stepped towards the microphone, keeping a tight hold on his guitar. He didn't dare look down at the front line fans, not wanting to be unnerved by direct eye contact. Looking out into the outer-space blackness between the spotlights, he took a deep breath and suddenly his fear slipped away.

'We are Cold Steel!' he roared.

Twin guitar screeches arced out of the speakers on both sides of Johnny, drowning out the audience reaction. Without warning, he'd replaced Maxwell in front of the fan club, and he knew the breach of fan-artist etiquette couldn't be more damning. Mike and Joe piled a solid rhythm filling over the riffs, and Johnny looked down and saw a liberal scattering of hands giving him the finger from the packed mosh pit.

He took a deep breath, picked up his cue and stood closer to the mic. Focussing his eyes on a single space of darkness, he sang the first verse of Sinners Sanctuary. He heard his voice come through the monitor, but it didn't sound like him, didn't feel like him. None of this felt like him. *I should be watching this from the mixing desk, not up here performing.*

First verse sung. Vince and Andy crowded in on either side, and all three of them belted out the chorus, normally reserved for Maxwell. Johnny launched into the second verse, his hands unmoving on his guitar. Vince and Andy prowled around the large stage space, drawing attention by striking ridiculous poses, alternately grimacing and grinning like Wolf Hoffmann clones. Mike embellished the drum lines and Joe launched into bass odysseys that would have made a seventies pothead sit up and beg.

Johnny kept his singing simple, staying within his narrow vocal range and hoping to Christ he was in tune. He stood frozen in front of the mic stand, his hands sutured to the guitar. He felt the music's rhythm, and verses flew from him instinctively. The song ground to a close and the joint guitar and drum note shot into the darkened mosh pit. Johnny looked down at his hand gripping the guitar neck, dimly aware that he was viced so tightly to the strings that they were digging into his fingers.

He fully expected to be booed off stage. Instead, a polite shimmer of cheers from the audience lapped around him and continued for several seconds. He looked down at the playlist taped to the floor. Power Games, one of the new songs, was next. It dealt with manipulative relationships and corrupt politicians. He knew the words, knew what the song was about, but his uncertainty returned and wave-crashed over him. Vince nudged him away from the microphone and growled into his ear.

'They've never heard it before, they don't know what to expect.' Slight headshake. 'They won't miss Maxwell on this one.'

'How did—'

'Christ, mate, we all know what you're thinking. We're not as stupid as you think we are.'

'Shit, Vince, I hope they find Maxwell. I'm bloody cacking myself here.'

'What do you mean?' Axeman grin. 'This is great practice for the tour.'

'You're having a laugh, Vince. No fucking way. This gig and that's it.' Johnny walked back to the mic stand, greeted by cheers and whistles. There were still fingers being sent his way from the darkened front row, but not as many as at the start of the set. *Where the fuck is Maxwell?*

Chapter 32

Maxwell trotted across empty grassland towards the turbines. Dry grass rustled under his scuffed training shoes and a low moan pulled his eyes upwards. The downward swoosh of a moving blade announced the inner edge of the wind farm. He looked up at the white carbon-fibre fingers rolling around the skyline, and quickly realised that in the daylight it was a whole lot easier to see them coming. Which was just as well: he had to get through and back to the hangar before that mad bastard caught him again.

He plunged into the turbine field, alternately looking up and then weaving around the pylons. He could see the hangar in the distance, nestled on the edge of what was once a runway. He settled into a fevered routine, fuelled by a desperate need to get through the field as fast as he could. Look at the blades, avoid the pylons, choose a path. Look at the blades, avoid the pylons, choose a path.

Deep inside the wind farm, and with the hangar still ahead of him and slowly getting bigger, he didn't sense anyone around him, heard no one approaching, was completely unprepared for the sliding kick at ankle level that pulled his legs away and sent him sprawling to the floor.

'How the fuck did you get away?' snarled Sawyer. Maxwell gagged on a mouthful of Suffolk grass, rolled over and struggled to stand up. Sawyer planted a boot in his chest and shoved him back down. 'You can tell me about it once I've hauled you back.' He looked at Maxwell. 'You sure know how to piss someone off. It's bloody miles back to base.'

'You can always let me go,' wheezed Maxwell.

'Bollocks. You know too much. You know about the bunker.'

'It's an *empty* bunker, you stupid twat.'

'You know what it was.'

'Fucking hell, it's all over the internet for anyone who gives a toss.'

'Maybe it's nothing to you,' said Sawyer. 'But it's something to me.'

Maxwell coughed and held his chest, trying to make himself look more incapacitated than he was. Sawyer looked down, dropped his pack on the ground and fished out a fresh length of rope. He concentrated on unwinding it. Still lying down, Maxwell edged forward. He placed his foot behind Sawyer's heel, locked his other foot against his kneecap and pushed.

'Hey!' Sawyer's leg was forced straight. Maxwell pushed against the knee joint's natural movement. Sawyer dropped the rope and spiralled his arms, fighting to keep balance. Maxwell kept pushing, knowing that soon Sawyer would either have to fall over or get his leg broken. 'Shit,' he hissed, as Maxwell strained and pushed. 'Bastard,' he grunted, and fell backwards in a haphazard, camouflaged heap.

Maxwell jumped up and made to sprint through the last swathe of turbines. He ran past Sawyer's sprawling form and a hand shot out and grabbed his ankle in a steel-vice grip. His foot stayed on the ground and his upper body crashed forwards until his immobilised leg whip-snared him back and he fell down again. This time he shot up straight away and faced Sawyer. The two men circled each other like a Friday night pub fight.

'Clever move,' Sawyer's fists settled in front of him with an easy familiarity. 'Feel like a shot at the title?'

'Do I fuck.' False bravado fused through Maxwell. 'Putting you down long enough to get away's good enough for me. Look, mate.' He lowered his half raised fists. 'You don't have to stay here. You can still work with us. We don't care how fucking nuts you are.'

'Are you calling me mad?' twitched Sawyer.

'Do you really think you're not?'

'Tell you what, beat me in a fight, and I'm mad.' A fist blurred forward and Maxwell jinked out of the way, feeling the rush of cold air as a camouflaged arm shot past his head.

'Really?' grinned Maxwell. 'A bit too quick for you, headcase.' He jumped backwards and only just avoided a blow aimed at his body.

'Cheeky bastard.' Sawyer ran straight at Maxwell, who danced to one side. Maxwell bunched his fist and lashed out at the back of Sawyer's head. Pain lanced through his knuckles, his punch landing on solid bone. Both men grunted, then faced each other, more warily this time.

'For Christ's sake,' gasped Maxwell. 'Give it up.'

Fists flurried between them, but swift, dancing movement avoided any contact. Maxwell wondered how long his luck would hold. Could he keep this nutter here until someone saw him and helped? Where *was* the help? Wasn't *anyone* looking for him? He kept his guard up and focussed, trying to anticipate what Sawyer would do next. He forgot where he was, what was around them.

Two blades whooshed groundward on either side, but neither of them noticed. Both men concentrated on trying to floor the other, lost in their silent oxygen tent of single combat. Time slowed down, and with adrenaline flooding his bloodstream, Maxwell felt a sense of invincibility percolating through him. He seemed to anticipate Sawyer's moves and managed to block or avoid all the shots that came his way, even though none of his own clumsily executed punches landed. Such was their concentration on the other that neither of them heard the turbine blade approach, never noticed the low moan getting louder, never felt the smack-blow of sudden unconsciousness that connected with a massive eco-thud and knocked one of them to the ground.

Chapter 33

'Baldy, Baldy, no love lost!'

The audience tagged Johnny's nickname to one of Cold Steel's songs. His sweat-drenched legs felt as if they were dissolving inside his leather pants. His voice had dried up and faded to nothing during Power Games, saved only by Vince, Andy and Joe harmonising the rest of the song. Now there was the rest of the concert to get though and nowhere to hide.

'Fucking hell,' growled Vince. 'Can't you at least *talk?*'

Jeers and whistles invaded the stage.

'Easy for you to say,' croaked Johnny.

'No, mate, that's *your* job.'

Slow handclap, and the impatience was palpable.

'Jesus H Christ,' hissed Vince. 'Fuck off to the back and do something about your bloody voice.'

He nodded towards the mixing desk, invisible in the hangar's darkness. A single spotlight snared him in its beam, bringing everyone's attention with it. He glared outwards and the chants stopped. He gripped the guitar neck in a tight power chord and slashed down on the strings.

Johnny shuffled to the back of the stage where Andy and Joe stood in the darkness. 'A bit early for his solo.'

'Like we've got a choice?' snarled Andy. 'What happened to your singing?'

'Yeah,' said Johnny. 'Like this whole thing was *my* fucking idea.'

'Come up with a better one and we'll do it,' said Andy. 'Until then, start performing. We're not seeing this band go down the shitter on account of you or anyone else.'

'Not even Angie Dale?'

'Don't piss with me, Johnny. Not onstage, not in front of the fans.'

Vince ground into his solo, working the crowd who cheered appreciation. He prowled along the stage line, his head shaking to the music. The audience clapped in time with his playing. Johnny took slow deep breaths, trying to calm the fear raging inside him. He had to sing again, he *had* to.

Andy strode forward and joined in the solo. The crowd's approval washed over the stage. Mike began a rapid beat playing, quietly at first, then louder, while Joe matched the beat. The lights flamed on and illuminated the stage. Johnny's time had come. He walked to stage centre, still gripping his mute guitar. He opened his mouth to sing the first lines to No Nation, but Joe, Andy and Vince beat him to it. He looked left and saw Vince mouth 'chorus' to him, and realised they were letting him in gently. He nodded, swung his guitar neck, jumped up and down and then spun around.

And drove the end of his guitar straight into Joe's face.

*

Cold Steel were booed offstage for the first time since their disaster in Tokyo the year before. Joe's legs dissolved underneath him, his yelp of pain unheard. But the bass line's sudden disappearance detonated like a shock wave. His hands covered his face and he rolled from side to side. Dixie rushed onstage and pulled him off by his feet, his bass guitar trailing behind him. Vince and Andy looked at each other and tried to carry on, but the music became tinny and shallow without Joe's presence. Johnny's shock and guilt corroded his movements, multiplying his sense of being out of place. He shuffled around the stage, hearing the jeers from the audience. He didn't know whether to stay and try singing at some point or retreat and leave Vince and Andy to face the fans alone.

The decision was made as No Nation sludged to a tepid end and the hostile chanting became louder than the music. The overhead lights crashed on. Vince and Andy looked back at Johnny, who thumbed left and jerked his head sideways. They walked off without a word and were joined behind the backline by Mike. Johnny risked a backward glance and saw Dixie and the road crew herding the audience outside.

'What the fuck?' hissed Vince. 'Who pulled the gig?'

'I did.' Rachel walked around the backline, an all-areas pass clipped to her jeans and her camera strapped across her Cold Steel skinny top.

'Oh?' said Andy. *'You're* the manager are you?'

'No. Johnny is, but he was too busy being the singer.'

'Yeah, and he played a right fucking blinder.' Vince looked around. 'Where's Joe?'

'Ryder's office,' said Rachel.

'I'm there.' Mike dropped his drumsticks and strode towards the hangar's admin section.

Johnny's insides turned to deep freeze. He'd tried to sing and failed, and the band had no singer. His thought process slowed to nothing. The rest of the band could harmonise, but none of them could replace Maxwell. What were they going to do? What was *he* going to do?

Dixie shuffled towards them and grabbed Johnny's guitar. His hand remained glued to the fretboard and Dixie yanked at the instrument. 'For fuck's sake, let go,' he said.

'What?' Johnny's eyes refocused.

'The guitar, let go of it.'

Johnny looked down and released the death-grip he'd had on the black Gibson.

'Half an hour,' said Dixie. 'Stage number two's next.'

'Oh Christ,' said Johnny. 'Shit. We can't, we just can't.' He looked around and saw Vince, Andy, Dixie and Rachel looking at him. They wanted to know what to do, and it was up to him. *Don't back out now, Faslane,* he thought, *this is the big time. You wanted this.* Seconds of silence dragged out. He felt eyes and expectation pressing down on him. He clenched his teeth, squared his shoulders and pressed his lips together. 'Any sign of Maxwell?'

Dixie shook his head, a mane of greasy hair blurring around his face. Johnny looked up and saw Mike's drum kit already being dismantled and moved to the next, smaller stage.

'Hey, guys.' Joe and Mike reappeared, Joe with an eye patch over his left eye.

'Fucking hell,' laughed Vince. 'Really?'

'Leave it, Vince,' snapped Johnny. 'Joe, I'm sorry, are you alright?'

'I'm good, man. But I'm not going anywhere near you on the next gig.'

'How's the eye?'

'Swollen?'

'Can you still play?'

'He's a fucking stoner,' said Andy. 'He usually plays with both eyes closed. Course he can bloody play. Question is, Johnny, can you sing?'

'Leave that to me,' said Rachel. 'Johnny, come here. The rest of you, piss off to the next stage, Johnny'll be along soon.'

*

Two minutes later, Johnny and Rachel stood alone. The band stood behind the backline of the second stage and the road crew set up the instruments.

'What now?' asked Johnny.

'You need to sing,' said Rachel.

'Come on, Rachel. You saw me, you heard me. Fucking hell, there's no *way* I can replace Maxwell.'

'Why not?'

'Why not? Jesus, Rachel, did you see me?'

'Sure.'

'And you're still asking?'

'Hey, you strapped on a guitar, you went out there and tried.'

'And I failed.'

'So you just quit?'

'Rachel—'

'It takes practice, that's all.'

'What, in half an hour?'

'Well,' she smiled. 'Maybe a little belief as well.'

'And there's *none* of that around here either.'

She held both his hands and her gaze drilled into him. 'Have you had *any* singing training?'

'No.'

'Well, I have.'

'You—'

'Shut up and follow me. Do, re, mi.'

*

Johnny joined the band on the smaller stage. He looked around and unconsciously hunched his shoulders inwards.

'Less room to move around,' growled Andy. 'But only if you can sing.'

'What—'

227

'If you go out there like last time, we're screwed.'

'Have we got a choice?' asked Johnny. 'Any singer is better than none.'

'And they know you're coming,' said Vince. 'Cold Steel's new singer is all over the social media.' He threw his phone to Johnny.

'Oh shit.' Johnny scrolled through a viral stream of fan comments on the band's website. 'Useless fucking bastard' were the kindest words that described him. 'Where the fuck is he?' said Johnny.

'Who, man?' asked Joe.

'Maxwell, you stupid bastard. Who do you bloody think?'

'It wasn't his fault he got taken.'

'Not that again,' snapped Johnny. 'Not now.'

'I had a feeling about the place, man,' Joe murmured.

'A feeling that couldn't have waited until daylight?'

Joe stared at the stage floor and shuffled his rope-sandaled feet and fiddled with his eye patch. 'Is that why you hit me with your guitar?'

'No,' said Andy. 'He hit you because he's a tosser.'

'A tosser who's only doing all this to help the band.' Johnny jabbed a look at Andy. 'Unlike some around here.'

'What do you mean?' Andy stomped towards Johnny.

'You want me to spell it out?'

'It's that or I'll beat it out of you.'

'Sure you will,' laughed Johnny. 'And then you'll just quit the band.'

'What?' said Vince.

'Angie Dale's big story,' sneered Johnny. 'Her idea, her creation.'

'Is that what all that shit with you and her is about?' asked Mike.

Stonewall silence from Andy.

'Is it true, man?' asked Joe.

'I'm still here, aren't I?' Andy spread his arms wide.

'For how long?' grimaced Johnny.

'Don't push me, you bastard,' hissed Andy.

'Or what?' said Johnny.

'Keep it up, you wanker.' Andy's fists bunched into hammers.

'Look, guys,' said Joe. 'This isn't where we need to be. We've got a gig in ten minutes.'

Andy and Johnny glared at each other.

'That's right,' snapped Johnny.

'And ten minutes after that we'll be slanged off stage without Maxwell,' said Vince.

'You'll be fine,' Rachel appeared from behind them and Johnny jumped and spun round. 'Just remember what I told you.' She smiled encouragement at him.

'What about it, lads?' Johnny faced the band and forced himself to stop trembling. 'You going to quit because we had a bad run? Is that all Cold Steel means to you?' He looked at Andy. 'Is that all any of you lot mean to each other?'

*

The band gaggled behind the backline and Johnny looked at Rachel. 'What's the net showing?'

'You really want to know?' She arched her eyebrows and passed him her phone.

'Cold Steel fan writes, "Who's the bald wanker in Maxwell's place?"' He grinned. 'I guess I can't do any worse this time round.' He passed the phone to Vince.

'Laugh it up,' grimaced Vince. 'This one says *you* should have been twatted onstage, not Joe.'

Johnny heard the jeers and whistles from the fan club soaking through the backline. A sense of imminent failure sent quickfrost through his bones. His resolve skimmed the dark chasm of retreat. He looked at Rachel. She smiled and nodded.

'You can do it,' she said.

'Fuck it,' said Johnny. 'What's the worse that can happen?' He picked up the spare guitar, looked over at Rachel and grinned like a hash-fuelled Flashman. It was false and he knew it. They were going to get slaughtered by their most loyal fans, who would then spread the misery online within minutes.

He cleared the backline and saw the audience for microseconds before the houselights blinked out. He felt the fear, and an overwhelming sense of unreality. He strode towards the waiting mic stand held in a single cone of light, stopped in front of it and took a deep breath.

'We are Cold Steel!'

Except the deep voice that shot through the sound system wasn't his. He looked at the band, then stage left, and as he did so, a shock blow to his right shoulder spun him round the other way.

'And this is Sinners Sanctuary.'

Mud-stained, unshaven, and sprinkled with an array of cuts and bruises, Maxwell grinned like he was about to sleep with a princess and swaggered to stage front, holding a spare mic. He grabbed Johnny's wrist and dragged him along like a schoolboy being taken to detention. He stopped just in front of the monitors and threw Johnny's hand skyward.

'Say hello to Johnny Faslane,' roared Maxwell. 'And he's not singing no more.' He spun Johnny round and propelled him offstage with a kick up the arse. Only too happy to be going, Johnny scuttled offstage like a retreating imp.

The concert, suddenly re-energised, surged outwards. Maxwell's voice wailed and soared around the hangar. He strode around the small stage with a fluidity that spoke of having been tucked up in bed all night with nothing to enrich his dreams but his performance the next day.

The band shifted into Power Games. The stage effects came alive, and unlike all previous tours, it wasn't one pirate ship that dominated the backline, but two. Both moved as though real, and both fired what looked like real cannon at each other. Gunpowder explosions punctuated the music and reverberated around the hangar. Smoke and flames gouted from the living ships, and as yet unseen crew members were flung into the air by invisible cannon balls that ripped through their wooden adversaries.

The band finally blended the new songs with the old. Halfway through the set, Maxwell added a rasping, gravely tone for La Casa del Dolor, a gritty acoustic song that matched the suddenly stark lighting. As its final chords shimmered around the hangar, the entire road crew surged onto the stage from both sides, dressed as either pirates or redcoats, and a massive, roughly choreographed fight took place.

Vince and Andy scythed through the opening riff-storm of Close Quarters. Fake bayonets and cutlass blades flashed, imitation blood spurted across the stage and spattered the band. Some of the road crew staged writhing deaths, some became walking wounded and dragged their same-side comrades away. Soon the band had the stage to themselves again. The ships shuddered apart to the sound of splintering wood fed through the speakers and camera booms floated around the stage.

Maxwell's sudden reappearance electrified the band like a devasectomised tomcat being turned out for the night. A full set, three encores, and the first concert had been cleansed from the fans' memories. They were ushered out of the hangar, and the band walked off the already being cleared stage. 'Where the fuck have you been?' asked Johnny.

'Not happy to see me?' Face-splitting smile from Maxwell. '"We are Cold Steel", eh? I kinda like it.'

'Just answer the fucking question.'

'Some mad bastard knocked me out and kidnapped me.'

'Some mad bastard called Shot Away?'

'Were you watching?'

'We pieced it together with a little help.' Shock vibrations juddered up Johnny's leg. He fished his phone out from a sweaty pocket and picked up.

'Johnny Faslane.'

'You picked the *wrong* time to go awol, mister.'

Chapter 34

'Lucy, we've—'

'I don't care what you've been doing. Your band's album is due for release today, and that means *you* stay available. Especially when Cold Steel, always Cold Steel, *only* Cold Steel, give us a completely different album to the one we were expecting.'

'Worth waiting for, though?' Johnny asked the only question that was important.

'Don't piss with me, Faslane. You know we've got more than just the music to consider.'

'Sure,' snapped Johnny. 'We can't let business get in the way of the music, can we?'

'Advice, Johnny. Leave the attitude with the band, because we've still got time to reverse our decision.'

Hope exploded in Johnny's guts.

'We're going with the remix,' she said.

'Christ,' he breathed.

'I would have told you three hours ago if you'd had your phone switched on.'

'Sorry, Lucy, it won't happen again.' Johnny paused. 'Twenty won't like it, knowing we shafted them on this.'

'*They* won't like it?' steamed Lucy. '*I* don't like it. Randall doesn't like it. Ozone don't like it, full stop, and you can bet your arse that Archimedes and Kurgan won't like it. In fact, no one likes this, apart from you and the band.'

'Do you want me to feel sorry about that?' asked Johnny. '*We* aren't the ones who did anything wrong. We *told* you that Twenty wasn't the place for Cold Steel. Jesus, even the band realised the place was wrong for them, and that's saying something.'

'No one's apologising, Johnny. Not us, not you.'

'*I* don't need to fucking apologise.'

'So get over it and move on. You did a good job with this remix and you got what you wanted. We've gone along with you this time, even if we didn't want to.'

'So why did you?'

'It's a big bad world out there, Johnny. We've got to think of our wedge, long term. So you're welcome.'

'*What?*'

'It'll be Ozone, not you, who has to deal with an unhappy recording studio, *and* all the artists that we'll have to send somewhere else. All thanks to a toxic relationship with Twenty, a studio which *everyone* knows is the best.'

'Maybe next time you'll listen to us.'

'Don't poke a tiger when it's pissed, Johnny. Just creep away and be glad you're still alive.'

'Is that a threat?'

'Friendly advice.'

'Christ,' said Johnny. 'What are you like when you're hostile?'

'You want to find out?'

'Shit, no.'

'Good,' said Lucy. 'So give your boys the news, then get on with the rehearsals. No more jerking around, either. And make absolutely sure Vince and Andy get the message. We want a focus on the music, nothing else, understand?'

*

'Was that about the album?' asked Maxwell.

'What do you think?' Johnny leaned against the Marshall stacks and the band crowded around him.

'So what's happening, man?' asked Joe.

'Cold Steel's next album,' said Johnny. 'Rock in a Hard Place.'

'We know what it's called,' said Maxwell.

'Recorded at Twenty Studios,' deadpanned Johnny.

'If only,' muttered Andy.

'Recorded at Twenty, produced by Hickey.' Johnny smiled. 'That's what it'll say.'

Hickey's mouth dropped open and a chunk of half-chewed burger fell to the floor. 'Holy crap,' he gaped.

'Get used to gourmet burgers from now on,' grinned Johnny. 'You're on producer's royalties.'

The band stared numbly at Hickey and awkward silence grated around the hanger.

'Thank you, Hickey,' Johnny glared at the band.

'Yeah, sure,' stammered Maxwell. 'Thanks, mate.'

Muttered gratitude from the rest of the band was enough for Hickey to smile as though he'd been given his own burger palace.

'So what about Shot Away?' asked Maxwell.

'What about him?' said Johnny. 'You were the last one to see him.'

'That turbine blade knocked him out cold.'

'Leave it to the police,' said Johnny. 'They'll find him soon enough. I don't want anyone going out there again.' He fixed Joe with a sawn-off stare. '*Anyone.*'

'You said it, man.'

Chapter 35

Excitement crackled around C Hangar and replaced rehearsal-fatigue. The stages were stowed in trucks that would take the Cold Steel tour around the world. Sawyer hadn't been seen since Maxwell's escape two weeks before, and the police hadn't found him. An endless sky stretched over Honham's infinite flat landscape, and Johnny looked on with tight-lipped satisfaction at the trucks. 'Ready to go?' he asked.

'We'll be off on time.' Wolf, the lead driver, looked down at Johnny. At six feet nine, Johnny thought he'd probably look down on everyone. Jeans and a Cold Steel tour t-shirt did nothing to hide his cage-fighter physique, and his growling voice howled frozen hostility direct from the Russian steppes.

'Locked?' asked Johnny.

'All the way,' growled Wolf. 'But there won't be any illegals going that way. They always head for the cold countries.' He shrugged. 'Go figure.'

*

Sawyer lay underneath the hedgerows close to the hangar. He'd been there all night, watching the convoy evolve, his faded camouflage blending him in with the gloomed undergrowth. Motionless beneath the empty sky, he watched people, vehicles, buildings. He wondered how something he'd known all those years ago could be both the same and completely different to the way he'd remembered it.

After he'd woken up in the wind farm, his head throbbing from the glancing blow he'd taken from the turbine blade, he realised it was time to move on. The bunker was blown, and police were all over the place looking for the damned longhair. Since then, Sawyer had been sleeping outside, scavenging waste food from bins and wondering what to do next. The thought of going back to his gym left him cold. Training up the band had been the first regular work he'd had for years, and once he'd got over their stupid looks, he realised that he actually liked them. *So go back,* he thought, then shook his head. *They'd never accept me after this.*

What next? Sawyer didn't know. He had nothing but the clothes he wore and what was stuffed in his pockets. He glanced at the truck drivers, slowly walking around their wagons, checking the sealed doors, kicking tyres, testing lights. Heading up and down the long line was the biggest convoy boss Sawyer had ever seen. He walked with easy confidence, spoke to his team in a relaxed manner, laughed with them and put them at ease. *A good leader,* thought Sawyer.

With the trucks checked, the crew moved inside the hangar and Sawyer sensed his chance. Half-remembered details from urban warfare, blind spots when approaching vehicles sludged through his mind. Would he need to know that here? *Unlikely,* he thought, *this is a civvy setup.* He scuttled towards the nearest truck at an oblique angle, ducked underneath the wheels and sat on the massive axle. He wasted no time, dug into his pocket and pulled out the fast straps. He secured himself to the axle, pulled against the straps in all directions and squirmed around to get as comfortable as the lump of metal he was sitting on would allow. Twenty minutes later, he saw feet approaching the cab, then heard the engine start up. Powerful vibrations hammered through Sawyer's entire skeleton and the truck jerked forward. He was out of Honham, undetected, but he had no idea where he was going.

*

Johnny pocketed his phone and looked along the row of loaded tour trucks; each one was screen-printed with a huge picture of a band member followed by the slogan 'Cold Steel Rocks the World'. He looked out to the wind farm, just about seeing the raised area at the centre. Was it his imagination or did he see tiny figures moving over it? He looked to the grass verge near the perimeter track, and a clump of neatly pruned hedges around what once would have been some essential airbase outhouse, now just a hollowed brick shed. Was there something, someone, moving under the hedge? He blinked and looked again. Nothing.

'Christ on a bike,' he muttered. 'This place.'

Inside the empty hangar, a lone people carrier waited to take the band to a small private airfield.

'So what about this clockwork plane that's taking us to Spain?' asked Andy.

'It's low key till we get there,' said Johnny. 'We break cover and do publicity just before the first gig. No hassles, and we keep control.'

'You're sure about that?' asked Vince.

Johnny smiled. 'It's secure all the way. What could go wrong?'

Chapter 36

'Don't you want to come with us?' asked Johnny. 'Always room for one more if we sit real close.'

Rachel looked at the single-prop PC-12 and shook her head. 'We're not even supposed to be at the same airport together, remember?'

'You call this an airport?' Johnny looked around the potholed runway next to a single-building terminal. 'Makes St Clements look like JFK.'

She grinned. 'There's a bit more leg room with an airliner. Besides, there's no danger of *me* being papped at the airport.'

'No,' he smiled. 'Your lot looks after their own.'

She kissed him and gently ran her fingernails along the back of his neck. 'I'll see you there,' she whispered. 'Don't get lost on the way.'

'As if.'

He climbed the rickety metal steps and the tiny passenger cabin pressed down on him.

'So much for first class,' grumbled Maxwell.

'What are you moaning about?' asked Johnny. 'It's clean, it's comfortable, it's only three hours.'

'The hotel had better be good at the other end.'

'Depends on you lot.' Johnny looked out of the small window and waved at Rachel. 'Focus on the tour.' He turned back to Maxwell. 'Stay out of trouble and you'll get decent cribs. Fuck around and it's B and B's and campsites. Your choice, lads.'

*

'Johnny, Johnny, wake up.'

Johnny's dream of umpiring at Centre Court, watching Rachel play a forehand smash evaporated, replaced by Maxwell breathing beer fumes in his face. He looked around the small cabin with bleary eyes. Outside, the plane's single engine droned on unchanged. They seemed to be flying level, no hijackers in sight and no smell of burning. 'What's the problem?' he asked.

'We've changed direction, we're landing.'

'Oh, for Christ's sake, Maxwell. That's what planes do at the end of the flight. Did you wake me up just for that?'

'But we've turned around, *right* around. And take a look out there.' He stabbed the window with a trembling finger. 'No town, no airport.'

Expecting to see Heyende's sleepy urban cling-hold around La Bidassoa as they approached San Sebastian airport, all Johnny saw were hills and pine forests. The plane was scarily close to the treetops: *too* close for his liking. 'I'll have a word with the pilot,' he said.

'We've tried,' sweated Maxwell. 'The door's locked and they're not answering.'

'It can't be anything serious,' said Johnny. 'This is probably how they land at this airport.'

'You sure about that?'

'Well, Christ, Maxwell, what else could be going on?'

'You tell me, mate, but I'll be a lot happier when we see the hotel.'

Johnny stood up and moved towards the pilot's door. At the same moment, the plane banked hard left and nosed down. Johnny fell forward and carpet burned his nose.

'I suppose that's normal as well, is it?' Maxwell had landed on top of Johnny.

'No, it's not,' replied Johnny. 'And I'm loving the foreplay.' He shoved Maxwell, who struggled back into his seat. The plane's propeller pitch changed and the sudden drop in altitude sucked at Johnny's insides. He looked out of his window; pine trees zipped past his view in a green blur, followed by a bump and bounce on what felt like a rough airstrip.

'Fucking hell,' juddered Vince. 'What are they like at customs?'

'I don't know,' croaked Andy. 'But I'm about to declare my breakfast.'

The plane shuddered to a stop and Johnny's nerves jangled around his dodgemed body. By the time he'd stood up and taken a few shaky steps towards the small cabin door, there came a clang of steps being fitted to the fuselage. The door was pulled open from the outside and a large man squeezed inside, clad in faded black jeans and a scuffed leather parka. Cropped black hair and stubble matched his clothing.

'Is this the airport?' asked Johnny, realising how stupid he sounded.

'Outside.' Leather Jacket spat the word with a Lithuanian inflection.

'What, you mean the airport's outside?'

Leather Jacket's long steps ate up the cabin space and he grabbed the front of Johnny's t-shirt. He reached behind him and an oil-shined kukri flashed through the air, coming to a wallstrike halt on the skin around Johnny's jugular. He skimmed Johnny's pockets and pulled out his phone, then gripped his shoulder and threw him out of the plane.

Johnny bypassed the small tubular steps and thudded onto the uneven airstrip. He sprawled in the dust for a few seconds before struggling to his knees, his leather pants collecting new stains.

'Get up, *gaidzio pautai*.' A twin to Leather Jacket grabbed Johnny's t-shirt and yanked him to his feet.

'Fucking hell,' he muttered. 'Can't you at least insult me in English?'

The man grunted and cuffed Johnny's head, turning what was left of his hair into a ponytailed comb-over. He saw the band being chucked out of the plane in a similar fashion to himself, finally followed by the pilot and crewman, who walked down the stairs and looked at Johnny. He saw their unspoken guilt. *Bastards,* he thought.

'Come on.' Kukri and his partner marched Johnny and the band off the airstrip, beneath the trees and into a roughly hewn log cabin. Inside, two more leather-jacket clones growled a hostile welcome, and they were shoved onto a hard wooden bench.

'Is this what you meant by low key?' asked Maxwell.

'This is *not* what I had planned,' whispered Johnny.

'That's good. I thought you'd ordered this treatment.'

'And now that you know that it's nothing to do with me,' said Johnny, 'maybe we can worry about who these bastards are and what they want.'

The cabin door crashed open and a middle-aged man in a black suit and white shirt walked in. Black cowboy boots sounded heavily on the rough wooden floor. Midnight hair striped with grey slicked back over a ravaged, wrinkled forehead, and dark, humourless eyes scanned the cabin's interior, missing nothing. A molasses moustache drooped down both sides of a thin, bloodless upper lip, while a gold cross on a chain dangled in front of his tie. Hostility emanated from him like a wall of iceberg hypothermia.

'So, you are Cold Steel.' A thick, rasping voice with a Spanish accent shot out the statement.

'Who are you?' asked Johnny.

'I ask the questions around here, my friend.'

'Perhaps,' said Johnny. 'But you won't get any answers until we get some. We give, you give. It's the only way.'

A humourless laugh sent arctic waves of fear over Johnny. 'I wonder if you are brave, or just stupid.'

'Both.' Johnny forced himself to meet the other man's stare and not waver.

A stonewall laugh and the man spoke again. 'Maybe I should employ you. You've got bigger balls than most of my boys. But to your question. I am Julio Ramirez.'

Johnny kept quiet but he felt himself twitch at the name.

'You've heard of me,' he said.

'Perhaps,' brazened Johnny.

'You lie. You give everything away with your movement. You don't have to say a word.'

'Good job I wasn't thinking anything.'

'You'd tell me soon enough, my friend. Here, I control everything, I know everything.'

'Control of what?' Johnny probed. 'A log cabin in the woods? Big fucking deal.'

'And do you know where these woods are? Do you know where these woods *really* are?'

Johnny shrugged. 'North Spain somewhere, maybe Southern France.'

'Maybe indeed,' chuckled Ramirez. 'This is Basque country. Spain and France both claim part of it, but neither really controls it. It is ruled by the Basques, who are neither French nor Spanish, but have enough blood of both nations in their veins to make all three sides fight hard for this land.'

241

'And that's got fuck all to do with us.'

'If you're expecting a rescue, it has everything to do with you.'

'What do you mean?'

Ramirez smiled. 'Up here, neither the French nor the Spanish will come looking for you, no matter how famous you are.'

'And I suppose you're immune from all that?' asked Johnny.

'If you do the Basques a favour,' shrugged Ramirez, 'they do you a favour. It is good business.'

'So, what?' asked Johnny. 'You want Ozone to pay a ransom for us?'

'You think they'd pay?'

'No.'

'No?'

'It's the music business,' scoffed Johnny. 'Even more corrupt than you, mate.'

'Then *you* need to pay.'

'What the fuck for?'

'To get to your concert on time. One million pounds, or you won't show up.'

'A million quid?' spluttered Johnny.

'Would you rather pay in Euros?'

'You can fuck off in any currency,' said Johnny. 'And what if we don't pay? What are you going to do? Kill us?'

'Careful, mate,' whispered Maxwell.

'Your solution is worth considering,' chuckled Ramirez. 'But to be honest, I don't need to. I've got something more important to you than your lives.'

'Really?' sneered Johnny. 'What's that?'

Ramirez shrugged and held out his hands. 'You,' he said. 'Cold Steel, the band. You live for your music, for performing. But we all know that you need to arrive on time for your concert if you want the music to continue. One million pounds allows that to happen.'

'And if we don't pay?' asked Johnny.

'Then you stay here until Ozone Records disown you and keep you from making music ever again.'

'That won't—'

'It will happen,' snapped Ramirez. 'You, Johnny Faslane, the highly regarded manager, you of all people cannot possibly be that ignorant of the facts. Cold Steel might be a famous band, but you have run out of chances with your record company. How long will they put up with you not turning up for your concerts?'

'So we pay you and that's it?' asked Johnny.

'No,' said Ramirez. 'You pay me. I let you go. And then you keep on paying.'

'Bollocks,' said Johnny. 'Why should we do that?'

'Because you owe me.'

'We *owe* you?'

Ramirez rubbed his chin thoughtfully. 'Is it so difficult to understand? You interfere with two of my organisations. You caused me to close down my product pipeline, my balloon imports and exports. Then you take Angel Face from me as well.'

'We didn't—'

'That's not what Angie Dale told me.'

'Well, she's full of shit. She—'

'She told me the truth about you. About the radio station.'

Fear tremored through Johnny's insides and he fought hard to appear calm. 'What? Another record company takes over a singer and that's our fault? And you're just going to keep us here?'

'That is all I need to do,' smiled Ramirez.

Johnny's confidence imploded like a burning airship. He realised how easily Ramirez had read the band's dilemma. Not turning up for a concert, even just one, and the band would be dropped, then gagged with a mass of legal agreements that not even a brigade of the sharpest lawyers would be able to cut through.

'Your time will be over,' said Ramirez. 'And I will have had my revenge.'

'It won't be that simple,' said Johnny. 'Do you think we'll keep quiet about this? You think Ozone won't listen to us?'

'Always brave when it is just you in danger.'

'What do you mean?' asked Johnny.

Ice-pick smile. 'Spare a thought for your road crew.'

'Yeah?' blustered Johnny. 'Where are they then?'

'They will be here soon. If you value their freedom, and *their* safety, you will agree to my terms.' Ramirez nodded slightly, barely visibly. His four men silently filed out of the cabin. 'If you leave this cabin's immediate vicinity you will be dragged back.'

'And if we leave the compound?' asked Johnny.

'You mean if you *try* to leave the compound.'

'We've done that before,' smiled Johnny. 'Escaped from an Ancadian base with half their navy after us.'

'That was there, this is here.'

'So it's a challenge,' shrugged Johnny. 'Works for us.'

'Then feel free to walk past the perimeter any time you choose. These forests are home to the separatists, and if they don't recognise you, they'll shoot you on sight. You'd live maybe twenty minutes at most. Last year three of my men strayed beyond the fence. They were never seen again.'

Chapter 37

Wolf crunched through the gears and coaxed the loaded truck up into the desolate saddle of mountains that separated France from Spain. Narrow windy roads and steep gradients tested the skills of his team far more than the free-flowing motorways. He reached for the radio handset and looked at the dense pine forest that hedged the road on both sides.

'Close up,' he growled. 'Convoy rules from here.'

A squawk of static and the nasal tones of the tail-end driver flooded Wolf's cab. 'What's the problem now, granddad? It's not like we're driving through the Congo.'

'Snotty, keep your idiot opinions to yourself,' snarled Wolf. 'I'm paid to get this cargo safe to each venue.'

'You're an old woman, Wolf. There's nothing to worry about up here but the trees. I thought old timers like you talked to them.'

'I'll remember you said that when we're on the way down. I've lost more wagons and drivers up here than I did in the Balkans.'

'Oh, Christ. Not *another* bloody war story.'

'Stop moaning, Snotty, do as you're bloody told, and no stops until we get to the next town.'

'Nothing up here to turn off for anyway.'

Wolf wheeled his truck round a vicious right-hand bend and stamped on the brakes with a curse. Three tree trunks stretched across both lanes of the carriageway. Tyres screeched, the anti lock failed, and the truck slowly skidded to a halt. The front light stacks gently kissed the remaining branches left on the trunk. He grabbed the handset.

'Tree trunk across the road. It's a hijack, turn around and get out.'

Wolf yanked the gear lever and pulled hard on the wheel, coaxing his rig through the complex manoeuvre of turning his truck around on the carriageway. He sweated under the chill mountain sunshine, concentrated on his truck. He didn't see the swaying pine branches, the dust clouds kicked up on both verges, didn't hear the running footsteps approaching the cab. He only looked around when he heard both doors being wrenched open and saw black-clad men pointing pistols at him.

'Take it out of gear, out of gear.' Orders were barked at Wolf. Keeping his breathing calm, he slowly slid the rig into neutral, moved over, and allowed the truck to be taken.

*

Johnny yawned and stumbled out of the poorly fitting door towards the open ditch at the back of the cabin, which served as a communal toilet. He sent a golden fluid-arc into the ditch, and the urine steam-cloud drifted upwards into the crisp pre-dawn air. Ramirez had left the compound hours earlier, presumably to let the band reflect on their helplessness, and Johnny knew that sooner or later Ramirez would win.

A low roar drifted through the pine-forested darkness, the trees slowly coming into visibility. Johnny zipped up and walked to the front of the cabin. He stood at the open area of the landing strip and roughly levelled track that led to the fenced perimeter. The noise increased and his spirits plummeted as he recognised the sound of diesel engines.

Headlight beams pierced the forest darkness, approaching the compound. The wood and barbed-wire gate was dragged back and the first of the five tour trucks barked their arrival with crunching gears and undipped lights.

'Oh, shit,' whispered Johnny. 'Looks like we're onto plan B.'

Chapter 38

'So what else did you see?' asked Maxwell.

'Just what I told you,' said Johnny. 'The tour trucks coming into the compound, then I was shoved back in here.' He turned to face Maxwell, and wrinkled his nose. 'What's that smell?'

'What smell?' Maxwell rolled his eyes. 'Oh, that. Christ, Johnny, is this really the time to be playing who smelled it dealt it?'

A sudden scratching underneath the cabin's rough planking erased Johnny's reply. He looked at the floor and saw one of the roughly nailed planks start to push upwards, accompanied by grunts of exertion and a pervading smell of rank sewage.

'Jesus,' said Mike. 'Has the shit ditch overflowed or something?'

Johnny stared at the creaking, straining plank. 'That's more than a Mister Whippy coming through the floorboards.'

'Do you think it's Ramirez?' asked Joe.

'He comes in by the front door,' said Johnny.

The planks creaked and buckled. A dirty, brown-stained set of fingers appeared around the wooden edge and pushed at the planking. Rusty nails spat out from the woodwork and the floor plank flew upwards. Splinters pinged around the cabin. Johnny ducked and turned away. He looked back and saw a newly created hole in the cabin's floor where the planks once were, and out of it climbed a man in a filthy camouflage uniform, smelling as though he'd crawled through every slurry pit in Europe. 'What the fuck?' Johnny gasped. 'Jesus, mate, who the hell are you?'

The man stood up and the band shrank away from the stench that came off him in solid, nauseating waves. 'Don't you recognise me?' He looked at Maxwell.

'I recognise the smell,' choked Vince.

'Oh, shit,' said Maxwell. 'It's Shot Away.' He looked at the effluent effigy with wide eyes. Beads of sweat appeared on his forehead. 'What the fuck are you doing here?'

'Never mind that?' gasped Johnny. 'Honham's bloody hundreds of miles away. *How* the fuck did he get here?'

'Why don't you ask me?' asked Sawyer.

'Holy crap,' breathed Johnny.

'Spanish crap, I'd say,' grinned Sawyer.

'Jesus H Christ,' spluttered Johnny. 'How, *why* did you get here? Fuck me, but you look like you crawled through every shit-stream in the planet.' His mind snapped back to the march he'd led the band on through a sewer pipe just a few months earlier. 'And if you did, I know what that's like.'

'Start with the why,' said Sawyer. 'I guess I couldn't keep the bunker secure, no matter what I tried.'

'Why'd you fucking bother in the first place?' asked Maxwell.

'You don't understand, mate.'

'It's a bit difficult to see it your way when you're hanging upside down like a chicken on the bloody slaughter line.'

'Whatever,' shrugged Sawyer. 'The place was blown, *I* was blown.'

'But why do all that in the first place?' asked Johnny. 'You had your gig with us. Training Cold Steel, keeping them fit.'

'After I'd cut loose and taken your singer down? Not sure I'd have been welcomed back with a big wet kiss.'

'He's got a point.' Andy jerked his head towards the door. 'Why don't you jog on that way?'

'Hang on,' said Johnny.

'No,' snapped Andy. 'We've got enough problems without having this mad bastard along for the ride.'

'We need all the help we can get.'

'What, from a shit-smelling psycho? You think he can help us?'

'Maybe he's here for a reason.' Johnny looked at Sawyer and raised his eyebrows. 'He did pretty well to get in here without being seen.'

'I don't fucking believe this,' groaned Andy.

'Let's hear the guy out,' said Johnny. 'We've got nothing to lose.' He nodded at Sawyer. 'Over to you, mate.'

'Yeah, man,' said Joe. 'Like, how come you came here when you're not down with us anymore?'

'I didn't know where you were going,' said Sawyer. 'I just hitched a ride under one of your trucks.'

'You did what?' gasped Johnny. 'All the way here under the trucks? Are you mad?'

'I'm completely shot away, mate, like the name says. I just wanted a way out, but every time those damn rigs stopped, there were people everywhere. I'd have been dropped and shopped before I got clear. No choice but to hang on and wait for the chance. Even on the ferry, everything was wired tight. I couldn't go anywhere.'

'So you climbed out from under the truck, hid in the shit ditch, then broke in here?' asked Johnny.

'That's the story so far.'

'Well, you might have got clear of Honham, but you're as stuck here as we are.' Johnny jerked his head towards the perimeter. 'Why didn't you head into the woods?'

'Because I'm only one.' Sawyer looked around at the band. 'Maybe we should work together on this.'

'You're a lone wolf,' said Johnny: a statement, not a question.

Sawyer stared at the ground before meeting Johnny's gaze. 'I didn't used to be,' he whispered.

'And now?' asked Johnny.

'I'm looking for a new home.' Sawyer looked around the cabin and nodded. 'This place'll do.'

'What the fuck,' said Johnny. 'You want to *live* here?'

'Ideas but no plans,' murmured Vince.

'Shut it,' snapped Johnny. 'He's on our side.'

'Yeah,' replied Vince. 'For now.'

'He owes us,' said Johnny. 'Right, mate?'

'I *owe* you?' said Sawyer.

'Sure you do. We gave you a free ride clear of Honham, and a new place to live.'

'And how is this nutcase going to help us?' sneered Andy.

'I say we take our chances while Ramirez isn't here,' said Johnny.

'You mean take our chances against the bloody gurkha knives?' asked Andy.

'As long as the guns stay on the other side of the wire,' said Johnny, 'we've got a chance.' He turned to Sawyer. 'We're going to need you to lead as many of the camp guards as you can out into the forest. Can you do it?'

'Easy enough,' said Sawyer. 'Can *you* do it? I've been trying to get you lot to work as a team since day one. I never managed it.'

'Not this again,' moaned Andy.

'This again,' said Sawyer. 'It's the real deal out there, and if you lads don't pull together as one, no one's going to help you.' He nodded at Johnny. 'What happens after I pull the heat away?'

'We find out where they've stashed our phones,' said Johnny. 'Call for help and hope to Christ it arrives before we get diced. There can't be more than a dozen of them anyway.' Sceptical looks speared his plan. 'Jesus, boys, haven't we just had a shit load of training from this guy right here when it comes to self-defence?'

'What about the crew?' asked Maxwell. 'They're here as well.'

'If we can break them out, even better. We'll definitely outnumber the bastards then. The main thing is to let someone, anyone know we're here, and get some serious help coming our way.'

'If we can get the crew,' said Mike, 'why don't we just fuck off?'

'Too dicey,' said Johnny. 'They control the forests, they've almost definitely got the roads sewn up as well, right?' Sawyer nodded in agreement.

'I suppose *somebody's* realised we're missing, man,' said Joe.

Johnny looked at Sawyer. 'How much time do you need?'

'Give me ten minutes and you'll start hearing some results.'

'Right.' Johnny peered out of the window. 'That cabin over there is the nearest. When the diversion starts, we rush the place, do over anyone inside and look for our phones. We'll go from shack to shack until we find them.'

Chapter 39

Rachel breezed through passport control at Bilbao airport's angular white concrete and glass terminal, nicknamed 'the dove'. She realised Johnny had a point. Cold Steel would never have made the transition through a commercial hub so easily. With a covert, insider's glance around the large, airy building, she spotted a dozen reporters without even trying.

She looked at her watch. Although the Airbus that had noiselessly whisked her to Spain had glided through the air much more quickly than that single-engine matchbox she'd seen Johnny and the band off in, they hadn't had to wrestle their way through check-in, passport control, customs, and the crowds, which, at Bilbao, had been thankfully less than Heathrow. If everything went to plan, they'd have landed and be at the hotel. She cleared customs and found herself almost immediately outside, a peculiarity of Bilbao's airport. She almost missed the usual straitjacket of shops and taxi drivers that were like a rite of passage to the international traveller.

She pulled her phone from her handbag and checked the screen, expecting a text from Johnny, or maybe a missed call. Nothing. An email? Still nothing. She stepped into a taxi and headed for the Novotel at the Exhibition Centre, then scrolled for San Sebastian airport and clicked.

'Aeropuerto de San Sebastian, *Hola.*'

'Did flight AAL one four arrive on time from England?' asked Rachel.

'No, *Senora,*' came the reply Rachel didn't want to hear. Her insides tightened and slow lead slurried into her veins.

'Was there a problem?'

'No, the pilot radioed to say there had been a change of flight plan.'

'Did they say where they were rerouting to?'

'No, *Senora.*'

'Was there a problem with the plane?'

'No, *Senora.*'

'Would they have said there was? Would you tell *me* if there was?'

'Of course. We have a policy of total transparency. We would have told you.'

'Do planes often reroute?'

'It is not common but it happens. We have safeguards within our voice procedures to rule out hijackings. The pilot used correct wording and the aircraft did not behave in any way to alert us to trouble.' A pause. 'Sometimes the passengers request an alternative landing location. That is the most usual reason.'

'Why would they do that?'

'I just work here, *Senora,* but some of the clients, they are rich. For them, to control where the plane lands, to change things to their desires, it is how they live. Perhaps the passengers on this flight are the same. no?'

'Perhaps.' Rachel hung up. Why would the band reroute? Why would Johnny let them? He wouldn't. 'Something's wrong,' she muttered.

The taxi drove along Ribera la Hiribidea, turned left onto Rio Castanos Kalea and slowed down outside the Novotel's sweeping forecourt. Rachel paid the driver, opened the boot herself and wheeled her case inside. Her high heels tapping on the smooth stone tiles, she stepped towards the clean lined laminate reception desk and gave her name. 'Has the Faslane group arrived yet?'

*

'They've fucking what?' Randall roared tantalum into Rachel's phone.

'I think they've disappeared,' replied Rachel.

'Then they're through,' snapped Randall. 'They redlined their asses like this the last time their tour hit Europe. If they don't learn, they don't earn. And after all that shit with their album, they've used their last chance.'

'It might not be their fault.'

'It's *always* their goddam fault.'

'That's not fair, Randall. Everything that happened at Twenty was between the studio and Ozone.'

'Kiss their asses, why don't you? But you wouldn't be so goddam sure of them if you had *my* stomach ulcers. I've spent a

252

lifetime covering for those bastards twenty-four seven, and it's time the assholes knew who the real boss was.'

'It's not just the band,' said Rachel. 'I can't get hold of Johnny either.'

'Then he's either in with them or he can't bring them to book. Either way, he's screwed his ace and he's grass.'

'You obviously don't know Johnny if that's what you think.'

'And why should I believe you?'

'Because the crew haven't shown up, either, and that's too much of a coincidence. Maybe the band *would* just take off, but not Johnny, the crew, *and* the trucks as well.'

'So you've been thinking about this. Tell me what's on your mind, and what the frig do you want from me?'

'Someone's taken the whole Cold Steel machine off the radar. Who hates Cold Steel enough to want to do this to them?'

'Jesus Christ,' laughed Randall. 'Who *doesn't*? I could spend all freaking night answering that one.'

'Whoever it is, they'll be talking to you about it.'

'Why me?'

'Because if Cold Steel don't show up for their tour, it won't just hurt the band, it'll hurt Ozone.'

'Ransom *and* blackmail?'

'A lot more plausible than the entire touring machine going off the grid just because the band want to screw around.'

'So we just sit on our asses while whoever you think might have dreamed this up gives me a call? And then when they do, I just bend over and take it up the madison to get Cold Steel back?'

'If we have to.'

'Jeez, lady, I hope you've got an alternative solution. I'm not about to surrender my starfish to a bunch of goddam family players at my stage of life.'

Chapter 40

Sawyer squeezed through the hole he'd made in the cabin floor. He snaked along the underside of the rough wooden building, held his breath and scooped through the latrine ditch. Some things never changed. Good camp practice always had the stench trench at the extreme edge, and human nature kept everyone as far away from it as possible.

Which was just what he needed.

Once he'd found the open-air thunder box, he'd found a way into the forest. But what to do when he got there? He had to play it right: this camp was like a present from the Gods, but only if he could empty the place.

Another reason to thank those longhairs. They weren't the bunch of pussies he'd taken them for when they first turned up at his gym. Weird, yes; wimps, no. And that balding, straggly-haired manager of theirs, he was weirder and ballsier than all of them put together. If only they'd cut their hair short and dress normally. Not that he could comment, wearing outdated, shit-stained camouflage, and far too old by a long way to be crawling through the undergrowth.

He emerged from the far side of the trench and stopped at the perimeter fence, foot-wide squares of rusting barbed wire. Slipping a small pair of wire cutters from his jacket pocket, he placed the jaws between the strand nearest his face. Gently squeezing on the handles, he applied more pressure until the wire sprang apart with a sharp twang. He lowered himself into the damp grass and waited a full minute, making sure there were no approaching footsteps through the undergrowth, then repeated the process three times before slithering through the grass and out of the camp.

Five metres from the fence he found what he was expecting: a narrow, barely defined path. Even in the wilderness, men followed routines. Sure, they'd vary their guard routes a bit; which troops wouldn't? But he reasoned that this close to the camp there was little activity from whoever the enemy were, and things would have dulled down to patrolling the same area with very little excitement.

Until now.

Close to the path's edge a rash of ferns stubbled the ground beneath the towering pines. He crept underneath the leafy umbrella and lay in wait, rehearsing his moves in his mind. Christ, how long had it been since he'd done this? Was he still good? How sharp were the opposition?

Forcing down his apprehension and trusting his training to take over, he controlled his breathing and tried to calm his hammering heartbeat. Still as a crocodile on a sun-blasted river bank, he waited, hoping it wouldn't be long.

After five minutes that felt like five hours, approaching footsteps padded along the path. Sawyer tensed and tried to work out how many there were. One was okay, two would be hard, three and he was fucked. He cursed his lack of knowledge, his lack of feel for the place, the people.

The footsteps got louder and Sawyer saw movement. Two of the bastards. Alright then, hard, but not impossible. A few seconds to notice their footsteps, clothing, gait, sounds they were making, how they carried their weapons. Work out how dangerous they'd be, then decide how to take them out.

One pair of trainers, one pair of scuffed, unpolished boots shuffled along the path and filled Sawyer's floor-level vision. Faded jeans travelled up two thin pairs of legs and the barrel of one rifle hung low, almost scraping along the floor.

Gash bastards, he thought, *but they still outnumber you.* He felt the familiar knotting in his stomach, the slight nausea that he knew would disappear within seconds. He tensed, ready to move.

The two dusty, shaggy-haired guards strolled along as though Sawyer wasn't there. He jumped up behind them, bounded towards them and his right leg flew upwards, kicking out at the first man. Combat boot slammed into crotch and the man dropped with a grunt. Sawyer kept moving, snatched the rifle from his collapsing victim and swung the butt as hard as he could into the back of the leading man's head. The second man went down, Sawyer grabbed his rifle and slung both weapons over his shoulder, reached down and grabbed a handful of magazines from his two groaning victims, then sprinted into the forest.

A hundred metres into the trees, he went to ground and checked his stash. The rifles were old Belgian FN, large calibre, but the wooden stocks and butts were smooth and the working parts slick with recent oil. The two lads he'd just decked might have been scruffy and easily dropped, but they kept their rifles clean. That meant they had someone in charge of them who was more switched on than they were.

He took one of the rifles to pieces, kept the bolt assembly, chucked the rest. Then he spread the spare magazines around his pockets and picked up the remaining weapon. 'Time to set the woods on fire,' he muttered. He set the selector to automatic, pointed the rifle to the sky and pulled the trigger.

*

Julio Ramirez sat at the edge of the swimming pool in his Bilbao villa. Perched on a forested hillside overlooking the port, he had a limitless view of the city and the point where the Nervion and Ibaizabal rivers formed the great estuary that snaked towards the sea. He thought about Cold Steel. They were tougher than he thought; they weren't caving in to his demands. His men had reported no signs of surrender, no offers to pay him off.

And that worried him.

A destroyed Cold Steel would have given him revenge, but no profit, and Julio was a man who liked to have both. If Cold Steel held out, even to their own destruction, they would have shown defiance, and that was intolerable. Maybe, he thought, maybe Johnny Faslane was wrong. Maybe Ozone Records *would* pay to have their band back.

*

'Fucking hell, that's gunfire.' Andy instinctively ducked and his head darted around like a meerkat on sentry.

'It's our signal,' Johnny peered through the cabin's single window, saw Ramirez' men looking at each other and moving towards the camp fencing. He reached for the door, and it door was flung open. A leather-jacketed man stood in front of them.

'Stay here, no moving.' He drew his kukri and glared at the band, then stepped out of the cabin and slammed it shut.

'Shit.' Maxwell peered out of the window. 'He's standing right outside.'

256

'So he's the first one we have to brain to get clear,' said Johnny.

'You fucking what?' gasped Andy. 'Did you see the size of that bloody knife?'

'There's six of us,' snapped Johnny. 'And Shot Away's facing people with guns. We don't know how long his diversion will last, so it's time to nut up or shut up.' He grabbed the door handle. 'Let's do it!'

*

'Randall Spitz,' he spat into his mouthpiece, expecting instant news about Cold Steel.

'Senor Spitz.' A Hispanic voice that Randall had never heard before oiled a soothing tone. 'We have a shared problem.'

'Don't give me goddam riddles,' snarled Randall. 'What the fuck type of problem do *you* got that's the same as mine?'

'An interest in Cold Steel.' The voice remained calm, unhurried.

'Oh, really?' growled Randall. 'Are you on Ozone's payroll, Mister?'

'Let us just say that Cold Steel are in my debt, and are being troublesome about making good on their obligations.'

'And that involves me, dickhead? I don't think so. I'm not their mother and I don't wipe their goddam asses. Talk to their manager about it, not me. And who the fuck are you, anyway?'

'I am Julio Ramirez, you have heard of me, no?'

'Should I have?'

'I was recently associated with Angel Face, an artist now with Ozone.'

'Angel Face, Angel Face.' Randall drummed fingers on his desk. 'Yeah, we got her now, the UK operation signed her. So what?'

'She and I had an understanding, and due to Cold Steel's interference, she is no longer a part of my organisation.'

'Listen, shithead. Angel Face was a vulnerable minor whom Ozone picked up for her own goddam protection as much as anything else. I heard she couldn't wait to get rid of the two-bit hood who ran her before us. That wouldn't be you, would it?'

'She is a child. She exaggerates.'

'The security report from Sun FM didn't. You don't sound to me like you do favours to anyone but you. And now you want a favour from me?'

'I prefer to call it a business proposition.'

'I'll be the judge of that. Say what you gotta say.'

'Cold Steel would appear to have gone missing.'

'Says who?'

'You can confirm that without me telling you. I would have thought a man in your position would already know this.'

'And you can make them reappear?'

'If I wanted to.'

'If I paid you to?'

'I did not want to have to use such vulgar terms, but seeing as you mention it, it can be that simple.'

'Maybe, maybe not. Prove to me you got the band, then maybe you'll have something to bargain with.'

'I know where Cold Steel are.'

'Don't say it, asshole. Prove it.'

Randall hung up and punched a number with such force his phone screen nearly cracked.

'Lucy Penhalligan.'

Randall couldn't help smiling at Lucy's Knightsbridge accent. If only he could find a mistress who talked like that. Never his wife, though: that ball-buster would laugh her ass off if he asked her to talk like a limey. 'Lucy,' he said. 'It's Randall. Who's Julio Ramirez?'

Chapter 41

Johnny pulled open the door, Maxwell leapt forward, grabbed Kukri and dragged him backwards. He flew into the cabin with a surprised grunt and thudded to the ground. Andy socked him in the jaw. 'Stitch that, you bastard,' he snarled. 'Now where's the next fucker?'

'Pick up that knife,' growled Johnny.

Maxwell stooped and swept up the unconscious man's kukri and Johnny led them out of the cabin. He scanned the area, his eyes taking in the half dozen log cabins skirting the rough airstrip. Around the edge of the compound, sapling fence-posts and barbed-wire perimeter blended in with the pine trees and ferns. 'Did that guy we just decked have a phone?' he asked.

'You said get his knife.' Maxwell drew his arm back and threw the kukri towards the perimeter. 'Keep it simple.'

'Let's keep it quick, too.' Johnny pointed towards the nearest cabin. 'That one's next.'

With his fist in the air and shouting like a mosh pit veteran, Johnny rushed towards the next cabin, the rest of the band howling at his heels. His smooth-soled cowboy boots slipped like a ball-head vacuum cleaner on the uneven ground. The band's thudding, running footsteps told him they were close behind. They hammered towards the nearest cabin, and with an inchoate roar, Johnny ran straight into the door. Rapid deceleration pushed a grunt of pain from his lungs before the rest of the band crashed into him, their combined weight throwing open the door and smashing into the guard.

Inside, a second leather-jacket man sprawled on the floor; Johnny and the band fell on top of him. Johnny felt smothered by a Cold Steel duvet and he dug his elbows backwards. 'Christ on a tightrope,' he gasped. 'Get off of me, you bastards, and let's see what the fuck's in here.'

Johnny struggled to his knees and peered around the small cabin, serenaded by the guard's snores. In a haphazard pile in the corner lay a heap of suitcases and holdalls.

'That's our luggage,' said Maxwell.

'Result,' said Johnny. 'First off, search that bastard for a phone. We need to make contact.'

He waded through the luggage, throwing aside bags that weren't his until he found his own. He rummaged inside. 'That's our baby!' He pulled out a tablet and flicked it on. 'Has he got a phone?'

A small object flew through the air. Johnny dropped the tablet and grasped the smartphone. His fingers slid over the screen. 'Shit, locked. Can we get the password from him?'

'He's out cold, man,' said Joe.

'Bollocks,' cursed Johnny. 'Plan B. Email to Rachel and Lucy, let's see if we can't organise a rescue.' His tablet booted up, he looked at the internet icon and groaned. No signal. 'Shite. Are our phones anywhere in here? Any of you lot keep a phone in your luggage?'

Hirsute head-shaking gave him the answer he didn't want to hear; then he looked on the wall and saw a bakelite swivel-dial phone. 'Worth a try.' He picked up the receiver and heard an analogue dial tone, then fiddled with his tablet, looking for the address book. Getting halfway through Rachel's mobile number, he heard no tone. 'Let's try dialling nine,' he muttered.

His finger blurred around the dial wheel again, and his agitation rose. He wedged the receiver to his ear, first hearing nothing, then dry clicks, then static, then his knees nearly buckled as he heard the ringtone.

'It's ringing.'

'Hello.'

'Rachel, it's Johnny. Look, we've been—'

'This is Rachel Shaw's mobile, I'm not available right now.'

'Shit!'

'But leave a message and I'll get back to you as soon as I can.'

'Rachel, it's Johnny. The plane was diverted, we've been taken prisoner. We're stuck in the woods somewhere and some mad bastard called Ramirez is holding us. Lucy from Ozone knows a bit about him. Call me as soon as you get this message, and try and get us some help.' He hung up and looked at the band.

'Stuck in the woods somewhere?' sniggered Maxwell. 'Shit, Johnny, that really narrows it down. We'll be rescued inside an hour.'

'Do *you* know where the fuck we are?' asked Johnny. Blank stare from Maxwell. 'Didn't think so. Right, let's move.'

Johnny brandished his tablet above his head like an enchanted broadsword and led the band to the next cabin. This time the guard inside saw them coming and pushed the door shut. Vince and Andy grinned at each other, grabbed a water butt that leant skewed against the cabin wall, and rammed it against the roughly hewn plank door. Again and again they battered at the door. From inside they heard desperate wails of despair. The door suddenly dissolved into fragments and the band poured inside.

'How did *that* piece of teamwork feel?' asked Johnny.

'Not bad,' shrugged Andy.

'Alright, I suppose,' muttered Vince.

Johnny walked inside, stepped over the freshly unconscious guard and his face split into a grin. 'Wolf,' he smiled.

Wolf looked left and right. The other drivers cowered behind him. 'We're all here,' he drawled. 'What's the plan?'

'You hear that shooting?' said Johnny. 'It's a diversion to pull the guards off us, and we don't know how long it'll last. Has anyone got their phones?'

Wolf shook his head. 'Whoever's holding us, they're not stupid. I saw the tour coach behind us, so the roadies are here somewhere.'

Johnny nodded. 'First thing we do is find them, then we need a phone. If we can get hold of someone, we're halfway there. I left a message with Rachel, but I don't know when she'll check her voicemail.' He looked out of the cabin doorway and saw black-clad figures scuttling towards the perimeter fence. 'Looks like the guards are out of here.'

'You think we've got them spooked?' asked Wolf.

Johnny heard random gunfire in the woods. 'The shooting might have.'

'So what happens now?' asked Maxwell.

'Wolf,' said Johnny. 'Take your lads and head for that cabin there.' He pointed to the nearest one. 'I'll take the band to the one furthest away. Pick up any phones you see, and if you get to the crew, bring them along. We'll meet in the middle.'

'Sounds good.' Wolf turned towards the drivers.

Johnny faced the band. 'Let's go!' He ran out of the cabin and along the forest-cut airstrip, and the band reached the far end at the same time as Wolf took the cross-country route to the nearest objective. Ragged optimism pulsed through Johnny. A rapid-fire stream of memories flashed through his mind: breaking down the other cabin doors, punching the guards senseless, the remaining ones retreating into the woods.

He careered towards the cabin and launched a flying kick at the door. It sprang open with no resistance and Johnny soared inside like an oversized parrot. He thumped against the far wall and collapsed with a grunt.

'Auditioning for a martial arts movie?' Maxwell grinned and yanked Johnny to his feet.

Johnny staggered upright and the rest of the band sardined into the cabin. He looked at a rough wooden table and saw a haphazard pile of mobile phones. 'Well, all right.' He limped towards the table and rummaged through the jumble of phones until he found his own, decorated with pictures of submarines.

*

'But I'm telling you they're missing, maybe kidnapped.' It had taken fifteen minutes of swearing through the local enquiry line before Rachel was connected to a senior police officer. Pacing the floor inside her hotel room, she fought to keep her voice calm and level. The story had taken a life of its own, and she didn't care. What she *cared* about was Johnny, and he needed her help.

'I can understand your concerns.' A tired-sounding officer went through what Rachel suspected was a scripted response. 'But this is a volatile area. We have just had reports of gunfire in the hills a few kilometres from here, and that has to be our priority.'

'And what if Cold Steel are caught up in it? Johnny's message said they'd been taken prisoner, somewhere in the woods. Maybe it's *them* being fired at.'

'Unlikely.' Her concerns seemed dismissed. 'There are many woods in this area. As for the shooting, we suspect a group of criminals have allied themselves with local separatists over the

262

past few months, and these alliances never last for long. We will soon put a stop to their argument, and then we can look for your friends.'

'You sound very sure you can deal with it.' Rachel's reporter's instinct picked up on an unsaid undertone.

'We're used to these situations.'

'Do they happen all the time?'

A humourless chuckle chilled Rachel's soul. 'There is violence and threats to peace everywhere in the world. And everywhere has its own way of dealing with such incidents, just as we do here.'

'And what do you do here?'

'We work in close harmony with the army. The police will seal off the affected area. It keeps those outside safe, and prevents those inside from escaping.'

'And what do the army do?'

'They deal firsthand with the gunmen. Anyone not wearing an army uniform is considered hostile and dealt with appropriately. Now, we have your phone number, should we need it. Please rest assured your situation with these celebrities will receive my full attention once this crisis has passed.'

The line clicked dead in Rachel's ear, and her heart trip-hammered. She *knew* there was a connection. She wondered what to do next.

Her phone rang and she jumped.

'Rachel, it's Johnny.'

'Oh, God, Johnny.' Her relief was like a solid blow. 'Are you alright? Where are you?'

'We're okay. Some bastard called—'

'I got your message. What's happening? Are you anywhere near the gunfire?'

'You can hear it?'

'No, but the police can, *and* the army. They've sealed off the whole area. Anyone not in an army uniform is fair game.'

'Shit, Rachel. We're not in *any* uniform. What do you think they mean by fair game?'

'They think they're dealing with criminals hooked up with separatists or something like that. Is this sounding familiar?'

'Holy shit, yes. Ramirez is some hood who wants us to give him our wedge. He said something about Basques guarding him.'

'Then you'd better get ready for the army to turn up.'

'Do they know we're here?'

'I tried to tell them, but I don't think they listened.'

'Oh, fuck. What we couldn't do with some media up here. TV cameras have a way of getting safety catches applied.'

'I'm worried about you, Johnny.'

'Really?'

'Of course really, idiot. You will stay safe, won't you?'

'You know me, Rachel.'

'That's what I mean. The only time you're safe is when the band are onstage, where they're *supposed* to be.'

'What?'

'I said—'

'I know what you said. Rachel, you're a bloody genius.' Static crackled over the connection. 'Can you get a TV crew up here?'

'Hey, rent-a-brain, I got into Spain two hours ago. I'm the only member of the tour setup that's not lost, I've been a bit busy trying to find you, and you think I can whistle up a TV crew just like that?'

'Can't you?'

Pause. 'I *might* know a few people.'

'Then get them up here, wherever here is, and don't forget to come along yourself.'

'What are you planning, Johnny?'

'A concert.'

'What?'

Chapter 42

Sawyer was enjoying himself. Half-remembered field drills flowed through his mind, training he once thought he'd forgotten, procedures he couldn't even remember, it all came back to him like direct current on overdrive. He flowed through the damp, green undergrowth as though he'd lived there all his life. He anticipated obstacles among the ferns and slid over them as silently and unseen as a python. He froze, statue-like, when he even sensed someone approaching, feeling the vibrations through the forest floor, gauging how many of them there were, not even needing to see them to count their numbers, and knowing exactly when to rise up behind the last of them like some re-animated stone monster.

Sometimes he'd send a scattering of rounds into the air if he judged his adversaries as inexperienced, easily spooked and likely to run into the trees like a gaggle of scattering geese. Others he silently removed from the back of the file, one at a time, trying to predict how many he could knock unconscious before they wised up to his presence. However he approached them, though, he could sense their fear, their uncertainty.

Each time he scythed through his opponents, he picked up one or two extra rifles, a handful of spare magazines, haversack, headgear, even small amounts of food. Noting turns of the path, the layout of the trees, even individual trunk and branch patterns, he quickly made the forest his home, finding and learning his way around as though he'd lived there for years. Beneath decaying tree trunks and overgrown bushes he created three caches, spreading out his captured weapons, ammunition and kit into evenly distributed piles. He could keep this lot of slack wankers on the hop for weeks if only he could score some regular rations. The handful of chocolate bars and chewing gum he'd rifled from their pockets wouldn't keep him going indefinitely. A secure base and supply lines were essential to any campaign. Not that his work here was essential, he was just the diversion: it was up to the longhairs to summon the rescue party.

*

'This is a really stupid idea.' Maxwell stood at the edge of the airstrip while Johnny pranced around and motioned the trucks towards level ground.

'It's not,' replied Johnny. 'You've just got a limited perspective.'

'And what the fuck does *that* mean?'

'It means get real.' Johnny crossed his hands in front of him, the truck stopped and the engine died, replaced by the background noise of intermittent gunfire. 'When the army get here, anyone who's not in one of their uniforms is the enemy. Now, do you *really* think they'll believe we're Cold Steel if we just tell them?' He shook his head. 'We'll have to show them.' He raised his arm and circled his hand. The road crew edged forward. 'Number one stage,' he called. 'Right here.' They looked uncertainly at him, as the gunfire was clearly audible. 'Now,' he snapped.

'We can set this thing up in our sleep,' said Dixie. 'But we're gonna need some current to make it happen.'

'Wolf,' said Johnny. 'That's your job. The road crew set up, it's down to you and your lads to find any wiring, tear it up and reroute it to the stage. There's power here to turn on the lights in the log cabins; let's hope there's enough to fire up a concert.'

'What about us?' Maxwell swung his arm, vaguely encompassing the band.

'First show of the tour,' said Johnny. 'Sound check as soon as the stage gets up. Any questions?'

Maxwell looked around at the forest and tilted his head. The sound of shots echoed around the trees. He grinned at Johnny. 'Seems pretty normal to me.'

*

'I'd sooner stay here,' Buster rested a protective arm over his camera and stared at Rachel. Clear green eyes peered out at her from underneath curly blond surf-hair. 'It's a big exclusive to miss.'

'They won't be coming,' said Rachel.

'A pre-tour press conference?' Buster's Australian accent boomeranged around the hotel's tiny press office. 'Of course they'll be here.'

'They would if they could, but they can't.'

'Can't? What the hell are you talking about? This is Cold Steel, girl, there's *nothing* they can't do.'

'Aren't you a little curious to find out why they aren't here?'

'Why don't you tell me?'

'It's better to find out. Think of the exclusive, Buster. I'm not telling anyone else.' She jerked her head towards the filling conference room.

'I suppose they *would* have been here by now,' edged Buster.

'Everyone else is wondering that as well, but *you'll* be the one who's there.'

'Are they in trouble?'

No answer. She stared silently at Buster.

'Is this going to be dangerous?'

Barely perceptible nod.

'Well, shit, Rachel.' Buster grabbed his camera and stood up. 'Why didn't you say so? But it's never dangerous for us journos, right?'

Rachel smiled.

'So let's go,' said Buster.

*

Captain Ricardo Silva crouched at the edge of the triangle of outward facing troops, his troops, the second Company, *5th Legion Tercio*. Digital woodland camouflage uniforms blended unmoving bodies into the undergrowth, invisible and silent. He felt the pride of leading his men: pride that went beyond national boundaries. His English mother made his citizenship problematic for the Spanish Legion, but his home-born father had given him the one thing he needed – fluency in Spanish. This was his third mission against the separatists, and also the strangest. 'Contact reports,' he whispered to Sergeant Cojones.

'Utter confusion,' replied Cojones. 'They're not organised, not even trying to resist. They're just throwing down their weapons and giving up. I've never seen anything like it.'

Silva nodded. 'Number One Company report thirty-five prisoners in their harbour. Soon we'll be prison guards as well.'

'Might as well get the police up here,' muttered Cojones.

Silva nodded. 'Not like the last lot. Something's changed.' He cradled his G36 rifle. 'We need to push these contacts if we want answers.'

'Radio message, sir.' A legionnaire materialised next to Silva and whispered to him.

'What is it?'

'Corporal Schmidt reports a motorcycle and two riders at his road block.'

'Significance?'

'They claim to be reporters. Corporal Schmidt advises they have cameras with them.'

'Tell Corporal Schmidt to be polite but firm. They'll be in danger if they enter this area, and the last thing we want is reporters taken hostage. Sergeant Cojones?'

'Sir!'

'Fighting patrol. Let's see if we can't find out what's scaring them.'

*

'What the hell is that?' Johnny gaped at sheets of polythene spread high over the stage as though it were a huge four-poster bed in the middle of a forest.

'What the hell is that?' Dixie pointed straight up at the sky.

Johnny saw grey and black clouds getting thicker and deeper by the minute. 'How long before we get piss wet through?'

'Do I look like a weather man?'

'What type of rain do you think they have up here?'

'The wet stuff.'

'Funny.' Johnny frowned. 'Is the stage good to go?' Roadies clambered over the flat stage, built on a foundation of empty speaker boxes.

'It would be if we had enough juice to power the lights and speakers.'

'You'll get it,' said Johnny. 'And I want a seventy-thirty slant towards the sound. We want to be seen, but we *need* to be heard.'

'Talk to Wolf,' said Dixie. 'He's the one you promoted to electrician.'

Johnny walked across the airstrip towards the less than smooth parking area where the trucks and tour bus were parked. Wolf towered over the other drivers who fought to unwind a wood-panel drum of thickly insulated cable. 'What have you got, Wolf?' he asked.

Wolf glared at Johnny. 'The good news is this.' He slapped the cable drum. 'It'll take enough power to fire up the stage. We can run it over to the festival generators and that'll convert through to the mixing desk.'

'The festival generators? You think they can push out stage levels of electric?'

Wolf shook his head and looked at Johnny. 'We're taking a chance.'

'Is this still the good news?'

'Yes.'

'And the bad?'

'The power at this camp is barely enough for the light bulbs. It'll never run up to enough for the stage.'

'Shit!'

'There *might* be a way,' said Wolf. 'But it's risky.'

'No choice,' said Johnny. 'What's the plan?'

'We splice this cable at one end, run it to the solenoids on the trucks and the bus, then start up the engines and leave them running. Between them and the generators they'll turn out more sap than we've got right now.'

'Wolf,' smiled Johnny, 'you're a bloody genius. There's no might about it, it *will* work.'

'Johnny, you're not a trucker or an electrician, are you?'

'Why?'

'The trucks weren't designed to be generators, and the solenoids definitely weren't. They'll give us power for maybe ten minutes. And then...' He looked at Johnny with raised eyebrows.

'And then?'

'They'll definitely burn a lot more fuel.'

'Christ,' said Johnny. 'Is that all? We're in Spain, not the bloody Sahara. We can fill up.'

Wolf shook his head. 'Running the trucks as generators,' he said. 'That's putting a lot of strain on the engines. They'll start getting hot.'

'Is that bad?'

'They could catch fire.'

'That's bad.'

'And the festival generators will either take the extra power, or they'll explode.'

'Shit.' Johnny rubbed his forehead and looked at Wolf. 'What do you think we should do?'

'That decision's yours, mate. I just do what I'm told.'

Johnny looked at the stage and the band, heard the shooting. 'How long will it take?'

'An hour?'

'You've got thirty minutes.'

Wolf nodded. 'Okay, we can do that if Snotty gets his thumb out of his arse for two seconds. Anything else?'

'Yes,' said Johnny. 'Make sure you're at a safe distance when you throw the switch. Things can be replaced a lot easier than people.'

*

Rachel sat astride the rented dirt bike and glared bayonets at the armed soldiers manning the roadblock. With cold efficiency, they'd stopped her and Buster, a quickly deployed stinger stretching across the road.

'How did you evade the police cordon?' the guard asked in strangely accented English that didn't have the normal Spanish inflections.

'What cordon?' she'd lied, with an armour-piercing smile that for once bounced off its target. They'd ridden to a police block two miles further down the road and turned back, but once round a corner and out of sight, Rachel had swerved into the trees. Riding pillion, Buster had nearly fallen off when they bumped through the undergrowth. By the time they came back onto the road, the police were far behind them.

'Wait here. I need to report this.' The guard walked behind the stinger to a humvee stretched broadside across the road. A heavy machine gun poked upwards from a roof-mounted turret. The soldier leaning behind it stared at them intently.

Dark clouds crept across the early evening sky, making the forest-hemmed roadway even darker. Cold, moist air stabbed through Rachel's thin jacket and she shivered. A fat raindrop slap-landed on her open face helmet and she yelped in surprise.

'Those lads are going to get soaked in about one minute.' Buster nodded towards the two soldiers who stood behind the stinger with slung rifles.

'And we're not?' snapped Rachel. 'Besides, they look like they could walk through a monsoon and not notice. And what is it with their accents?'

'Were you expecting a pair of Geordies? At least they spoke English.'

'And how! They sounded like Germans.'

'They probably were.'

'What do you mean?'

'Look at their shoulder badge,' said Buster. 'They're Spanish Legion.'

'What?'

'Spanish Legion. They're like the French Foreign Legion, they accept foreigners.'

'Bullshit.'

'It's true,' said Buster. 'There must be something pretty serious happening up here if they need these lads on the ground.'

Sounds of gunfire drifted through the closely packed trees. Raindrops soaked into Rachel's jeans and her heart-rate sped up. 'Christ,' she muttered. 'We've got to get past this road block.'

'How?' asked Buster. 'Spikes across the road, a hummer in the way, armed soldiers.' He chuckled. 'We could always fly.'

'They've seen the cameras,' said Rachel. 'They know we're press, and we need to disappear soon.' She spun the bike round and pulled open the accelerator.

'Where the hell are we going?' Buster squeezed her waist as the bike sped off down the road.

'Back into the woods,' said Rachel. 'This rain'll cover us.'

'That won't work against these guys.'

'Sure it will.' She swung the bike hard right and they lurched between two tree trunks and into the forest. 'That road block is static. They can't chase us.'

'No,' replied Buster. 'But they can call for help, and what if they shoot at us?'

'Man up,' said Rachel. 'This is woman's work.'

*

Suddenly, Sawyer saw the same people he'd just sent running scared into the woods. They were coming back at him. They hadn't reorganised, they weren't in control, they were just being herded back the way they'd come. 'There's a new player on the scene,' he muttered. He sank back into cover and waited. The sky suddenly darkened and he saw clouds rushing in to blot out the sunshine. The wind blew colder and he felt the moisture in the air. Seconds later, the first raindrops fell. Through the reducing visibility, small movements ghosted in and out of his vision. He thought he saw something, then looked again and couldn't be sure.

*

'It's wired up.' Wolf strode towards the stage – an expanse of flat space with drums at the back and a wall of speakers behind. The band stood in a tight clump of uncertainty.

'Right.' Johnny turned to them. 'Don't just stand there like a bunch of nuns at a pole dancing class. It's opening night. Let's go.'

'We usually play to an audience, man,' said Joe.

'They'll be coming,' said Johnny. 'Just as soon as you bring them here with the music.'

'And what if we attract the wrong kind of attention?' asked Maxwell.

'Concentrate on the gig,' replied Johnny. 'I'll take care of the rest, as usual.'

Cold wind gusted under the rain shelter, and the first raindrops pattered against its plastic sheeting. Maxwell looked up. 'That's not good,' he muttered.

'Hey,' snapped Johnny. 'You're Cold Steel. You're not shaped by destiny, you *make* your destiny.' His words ricocheted back at him with a stark bareness that matched the closing weather. 'Fucking hell,' he shouted. 'It's only rain! Do you want to get shot or rescued? Jesus, if Blackbeard saw you right now, he'd be turning in his topsoil.'

'Look, mate—'

'Don't "look mate" me,' snarled Johnny. 'That fucking nutter we've had in tow since the studio has come up with the goods, in case you haven't heard the shooting. Sooner or later someone's going to come up here, and unless we convince them we're not a bunch of bandits or gangsters, we're screwed. And if there's one thing that isn't any of the above, it's a fucking metal band.'

'We *are* a metal band,' said Vince.

'You might look like one,' said Johnny. 'But that won't convince the Spanish Army. I don't want you looking like a metal band, I want you sounding, moving, walking, talking like one, okay? So, how about Sinners Sanctuary, and how about doing it right fucking now?'

Johnny glared at the band and faced five seconds of sullen resistance before Mike sat behind his drums and Joe picked up his bass. Maxwell shrugged and walked towards the mic stand. Vince and Andy still faced Johnny. 'And what's with you two?' he asked. 'Do you need a written invitation? Sawyer was right. At times like this, lads, it's fucking pathetic.'

'What are you going to be doing while we're up here?' asked Andy.

'Stopping them getting too close.'

'How?' asked Andy.

'Don't ask stupid questions.'

'It's not—'

'Just get up there and play.'

*

The rain started to fall. Silva led the patrol out of the company's harbour. Someone had turned his quarry from an unpredictable, talented adversary into a bunch of directionless, scared amateurs. He led his men forward cautiously, listening for sounds, looking for signs in the forest. Movement, noise, even smells.

He edged forward, alive for any movement, any sign. He felt the rain soak through his camouflage uniform. Minutes later, it hosed down, masking the smaller sounds around him and obscuring his vision.

An unexpected noise cut through the descending weather. Heavily beating drums and high-pitched screeching, overlaid by an unfamiliar voice singing words he didn't understand, with the odd, clearly identified English phrase. He went to ground, and with a small hand movement summoned Corporal Uñas. 'What the hell is that noise?'

'Music, sir.'

Silva looked up at the rain. 'Why would we hear music up here?'

'I don't know, sir.' Uñas rested his rifle and tilted his head to one side, sending streams of rainwater cascading off his helmet's convex dome. 'But I know what they're playing.'

'What?'

'It's a Cold Steel song, sir.'

'Cold Steel?'

'An English metal band, sir. I've got tickets to see them tomorrow night, if we finish here before then. They sound a lot like the real thing, whoever they are.'

'Analysis?'

'Unprecedented, sir. The last thing we could encounter up here would be performing musicians.'

'And the separatists? Do they have this type of… recreation noted in previous contacts?'

'None, sir.'

The rain beat down even more heavily, and Silva turned to Uñas. 'What about those god-awful motion prongs? Did they pick up anything?' He couldn't hide his scepticism of the small boxes his unit had recently been issued with, comprising a pair of what looked like tent pegs wired to a small box with a screen, which supposedly detected footsteps and gave a direction of movement.

'They *do* work, sir.'

'They're no match for a clean rifle and a steady eye.'

'They *did* give us a fix on the target, sir.'

'Really?'

'Yes, sir, the target's heading towards that, er, music. Multiple footfall, overlapping trajectories, but all going in the same direction.'

'Then we head that way and deal with both threats, Corporal, no matter how much they sound like that band you like.'

'I thought you'd be a fan as well, sir – they're from your old home.'

'The Legion's my home now, Corporal. Extended line, we'll drive them ahead of us.'

274

Chapter 43

'Soon we shall have those longhairs back where they belong, and making us some real money, eh, boss?'

'Shut up and drive, Carlos,' snapped Ramirez. He stared at the tree-lined road and cracked his knuckles with bone-breaking force. Things were *not* going as he'd planned. He'd thought the band would cave in without a fight. He was certain the record company would, but Randall Spitz could have scared even his own enforcers. 'We may need to hold them a bit longer,' he muttered.

'What?' Carlos stared at Ramirez.

'Watch the road, idiot. I need to think. STOP!'

Carlos stamped on the brakes and Ramirez straightened his arms against the dashboard. Tyres locked and the jeep screeched along the narrow forest road. Up ahead, Ramirez saw a police roadblock turning away a couple on a dirt bike. 'Shit! The police are here.'

'You think they look for us?' asked Carlos.

'Us or the Basques. Either way, we're compromised. Turn around, back to the town house.'

'What about our boys?'

'They know the rules, they're on their own.'

*

With a truck's side panel like a solid wall between him and the stage, Johnny made himself heard. Power rain soaked him through and made his leather pants double in weight. The remains of his hair were plastered to his head, and he squinted at the road crew and drivers who semi-circled him and listened to his rapid-fire instructions.

'Right.' His voice knifed through the rain. 'That firing in the woods has brought the cavalry, but right now they don't know we're here, and they've got no orders to rescue us. They'll be shooting first and asking questions later. Much later.'

'That's not good,' said Dixie.

'No,' agreed Johnny. 'And that's why we've jacked up a concert. Cold Steel playing live, here in the woods, in the pissing rain, it's bound to make anyone think twice before shooting us, and that'll give us time to hold up our hands and talk our way out of here.'

'So we just sit back and wait?' said Dixie.

Johnny shook his head. 'Suppose those bastards that brought us here come back before the good guys?'

'I guess you're about to tell us,' said Wolf.

'That's right.' Johnny slapped the side of the truck and winced; it hurt more than he'd expected. 'And we need what's in here to do it.'

*

'Jesus, Rachel. Slow down a bit.' Tree trunks buzzed past Buster's knees, which poked out at right angles. He perched on the back of the dirt bike, clinging to Rachel, and wondered when he'd last been this scared, cold and wet all at the same time.

'Do you want that exclusive or not?' Rachel's words whipped back past her black hair, which escaped the rim of her crash helmet and kept brushing in Buster's face. She didn't look back to see if he'd heard. The bike bucked and bounced over the tree roots and fern bushes. They'd gone in a wide arc around the army roadblock, then stopped once, listened, heard the band playing and rode straight towards the sound. The rain lashed into Rachel's face and made her squint, tyres slipped on wet vegetation and her arms soon tired from fighting the bike's tank-slapping handlebars. The single headlight sent a powerful beam through the downpour gloom, the bike's straining engine buzzed and chattered through the gear changes, but Rachel didn't stop.

Suddenly the trees disappeared and she saw a roughly cleared border surrounding barely visible fence posts and rusting barbed wire fencing. Without slowing down she scanned left and right, saw a quagmire track and veered towards it. Beyond the fencing a thick pole of light shot upwards, and over the bike's engine she heard the band's music. 'Fire up that camera, Buster,' she shouted.

A cross-pole barrier had been pulled back where the track entered the compound. Rachel pointed the bike at the gap and they shot through. The stage and trucks loomed on her left through the rain, while to her right she saw a band of armed men running towards her.

*

Wind-blown pine needles and stones made bullet-hole punctures in the overhead rain shelter. Maxwell shower-flicked the cold water off his hair and shivered as the wind stabbed into him. The band flamed through Sinners Sanctuary, then steamed straight into Power Games.

The lyrics to Power Games, though new, flowed effortlessly after the month-long hangar practice. Maxwell stared at Vince and Andy in mild surprise. They were standing side by side; was he going blind or were they actually smiling? At each other? Behind them, Joe and Mike shared a watertight back section over which the guitars and vocals soared.

Power Games flashbanged to a high velocity halt and Maxwell dropped into the quieter first verse of Rock in a Hard Place. Mike's drums joined in, slowly at first and then faster, deepened by Joe's bass. Slow-fire guitar picking from Vince led the guitar rush, followed by Andy's mild distortion riffing. The tempo built, sheathed by Maxwell's increasingly powerful singing; he felt the music warming his insides, building into a bonfire within him, and he almost forgot where he was. The first verse drew to a close and he stamped on the vocal accelerator. He looked out to the woods and saw a disorganised group of men running towards the stage. Off to his right, but approaching fast was an off-road motorcycle with two people on it.

*

Rachel yanked on the brakes and the bike slid to a stop, spraying mud and stones over the approaching men. Wide eyes stared out at her from rain-pale faces. The man nearest to her shouted and pointed at her and Buster. Seconds later they were surrounded, dragged off the bike and covered from all sides by quickly levelled rifles that looked like a living history of firearms.

*

'I'm really not sure about this.' Dixie looked at Johnny, fidgeted inside his red coat and gripped his stage musket. 'Isn't this going to make us look like soldiers? And won't that really wind up the *real* soldiers when they get here?'

Johnny adjusted his eye patch and nearly tripped over the imitation cutlass that he'd stuffed inside the wide belt that now doubled around him, and was fastened with a rhinestone buckle.

'We look like redcoats and pirates. And behind us are a metal band.'

'Redcoats with guns,' moaned Snotty.

'Muskets,' snapped Johnny. 'Which even to me seem a little antique, so you can be bloody sure a soldier would know that. Besides, we aren't dressed like this for the benefit of the good guys.'

'Why then?' asked Snotty.

'Simple,' said Johnny. 'The army'll take one look at us dressed like this and they'll either piss themselves laughing, or realise straight away that we're not gunmen out to cause trouble. But the bastards who took us won't have a fucking clue what we're about, and if they get here first, hopefully we'll be able to make them stop and think long enough for the good guys to arrive.'

'The good guys,' said Snotty. 'Being the army who've been ordered to shoot anyone who isn't them?'

'Stop being a pussy.'

'Can't we just hide?' asked Snotty.

'If we did that,' said Johnny, 'and the bad guys get here first, they'll shut down the band and do Christ knows what to them. And then us.'

'And why can't we just drive away?' asked Dixie.

'Along roads controlled by a bunch of mad bastards with guns? I don't think we'd get very far.' Johnny looked at Wolf, who nodded and shifted uncomfortably in a red coat several sizes too small for him. 'We've got no bloody choice,' said Johnny. 'So let's get with it and do what we've got to do.'

A buzzing whine made Johnny look out through the rain. Along the now mud-slicked track that led into the compound rode a small motorbike with two people aboard. A hundred yards away it stopped and the pair got off. The movements of the lead rider jarred familiarity as he looked. He recognised her and moaned anguish. 'Rachel,' he shouted, jumping up and down and throwing his arms over his head. 'Over here.'

Rachel pulled off her helmet and was instantly lost to view by an approaching bunch of soaked, heavily armed approaching men. 'No,' gasped Johnny. 'Hey, leave her alone,' he shouted. 'Hey, you bastards.' His insides turned to solid lead, his hands shook, and he forced down his last meal, which threatened to reappear. His legs buckled and he dropped to his knees.

'You okay?' asked Wolf.

'Oh, shit,' gasped Johnny. 'They've got Rachel, the bastards have got her.'

'You mean that's *your* Rachel? She's here?'

'Christ,' sobbed Johnny. 'This is my fault. I told her to get here. Fucking hell, what have I done?'

'Hey.' Wolf grabbed Johnny's trembling shoulders. 'You didn't mean for her to get taken. It's not your fault.'

Frustration and anger slowly built inside Johnny, beginning as a warm infusion rising up from the soles of his cowboy boots, through his sodden leather pants, soaking up into his chest and sending a throbbing pulse through his head that competed with the band's driving music. He stood up and yanked his cutlass free from his belt. 'That's one of ours out there, lads,' he roared. 'So let's get her back. Come on!'

He didn't wait to see if the road crew were following. With the rain shutting down his vision, he ran towards Rachel. It was the first time he'd ever known her in danger and he acted without thinking. He splashed though puddles with his boot-soles slipping on rain-slicked stones, kept his stage cutlass high above his head and roared wordless curses at the bastards holding her. His arms windmilled and the cutlass clanged on loose stones, sending a numbing, jarring pain up his arm. He kept hold of the now bent and useless fake weapon, forced his legs to keep moving, and sped up, still heading towards Rachel. He looked at the mob in front of him, which started to look his way. One of them raised his rifle. Johnny hefted the cutlass and brought its blunt blade downwards. He closed his eyes and the gunman pulled the trigger at the same time as the blade struck the rifle's barrel. Johnny's wild swing sent the rifle pointing towards the ground and a chattering burst of auto-fire piled harmlessly into the mud. He grabbed hold of the rifle and yanked, pulling it free and throwing it to the rain-slicked floor. Rachel pulled the gunman's shoulder, swung him around and punched him with teeth-loosening force. He dropped to the ground in a soggy heap. Johnny looked breathlessly at Rachel, then heard thudding footsteps and saw a sea of ill-fitting red-coated roadies and drivers crowd around them, brandishing non-functioning stage muskets and putting a shaggy-haired, musketed human barrier between Johnny and Rachel on one side, and the gunmen who had emerged from the forest on the other.

'You mad, crazy bastard.' Rachel hugged Johnny. His rain-chilled body felt the fusing defibrillation of her warm flesh pressed against him. 'God, I was *so* worried.'

'Really?' He breathed in the smell of her wet hair.

'You think I'd do all this for the story?'

'Not any more.' Johnny's teeth chattered and the rain hammered down on them. 'And do you think *I'd* stand by and let one of this lot sweep you off your feet? You know, being out here just *might* have been dangerous.'

'I've got my press card, I'd have been fine.' She nodded towards Buster. 'You wanted TV, you got it. Is the live link working, Buster?' She spoke more loudly than Buster needed to hear. He panned around with his camera steady on his shoulder.

'Great pictures, Rach.' His lager and sunshine accent cut through the rain, and Johnny saw his crossed fingers as he spoke. '*FUEGO!*'

Three perfectly synchronised shots crashed through the driving rain, fired by what sounded like a hundred rifles. The crashing echo bounced back from the wall of trees surrounding the compound. Soaking wet camouflage figures moved through the gunmen in pairs, one man pushing the irregular, demoralised gunmen to their knees, contemptuously knocking weapons to the floor, while the second man covered him with an expertly levelled assault rife. No words were spoken, adding to the silent efficiency with which they worked. Soon the only people standing were the suddenly arrived soldiers and the red-coated roadies surrounding an eye-patched Johnny, who stood with an arm around Rachel. Buster continued filming, shivering beneath his soaked Hawaiian shirt.

'Who the hell are *they?*' Johnny nodded towards the soldiers who stood and growled over the kneeling gunmen.

'Spanish Legion,' Rachel smiled.

'I suppose you know their names as well,' chuckled Johnny.

'Easy enough to find out. But now that I'm here and doing my job, maybe you'll get the band back to where *they're* supposed to be.'

Through the rain Johnny heard Aphid Guitar screech across the waterlogged wilderness. 'What do you mean?' he smiled. 'They're onstage and playing live. Where else should they be?' He walked through the redcoat barrier, held out his hands and smiled at the nearest pair of soldiers. 'Does anyone here speak English?'

Chapter 44

'But why was your flight diverted?'

Inside the hotel, the conference room's pristine newness couldn't have been more different to the compound and rough cabins the band had been in earlier that day. Freshly showered and in clean clothes, Johnny smiled, but his numbed mind still clanged with Randall's blunt telephone warning just minutes before. 'Don't say a goddam word about Ramirez, you get me?'

'But, Randall—'

'And don't but me, asshole. If we give that cocksucker any goddam publicity, every two-bit hood in the universe will think he's got a shot to hold you or any other band for ransom. We know where he is, and we're about to close his hole, for goddam good.'

'Who's we?'

'Not you, dickhead. Now give the press conference, say whatever the hell you want about your games in the woods, as long as there's no mention of Ramirez. *And* get your goddam fairy boys to the venue on time, *every* motherfucking time. You copy?'

'I understand, Randall.'

'You'd better, you bastard.'

Ten minutes later, Johnny faced the first questions from the gathered press, seeing barely masked disappointment that the band had actually turned up. 'Technical issues,' he answered, and saw the reporter's irritation.

'That doesn't tell us much, Johnny.'

'Not much to tell,' he replied. 'So let's get back to the album. It's already the number one download in Spain and seven other European countries. Don't you want to talk about that instead?'

'Because *we* bloody well do,' growled Maxwell who. unlike Johnny. was still filthy, brimming with nervous energy, and flanked by the rest of the band in an equal state of natural disorder. 'Cold Steel, Rock in a Hard Place. It's about us, all of us.'

'Us?' asked one reporter. 'Who do you mean?'

'This band,' grinned Maxwell. 'This music.' He thumped his chest. 'Our fans, our road crew, everything. If you want to know what it means to have metal in your soul, no matter what else is happening in your life, then this album, this tour, this band, will have something to say to you.'

'And what have you got planned for the tour, Maxwell?'

'Come along and you'll see.'

*

The last olive green truck swayed along the still muddy track. Its load of disarmed prisoners stared forlornly out of the back, watched over by a razor-eyed legionnaire. Captain Silva's eyes traversed the compound, which already looked abandoned. The cabin doors swung open after his men had swept through every building and rip-searched the entire area. Camouflage cloth sacks sat like collections of eco-rubbish awaiting collection, containing discarded separatist equipment and belongings. His company knelt in a tight harbour; low grey clouds still pressed down on the treetops, although the rain had stopped falling. Any dip in the ground still overflowed with rainwater, and the damp air threatened more to come.

'I suppose this place will be bulldozed and trees will be replanted.' Sergeant Cojones stood at Silva's side.

'What a waste of an ideal jump-off site,' said Silva. 'If we had a permanent presence here, we'd make sure the separatists never got to use it again.'

'After the cutbacks?' grunted Cojones. 'Not a chance.'

'All we'd need is one squad.'

'We're lucky to get them to pay for our ammunition,' grumbled Cojones. 'Let alone extra soldiers.'

'Even just *one* man to keep this place secure,' despaired Silva.

'Captain! Captain!' Silva turned round and saw a pair of legionnaires walking towards them. They escorted a man in faded camouflage, with cropped greying hair and a stubble, and an old FN rifle unloaded and slung over his shoulder.

'What's this?' asked Silva.

'He gave himself up, sir,' replied the legionnaire. 'We walked right past him and didn't even see him. Best fieldcraft we've ever seen. I think he's speaking English.'

*

Damas Infernales stood up in their small dressing room and checked each other's stage outfits. Immaculate business suits, stage

283

make-up, razor-edged eyeliner, perfect long hair. And fingerless leather gloves.

'We look good.' Candelaria couldn't hide the nervous quiver in her voice.

'We'll sound even better,' said Roxana.

'Cold Steel,' laughed Guiomar. 'They'd better put on a good show after us.'

Without a manager to lead them to the stage, Damas Infernales walked along the narrow backstage corridor. Alternate concrete and sheet metal walkways were lit by random strip lights. Outside, selfies and photo bombs flashed around the crowd floor, the metal playlist soaked into the smell of spilt beer and tapas and expectation built like the inside of a pressure cooker on fast heat. The band reached the edge of the stage. The road crew gave the thumbs up, and passed guitar to Candelaria and bass to Roxana. Candelaria felt the tingling, trembling nervousness of impending appearance. The floor manager nodded, and as the house lights winked out, a surge of cheers surfed over the stage. Candelaria led the band out to face the home crowd.

One by one, spotlights stabbed through the darkness. Candelaria looked out at the audience, smiled and threw a fist into the air. The crowd's roar built, and she saw right arms punching the air as one, many clenched around fingerless gloves, many more wearing business suits. The lights burned white on the stage and the home crowd roared out a hammerblow welcome.

*

Candelaria changed a broken string onstage, while Roxana covered with an improvised bass solo. An exchange of grins spoke of crisis passed. Candelaria stepped to stage front. Cheers washed over them and they blasted a riff-heavy cover of Money for Nothing, sung entirely in Spanish. The audience joined in for the chorus and drowned out the band. Candelaria looked back at Roxana and Guiomar and felt the chemistry, the link with band and audience. They'd been given an hour to play, longer than most support acts, and they crammed caustic metal into every minute.

*

The between-band playlist powered from the Bizkaia's speakers. Dixie looked over the stage and appraised the smallest detail. All

284

lights secured and safely wired up. The two massive pirate ships rested, hidden behind backcloths. The drum riser stood silent guard over the empty stage and guitars rested at either end in their protective stands. Pyro stacks nestled ready to go, still hidden from view. Expectation built among the twenty-six thousand fans who stretched back endlessly into the arena.

'All set?' asked Johnny. 'Christ, but they were good.'

Dixie nodded slowly, his eyes taking in the stage, segment by segment, looking for anything that had been missed or overlooked. 'This gig's been a long time coming. By shit, Johnny, we nearly didn't make it. Again.'

'We're here now,' said Johnny. 'This time the tour starts right, and stays that way.'

*

Johnny led the band from the dressing room and up a ladder-steep staircase. The playlist pulsed through thin walls and he felt the band's nervousness at the first concert just seconds away. He turned the final corner, saw the fans near the front of the stage and Hickey illuminated in the middle of the arena at the mixing desk, like a strobe-lit island in a dark sea of fans. Johnny nodded; seconds later the hall lights went out and darkness announced the start of the show. Cheers erupted from the unseen thousands, red and white lights flared across the stage and the band walked into view. Maxwell smiled like a returning Caesar and held his fist high, his bare chest already sweating under the harsh spotlights. He grabbed the microphone and looked out into the anonymous multitude.

'Barakaldo,' he roared. 'We are Cold Steel.'

THE END

Cold Steel on the Rocks

Rick Brindle

When the pirate Blackbeard buried his treasure, he could never have imagined that it would fall to the heavy metal band, Cold Steel, to come looking for it.

Cold Steel, high-octane British rockers who came close to legendary status, until the release of their fourth album, when their excesses send them spiralling into terminal decline.

Struggling small-time band manager Johnny Faslane, in the right place at the right time, lands the dream job of managing Cold Steel, and then has the seemingly impossible mission of turning the band around.

Cold Steel's singer, Maxwell Diabolo, claims to have a treasure map that he thinks will lead him to Blackbeard's lost riches.

With the band bent on a terrifying path of self-destruction, Johnny wonders if they will even complete the tour, much less get to the Caribbean to embark on a treasure hunt.

Against all expectations, the tour ends on a high and they sail halfway around the world chasing a long-dead pirate's map. Once there, it seems as though they were safer on a decaying tour. Facing their ultimate challenge, it will take all of Cold Steel's talent to escape a fate of their own creating.

'Cold Steel on the Rocks is **the** heavy metal book the world needs to know about.' - Goodreads.

Printed in Great Britain
by Amazon

47081515R00170